A KINGDOM OF BLOOD AND MAGIC

CHIARA FORESTIERI

SPECIAL THANKS

There's an additional acknowledgments section at the end of the book but before get started I just wanted to thank all of my extraordinary ARC Readers. It often takes a leap of faith to invest time and energy into going on a journey curated by the mind of a complete stranger with little to no evidence to prove that it will be an enjoyable one.

So thank you, brave souls. I love you and you have my eternal gratitude.

As a show of my gratitude, I would love to encourage my readers to support these wonderful humans by following their insta/booksta-grams. They are truly kind human beings with original content.

Well Read Alchemy - @wellreadalchemy
Booktastyc Book Club - @booktastycbookclub
Holly - @wandersthroughbooks
Rhi - @reads_with_rhi
Rissa - @reading_rissa
Gem - @bookscaffeinecurls
Candi - @cjamz_books
Josephine - @witchybooksta
Mama - @mama_reads24
Brittany - @smuttybooksreader
Amanda - @crookedhouseofbooks

Amanda Marie - @amandapagereads
Lily - @smutly.romance
Kelly - @kellyjeanchandandler
Brie - @thatreadingwitch
Kelly - @kellyjeanchandandler
Megan - @_ins0mniac.reading_
Haley - readwith.caffinatedmommy
Chelsea - @bookmama2375
Amber - @poursome_booksonme
Liz - @breakawayreads
Jessie - @jessiereadsfantasy
Sarah - @lostinthelibrary23
Amber - @amberbeer701
Rylie - @rys_reading_room
Thalia - @SimplySommelier
Maria - @bookishfairytail
Eva - @evas.book.nook
Iola - Iola Fazzari
Yasmin - @yazg.books
Kat - @arcane.pages
Erin - @bookdragonerin
Breanna - @boo.kitup
Kristin - @grimreber
Katherine - @worthyofafareread
Elise - @gamblersgirl02
Jessie - @jessiereadsfantasy
Dani - @kindle_n_coffee
Tay - @read.withtay
Stephanie - @paintandpages_
Sarah - @sarahsbookcollection
Katie - @bookishk92
Samantha - @foxxybookreads
Alys - @alyslovestoread
Jennifer - @twisted.page

Alicia - @enelyae.is.reading

Additionally, I want to thank the beautiful Megan Clark - @megantheereader - for suggesting the brilliant name *The Dancing Dryad* as the name of the tavern we visit in chapters 8-12.

Thank you so much to all the brilliant and insanely supportive bookstagram girlies that helped keep me inspired, showed me that people are actually interested in my work, and given me the most delicious and soul nourishing book recommendations.

TRIGGER WARNINGS

Dubious Consent
Being Held Captive
Bondage
Blood Play
Explicit Language
Graphic Scenes Depicting Sexual Acts
Torture, Gore, & Violence
Mention of Trauma
Mention of Suicidal Feelings (This occurs earlier in the book and is
not repeatedly mentioned)
Mention of R*pe
Mention of infanticide (that doesn't actually occur)
Mention of genocide (historically within this fictional world)

If you find all of that palatable in your literature, you'll do just fine
with the rest. Let's leave some mystery between us, shall we? :)

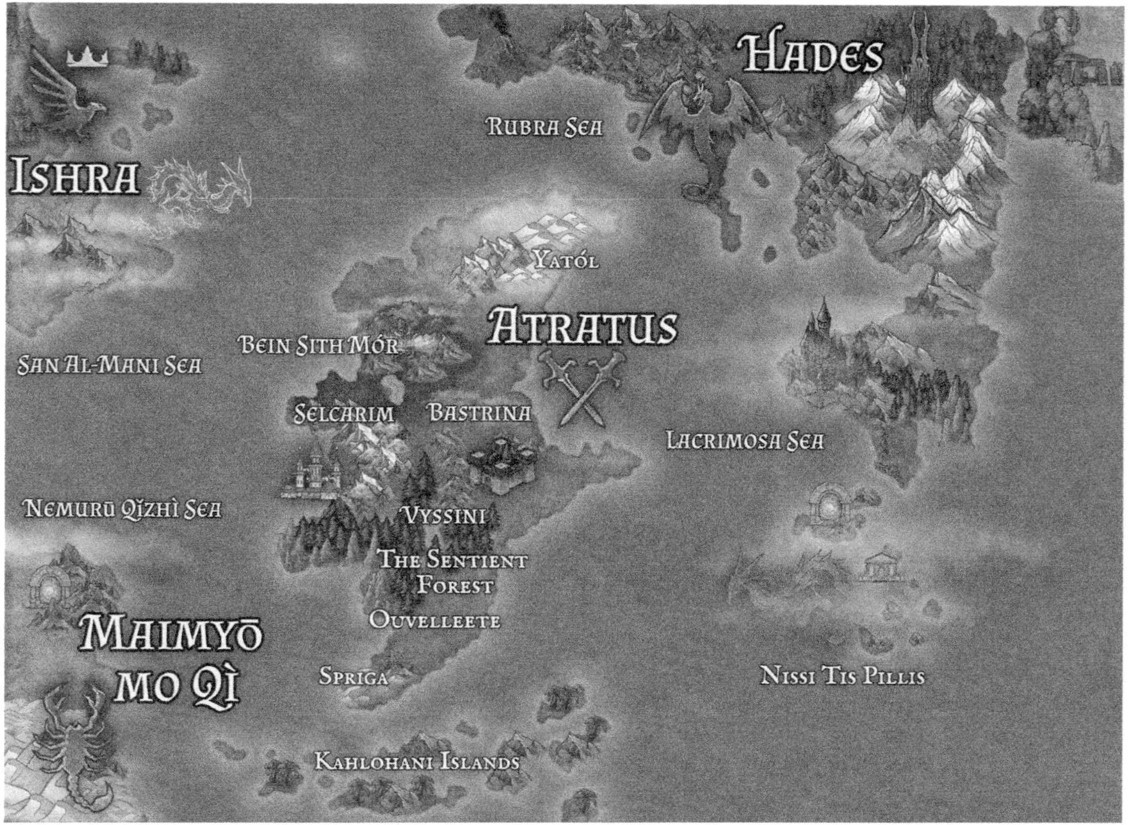
Hades
Rubra Sea
Ishra
Yatól
Atratus
Bein Sith Mór
San Al-Mani Sea
Selcarim
Bastrina
Lacrimosa Sea
Nemurū Qīzhì Sea
Vyssini
The Sentient Forest
Ouvelleete
Maimyō Mo Qì
Spriga
Nissi Tis Pillis
Kahlohani Islands

GLOSSARY

Aequili *(ay - kwee - lee)* - literally meaning 'balanced', is a term used amongst sanguinati that refers to a person of both sexes.

Akash *(ah - kahsh)* - the divine essence of the world that births, permeates, and destroys all things.

Anim Gemla *(ah - neem - game - lah):* the sanguinati term for *soulbound.*

Archestratim *(ark - eh - strat - um)* - an immensely powerful winged immortal from one of the divine realms.

The Arrival - refers to event, several thousand years ago, when beings from another world entered through a tear in the fabric between worlds.

The Atratus - The serpentine river named after the kingdom through which it runs where the bodies of the dead seem to vanish.

Bastrina - the capital city of Atratus where Queen Zurie's palace is located.

Dakrun *(dah - kroon)* - Kahlohani for 'bandits'.

Dream Leaf - a plant medicine, usually smoked or brewed as a tea, used to induce feelings of euphoria, deepen sleep, and enhance dreams.

Donatris *(dohn—ah-treess)* - Donor, used by sanguinati in reference to a person - whether mortal or immortal - who provides blood directly from the vein, usually at a blood parlour.

Erosyan Disciples *(ero-zee-in)* - those who worshipped the gods and goddesses of pleasure, lust, and desire; dedicated their lives to providing pleasure to others.

General Theikos - *Malekai Theikos*

Ilanwei *(ee - lahn - way)* - Kahlohani term for the clicking noise made used to communicate with horses.

Irae Kalini *(eye - ray - kah -lee - nee)* - Mareina Kalini

The Hand of Irae | *The Royal Irae (eye—ray)* - Queen Zurie's personal mercenary.

Kahlohani Islands - An archipelago in the majestic Kahlohani Sea that lies south of the Atratusian continent that is renowned for its fearsome tribal warriors.

Ku'kāne *(koo - hah - nay)* - Kahlohani for 'my son'.

Leath-Anama *(layth - anah - mah)* - Reilandish for 'Soul Halve'.

Lohane thili *(low - hah - nay - thee - lee)* - Kahlohani for 'soulbound'.

Maha Loha *(may - hah - low - hah)* - Kahlohani for 'my love'.

Maha Mo'ina Li'ili *(mah - hah - mo - ee - nah - lee - ee - lee)* - *Kahlohani for 'My little nightmare'.*

Medí Kosmoi *(med - ee - kohs - moy)* - *Aurealingan* for 'middle worlds'.

Nephilim - an immensely powerful winged immortal from a divine realm that guards the hell realms. Distinguishable from other *seraphi*

races by their horns, tail, and armor (the dark plating often found on their brow, chest, legs, and back).

Ouvelleet *(ou - va - leet)* - A town south of Bastrina, just beyond The Sentient Forest.

Poa Hanei *(po - uh - hah - nei)* - Kahlohani for 'soulmate'.

Reiland *(ray - land)* A northern island of lush rolling green hills, marshes, and seasides.

Sanguinati *(sang — gwee - nah - tee)* - an immortal being sustained by blood similar to the traditional 'vampire' but is not hindered by sunlight, is not allergic to silver, and will not die by a simple wooden stake to the heart.

Wielder - any individual or entity capable of wielding magic.

Seraphi Ousia *(seh- raff - ee - Oo - see - uh)* - Fragments of resting divine spirits.

Seraphi *(seh - raff - ee)* - a broader term for beings and deities originally from one of the higher realms, such as the *Nephilim.*

Syntrifa (seen - treef - fah) - The aurealingan term for fated mate.

Tessari mú *(tess - ah - ri - moo)* - An aurealingan term of endearment meaning *my treasure.*

Yatól *(yah - tohll)* - A northern province with a harsh and extreme climate that possesses mountains, dense forests, and a sprawling desert.

For anyone who has ever felt like they weren't enough.

You are more than enough.
You are worthy.
And you deserve the most wondrous things this bizarre and beautiful realm has to offer.

You are loved.

CHAPTER
ONE

MAREINA

The celestial glow of the moons spilled into my bedroom as I peeked outside the curtain before climbing into bed. Every hair on my body stood on end at the sight of the ominous, shadowy, hooded figure standing - or perhaps, floating - brazenly out in the open beneath a beam of the aforementioned moonlight.

Taunting me. Or so I'd begun to think.

Mors is coming for you, it seemed to whisper in my mind silently.

Fuck. Off, I replied. Also, silently and from the protective shell of my own mind lest the creature hear me and seek out its vengeance.

Despite the fact that my home was a formerly abandoned fortress ruin that I'd put my heart and soul into reclaiming and infused with every protective ward ever conceived, it did absolutely nothing to keep The God of Death's *Pharalaki* off my property.

My days were consumed by death. If there was a place I'd hoped to escape it, it would be my secluded haven, sitting at the edge of the Falcweard Mountains on the furthest outskirts of Bastrina, the capital of the Kingdom of Atratus.

My heart galloped in my chest as the *Pharalaki* glided closer as if lured by my gaze. I quickly flung myself into bed, tightly tucking myself beneath the covers.

For all the lives I had taken, one would think I would be immune to death.

No such luck.

It wasn't dying or the pain that would likely come along with it that terrified me. *Akash* knew I had faced that too many times to count.

No, no. As if some infantile part of my brain had never matured, the sight of those dark, whorling specters cloaked in darkness never failed to send icy tendrils of terror seeping through my veins.

My gaze remained fixed on the window, half expecting the *Pharalaki* to walk straight through it.

You deserve no less.

Time passed slowly as I tried to keep my mind from wandering down deeply carved paths long engraved into my psyche with an unforgiving blade. Finally, just as the moons began to slip beneath my window, my eyes slid shut, and I drifted into peace and nothingness.

Blackness as in the cool, blessed respite of night.

A blanket of calm.

As I did almost every night, I found myself floating here for an interminable amount of time- as this seemed to be a place that lay beyond time.

A distant pinpoint of light caught my attention, and I felt myself drawn to it, like a moth to a flame. As I did, that pinpoint of light seemed to break apart into dozens, hundreds, thousands, infinite points of light. Stars. Blazing in the limitless cosmos.

A deep, soothing voice that rumbled like distant thunder filled my mind, speaking a language I'd never known yet understood perfectly.

"O ziton irini feri polemon, al o kaloumenos 'O Vasiléfs mou' synaxi. Protá dio emisfaíria tou auto olo én genisete, ke tote panta pesite."

"The one who seeks peace will bring war, but it is the one you call, 'My King', who will unite. If two halves of the same whole become one, all your kingdoms will fall."

"Mi lanthonéti, oti kei mortatum ei aeternitate m*a skhimata dothate. Essita me, Guardatore Vitum, na evrīs tin oikisí sou."*

"Born between realms, forget not that you are eternity given form. You are never alone. Seek me, the Guardian of Life, to find your home."

The voice began to grow stronger, louder, sounding like one and many, as a great weight began to press upon me. I felt myself being pulled towards a distinctly black space in which everything, even light, was absorbed.

The voice within my mind grew so powerful that every molecule in my body began to shudder just as pain burst through me, swiftly and enduring until light consumed me. The pain disappeared as quickly as it had come.

The voice returned to a whisper, no longer inside my mind but outside of what was both distantly familiar and a strange, unsettling corporeal form that felt like a cage to my spirit body.

Water lapped at my feet at nearly the same temperature as this body. I found myself sitting up in a cave from what little I could make out in the brightness of the light that appeared to be emanating from some fixed point across the room.

The voice seemed to multiply and strengthen, otherworldly and consuming. I found myself drawn towards this fixed point, getting closer and closer until the light dimmed and the voices calmed once again until the cave became utterly silent... as if whoever's the voice it was holding their breath. Waiting.

A pythos sat atop a tall stone pedestal. The energy around me seemed to hum and vibrate in anticipation as my hand reached toward it. A distant voice roared as the skin of my physical body appeared to burn and evaporate away the nearer my hand drew to it. Muscle and tendon were seared away to reveal bone that burned away until all that remained of my hand was the silhouette of my hand and forearm, revealing my energy body and, within that, the cosmos as I'd travelled from...

The voice encouraged me forward as the chanting returned and grew in volume. Biting back the pain, I pressed forward, my fingertips only millimeters remained between my fingertips and the pythos...

My eyes blinked open, squinting at the sliver of dawn rising above the horizon. A current of energy still poured through me from the reoccurring dream I'd had on and off since I could remember, though it had grown far more frequent over the last year.

It had begun to drive me mad despite it being something of a reprieve from my usual reoccurring dreams. Or, more accurately, nightmares.

For the last ten months, I'd spent countless hours haunting The Queen's Library to no avail. I'd even snuck into her vaults that contained priceless artefacts that were thousands of years old, and nothing had come close to the pythos in my dreams.

Accompanied by an all-too-familiar ache that permanently settled between my shoulders, a thread of anxiety wove through me as reality settled in. What I knew the coming day held.

Execution day.

TWO

MAREINA

Each step felt like the passing of long seconds as I approached the entrance to the amphitheatre. A hulking fae male, Galvor Laith, with bright blue eyes and light brown hair, stood in front with his hand resting on the hilt of his sword. He'd always been one of my *least* favorite of the few guards I was forced to interact with due to his crass and smug manner in which I'd frequently found him interacting with others. If anyone deserved to be stuck in Leilani's time loop, it was him.

He was also one of the few guards who dared to meet my gaze and the only one who had ever dared to make sexual advances. Perhaps because I'd known him for too many years... We'd fought in the war together, and whereas I had risen in rank... He had not. The only reason a horrible *accident* hadn't yet befallen him was the fact that he had once saved me from a nearly fatal wound, and he clearly still felt like I owed him something.

His voice sounded like a boulder scraping across stone.

"Lovely Mareina..."

My annoyance rose swiftly, there before he even spoke.

"Galvor."

He stepped in front of me just before I could cross the threshold, making me bump into his wall of muscle. My lip curled as my gaze lifted from his pectorals to his face - generically handsome in that fae way but did absolutely nothing to inspire my libido.

"Unless you want to face Zurie's wrath because *you* made me late, I suggest you step aside."

"Now, why would you want to do that? You know I always look forward to our interactions. I just wish I could do something more to show you the... height of my desires for you."

Galvor's hand drifted over the front of his trousers, drawing my gaze to where he then gripped his cock. The thick outline of which I could clearly see.

"Come on, Mareina... After all these years, you can honestly say you feel *nothing* for me? Even after I saved you?"

A scowl twisted my features as I gradually drew my gaze to his heavy-lidded one. My hand lashed out to fist the low knot of his brown hair, yanking his head down and to the side to expose his thick throat to me as I drew the dagger sheathed at my thigh and pressed it against a thick, pulsing artery.

"Do something like that again, and I'll forget that you suffered that blow for me."

The whites of Galvor's piercing blue eyes widened with surprise before he raised his hands in surrender, and a smug grin tilted his lips.

"Understood."

His grin fuelled the flames of my ire, inspiring me to press the blade firmly. Blood trickled.

Before my hunger got the best of me, I released him, and he stepped aside. I licked the blade before spitting his foul blood onto his boot.

He chuckled, entirely nonplussed.

"You let me know if you change your mind... Just... ugh... Don't say anything to the General about this, please."

I huffed a laugh. Malekai would fucking *kill* him if I told him about this.

"Don't worry, Galvor. If I want you to die, it'll be by my blade."

"If it had to be anyone's blade...," he called out after me as I entered the cool, darkening depths beneath the amphitheater.

I heaved a sigh, feeling the weight of what was to come settle upon my shoulders, treading for too long minutes up the long, silent corridor that would eventually lead me to the outdoor stone dais. I

As I neared the end, I could hear Miroslav's baritone voice distantly echoing through the amphitheater above, working the crowd. By title, he served as Zurie's seer and advisor, though he seemed to relish going above and beyond his duties. First and foremost, the fact he slaughtered thousands of soldiers with little more than a thought during The Atratusian War. I'd also heard he'd appeared all too serendipitously out of nowhere after the untimely death of Queen Zurie's former advisor. She trusted him implicitly and relied heavily on him. So much so it made me wonder if they were clandestine lovers, though I'd never seen any evidence of it.

"... They threaten our sovereignty! Through their selfish, reckless actions, they attempt to create dissonance within the haven of our Kingdom! It weakens us! We must stand united lest they start another *war! We must end The Uprising!"*

The crowd's cheers and stomping in the amphitheatre above was deafening. Pebbles and dust rained down from the ceiling and the walls until they quieted.

Fools, my treasonous mind whispered.

After several long, gut-churning moments, I reached the doorless entryway that rose onto the dais, squinting my eyes in the bright sun, shining its jovial indifference on us from a cloudless sky. From her throne above, I felt her gaze on me like pricking needles.

"And here to ensure that justice is served, that our Kingdom's freedom and power remain, is The Wrath of Queen Zurie, herself... The Royal - Irae - Kalini!"

The crowd's roar was deafening as I stepped through the darkened archway that led onto the dais, my expression impassive and indifferent despite my inner turmoil.

My gaze clashed with Miroslav's silvery eyes, where he stood before a row of fae, sanguinati, elves, and other immortals, all kneeling with their hands bound behind their backs.

My gut gave another sickening twist as I tried not to meet their eyes and failed. Like the gravity of the sun, my gaze always fell to theirs. Eyes holding a painful melange of grim, defiant resignation, pride, fear, and sadness.

It should be me kneeling here instead of you, I know. I'm sorry. I'm so fucking sorry.

I knew none of them could hear me, yet my irreparably tarnished soul compelled me to direct the words silently towards them. Just as much an apology to them as it was a plea for forgiveness. Forgiveness that I didn't deserve.

My grip tightened on my sword as I steeled myself for what would come.

Nine.

Nine more lives I had to take. I'd never attempted to keep count during the war. It would have been a futile endeavour. However, after being promoted to Zurie's Wrath 70 years ago, I couldn't help but keep count on execution days.

1,504.

1,504 heads had rolled on this dais in the last 29 years. 1,504 more lives that I had taken on this gods-forsaken stage in front of thousands. Approximately 23,600 more pints of blood on my hands. I had reoccurring nightmares of drowning in their blood.

And my guilt.

I was no longer so loyal, disillusioned, and brainwashed into believing that what I was doing was for the betterment of The Kingdom of Atratus.

My eyes locked with the first of the waiting dead. A dryad female. Tall and beautiful, despite being covered in dungeon grime with skin a brownish green like the forest from which she, or her ancestors, had been born. Her eyes were blessedly dry. In place of tears was disgust and defiance.

Her eyes slid to the powerful male kneeling beside her. A sanguinati, like myself. And thanks to my heightened sense of hearing- a typical sanguinati gift- my gut gave another sickening churn as it effortlessly tuned out Miroslav's impassioned speech, along with the crowd's cheering, and sharpened to hear the words whispered between the dryad and her lover.

"I will find you in the next world, my fate."

Her eyes slid shut, head bowing forward in resignation to her fate. Her mate attempted to burn his hatred into me through his stare alone.

Metal sang through the air as I rose and brought down my blade. The dryad's mate roared his agony so loudly it drowned out the ensuing crowd's cry of victory.

The sickening *smack* of her head hitting the stone dais echoed as I swung my blade in its diagonal arch to sever the howling male's head from his body. Agony swiftly silenced, his head rolled across the dais, stopping beside hers as if drawn. Eyes still open, he met my gaze even in Death. Their bodies fell forward one directly after the other, like two toppling dominoes.

I didn't have the strength left to meet the remaining gazes. I swiftly mowed through the last of the seven Resistance members who had gotten themselves caught.

Though I'd never speak it aloud... I admired these rebels. They were doing what I longed to do but had no idea how.

How to sever this unbreakable tie to Zurie...

How to escape her wrath and, thusly, my death.

Despite the raucous noise filling the amphitheatre, I could only hear the soft, wet kiss of a blade meeting flesh and bone, the slap of the head smacking against stone, and the solid thunk of a body hitting the stone dais.

Shlick.

Smack.

Thunk.

Shlick.

Smack.

Thunk.

By the time the last body fell, my chest was heaving. Not from physical exertion but from the swelling tide of emotion. Guilt so powerful it had nausea crawling up my throat. My hand shook as I gripped my blade and quickly gave Zurie a cursory but mandatory bow before striding off the dais. The crowd roared behind me all the while.

The moment I made it around the first corner of the corridor exiting the arena, the contents of my stomach fled me. Mostly bile, as I hadn't been able to eat much this morning in anticipation of the morning's event.

I swiftly *willed* it away as I attempted to catch my breath. Approaching footsteps echoed softly moments later. The sensation of familiar magic reached out to me in a comforting and inquisitive caress.

I rushed down the corridor, hoping the lingering scent of my vomit wouldn't be noticeable at a distance, and nearly slammed directly into the approaching fae male who towered nearly an entire foot over my five foot ten inches.

"Hey," Malekai asked, bracing my shoulders with his large hands to study me, "You ok? You look pale..."

My voice came surprisingly steady. The heat that always radiated from Malekai's skin, no matter how icy the weather, poured into me from where he gripped me, easing the chill that had come over me.

"Of course."

Malekai's expression pinched dubiously.

My throat worked on a swallow as I stared up into his remarkably handsome face, tight with concern. Malakei, just like everything else about him - from his perfectly coifed flaxen hair, sun-kissed skin, and facial features that were otherworldly in their perfection - was like liquid gold. Complimented by the mesmerizing greens and blues of his eyes, only paralleled by the crystalline seas of Atratus' southern shores.

My eyes scanned the long corridors to confirm what my ears and magic told me: no one was nearby. Even so, my words came out little more than a whisper.

"I just..."

I shook my head, already knowing his thoughts. We'd had countless conversations regarding how I had grown to feel - to know - we were fighting on the wrong side.

My chest ached with disappointment as the words left my mouth, knowing very well Malekai didn't share my concern. His loyalty to Zurie remained as unwavering as the coin she put in his pockets. Yet, on the same token, I also knew he was loyal to me. He would betray her if it meant protecting me if it came down to it. If it meant sacrificing his own life to do so. His loyalty to me was only matched by my own to him.

Thanks to the last 100 years of serving in Queen Zurie's army together.

We had saved one another's lives on nearly countless occasions during the war against the Kahlohani people for their precious land and natural resources.

The primary resource being the precious *aetra* plant.

After Zurie had exploited and fully depleted the mainland of its natural resources, the Kahlohani Islands were now the only place in which the realm's most precious natural resource flourished. *Aetra*, which could be digested fresh, boiled down, and reduced for various uses, had magical and medicinal properties.

For the fae, like Queen Zurie, it made their magic near inexhaustible and enhanced them exponentially. It made them god-like. Even though they naturally possessed a remarkable control of magic, it was a finite thing. The magic in their blood and in their essence had its limitations. Like any muscle, it could become exhausted. And they wanted more. Few races of beings could rival their power without the assistance of *aetra*.

And without any other natural resources left for Zurie to exploit and make profit, *aetra* was her lifeline. It was all that remained to ensure her grasp on the throne.

There were a handful of wielders that aetra had no magic-enhancing effect on. As a Sanguiniti, I was one of them. Blood was the only thing I required for my power to be... formidable. However, it did make a difference what type of blood I feasted on. Human and animal blood, due to the minuscule amounts of magic it contained, did little to sustain me or enhance my power. I needed the blood of a *wielder. Any individual or entity capable of wielding magic.*

Malekai, unlike most fae, didn't need *aetra* to enhance his magic. The power he possessed was terrifying enough without it. He'd tried it before, and I witnessed its adverse effects on him first-hand. It was overwhelming, as though his power consumed him. He had an ungodly way of manipulating fire... That combined with the sheer brute strength, swordsmanship skills, and the keen intelligence he possessed... I'd always wondered if perhaps he had some distant   ancestor   that   had   been something *other,* something *more* than just fae. Especially considering his family had come from Hades originally. Anytime I'd asked, he'd always just shrugged it off.

After leading countless battles that resulted in victory and extraordinary displays of power, bravery, and valour, he was promoted to the Queen's General. And he'd taken me with him.

After some insistent whispering in the Queen's ear, she'd promoted me along with him, and for the last 29 years, I'd served as her *irae.*

Her *Wrath.*

To put it simply, I was her personal mercenary and executioner. I was the first female in her 480-year reign as Queen to serve as such. *The Royal Irae.* Something that would never have been possible without Malekai's influence on her.

It was a job I had once been profoundly grateful for, back when I believed that what we were doing was right. Now, however, I felt that each task Zurie assigned me further damned not only my soul but the Kingdom.

"Providing an equal distribution of power," as Zurie so loved to claim.

It was a lie.

While, yes, *aetra* was available to the public, only the wealthiest could afford it. Especially now that the only place it grew was the Kahlohani Islands.

Before Zurie had exhausted Atratus' other natural resources, *aetra* hadn't been particularly popular despite its miraculous properties. It had grown in great abundance, freely, like a wildflower, with its creeping vines, lilac petals, and golden pollen. It wasn't until Atratus' other natural resources began to dwindle that Zurie began manipulating the masses into believing that they *needed* it. That their impoverished circumstances were due to the fact that they didn't have enough of it.

Objectively speaking, it was a rather genius plan. And it had worked beautifully.

Once the demand increased, it did so exponentially and rapidly, and we soon learned that *aetra* was a rather sensitive plant. It required soil rich in magic and naturally occurring nutrients. All of which was swiftly depleted by her over-seeding and over-harvesting.

While the soil of the mainland had steadily been sucked dry for the last two thousand years, the Kahlohani Sea's nearby archipelago had remained almost entirely untouched. Its tropical climate was favorable, and its virgin soil, rich.

Zurie and her allies had claimed that chaos would ensue without *aetra* being accessible to the masses. That we needed to conquer the Kahlohani Islands so *aetra* would be abundant again. That innocent masses would be made vulnerable and victim to the few wielders who possessed exponentially more power than the rest.

That all happened anyway, except for the fact that *aetra* had little to do with it. The wielders who already possessed considerable magic only became more powerful, and those who wielded less magic were forced to abide by their rules and settle for the exceedingly limited resources and opportunities provided to them by the wielders in power. In order to accomplish this, she had chosen to enslave the Kahlohani, who had made the mistake of remaining on the islands and forced them to exploit the land to overgrow and over-harvest it in order to meet the realm's demands.

Zurie, if anything, was vicious. Her viciousness and mercilessness were inspired by her deep-rooted fear of losing control and power. And with *aetra* unavailable to almost everyone, most were rendered powerless against her because no one had access to it unless she allowed them to. Only Zurie controlled the growth and harvesting of *aetra*, and only her chosen loyal lords and ladies could afford to buy it. It was the most expensive and precious commodity in the entire Bellorum Realm - worth more than gold and jewels.

Malekai exhaled heavily, as though willing himself to be patient, as one would with a child, before leaning in and speaking in a hushed tone.

"You know how I feel about this, Mareina... There will always be those with power and those without. And I thank fuck that I'm one of the ones with it. But it doesn't make me evil. We're all just trying to survive. And the people who meet their ends at your sword put themselves there... And they are all that stands between you and your own end. If it wasn't Zurie, it would be someone else... It is the way of the world."

I disagreed. It didn't have to be that way. His words, in fact, only inspired my anger at his willful delusion. Perhaps it was his attempt to claim his sanity because I was indeed losing mine.

A grin curled Malekai's lips.

"Want me to just kill her for you, and then we can watch the world burn together?"

I huffed a laugh to mask the longing those words inspired within me. Malekai had jokingly suggested it to me on a number of occasions. More frequently as of late because he'd witnessed me become increasingly morose. And he knew just as well as I did that abandoning Zurie also meant forfeiting my life.

But as much as he joked, we were both trapped. And what were our alternatives even if we did escape? Malekai wasn't about to sacrifice his life of luxury. As much as I hated it, we *needed* Zurie. If something happened to her, she had no heirs, and whoever on her council took her place... Well, they would likely be just as bad, if not worse.

"Oh no, but who would pay for all your trips to *Satia Fama* then?"

Satia Fama literally meant *sated hunger* and was the name of his favorite brothel. It also had a section reserved as a blood parlour and was renowned for its sanguinati beauties.

Malekai's brows lifted as he pulled back to look down at me with a challenging look, absently twisting at the gold and ruby ring that always adorned his middle finger.

"I wouldn't need the *Satia Fama* if we were together."

My gaze fell from his at the heavy weight settling on my chest. It wasn't like I hadn't considered it for the last hundred years... Like I hadn't had an ache in my chest at the Malekai-shaped hole I had in it because some part of me longed to give in.

But Malekai was all I had. And I wasn't willing to destroy what we had by turning it into some fling. When we'd met, I'd already been in a relationship. We'd become best friends. And when she died during the war, Malekai was there to pick up the pieces. At the time, I'd been so busy grieving and trying to keep us alive that a tryst with him was the furthest thing from my mind. Not to mention, I was absolutely fucking terrified that I'd lose him too.

Malekai hooked a finger beneath my chin.

"Hey... *Katadamna Kaza.*"

Malekai's parents were originally from the southern coast of Hades, where they still spoke *Aurealinga*. It was a phrase he'd first told me a few years after we'd met, nearly a century ago, when he'd taken a bolt to the chest for me and nearly been killed because of it.

A few days later, I took a sword to the body that nearly stole my head to save him. He'd been furious and cursed at me for being so reckless. I'd merely given him a bloody grin and parroted his words.

More than a century later, the words still brought a swell of love and gratitude to my chest. Anytime we were forced to part ways, had an argument, or merely wanted to show the other affection, we needn't say anything more than those two words to be understood.

A sad smile tilted one corner of my lips at our declaration that spoke of undying love and loyalty.

"Katadamna kaza."

Damn the cost.

CHAPTER

THREE

MAREINA

I'd *just* sat down when the hairs on the back of my neck rose. Feeling the heat of someone's gaze, my eyes lifted from the table I was sitting at to find one of Mors' cursed *Pharalaki* dressed in his signature black robe. Unease seeped into my veins like a poison, and an icy fist squeezed my throat.

It took up the corner across from me in the tavern's dining room. The blasted things were made out of shadow. They didn't drink wine or beer.

What the fuck does it want?

You, that shameful, guilt-ridden part of me whispered.

I'd cheated Death, *Mors,* entirely too long. Had sent him far too many souls over the last 100 years for him not to take notice.

The shrill tinkle of feminine laughter coming from the booth behind me made my hackles rise. I twisted in my seat to settle a threatening glare at whoever was sure to give me a headache and found a scantily clad female dressed in white, a scarlet Erosyan collar on her neck, sitting on the lap of some male, her head tossed back in feigned, uproarious laughter.

There's no way that slimy fuck is that funny.

By no means was I against the *Erosyan Disciples*. Those who worshipped the goddess of pleasure, lust, and desire dedicated their lives to providing pleasure to others. My father was one, and as of the last 60 or so years, he'd become the high priest at the Erosyan Temple here in Bastrina. They'd taken us in when my mother had abandoned us shortly after I'd been born. A wound that had long since healed the best way it could and had turned into a *keloid scar*. Apparently, she'd disappeared one night and left nothing more behind than a note reading, *"I'm sorry."*

My father had come from poverty and had next to no material wealth, like most Atratusians. And by the time he'd had me, his family, loving as they were, had long passed. Without my mother to care for me so my father could work, we'd become destitute quickly and found ourselves on the steps of the Erosyan Temple. A place known for rehabilitating those in need... At a cost, of course.

Even so, thanks to the Erosyan Temple, I'd been readily enfolded into one enormous family despite all its flaws. They'd fostered my singing abilities and encouraged and trained me.

Before I'd even reached adulthood, I'd sung in their pleasure halls as my way of contributing. It had been the most fulfilling thing I'd ever experienced. It still remained to be one of them. However, despite all the love and nourishment that had helped me blossom and grow at the Erosyan Temple thanks to its disciples... More than a few patrons had given me the kind of scars you couldn't see. However, I knew the only reason I didn't have any physical scars was purely because of my sanguinati healing abilities. My singing had drawn too much attention. The *wrong* kind of attention.

And while some patrons were respectful.

Some were not.

They'd taken what they wanted.

It was why I had left and joined Queen Zurie's army. It had been my only means of escape outside of rendering myself even more vulnerable by sleeping on the streets. Joining her ranks had given me the skills to protect myself, and I vowed to never be made a victim again.

But I had yet to sing since. Not in front of anyone, at least.

Occasionally, in the comfort and security of my home, I would sing in the small hours of the night until tears poured from my eyes in cathartic release.

I turned back around in my seat to find the *Pharalaki* had disappeared, and I finally exhaled.

A heavy sigh left me as I raised the glass of amber liquid to my lips, briefly locking eyes with another of the pub's patrons wearing an expression similar to mine.

My eyes scanned the crowded pub, desperate to find another open table or booth, just as Malekai strode in. Like a magnet, his eyes found mine instantly. Just as every female and several males' eyes were drawn to him.

Unconcerned with his ever-present admirers, his handsome face split in two at the sight of me. He had a way about him that always seemed to illuminate every room he entered, whereas I tended to darken it. He had the sort of beauty and perfection that was almost annoying. Truly, Malekai was an unfairly good-looking male.

The heads of his onlookers craned to follow his long strides. The crowd parted like the sea as he made his way towards me. I couldn't help but roll my eyes, watching them before I rose to greet him.

"Perhaps there'd be some merit in—

Another peal of high-pitched laughter accompanied by a masculine rumble stabbed my ears again, making my jaw clench. Malekai lifted a dark golden brow as a grin tilted the corner of his mouth.

"— finding another place to sit... Or another pub, entirely," I finished, head throbbing.

Malekai leaned around to peek at the Erosyan female and her client before looking back at me.

"But they're having so much fun... Perhaps we should join them?"

My hand lashed out as Malekai shifted, gripping his large bicep as I spoke through gritted teeth.

"Don't. You. Dare."

I downed the rest of my drink and slammed the empty glass back on the table. The burning warmth of it sliding down my throat helped relax the tension in my neck that throbbed at the base of my skull and had begun to radiate behind my eyes.

Malekai tsked, cooing to me in a husky voice.

"Always such a curmudgeon, my darling."

My eyes narrowed sharply.

"When was the last time I stabbed you?"

Malekai's eyes twinkled with mirth. "Too long ago, I'm sure."

"You almost sound like you want me to stab you."

"I thought you'd have realized a long time ago that I'm a devout sadomasochist."

I huffed a laugh, shaking my head at him. "You are *so* twisted."

Malaria's voice dropped to a husky purr. "Nothing wrong with a little pain and pleasure, sweetheart."

Sweetheart.

He was, quite literally, the only male who had ever dared to call me such an endearment. The only one I'd ever let beyond the wall I'd systematically built over the years that could even feel comfortable calling me such a soft name. Admittedly... I fucking loved it when he did. After so many years *of literally* fighting to survive, I longed to trade in my sword to become soft, tender, and pretty.

A familiar heat that only he inspired coiled low, but I merely pursed my lips and narrowed my eyes as if to say, *touché.* Malekai gave a hearty chuckle as I swiftly turned, throwing the hood of my cape over my head.

Malekai and I wandered the serpentine, cobblestone footpath along the River Atratus' black waters. Named after the Kingdom through which it ran, it was one of the only relatively safe places in the city beneath the Queen's palace. Not many dared to venture near the waters of the Atratus because it was a notorious dumping ground for the 'recently deceased'. The Atratus had a way of making things disappear. How exactly, no one precisely knew, but that seemed to only add to the fear the Atratus inspired.

Not that Malekai and I had any reason to be fearful. Despite the crime that plagued the city, Malekai was well-known and feared as the Queen's general. And I, thankfully, still possessed some relative anonymity by comparison, thanks to the fact that not many knew my face. I would find no small amount of satisfaction in ridding the world of one more twisted opportunist looking to prey upon 'vulnerable' females.

My gaze snagged on a dark, hooded figure in the distance facing the stone riverbank's wall. Dressed in the rich black robe of Mors' acolytes. They hadn't noticed our approach yet. I slowed, silently nudging Malekai and nodding towards the figure. We came to a stop, watching. Their back too broad for us to see what it is they're doing.

Taking a piss, maybe?

It would be a little unusual for one of those zealots to be doing something so uncouth.

The acolyte turns and scurries across the street, where another of the hooded acolytes waits. *Technically,* we should have done something about it. Vandalism was something Zurie didn't take kindly to, but... Neither of us actually cared.

Not to mention, they made my skin crawl.

The acolytes disappeared down the alley. We soon reached where the acolyte had been standing to discover they'd painted Mors' symbol in white, stark against the dark stone.

An inverted torch with wings.

The inverted torch was supposed to represent the extinguishing of life and the wings being liberated from the body that shackles us to this realm and carries us into the next.

I glanced back down the alley to find an even larger depiction of the symbol.

"So creepy."

Malekai chuckled, piquing a brow at me as he blew out a lungful of dream leaf smoke.

"To *you*? The fearless and feared Royal Irae?"

I gave him a challenging look. "They literally pray for the world to end."

"Have you been sleeping much lately?"

Malekai's question caught me off guard, the concern in his voice blatant. I took a deep breath, eyes locked on the triple moons' glittering reflection on the Atratus.

"No less than usual."

A corner of Malekai's mouth tilted low.

"So not at all then."

I shrugged. "Not always."

Malekai remained silent for a moment, taking another puff from the dream leaf cigar he'd rolled before passing it to me. The dream leaf helped ease the tension in my neck, alleviating my headache. Unfortunately, its effects wouldn't last long enough for it to help me sleep, as its name would suggest.

Dream leaf was often smoked or brewed as tea; the effect could last several hours for humans. It would last an hour or so for the fae, like Malekai and other immortals. But thanks to being sanguinati, it only lasted me 15-20 minutes. It also made me awfully hungry, and my canines had begun to ache, longing to bite and drink.

My heart stalled in my chest at the sight of the palatial building that came into view from where we stood on a bridge that held a rather impressive view of the city. The Erosyan Temple, for the last eighty years, had been a glittering, white and garnet domed, stone cathedral... Objectively speaking, it was indeed an impressive sight.

However, when I had lived there, it had been an enormous but claustrophobic wooden and carpeted maze of rooms and secret hallways...

A few short years after I'd left, much to my satisfaction, the whole place had been reduced to ashes... It was no surprise, considering patrons smoked all manner of mind and mood-altering substances, not to mention all of the bowls of cloying incense that someone could easily have accidentally nudged too close to one of the heavy drapes.

I'd only wished that I'd thought to burn it down myself.

Gods. How did we even end up here?

Fucking dream leaf.

Malekai followed my gaze, expression tensing when he found my focal point and wrapped an arm around my shoulders. The muscles in my body seemed to relax all at once, and I hadn't even noticed how tense they were. He wordlessly guided me in the opposite direction, pressing a kiss to the top of my head.

I'd never told Malekai what had happened in the Erosyan Temples, but I imagine he assumed *something* had occurred. On the few occasions he'd asked about my time there, I'd always deviated from the more traumatic of events. The horrors that'd occurred there had caused me to curl in on myself and hide. I'd spent the last 120 years carefully crafting my disguise- the hardened, cold warrior that had risen to the top of Queen Zurie's ranks.

Speaking aloud the things that had, at one time, broken me was unthinkable. Not to mention, confessing to Malekai what had happened would cause him pain. And there was nothing that could be done about it. The ones who had stolen what they'd wanted from me were lost to the realm, and I had no way nor desire to find them, with only one exception. Whom I had found and killed.

A year after joining Zurie's Army, I discovered that wreaking vengeance did nothing to heal hidden wounds. In fact, it only served to make them more raw.

The male's death had come to me easily. He hadn't even remembered me. He'd not only been the first male to have entered my body, despite that I'd nearly clawed his eyes out trying to stop him, but he was also the first person I'd ever killed. I'd followed him home after happening upon him in a pub to see him for the sad, sick male he was. When my sword had removed his head, it felt more like a mercy kill than anything.

Malekai passed me his cigar before bringing his hands to the tense muscles of my neck, squeezing and kneading and making me groan in relief as I exhaled the dream leaf in a billowing cloud. A wave of gentle euphoria washed over me, easing the tightening in my chest and carrying the painful memories away. A blessed giggle bubbled up within me.

Malekai chuckled behind me, further fueling my laughter.

"What's so funny, *tessari mú*?"

My treasure.

I chuckled all the more. "I have no idea."

Malekai's chuckle grew into something warm and hearty before he turned and pulled me into his arms. The perennially effusive warmth radiating from his chest instantly eased the tension in my muscles. I peeked up at his smiling face, grinning from ear to ear. The sight quite literally stole my breath away.

He spoke through his laughter as his eyes scanned every part of my face as though committing it to memory.

"Let me see that gorgeous smile..."

Our gazes held for several moments, my heartbeat galloping with increasing speed. Our laughter gently faded, our lips parted...

Oh, gods... How I'd wanted this for so long...

But something... Something clenched around my fluttering heart like a fucking iron fist.

My mouth snapped shut, and my gaze fell from his.

Malekai's grip on me tightened, drawing his hand to my face to return my gaze.

"Mareina..."

"We should get going... It's getting late."

Gods, I was an asshole.

"Let's get you home then..."

Malekai stepped back, leaving cool air and an all-too-familiar ache in my chest to take his place.

Tense silence settled into companionable silence as we walked. Malekai flicked out the remainder of his dream leaf cigar and wedged it between a crack in one of the mortared stones lining the river wall, likely so that a *transient* person might enjoy it.

I peeked an eyebrow at him. "Feeling generous suddenly?"

"Not at all... Would just be a shame to waste it, and half-smoked dream leaf tastes like shit."

I gave a small huff of intrigue.

The rest of our walk was silent, my gaze occasionally sliding to him to find his gaze fixed in the distance and twisting the ring of his middle finger. It was his one tell that consistently belied his tension. Only displayed when it was just the two of us.

"You think you'll be able to sleep tonight?" I asked once we reached my doorstep.

Malekai shrugged, caressing my hair, taking me in one last time before leaving.

"Probably not."

"Are you going straight home or..."

Are you going to Satia Fama?

His favorite brothel.

He huffed a laugh. "What would you have me do? Suffer from blue balls until the day I die?"

I chuckled, rolling my eyes and smirking despite the jealousy that spiked through me. The words I forced out felt like shards of glass.

"Well... I hope you have fun..."

He grinned knowingly, taking my chin between his thumb and forefinger to tilt my head as he lowered his to press a lingering kiss on my forehead.

"Katadamna kaza," he murmured, lips grazing my brow.

I reached out, pulling him back towards me, wrapping my arms around his waist. He was the only person I allowed even that modest intimacy with. I trusted him more than anyone I'd ever known. Nearly a hundred years of fighting side-by-side, saving one another's lives, and trauma-bonding will do that.

"Katadamna kaza."

CHAPTER

FOUR

MAREINA

S leep evaded me. Though it was perhaps for the better. It meant I wouldn't be haunted by the reoccurring nightmares depicting even further twisted versions of my past, nor the bizarre reoccurring dream of some god - whether long forgotten or imaginary, I had no idea - begging to be unleashed.

By the time the moons had sunk to the horizon and the watery light of dawn's twilight began to seep in through my bedroom window, I'd given up trying. I also hadn't fed properly in at least a week. I ate food, like most anyone else, but it wasn't what truly sustained me. Even if thoroughly enjoyable on occasion, it never left me feeling truly sated or nourished.

I swiftly bathed in scalding hot water, hoping uselessly that it would somehow lessen my hunger pains. Since The Atratusian War had ended 88 years ago, I felt as though every life I'd taken took a piece of my soul with it, and now I had nothing left. Deep within the darkest part of my subconscious that haemorrhaged into my waking consciousness, I knew that I didn't deserve to live. Much less enjoy the satisfaction and nourishment that blood would give me.

I braided the length of my long black hair, studying my olive complexion. Over the course of too many sleepless and hungry nights, I'd begun to pale, and my high cheekbones were becoming a little too sharp. A symptom of my lack of feeding. Perhaps it was time to visit a blood parlour. Another sort of pleasure palace that I avoided, knowing full well that whatever went on at the Erosyan Temple, it would be even worse at the blood parlours, but at least they weren't haunted by my memories or the ghosts within.

The sun had just begun to peek its warm, purple and orange rays over the horizon, reflecting starkly off the black waters of The River Atratus by the time I made my way to Zurie's palace. It was a sharp, white, jagged thing that cut into the skyline like spiralling daggers. Aesthetically, it was an assault on what would be a majestic land-scape where it was positioned in the valley with the mountains as its only backdrop. Architecturally, it was an astounding and intricate sprawling mass of twisted spires with detailed sculptures carved into the edifice itself.

Still, I found it mildly hideous and rather abrasive to look at.

Approaching the imposing gates, I slipped the hood of my cape off. The horde of fae guards stepped aside silently as I approached. Though their heads remained forward-facing, I could feel their eyes following me like an unwanted touch as curiosity and wariness radi-ated from them.

Sanguinati rarely reached the upper echelons of society. Gener-ally, they were regarded as too dangerous, too cunning, and too savage to be trusted. Mainly because we generally didn't have any need for *aetra*. And our magic didn't diminish with use.

Objectively speaking, I couldn't blame their wariness. We required the blood of beings who possessed magic.

Beings like them.

The fact *they* were our prey, and not humans, who were viewed as little more than labour livestock by most wielders nor most animals - naturally caused a rift between our kinds. Even though it wasn't necessary, or even common these days, that we took a life every time we fed. Quite the opposite, in fact. Thanks to our venom, feeding was most often an exceedingly pleasurable experience. It was only in rare cases when a sanguinati had gone too long without feeding that they risked being lost to blood lust.

It had taken a year of Malekai's incessant persuasion for Queen Zurie to consider me for the esteemed and feared position of Royal Irae. Queen Zurie had made her distaste of sanguinati evident to the both of us.

Though they certainly had their place in her army because of our tremendous power and inexhaustible supply of magic. It was said that the sanguinati were the descendants of the Omnisseras. An ancient race of primals that had seeded our realm, Bellorum, with their spawn before they'd either left or died out.

The palace was still blessedly quiet when I arrived. I looked forward to spending my early hours in the training arenas to work off some of my mounting tension. A grin leapt upon my face when I saw the deadly obstacle course empty, excitement brimming, as I unclasped my cape and let it pool around my feet.

I approached the white marble waist-high obelisk carved with ancient ruins- a blood altar- and drew my dagger across my palm to spill my blood into the sharpened point of its apex. As my blood trickled into the veins of the marble, hungry magic began to emanate from it, licking against my own as though trying to steal more than I was already offering. A low, metallic groan and a monstrous yawn sounded in the distance, signifying the now-waking labyrinth and all the beasts that roamed within.

The labyrinth's obstacles and creatures were ever-changing. There was no memorizing the way out or anticipating what obstacle or creature might come next. It was chosen for you each time, and each time was different. And many who went in died. It was the final requisite to becoming one of Zurie's infamous royal guards, infantry-men, and the like.

"Why you'd choose that haunted death trap as a way to blow off steam is beyond me."

My heart leapt at the sound of that voice.

I turned to find Malekai sitting perched on the leg of a stone sculpture of a sphynx behind me. He brought a bright yellow pear to his lips, taking a large bite that made juice run down into the dimple of his perfectly sculpted chin. I couldn't help the scoff that escaped me at the sight of his shirtless chest glistening with perspiration from his own training. *It was honestly cruel for any male to be that good-looking.*

"It's been nearly two weeks since Zurie sent me off to do her 'bidding'."

As much as I hated it, her tasks were also a source of therapy for me... So long as they proved to deserve her wrath, which was often the case, thankfully.

Malekai finished the rest of his juicy snack in two large bites - core and all - before hopping off the Sphinx, falling about a dozen feet before landing with feline grace and prowling towards me. His voice was a velvety purr.

"Train with me."

He gave me a wicked grin that promised... so many things.

If I'd only be willing to accept them.

If only I deserved them.

Deserved him.

I opened my mouth to reply, stopping short when his brow furrowed, and he drew close. Frowning for a moment and studying me a little too intensely.

"You haven't fed since then, have you?"

Any potential lie caught in my throat. I'd never been a good liar. And he was the only person in this world that I loved. Despite all my unforgivable transgressions, I didn't have the intestinal fortitude to be dishonest with him.

"I'm fine... I don't need to feed that often."

Apparently, lying was *not* beneath me.

Malekai's nostrils flared to discover the answer for himself. He had an exceptional sense of smell, and apparently, he could scent when I'd gone too long without feeding.

"Mareina," he growled.

I heaved a sigh, ignoring that pinching feeling in my back, as I pressed a palm to his heated chest in an attempt to assuage his frustration and *my* guilt.

"Look—

The sound of a door opening had both our heads snapping towards the training room. I stepped back, returning my hand to my side. A few heartbeats later, a royal guard appeared.

"General Theikos. Irae Kalini. Apologies for the interruption. Her Majesty requests your presence in her private garden."

Malekai gave him a sharp nod. "Thank you, Sekhat. We'll be right there."

At that, the guard brought a fist to his chest before returning the way he came, leaving us to our heavy silence. As much as I normally avoided *Her Majesty,* I was grateful for the interruption.

"Let's go see what it is precisely that has caused her to crawl out of her harem, shall we?"

Zurie rarely found reason to leave it, and when she did, it was only begrudgingly.

I gave Malekai a pat on one of his impressive, golden pectorals before attempting to turn on my heel —

"Mareina, we aren't through with this discussion," he ground out, grasping my arm firmly and pulling me back towards him. I looked down at the offending hand before returning his gaze, raising an eyebrow.

"I'll feed. Obviously. It's not like I have a choice in the matter."

"When? You can't keep throwing yourself into the jaws of death when you're not at peak performance. You aren't invincible. And if you think I'm going to let you, you're gravely mistaken."

A frown sank its way onto my face.

Malekai shook his head at me with growing impatience.

"Would you allow me to do the same?"

My shoulders sagged in defeat. It was a rhetorical question, obviously. He already knew the answer. It didn't feel so long ago that the tables were turned. And Malekai no longer drank because of it. We'd nearly lost the war despite the Kahlohani's dismal odds.

Most of his family had died long before Malekai's parents migrated from Hades, like my father, centuries ago. The only living relative Malekai had by the time the war started was his mother. They'd shared a deep bond. When she was raped and murdered during a raid in their village, he'd blamed himself for not having been there to protect her.

He'd left his mother to fight the war to protect her along with the rest of their family, but now he felt certain it was because he left that she, along with the rest of their family, had died.

It was then that he had taken on a nihilistic way of living. He still did in many ways, but at least now he didn't drink and wasn't actively trying to get himself killed. Trying to help him recover from that had nearly destroyed our friendship.

"I promise I'll feed tonight. So long as it doesn't interfere with whatever Zurie needs me to do."

Malekai narrowed his eyes at me, and I swore I saw a flame spark somewhere within the depths of them.

"If you think I won't tie you down and force you to feed, you clearly underestimate me."

I bit my cheek, suppressing my grin and my gut reaction.

"If you think that's a deterrent, you highly underestimate *yourself.*"

His lips parted briefly before his jaw quickly snapped shut, and he tried to suppress his own grin.

Zurie's garden was a hidden but expansive courtyard that included a dazzling variety of flora set in perpetual bloom, thanks to her magic.

And aetra.

Two guards posted at the entrance shut the elegant carved

double doors behind us, sealing us in with the tiny little demon that ruled this realm.

In the distance, Miroslav, who was a slash of black against the vibrant garden, stood beside Zurie, a mask of innocent beauty garbed in pale blue.

"I don't need to threaten you for you to understand that if I discover any betrayal, you'll be made an example of," Zurie whispered in a deceptively soft tone.

Miroslav stood frozen still, staring down at Zurie, and it was only when I homed my hearing in on him that I realized he wasn't breathing. Sweat beaded from his forehead as veins bulged in his neck. If I didn't know better than to hide my eavesdropping, I'd have gaped in shock at the sight. Miroslav was the most powerful male I'd ever seen- and that was without the assistance of *aetra*.

As one of the few remaining Orisha— beings with deity-like powers that hailed from the mountains and deserts of Yatól, *aetra* had no effect on them. I'd witnessed him kill thousands in an instant during the war with little more than a thought. Without him, it was likely Zurie would have lost the war.

The Kahlohani had not only been fearsome but also strategic. They'd always seemed three steps ahead of us, in addition to having a formidable ally- The Selcarim Army.

Selcarim was a western coastal region that was ensconced by a mountain range so treacherous the only way to cross it was to go *through* it and *under it*. The only people who could find and make it through the tunnels, winding and hundreds of miles long, were the Selcarim people themselves. The region had a plethora of myths and mysteries that surrounded it because anyone who wasn't from there had never ventured there and returned, except for their natives.

Additionally, there was *supposedly* no land worth mining; thus, Zurie had no incentive to infiltrate it. Self-governed, it was the only land on the Atratusian mainland that remained independent of Zurie.

It wasn't until Miroslav began actively participating in the war, not too long before he showed up, that the War had swiftly ended. Traditionally, a royal seer or advisor didn't risk stepping foot on a battlefield. However, after 12 years, Zurie finally decided to risk her most powerful, newfound ally. Before then, I don't think she even had truly grasped the extent of his power. In a matter of weeks, the Kahlohani had been forced to surrender.

To see him made victim to Zurie was deeply unsettling, even though I had no doubt the male deserved it. While she was one of the most powerful fae in Atratus, I couldn't help but wonder just how much of that display was in thanks to the amount of *aetra* she consumed. Unlike Miroslav, she kept a vial of it on her at all times. Though she made a point to be discreet about her usage of it, she always bore the telltale signs of someone who was on it: the scent of the flower seeped from their pores in its signature earthy, floral musk, and her tongue was often stained darkest purple.

Thanks to the fermentation process required in order for it to maximize its magic-enhancing potential, the flower and its pistils had to be prepared as a concentrated tincture, which intensified the natural purple of the flower and stained anything it touched.

Her gaze snapped to us, and she released Miroslav, who quietly drew in a deep, steadying breath before wiping away beads of sweat on his forehead.

Zurie gave Malekai and me a small, forced smile. "See that you escort Irae Kalini and her steed to the location of her next task tomorrow, Miroslav."

"Yes, Your Majesty."

Miroslav gave Zurie a stiff bow before turning to leave, his eyes briefly meeting mine and giving me a quick nod.

As we approached, the Queen came to stand in front of a large pond, holding a small sack from which she drew bloody chunks of meat with her blood-tipped fingers. The fish, I had never discovered what kind specifically... All I knew was that they had come from another realm. Supposedly the realm of her ancestors.

The water sloshed violently as the creatures fought for each bit of flesh she tossed in. She wore a placid look on her face as she appeared to stare *through* the pond and fish, not bothering to look up at us as we approached. I found my gaze drawn to the matte grey and brown, sharply finned creatures thrashing beneath the surface.

As we neared, Malekai and I both bowed at the waist, exchanging a brief glance as we straightened. Zurie stood a full foot and a half beneath Malekai's 6'8, with long light brown hair that hung in two thick braids over her shoulders, framing her heart-shaped face with its pointed chin. Large, blue, doll-like eyes and long eyelashes gave the illusion of innocent youth.

Zurie was older than anyone I personally knew, but perhaps that was because having come from the military, most individuals I knew had a great propensity to die. And to speak of her innocence would be like trying to dress a wolf in sheep's clothing.

"Beautiful, are they not?" Zurie murmured softly in her delicate, ultra-feminine voice.

"Yes, Your Majesty," Malekai replied promptly as his eyes remained on me, "They indeed possess a... savage and terrifying beauty."

Her gaze rose like a blade, drawing our eyes to her deep blue ones. Her gentle features are a sharp contrast to the twisted creature within.

"Terrifying? Why, I don't find them terrifying at all, General. Hunger does not equate to malevolence. A rabbit grows hungry and devours a carrot. Do you find rabbits terrifying as well?"

As if to punctuate her sentence, one of the fish thrashed above the water just as she tossed another bit of flesh into the pond, giving us a glimpse of its multiple rows of jagged, razor-sharp teeth.

"Perhaps it is merely their... physical characteristics that I find off-putting. Not their nature," Malekai amended.

The queen grinned, revealing a set of fangs, remarkably sharp for a fae.

"Oh, but that is precisely what I find so breathtaking. Simple symmetry and color alone are dull," Zurie explained, closing in on

Malekai until she stood only inches in front of him, "Irae Kalini... General Theikos is a rather beautiful male, yes?"

As she spoke, she drew a delicately clawed finger across one side of his jaw, making it flex, along with my own. Both mine and Malekai's hackles raised in response to her unwanted touch.

At my hesitation, her gaze snapped to mine, gripping Malekai's jaw in her hand.

"Speak, Irae. Surely, you have an opinion."

"... Yes, his beauty is... remarkable, your majesty."

Her sharp grin broadened, a malevolent glint in her eyes. The telltale signs of *aetra* staining her gums added to her menace.

Zurie's grip further tightened on Malekai's jaw with each passing word, her nails sinking into his flesh, causing blood to blossom and spill down his neck. That pressure in my shoulders burned so fiercely that my hands shook with the need to gut her where she stood.

"But don't you find his beauty so much more captivating...," she continued. Malekai's brow hardened as the tips of his unusually long fangs elongated further, pressing into his bottom lip, "When he has fangs?"

I silently debated whether or not I could summon my sword and close the distance between us fast enough to survive killing her. Malekai would be furious if I didn't.

"With or without fangs, what I find most captivating about General Theikos is his valor and loyalty. His soul."

And yours is fucking hideous.

Zurie's only response was the pursing of her lips as she finally released him, patting his chest like a *good boy* before wiping her bloody hand on his shirt. She held his gaze, looking up at him seductively from beneath her long eyelashes as she licked the residue of his blood from her fingers with her *aetra*-stained tongue. Her brow pinching suddenly.

"Your blood is rather peculiar, General... Where did you say your family is from?" She asked, studying him with far too much interest.

"Hades, Your Highness."

Humming thoughtfully, she grinned as though having reached a conclusion.

"Perhaps you would like to join me in my chambers this evening, General?"

Jealousy heaped coals onto the fire of my rage.

Malekai somehow managed to not miss a beat and gave her a seductive smile despite the gouged wounds still actively healing on his face.

"I am truly honored that you would extend such a prized invitation to me, your highness."

Her grin broadened for a few moments before falling as she began to pace in front of us.

"In the meantime, I have some rather upsetting news."

Zurie lifted a palm, and a letter appeared.

"General, I need you to select a small company of your men to ride for Vyssini. I've received word that a few of the villages just south of Vyssini have begun rioting against the lords in the region. One of the mobs even managed to burn down one of their estates. I want the head of every rioter put on a stake in the town square as a warning. Prepare your men. You leave first thing in the morning."

Malekai's jaw feathered, hesitating only briefly before nodding his acquiescence. My stomach churned for him.

"Additionally, I've received word that yet another estate has been sacked and that Hallofrin no longer has a Lord to govern it. I'll need you to send a separate company of your soldiers to prevent any additional turmoil in the region."

"Yes, Your Majesty."

"And General, I hold you accountable that these *Akash*-forsaken outlaws are *still* wreaking havoc in our lands and slaughtering my Lords and Ladies. The lootings have become more and more frequent *despite* your efforts. Illumine me as to *how* exactly that's possible."

"Your majesty, I have sent my best males and females to investigate - they leave nothing behind but spilled blood and..."

"And what, General?"

"They share the spoils with the servants."

Zurie's eyes flared wide briefly, and a vein began to bulge in her forehead as she spoke in a dangerously quiet voice.

"Do you like your place in this realm, General Theikos? The luxuries it affords you? The countless nights of debauchery at *Satia Fama* that you indulge in?"

Malekai's expression gave nothing away as he spoke evenly. "Yes, Your Majesty."

She studied him for a moment, a look of dissatisfaction pinching her features.

"But you're not entirely motivated by those things, are you? What about the comfort and stability afforded to Irae Kalini? Or the money you're able to save in the hopes of one day retiring and... taking my Irae with you?"

My heart stuttered and clenched at her words as Malekai's jaw clenched.

Zurie chuckled. "How precious that would be... What a fairytale I'm sure you've imagined for yourself."

Malekai remained silent, though I couldn't help but notice the hand fisting at his side restlessly as though it wished to grip the ruby-tipped pommel of his blackened steel sword. Tiny flames sparked around fingertips as though he could barely suppress his power rising to the surface.

Zurie chuckled, humming to herself. "Well, I can assure you that none of that will be possible if this Uprising gains traction. What do you think will happen if every fucking *minori wielder* all over Atratus bands together against us? Hm? Even enough ants can overcome a lion. And then *none* of your little fantasies will become a reality because we'll all be dead. The Kingdom will lay in ruin. Given to lawlessness and impulse just as it did *before* my ancestors came here and *built* this fucking throne."

Ruin.

Before Zurie's ancestors arrived, this place had been a place of wild bounty, even if it hadn't held the comforts that more modern times were afforded.

Malekai remained silent still as Zurie's gaze bore into him.

"And what we need is to burn this blight at the root. *Find* these *minori* scum outlaws. *Find* the leaders of this Uprising. I want their dreams shattered like glass upon the cold, unforgiving ground. This kingdom will learn the consequences of challenging a queen: a slow, agonizing death."

Each heinous word she spoke only further served to increase my hatred of her.

How difficult would it be to kill her here and now?

Even if I died doing so... It would be worth it. Judging by the dark purple stain on her lips, I'm not sure I would be able to pull it off.

Gods, who would take her fucking place?

Miroslav?

One of her vile Lords or Ladies?

None of those prospects stood in our favor.

Malekai's reply was firm but bared an unmistakable hollowness to it. "Understood, Your Majesty."

Perhaps Malekai's conscience was starting to wear on him... Though it was doubtful. He'd expressed as much.

At Zurie's silence, Malekai bowed and turned, briefly locking eyes with me before striding out of the courtyard garden.

Zurie took a deep breath as she began to slowly pace in front of the pond housing her *hungry* fish. I couldn't help but imagine pushing her in, them shredding her to pieces.

Instead, I waited silently, thoughts having followed Malekai out of concern. Concern at Zurie's sociopathic display, how he would handle Zurie's *invitation*, and now his latest assignment - public executions.

Zurie's eyes lingered on Malekai's back until he disappeared, and she finally turned to face me. She took her time running her gaze over me as though examining some kind of puzzle with too many missing pieces.

. . .

"There is a... a hybrid male. Half-fae, half-human. From what I'm told, he always wears a glamor... His name is Nakoa Solanis. Apparently, he lives somewhere in The Sentient Forest. I need you to find him, kill him, and bring me the body... Have Miroslav fold you and the body to the crypt."

Several heartbeats passed, anticipating that perhaps she would elaborate. She had never requested I bring the corpse of her 'victims' back with me... Perhaps she wanted to make an example of him by mounting his head on a pike in front of the castle.

The beginnings of a sneer began to curl her lip at my lack of response.

"Yes, your majesty..."

"It's suspected he's the leader of this group of outlaws terrorizing the members of my court... From what I've heard, he's heavily allied... Likely due to all the *charity* he's shown the paupers of the region, so I would recommend even further discretion."

Dread knotted my stomach.

I had few qualms with ridding the realm of the scum who usually found themselves tangled in Zurie's web...

But someone who was... decent? Who was actively helping vulnerable people? People who came from adverse circumstances like I had?

Zurie may as well have had her clawed hand wringing my neck. My words came out hollow but firm, forced out, as I buried my guilt deep in the chasm of my soul so that I could finally breathe.

"I will speak of it to no one."

"It is also rumoured that his magic is considerable..."

"... Because of *aetra*?"

She hesitated to respond. "... No."

It was exceedingly rare for humans to have access to magic. I'd only ever heard of the rare witch being endowed with such a gift.

Her lips pursed as she ran her gaze over me. Something like

distrust flickered in her eyes despite all my years of loyalty. I knew it was more than just being sanguinati. Though we were renowned for being savage, impulsive, and guileful creatures... the fae were certainly no better.

More than that, she knew I'd been raised in what some considered to be a glorified brothel, the daughter of a male 'prostitute'. Abandoned by even my mother, who I knew almost nothing about. And *that* would forever be the lens through which she saw me. *Unworthy.*

Although no one actually knew much of Zurie's lineage beyond the last few generations. Her great-grandfather had been the first King of Atratus. From what I'd read in historical texts, these lands and its people were still wild... Until *the arrival.* When the fabric between worlds was briefly split open, and *they* stepped through.

"You have five days."

"Yes, Your Majesty."

CHAPTER

FIVE

MAREINA

I took deep, anxiety-soothing breaths in an attempt to stranglehold of the last remaining thread of my sanity as I left the Queen's study.

I can't keep doing this...

Perhaps when I find Nakoa... I could just... Let him overcome me.

Then I wouldn't have to feel this anymore.

Wouldn't have to live *with this anymore.*

If I were to ever leave Zurie's service as her Irae... I'd be killed. Just as every other Irae had, Malekai and I had only realized some years after I'd been hired. Though it had always been presumed to be a tragic demise in an act of service to her...

Lost in the downward spiral of my thoughts, I made my way hallway after hallway, hoping to catch up with Malekai before I left... Both of us were leaving to perform relatively dangerous tasks, and we'd always promised each other never to part, no matter how brief, on bad terms.

As I rounded a corner, I was jolted back to the present by the towering, stone-hard body I'd just slammed into. My lips nearly curled in disgust.

Miroslav.

He and Zurie were practically glued at the hip. With skin nearly the color of ink, he was always dressed in black or darkest blue. He possessed the unsettling otherworldly beauty that the Orisha always had. The immensity of his magic poured off of his lean, muscular, seven-foot frame in waves. Combined with his smug grins and amused indifference... He had an arrogance I found teeth-grindingly disdainful.

In all my journeys, the few Orisha that I had met, despite their tremendous power, had never been arrogant. They were exceedingly rare to come across. They were among the few native peoples of Atratus. Before the fae, sanguinati, and other foreign wielders had come - they had then been considered gods. They could survive for millennia and were nigh-impossible to kill, though they did not manage to procreate very often due to the fact that they could only bear children with someone biologically *made* to do so - a fated mate, which had become increasingly rare though they weren't entirely uncommon. Now, there were perhaps less than a dozen Orisha left in the entire realm, as far as I knew. And had made themselves scarcely seen or known.

"Forgive me, Irae Kalini," he crooned in a dark voice, "My mind was elsewhere."

Wishing to not prolong our interaction, I made haste, stepping around him to continue down the hallway.

"As was mine, my apologies. I'll be ready... Soon. Ish."

If I was going to do this, I needed to do it quick.

"Irae Kalini?"

Steeling myself, I turned.

What had the Queen suspected of you?

Miroslav studied me intently as if searching for something, his piercing silvery eyes glittering like diamonds. His expression, for once, held no smugness. It only made it all the more alarming. His brow tensed briefly before a corner of his mouth lifted, and he took a step toward me.

"Join me. By the lake."

"I would really rather not."

He chuckled. "It would be in your best interest."

Unease spiked within me, making my chest tighten. The last thing I needed was some doomed prediction. At my hesitation, he extended his large, upturned palm. After staring at it briefly as though it were a venomous thing, I placed my hand in his, allowing him to *fold* us. Darkness consumed us. The deeply alarming sensation of space and matter collapsing entirely filled... what remained of me. For a fleeting moment, it seemed we'd ceased to exist. Before my heart completed a singular beat, however, that darkness was replaced by the light of day and the lake at the rear of the sprawling palace gardens. His ability to *fold* space in such a way that enabled him to jump in and out of various locales in the blink of an eye - was unlike any other I had ever seen. There was seemingly no limit to the distance or the number of people who he could take with him.

Such is the power of an *Orisha*.

A shield rose around us, silvery and iridescent, and I couldn't help but momentarily admire it even as my words broke free.

"Am I going to die?"

Please say yes, a scornful voice whispered.

Miroslav brows lifted, yet still somehow managed to look bored.

"Aren't we all?"

I took a deep breath to muster patience just as Miroslav, out of thin air, withdrew a small vial that held a shimmering translucent liquid.

"Take this before you attempt to complete your assignment."

My brow furrowed with suspicion.

"What is it, and why?"

His lips curved downwards as though in apology.

"... I cannot say."

"And you expect me to trust you... And just... Imbibe this mystery liquid."

Something in his gaze seemed to search mine, a sudden openness and... concern on his face that I found far more unsettling than anything else. Never before had I seen him without his features trained in equal parts detachment and amusement, as though everything was merely a form of entertainment.

"I know you don't trust me..."

Distrust is putting it mildly.

I hadn't been one for pleasantries or false reassurances since I'd left the Erosyan Temple, and this male certainly wouldn't be the one to change that. My mouth pressed into a hard line.

"And I understand why... If I swear it in blood that it will do you no harm, will you promise to consider taking it?"

"And you can't tell me what it is?"

"No, but I can tell you it will change the course of *our* lives for the better. One in which you may even one day find your mother..."

My breath stilled at that faint flicker of hope but promptly extinguished. Bubbling anger followed at his manipulation.

I chose to ignore it.

"What was Zurie referencing when she spoke to you about betrayal?"

A subtle grin quirked his lips, something twinkling in his eyes.

"You'll find out in a matter of days..."

I nearly reared back.

"And are you betraying her?"

Miroslav's grin became luminous.

"Indeed, I am."

My jaw nearly hit the floor.

"Why? I'd have assumed if anyone was loyal to her, it would be *you.*"

Miroslav's expression hardened with restrained sadness.

"Every horror I have committed, I did so to protect those that I love."

Imagining Miroslav *loving* anyone was... Something I hadn't fathomed.

"To what end? Are you trying to usurp the throne?"

Miroslav huffed a mirthless laugh.

"No, Mareina. I have no designs nor desire to bear the burden of a throne. The only future in which we can all be free required me to shackle myself to that monster. It will haunt me in this life and the next, but at least my *soulbound* will be safe."

I stared almost disbelievingly, brow furrowed and rendered speechless for several moments.

"And why exactly are you trusting me with this knowledge?"

"Because I know you want Zurie to meet her end as much as I do."

Disbelief and wariness wove through me. This male had always appeared to be nothing but loyal to Zurie. Had it all been by design? He had committed such horrific acts...

As have you, my conscience promptly reminded me.

I'd wanted to find a way out for decades... But Zurie had me on a leash...

"... It would be no more of a challenge for you to end her life than it is for you to draw breath," I mused in accusation.

Miroslav gave me a sad smile.

"That, unfortunately, is not true. When she hired me as her seer and advisor, she made me swear a blood oath."

Of course, she did.

How wildly unfortunate.

At my scowl, he continued.

"Drinking that vial will incite a positive and powerful change not only in your life but throughout Atratus."

After staring at it, and him, for several moments, I slipped the vial into my brassier.

"Swear it in blood."

Without hesitation, Miroslav willed a gleaming black obsidian blade into his hand and swept it across his palm. Silvery tendrils of magic wafted off the dark red of his blood as it spilled onto the grass.

"I swear that no harm shall come to you by drinking the contents of the

vial I've given you, that my words are true, and that doing so will lead you to your true home and to the Guardian of Life."

My breathing stilled at his words, and his gaze flicked to mine. A small, knowing grin perched on his lips. The tendrils of magic buried themselves in the soil, and I felt something pulse briefly beneath my feet.

Shock and unease warred within me. *Had he been sifting through my mind? My memories? Had he somehow planted that dream in my mind?* I had never heard of such a gift, but I imagined if anyone had it, it would be an Orisha.

As if reading my thoughts, he shook his head.

"The pythos you see in your dreams is very much real, as is that voice."

My mind reeled. It seemed as though *Akash*, the divine essence of the world that was the creator that permeated and destroyed all things, was trying to reveal something, but I felt like I was looking through a foggy glass, still unable to see what it was exactly.

"Whoever has sent me that dream has filled me with a visceral longing that is not my own... The longing to go home... *Your longing...*"

Home.

I'd never felt like I belonged here in this realm. And it had been an excruciating existence. Malekai being the only enduring exception to that.

"What would it be like to go *home*."

Wherever that was.

My parents were from Hades... A neighbouring continent. Its ruler a formidable *Aequili* sanguinati...

A person of both sexes.

One whose grandfather had committed genocide against the *Drakonati* people.

Inconceivably powerful wielders who possessed a dragon form.

Something about *that* place being home didn't quite sit right, either.

Miroslav began to answer my questions before they even finished rising within me.

"I have searched tirelessly since the dreams began 120 years ago, reached to the furthest corners of our universe to no avail, searching for the *'Guardian of Life'*, only to be left with more questions and uncertainty. The only explanation I am left with is that it is a being from somewhere beyond... A god or primal, perhaps. Its ultimate goal is the only thing that was made clear to me: that it wishes to enable a great change in this realm.

"It has shown me visions of a great purge. A cleansing. I have been shown scenes of death and destruction that ultimately leads to peace and prosperity... And why it has chosen you to reveal these messages is something that you will come to discover in your own time, but know that it is not without reason."

I was rendered beyond speechless. I could viscerally feel a path being made, as though by Akash herself. Where it would lead, I had no idea, but some core part of me knew, without a doubt, that I had to follow it. And something like the faintest twinkling of hope flickered somewhere in the distance on that path. One of change. So that not only would I no longer have to sell my soul to survive... But countless others. Like all of those serving in the Erosyan palace. Or simply just the majority of the Atratusian population living in poverty because all of the wealth and resources were reserved for Zurie and her aristocracy.

Miroslav rested his large, slender palm on my shoulder, *folding* us to the stables where I would prepare Chihiro for our journey. Even though Miroslav would be folding us to the town where Zurie's target, Nakoa, would be, I would still need him once we arrived.

"Malekai is looking for you, by the way..."

I was too shell-shocked to be any further disturbed that he effortlessly seemed to know everyone's inner workings and details.

My voice came out distant.

"... Probably."

"I needn't advise you on why you mustn't mention any of this to him just yet..."

I jolted slightly at the intrusion of him speaking within my mind. He had never done so before. It was an exceedingly rare gift, but again, I wasn't surprised that he possessed it.

"Yet?"

Malekai was the last person I would speak to about this, even if he did love me unconditionally. He may have half-jokingly offered to kill Zurie for me, but I knew that if it came down to it, there would be a lot that would have to occur for him to actually sacrifice his luxurious lifestyle. And short of betraying me, he'd do just about anything to protect it, including, but not limited to, telling Zurie what Miroslav was apparently trying to do.

It probably would be best because this is fucking insane.

Not to mention, he and Miroslav had never taken a liking to one another.

A few of Zurie's soldiers strolled past, their conversation quieting at the sight of us, dropping their gazes.

"After you're finished preparing, I'll find you and drop you outside of the tavern where Nakoa will be... I'll see you when the time comes."

CHAPTER

SIX

MAREINA

till trying to collect the pieces of my mind that had just been blown away, I moved on autopilot. Riven's eyes widened at the sight of me before rushing over. The stable boy was a young satyr male that I guessed was only 19 or 20. He hadn't been with Queen Zurie but a few years and was only just beginning to outgrow the signs of adolescence.

"Irae Kalini! I wasn't expecting you! My apologies, but Chihiro is grazing. Shall I fetch him for you?"

I couldn't help the grin that tilted a corner of my lips at his sweet nature, *willing* several silvers into my palm and offering them to him.

"It's not a problem, Riven, I can go find him. Would you mind just collecting a couple satchels of food for him, enough for four days, if possible?"

Riven's mouth parted, his upper lip still only capable of growing the sparsest of moustaches, and his warm brown eyes rounded at the sight of the silvers.

"Oh- No- I mustn't—

Riven started as I took his hand, placing the money within.

"Don't be ridiculous. How long would it take you to earn this amount otherwise?"

Riven's mouth tilted downwards even as his shoulders straightened, and he lifted his chin.

"It's a full month's pay."

I nodded, heartstrings tugging.

"And do you have anyone at home to take care of?"

Riven's throat worked on a swallow.

"Yes... My mother and baby sister."

"Is your father around?"

Riven's energy became heavy, and I knew the answer before the words left his mouth. His grief was a palpable thing.

"No... He passed away shortly before I was hired into Her Majesty's service."

Oh God. This was why he had started working here so young.

I willed a palmful of gold coins into my hand. Riven's eyes widened further, soon brimming with unshed tears. I knew this look. This feeling. Before my father and I had been taken in by the Erosyan Order, we had been destitute like so many of their disciples.

Riven opened his mouth to protest, and I held up a palm.

"Hush, child. You're in no place to refuse me."

The Queen's army, while we weren't paid nearly as much as we were worth, had not only rescued me from the Erosyan Temple. It gave me a modicum of financial stability and independence. Over the years, as I rose in rank, my earnings increased, and now that I was The Royal Irae, I had more money than I knew what to do with. It was how Queen Zurie's attempted to ensure my loyalty and discretion because *Akash* knew it wasn't out of generosity.

I also knew that without a doubt, part of her resentment towards me was that I didn't need *aetra* to wield magic that nearly paralleled that of an Orisha's - the god-like beings, like Miroslav, who came from deep in the mountains and deserts of *Yatól* had been here long before even the fae.

Zurie both needed me and despised me. We both knew that no

one could carry out her duties as effectively as I could. Her former Iraes were known to die within a few years. And I had survived for seventy more than anyone before me.

The lush, rolling, grazing pastures behind Zurie's palace were breathtaking. Adorned with fields of wildflowers lay an unobstructed view of Mount Othrys, the largest of the Falcweard Mountains, and its snow-capped peak. I walked unhurried and in awe of the surrounding majesty. The reeling of my mind at what had just occurred with Miroslav and the immensity of what I could intuitively feel was coming despite not yet knowing what it was finally beginning to calm.

Akash, the divine presence in all things, washed over me in a wave of peace. Without conscious thought or intention, I found myself kneeling in the grass and flowers, spreading my palms across it as my eyes slipped shut. I simply *felt* the magic in the ground beneath me. *Akash*. My heart swelled in recognition and gratitude.

I sat back on my heels, just *being*... Feeling the energy, the magic of the land course through me and out of me in what was revered by our wild ancestors as a healing energy exchange. I'd read that often before battle, or if someone were suffering from an emotional or spiritual malaise, they would do this very thing beneath the oldest, thriving tree they could find.

The sound of distant, lazy hoof steps had my mind returning to the present and a grin parting my lips. My eyes still closed with the sensation of my soul *needing* this sacred exchange of magic. Several moments later, a velvety muzzle pushed against my cheek. Finally, I opened my eyes to see Chihiro in front of me, head swaying as he huffed softly in demand for my attention.

His coat, black as a starless night sky, had been perfectly groomed. Even the long tufts of hair around his legs that draped over his hooves shined as though they'd been conditioned.

Riven had clearly been spoiling him. My heart swelled a little more in appreciation at the thought of him.

I stood, taking his large head in my hands and pressing my forehead to his as I caressed his cheeks and neck.

"Yes, I missed you too, dear friend. How long has it been? Hm? A whole week?"

Chihiro huffed a breath that sounded remarkably indignant.

"I know. I'm sorry... Wanna go for a ride?"

A familiar magic caressed my intangible senses, making my head snap up, startling Chihiro. Relief filled me as I saw Malekai striding towards me. His own relief was visible on his face, replacing the frustration that had stricken it earlier. The wounds on his face from Zurie were, blessedly, now fully healed.

We had experienced too many near-deaths together for either of us to ever feel certain that each time we parted couldn't possibly be our last. Malekai's long, muscular arms curled around me and pulled me against him, tucking my head beneath his chin as my arms wove around his waist.

"I was worried I was going to have to leave with you still angry at me," I murmured.

He pressed a kiss to the top of my head. "You should know better by now."

"I'm sorry for stressing you out..."

Malekai frowned, tucking a few rogue strands of hair behind my ear from the gentle breeze.

"Will you go to a parlour before you leave?"

My gut twisted at the thought.

"You know how I feel about those places, Malekai."

"What if there was an alternative?"

I huffed a sigh, already knowing where this was going.

"We've been through this already."

"But I'm giving my blood to you willingly and for no other reason than wanting to protect you. It's not like you haven't fed from me before."

"That was when I was on the cusp of death. You *know* that my venom doesn't have the same effect then... I'll just feed from Zurie's latest victim. Like I usually do."

Malekai's frown deepened. "But that still leaves you vulnerable. What if something happened? You're in a weakened state. What if they're not alone... Or they're stronger and faster than you. More skilled. As much as it might seem otherwise, you *can* be killed, Mareina."

"I've been doing this for nearly a century, Malekai. One male isn't going to sever the cord tethering my soul to this body."

"... You and I both know it only takes one well-placed blade... Not to mention, he might not be alone."

He wasn't wrong. We had both witnessed enough of our comrades killed by *minori,* the so-called 'lessers' among *wielders,* and even humans to know just how true those words were. Silence weighed heavily between us. My graze trailed Chihiro as he walked off to graze on more wildflowers. I had fed from Malekai before, out of desperation - moments when I'd been gravely injured. Like the fire he wielded, it was more potent than any other fae blood I'd ever had. But in a situation like this, it would never be as simple as just drinking his blood.

All sanguinati released a venom when feeding, and if a tremendous amount of adrenaline wasn't being pumped through the body to counteract it - i.e. during a fight to the death or when you were actively dying— The venom had a potent effect on both parties. One of its side effects was euphoria and a rather savage arousal.

Which was, of course, only in addition to the bloodlust that I knew would ensue because I'd been over two weeks without feeding at this point. Almost always, waiting for Queen Zurie to entrust me with a task in which someone would end up dead anyway, and I'd have enough adrenaline pumping through me to negate the effects of the venom.

I knew and could *feel* Malekai's love for me. And it went beyond the platonic love of friends. I knew that *Satia Fama* was practically a second home to him and that he took *countless* lovers... But I also knew that it didn't fulfill him.

It was ineffectively a bandage and a distraction from what he wanted from me. And I wasn't sure I could ever be what he needed and deserved.

If I was completely honest with myself... I knew that *I* didn't deserve Malekai. And once he came to see just how all-consuming that chasm in my heart and soul was...

My thought worked on an audible swallow, my gaze dipping.

Out of fear and self-preservation... Always hiding my true self... Malekai knew me better than anyone, but there was still so much I'd never be able to reveal to him...

My past.

My vulnerabilities...

All those times, now so long ago, when I had been a victim and powerless.

He had only ever seen me as powerful. A force to be reckoned with. Made victim to none. He had never met the broken young female who had been so easily beguiled by the patrons at the Erosyan Temple, manipulated and used to be quickly disposed of, or worse, raped and beaten.

The runaway who had been forced to live on the streets.

The thief that had nothing to her name and had to steal food and clothing to survive.

The master manipulator that exploited those seeking to prey upon her vulnerability.

The heinous murderer who had sought bloody revenge on those who had harmed me.

The crumbling ruin of the person I had become.

Until I had come across a warrior recruiting for Zurie's army.

Seline.

She had been a fellow sanguinati. Beautiful and intimidating. I had envied her when I saw her. The attention and respect she wordlessly commanded.

She and another male had even sparred as a demonstration to the public to inspire people to join Zurie's ranks. She had viciously dominated him - despite him being twice her size - with power, skill, and remarkable grace.

I'd joined that same day.

Initially, Seline and I had become friends.

Until it blossomed into something more.

She was my first love. She helped me grow into the female I am now. Had come to know me better than anyone else ever had. After a few years, I began to slowly pepper her with truths of my past that I had hidden in shame.

Initially, I'd assumed she felt apathetic about what I'd told her until a tangible change gradually occurred. She confessed that when I spoke about my past, it made her uncomfortable and made her see me in a different, tainted light. She'd had rigid moral beliefs and had come from a wealthy family - one of the few sanguinati families within Zurie's Aristocracy. They had also been wholesome and nurturing towards their daughter, Seline. Had provided her every-thing she could ever possibly need and more. She couldn't fathom 'allowing' anyone to touch her because of the things they'd promised her. The hope they'd given her. Like an escape from hell, such as being homeless and stealing to survive.

Seline had harsh views of such *manipulative* behavior. She associ-ated the derelict of Atratus with laziness and weakness. She saw the fact that I had experienced sexual violence merely as an unfortunate symptom of having stayed in that environment after I'd been old enough to leave. The Erosyan Temple. The only home, family, and friends I'd ever known before I'd met her.

My heart had both shattered and hardened at the same time.

Malekai had come from a similarly wealthy and healthy upbring-ing. I didn't doubt that he would have a reaction similar to Seline's. They'd had a lot in common and became fast friends when we'd met. I'd often wondered if they would have been together had I not been around. They would have been a perfect match, both having come from wealthy families yet still choosing to become warriors in Zurie's army.

Seline and I had just begun to heal our relationship when she'd been killed at the beginning of the war. Malekai had been the only one to help me pick up the remnants of my shattered heart.

I also feared that the moment I opened myself up to him that way, he'd be taken from me. Just as so many things in my life that I loved had been. My mother. My best and only friend before Malekai, Fara. My first love, Seline... All of my closest friends in the military, who, in every way except blood, had become my family. Malekai was the only person I hadn't lost. If I allowed myself that happiness, I felt like perhaps the rug would finally be ripped out from underneath me. That *Karma* would finally catch up with me.

'*Well, Mareina, it appears you've used all your happiness tokens, so now, surely, it is time for someone you love to die.*'

Because after all that I had done, I certainly didn't deserve that kind of happiness.

Yet somehow, by the grace of *Akash*, we both survived the losses, the deaths of countless friends, and the war... and a century later, we were still here, despite all the trauma and survivor's guilt.

With each death of a loved one, a hole had been carved in my heart that could never be filled. And if something happened to Malekai... I didn't think I could survive this world. I wouldn't want to. A world without Malekai would condemn me to a world utterly void of love.

Ever in tune with my thoughts, Malekai stepped forward, gently bracing me by the arms as he peered down into my face.

"Mareina, *please*... If you don't care enough about your self-preservation to feed beforehand, then please do it for mine. If something happened to you..."

Malekai's face hardened as though trying to stifle emotion.

"... I swear to *Akash* that I will literally throw myself onto my own fucking sword just to chase you into the afterworld and strangle you. I refuse to be in this wretched realm without you."

I couldn't help but chuckle as I leaned into him, wrapping my arms around his waist.

"Fine," I acquiesced.

Malekai heaved a sigh of relief, squeezing me firmly against him as he pressed a kiss to the top of my head. My eyes stung with the love I had for this male.

Malekai, of course, just happened to tilt my gaze up to his the moment a rogue tear slipped down my cheek.

"Hey now..." Malekai's voice was the best kind of embrace. The kind that you felt deep in your bones. In your soul. "Wanna tell me what has you all worked up?"

I shook my head, feeling a little ashamed at my sudden, random swell of emotion.

"That's ok... So long as you know, I will always be right here for you. And nothing will ever get in the way of that because I won't hesitate to murder *who* or *whatever* dared to do so."

I buried my face in the immovable wall of his chest, savouring the intense warmth that radiated from his body and his sea salt and embers scent. He smelled like the sun, the sea, and bonfires with every ounce of the comfort each could bring.

"Will you accompany me to the parlour?" I asked, pulling away to take in the reaction I knew he would have. Like the masochist I apparently was.

His disappointment was evident, but he simply pressed another kiss to my forehead.

"Wherever you go, I will follow, Mareina."

CHAPTER

SEVEN

MAREINA

The House of Rubra was arguably the least seedy blood parlour in Bastrina. For one, it didn't have a shared feeding room where orgies took place. Instead, while it maintained a modicum of the signature gaudy opulence that virtually all blood parlours were known for, all of its rooms were private and consisted of more than just an enormous bed.

Malekai and I entered through towering, dark wooden doors into a quiet stone foyer boasting a chandelier flickering with candlelight - the only light in the space. An elegant figure appeared, dressed in a long sheer dress that left little to the imagination, whispering against the stone floor as she strode down the hallway.

"*Sanguis felix,*" she purred. *Happy blood.* It was an ancient but frequently used greeting between sanguinati intended to wish the recipient healthy blood that brought them good fortune. Her face was beautiful and doll-like in its perfection. Her full, pouty lips, large doe eyes framed by lush dark eyelashes, and high cheekbones complimented her lithe yet voluptuous figure. I couldn't help but feel a twinge of jealousy when her eyes roved over Malekai with blatant hunger.

59

"Sanguis Felix," I managed, not bothering to force a smile on my face. Her gaze snapped to mine as if catching herself, and she managed a polite, if not apologetic, smile. Somehow, Malekai's gaze, bless him, remained steadfastly fixed on me as he pressed his large palm against my lower back to reassure me.

"How may I serve?" She asked.

"Just one room and one *donatris*, please." *Donor.*

She nodded, causing the straight plaits of her long brown hair to shift over her dark skin. "Would you prefer male, female, or aequili?" *Aequili*, meaning 'balanced', was another term used amongst sanguinati that referred to a person of both sexes.

"Female. Thank you," I replied quickly, hoping to not further upset Malekai.

Her gaze flicked between the two of us.

"And will your companion be... participating?"

While she could surely tell he was fae and wouldn't be drinking any blood, she was trying to ask if he would be partaking in the sex that almost always ensued during feedings.

"No."

The disappointment in her eyes was evident. I felt another curl of jealousy, turning my gaze to Malekai, whose stare remained on me, his hand rubbing soothing circles against my back.

Her nostrils flared, probably scenting my hunger.

"How long has it been since you've fed?"

"15 days."

Her jaw dropped before snapping shut, lips pursing in distaste. I couldn't blame her. It was irresponsible of me. Her eyes flicked to Malekai.

"You're aware you'll be charged triple if you go into bloodlust?... And you will restrain her when the bloodlust takes over?"

Malekai finally met her gaze. "You have my word."

She gave a slight nod and turned, striding down the long hallway. Malekai and I followed several steps behind. As we got closer to the mostly soundproof parlour rooms, we could vaguely discern the sounds of ecstasy being inspired from within. After several moments, our host stopped beside a large, ornately carved door and swung it open with a gentle push of her magic.

"Your donatris will be with you shortly."

At that, she turned and strode towards a door at the end of the hall that I imagined led to the donatris residences. Due to the fact that a sanguinati, or any other immortal, in need of blood could come at any hour, blood parlours often housed their many donatris so they could remain on call.

Malekai ushered me further into the private room. The lighting was dim, lit with candles whose flickering flames created shadows on the walls. A large, ornately decorated palette bed adorned in shades of rich red and exotic designs lay at the back of the room. A couch and a small chaise longue with a cushy chair across from it. The chair for the patron feeding, and the chaise longue for the donatris to lay down while their blood was drained.

A considerate choice of seating for the rare, and likely deranged, individual who would actually choose to not engage in any sexual activity during a feeding.

I moved to step towards the chair as Malekai shut the door behind us. As soon as I sat, he knelt in front of me, searching my face.

"You alright?"

"Yeah... I just... Hope the donatris are treated well here by the patrons."

"I'll pay her well."

"You don't need to do that. I'm already more than grateful to you for your concern and for ensuring I'm safe before leaving for Ouvelleete."

Malekai gave me a bored look.

"Mareina, you literally can't stop me short of tearing my throat out, which would defeat the entire purpose of us coming here in the first place."

I sighed, shaking my head.

"If I go into bloodlust..."

Thankfully, Malekai was here to prevent things from getting out of hand, but even so, it was a risk as to how much I would take from her before he could stop me... And it would take time for the donatris to heal. Magical assistance and potions would help, but the consequences of teasing death were never a pleasant experience.

"I'll make sure you stop."

"And what if I try to bite you?"

A devilish grin swept across his face, and I swear to *Akash,* the action alone made my clit tingle.

"I wish you would."

Despite my heavily guarded and suppressed feelings for him, my core clenched with need. It had been an unfairly long period that I had gone without the touch of another.

Gods, and did I crave him. Like a flower seeks the fucking sun.

The words felt like gravel scraping against my tongue and throat.

"I wouldn't be in my right mind... I—

The door of the feeding room opened as a petite, curvy female with milk-white skin and scarlet hair dressed in another sheer dress stepped inside. I scanned her body for any signs of recent feedings but found none. I let out an audible sigh of relief at the sight of her fae ears and the scent of her fae blood. At least if my bloodlust got the best of me, she would heal faster than most.

Her eyes briefly locked with mine before returning to the floor as she made her way to the chaise longue. I could hear the hammering of her heart, unable to hide her nervous energy.

Her exposed, soft, pale skin did nothing to hide the faint blue lines of her veins beneath. The sight, coupled with anticipation, had my fangs aching and my hand gripping Malekai's. She quickly laid down and extended her fleshy, delicate arm towards me. I couldn't help but notice she was trembling faintly. Compassion and predator warred within me.

"Are you... Nervous?" I asked, my voice shifting to something husky with hunger and need.

She shook her head, eyes briefly flicking to mine. "You're... The Irae..."

My brow furrowed, feeling both wary and relieved, even as my fangs descended. The sweet, musky, cinnamon taste of my venom flooded my mouth. Words of reassurance rose to my throat, but before I could get them out, I found my hands gripping the donatris' wrists to the point of bruising. The action pulled me forward and yanked her halfway off the chaise longue as I sank my fangs into the donatris' wrist.

She let out a yelp, nearly tumbling to the floor. Malekai caught her, helping her regain her seating - something I only distantly noticed - before he re-situated himself beneath me, holding me in his lap. Waiting to pull me off of her.

My venom had delicious heat curling through my body as, simultaneously, the sensation of each and every cell in my body finally being nourished and reanimating felt like they were roaring back to life. I moaned, panting heavily from around my mouthful of her wrist, greedily gulping down her blood.

Her trembling ceased, replaced by the slow, wanton movements of her hips against the air as her back arched, letting out a breathy moan. "*Oh gods...*"

The scent of her arousal curled through the air, only further pushing me over the edge, as gradually the only things my mind could recognize were her blood, my hunger, the tingling pulse of need as my empty core greedily clenched around nothing, and the *breathtaking* length hardening against my ass and the back of my thigh.

Distantly, I heard a masculine growl, but my mind remained anchored to her blood and my arousal. My hips began to grind against Malekai's hardness. His arms tightened around me as if to still my movements, tearing a growl from my throat as I continued to drink. My mind was rendered entirely blank except for this burning *need.*

Her moans and sighs escalated as she achieved orgasm, spurring me further, but I felt as though I were chasing something that remained just out of reach.

Gulp after gulp, my hunger and desire only grew. The donatris' arm slackened in my hands, and I could faintly make out some distant, male voice. Unyielding arms came around me and attempted to pull me away from my source of sustenance. Making me sink my fangs in further. My hands grip tighter.

A powerful hand grasped my face and began manually *prying* my jaws apart. He stood, clutching me tightly against him and pulling me away from my meal. *Furious,* I released my prey, twisting and snarling in the direction of the one who had dared to interrupt my feeding as I launched myself at them.

The male went tumbling backwards, and I used the opportunity to mount him, swiftly gripping his face to bare his throat to me. Before I could sink my fangs into his blessed arteries, his fist curled around my throat, holding me at arm's length. The pulse between my legs continued to throb persistently. Of their own volition, my hips resumed thrusting firmly against the remarkably long, thick, *hot* length that was pressing itself against my sopping wet core.

There.

Some semblance of satisfaction even as the tension in my body heightened with need.

"Fuck... Yes..."

He gave me a grin that was filled with equal parts reverence and...

Hunger.

"Mareina...," Malekai ground out.

At the sound of his voice, recognizing again that it was *him* beneath me, waves of euphoria returned to me as my venom continued to work its way through my body. The desperate, tingling throb of need and pleasure was so intense I was certain I could die from it.

"Malekai... Please."

"*Fuck,* don't use that word on me. I only have so much self-restraint."

Slowly, his hand left my neck as if to be sure I wasn't about to tear his throat out. His grip shifted to my hips, stilling my movements, frustration warring on his features.

"If you don't stop, Mareina—

"Oh *fuck,* why in the gods' names would I stop?"

Malekai chuckled before flipping us to lay me beneath him as he gripped my wrists in one hand and pinned them above my head.

"Careful, *tessari mú.* I want nothing more than to pin you down and fuck you so thoroughly you cry tears of joy."

"*Oh gods, yes... That... I need* that... Tell me what you would do to me... *Please.*"

Malekai's grip on my hips loosened slightly, enabling me to continue grinding my clit against his enormous cock.

"You really wanna know?"

I nodded, whimpering shamelessly against him as I continued to work my hips. I *willed* away our leathers and promptly gasped as I peered between us. My eyes widened in shock at the sheer size of him. The male was hung like a fucking horse.

Malekai's lips parted, and his grip on me became bruising as he took me in. The venom's effects were gradually receding. The dizzying euphoria had dimmed slightly, leaving behind that tingling and desperate ache to be filled.

By him.

Desperate, my back arched and strained towards him, hips working against his monstrous length and girth.

The thickly veined shaft of his cock was a few shades darker than the golden tan covering the rest of him. The crown was a blend of deep gold and red, with a broad, bulbous crown featuring a prominent ridge that promised to stroke the sweetest places inside me. The pearlescent strings of pre-cum already dripping from him had me salivating.

Oh, gods, and *it's fucking gorgeous.*

Malekai gave a dark chuckle and a hum of purely male satisfaction.

Oh, fuck. Had I said that aloud?

"So eager for my cock, aren't you, tessari mú?"

My core clenched in response.

"Gods, yes... Need you. So fucking Badly."

He growled low, bending to my ear, nipping at the lobe. The deep velvet of his voice dropped to a rough husk.

"If you weren't out of your mind on venom right now, I'd fucking devour you. I would lick and suck every drop of that honey dripping from that beautiful little pussy until you came, crying out my name. I would split you in fucking half with my cock until you gushed with climax. And only after you came at least twice more, would I allow myself release. I would fill you with my cum - your throat, your pussy, even that voluptuous ass of yours. Because it all belongs to *me*."

Every muscle in my body coiled tight, getting ready to snap with release, even as, at the same moment, I was utterly captivated by his words and the fantasy they'd created in my mind.

My words were barely a coherent string. *"So perfect... Malekai... Yes... Gonna..."*

Every fragment of my being ached for him.

Malekai's grip on my hips tightened again, stilling the undulations of my hips. Making both of us growl with frustration and need.

"But that isn't happening. Not until you want me *without* the influence of venom... Do you understand?"

Pain speared my heart.

Oh, gods... Did he think that was what this was?

My heart shattered at the idea.

A tremor worked through his entire body at his restraint, that wondrous heat radiating from the steel length against my core. The fingers of his free hand curled even deeper into my hips, hard enough it would leave bruises.

Bruises I wanted from him.

The realization terrified me. Had me coming further to my senses.

Fuck.

I wanted him to mark me.

I wanted to be his.

"Mareina... Nothing means more to me than you and your trust. I won't jeopardize you for anything."

Malekai drew back to study my reaction. My expression was starkly the opposite of my desirous, euphoric expression only moments ago. It was heartbroken. Heartbroken that he thought all of this was only because of venom.

"Oh gods, Mareina..."

Malekai released my wrists and pulled me onto his lap, holding me firmly against him and stroking my hair. Even as his divine warmth enveloped me, my eyes stung with tears.

"Are you upset with me?" He asked hoarsely.

"Gods no. I'm heartbroken and ashamed that you think this was all because of venom."

I felt his throat dip from where it pressed against the side of my face, his chin perched against the top of my head that he cradled in one hand.

"Wasn't it?"

That familiar fear coiled through me. The fear of losing him. Because I knew I didn't deserve him.

"No. Not even remotely."

He gave a noncommittal grunt.

There was so much more I wanted to say, but...

A soft feminine groan sounded from the other side of the room.

"Oh, gods... the *donatris*..."

His voice came out little more than a growl.

"She's fine. She's fae. All she needs is a long nap."

I heaved a sigh, still feeling guilty and ashamed that I'd led him to believe it was only because of the venom.

Because for a century, I'd never once given in to his advances.

I was desperate to make amends... But was I willing to risk every-thing - because Malekai was *everything* to me - for what would likely be a temporary thing, perhaps years long, but temporary none-theless, for what would otherwise be a lifelong friendship?

Being pressed against him like this, skin-to-skin, with nothing between us and held in his arms... It was the most divine sensation I'd ever been gifted with.

And I knew I'd never be able to go without it again.

Before my rational mind or fear could get the better of me...

"Can we... talk when I get back?"

He drew back slightly to take in my expression, brow pinching with concern as he stroked my hair.

"Of course... Are you ok?"

I nodded, eyes burning again. My gaze dipped to Malekai's perfect, cupid's bow mouth. Everything within me urged me to close that small distance between us. When my eyes flicked up to his, I saw that his gaze was fixed in the same place on me. When his eyes lifted to meet mine... Something tightened between us.

"Mareina?"

I exhaled the breath I'd been holding. But now was not the time to pour my heart out.

"Yes... Sorry. I'm... fine. I just... Don't wanna leave you."

A grin curled his lips, and the tension between us lifted all at once.

His fingers carded through my hair, gripping it and pulling my head back to bare my throat to him.

Fuck. Yes. This was everything. I needed this.

I silently vowed to myself and Malekai, right then and there, that I would come back and make this right.

Malekai's fangs grazed me as he growled his pleasure at my admission against the curve of my neck. His cock, still hard and leak-ing, twitched insistently against my seam and my ass.

"Just hurry up and get the fuck back here. Or I'll come kill that hybrid fucker myself just so I can drag you home to me."

I grinned against his throat.

My body hummed in anticipation.

I could finally breathe again for the first time in I didn't know how long, only partly because I had fed. The clouds dimming my mind and my mood had finally faded. Feeding again had returned me to my sharpest senses and endowed me with a wellspring of energy.

"Thank you. For making me feed..."

Malekai's huge body sighed heavily against me.

"Whether or not *you* know what's best for you, I will always do what I need to to keep you safe, tessari mú."

EIGHT

Miroslav was already waiting outside The House of Rubra when Malekai and I stepped out. Miroslav bowed as he turned from where he'd been staring, seemingly, into the distance as his eyes met mine.

"Irae," he said before shifting his iridescent gaze to Malekai and studying him for a moment, something like wariness briefly filtering through.

"General."

"My Lord."

"I'll wait by Chihiro."

My eyes followed as Miroslav strode across the cobblestoned street where Chihiro stood nibbling away at the leaves of a bush, peeking between the sharp wrought iron fence posts where I'd tied his reins.

A tendril of dread curled through me at the sight of the wall painted with Mors' symbol. The inverted torch with wings.

I tore my gaze away. As usual, the sight of Malekai alone allowed me to exhale my relief.

He gave me a concerned look.

"Something wrong, *tessari mú?*"

I shook my head. Thankfully, he didn't press the subject. Instead, he merely pulled me against him and stroked my hair.

I could have purred.

"I'll see you when I return from Vyssini next week, ok?... Be careful with this male in Ouvelleete... Don't make the mistake of underestimating anyone. Even if he is half-human..."

I couldn't help the smile quirking my lips. I had faced countless *wielders, minori* or not, and had always emerged victorious. Even so, Malekai never failed to fuss over me each time before I left.

"*You* be careful."

"Mareina, I'm going to have an army of 30 men in Vyssini with me... *You're* the one who's going alone..."

I fisted the front of his fighting leathers and stood on my tiptoes to press a kiss to his cheek.

"Thank you for your concern... I'll be careful. I promise."

Malekai kissed the top of my head as a question rose to my tongue. A question I already knew the answer to but couldn't stop myself from asking...

"Malekai?"

"Hm?"

I lowered my voice, eyes darting to our surroundings, and raised a barrier.

"How do you feel about The Uprising?"

"What do you mean?"

"Do you... sympathize with them at all? What they're fighting for..."

Malekai's brows pinched as he pulled back to study my face.

"Why? Do *you?*"

I sighed, rolling my eyes. "Answer me."

He took a deep breath, gaze wandering as though this were the first time he'd given it any thought and, though not unexpected, another stone of disappointment dropped into the pit of my stomach.

"I think the people fighting in The Uprising are poor and miserable and are looking for a way out. Even if it's the wrong way."

That stone in my stomach seemed to sink further.

"And... Do you feel as though their actions are justified?"

"I *understand* it. I just feel like they aren't smart enough or strong enough to overcome their own adversity."

I took a deep breath, exhaling loudly and shaking my head.

"That's sad," I murmured, more to myself than anyone else.

"Indeed it is," he muttered for an entirely different reason than my own. His blatant lack of empathy was one of the exceedingly few things that had always held me slightly aback from giving in to him. Not that I could point any fingers... I was Zurie's most notorious murderer.

"If they really wanted to make a better life for themselves, they would have or could have... You're the perfect example of that. Look how far you've come since the Erosyan Temple."

I shook my head, pulling away.

You actually have no idea.

"Not everyone can join Zurie's army, Malekai. Not everyone is a warrior. Not everyone is willing to die in battle or sell their soul to be Zurie's wrath."

The anger in my words was directed more at myself than him, and he knew it.

I also knew I'd never change his mind. He'd come from tremendous privilege. He didn't know any better. He'd gone against the grain, denied his parents' wishes to join their world of aristocracy and politics, and had chosen to become a warrior. He had joined the war efforts to protect his people. And he had worked just as hard as I had to get here. I loved and admired him for that.

I highly doubted that I would have chosen this path if I hadn't been through what I had... If I'd had, literally, *any* other resources or opportunities, I couldn't fathom I'd have joined Zurie's Army.

Such was the origin of most of those at her command.

Sweet, sweet irony.

And regardless of his views on society, I knew better than anyone that he didn't enjoy murdering anyone. I knew that executing and putting the heads of those in The Uprising on pikes would plague him. He seemed to manage his conscience successfully by justifying his actions with the reasoning that he was doing it to protect Atratus. That he was doing little evil for the greater good.

I was no longer holding that delusion.

"You didn't sell your soul, Mareina... You chose to rise above the shitty circumstances that you were born into, and sometimes that means standing on the shoulders of others."

I disagreed, and his words did absolutely nothing to alleviate my guilt.

"And if you did sell your soul, then mine is right there with it, and there's nowhere in all the realms I'd rather it be."

I huffed a mirthless laugh. "I'm pretty certain it's in the lowest of all the hell realms."

Malekai gave me a challenging look. "Whether it's in the hell realms or the divine realms, I don't actually give a fuck so long as it's with you. "

I held his gaze, seeing the truth in his words, before I resigned myself to resting my head on his chest.

The weathered lump of coal that remained of my heart gave a fluttering thump. Like it was trying to sprout wings.

His arms came around me, firm and unyielding.

"If you want me to burn the world down for you, Mareina, all you have to do is ask."

"And what does that mean exactly, Malekai?"

Malekai's brows lifted as though surprised I'd asked. As though I were actually considering it.

"Whatever you want it to. You wanna leave all this behind and hide somewhere in the Yatól or *Bein Sith Mór* Mountains? Let's go. You want me to kill Zurie, so you don't have to worry about her chasing us? I'm not entirely sure I'd survive, but I'd certainly fucking try for you. If you asked me to cut off my right nut just because you were feeling peckish, I fucking would... I mean... I'd try to convince you to maybe snack on something else first, but if it meant that I got to be with you, I'd do it at the drop of a fucking coin."

I longed for a future with him. And as soon as I got back, I would give him everything I had left within me and fucking pray to the gods that it was enough.

What I didn't want, however, was for him to risk his life in the process by trying to kill Zurie.

You don't deserve him, that insidious voice whispered in my mind.

That familiar fear returned.

Would I just be throwing away everything for fleeting satisfaction?

A second tendril of fear returned. The one that swore as soon as I gifted myself this happiness that it would be stolen from me.

Malekai nudged me with his head to draw me out of my thoughts.

"Please, let's not part on a sour note. You know the rule, Kalini."

Never leave on bad terms.

A corner of my mouth quirked. Something about the way he used my surname always made me soften towards him. It brought back all the *good* memories of us in the army together. All of the history we had. All the times we'd saved one other's lives.

"Fine... I'm not sour," I relented dourly.

He chuckled, imitating me in a whiney voice. *"Fine, I'm not sour."*

My smile broke free as a chuckle finally rose and escaped.

"There she is," Malekai purred, pressing another kiss to the top of my head. I squeezed him in return before finally stepping out of his arms to mount Chihiro, swallowing back my emotion.

I prayed that it wouldn't be too late to make things right by the time I returned.

Malekai *willed* an apple into his hand and gave it to Chihiro, caressing his muzzle.

"See you next week, Kalini."

"Katadamna kaza," I promised.

That stunning fucking grin of his lifted, unilateral dimple made a

74

glorious appearance. It alleviated some of the pressure building in my chest with it.

"*Katadamna kaza,* Mareina."

Miroslav folded Chihiro and me to an empty road an hour's ride from *Ouvelleete's* town center. Far enough away from prying eyes that might recognize him and warn Nakoa that Miroslav had been seen nearby - a dooming foreshadowing if there ever was one.

I swiftly *willed* a pretty, off-the-shoulder dress to replace my fighting leathers. It was a dark green corseted dress with a low neckline and billowy long sleeves. One of the only dresses I owned. Not because I didn't like them. In fact, perhaps because of my profession and the fact I rarely got to wear one, nor had the opportunity to really embrace my feminine side, I relished wearing one.

Thankfully, my face wasn't widely recognized because it was almost always concealed by the hood of my cape when performing public executions. I deliberately remained in the shadows whenever Zurie made public appearances. On the other hand, Miroslav was always displayed prominently at her side.

"Malekai plays a larger part in all this than you'd imagine," Miroslav volunteered casually.

His words promptly snapped me out of my thoughts.

"All of... What?"

Miroslav's gaze shifted to the darkened tree line of the forest.

"The Dancing Dryad is the name of the tavern where he'll be. Make sure to only drink the vial before you're going to perform the task. And I'd recommend being somewhere... *private.*"

Of course, he wasn't going to answer. But now, just as he'd intended, my mind had something far more worrying to dwell upon.

"What the hells do you have me drinking? I mean, as I'm sure you already know, I have better sense than to murder anyone publicly, but now you're making me worry."

Miroslav's face was utterly impassive.

"I can assure you that you have no reason to be whatsoever... Also, try not to let your temper get the best of you."

He promptly disappeared before I could get out the words forming on the tip of my tongue.

I grumbled a few curses under my breath before turning to mount Chihiro. My eyes scanned the blazing horizon of the setting sun, illuminating a breathtaking view of the gently rolling hills and surrounding forests that eventually bled into The Sentient Forest.

Why in the hells would he be so insistent about me drinking this potion? And most of all, what the hells did it have to do with me finding my *home*. And what in *Akash's* name did it have to do with this male, Nakoa Solanis?

Images of what had happened with Malekai began to sneak back to the forefront of my mind. *Gods.* My core clenched with breath-stealing need.

While I expected nothing less, I wasn't entirely sure how grateful I was that he had maintained his decency to not let me give into the venom-induced lust... It was the first time that we'd come *that* close... Though it was something that had already occurred countless times within the privacy of my mind.

As it did every time we parted, my heart squeezed with the familiar ache of longing. He would be leaving for Vyssini in a matter of hours, in the early morning hours. I sent a quick prayer to *Akash* for his safe and swift return.

Now, so far outside Bastrina where no one would recognize me dressed as a common female and no longer in my fighting leathers, the gazes of many males I passed became leering. After all, a single, unfamiliar female traveller was a rarity. While I wouldn't instigate anything, I certainly wouldn't shy away from it. Perhaps it would even enable me to enjoy a second meal in one day. Though, I did have to be mindful to be discreet.

Just at the edge of town, thanks to the music pouring out of the tavern, an old, carved wooden sign with fading and chipped paint that depicted a curvy dryad holding a mug of beer, her hips mid-s sway caught my eye. I squinted, barely making out the name, *The Dancing Dryad*. Almost illegible and illuminated solely by a dusty, cracked fae light lantern.

After dismounting Chihiro, I tied his reins and one of his feed-bags to the railing above the water trough off to the side of the Inn's tavern.

"I won't be long, I promise," I cooed, stroking his cheek and neck. At the sight of his food, Chihiro plunged his face into the bag of goodies Riven had packed for him: apples, carrots, and grains. Bois-terous live music poured out from the windows and door of the tavern, along with the amber glow of lanterns. I quickly willed my hair into a loose updo that allowed a few tendrils of my black hair to grace my neck.

A black smudge on the horizon snagged my gaze as I turned towards the tavern.

A *Pharalaki*.

The dark, Stygian hooded figure seemed to float towards me in the distance. My heart began to pound a fearful beat.

Fuck.

Would I even get a chance to find this *'home'* this long-lost diety promised me before fucking Mors came to collect my damned soul?

Something like panic was trying to crawl up my throat. All my earlier audacity at the thought of letting this male kill me vanished, and life-preserving instinct kicked in at the sight of the *Pharalaki* rapidly closing the distance between us.

I spun on my heel and sprinted around the building towards the tavern.

My lungs panted their fear as I bodily slammed the door behind me. Thankfully, the music was loud, and the crowd was louder. Only a few people noticed my frantic entrance, throwing me odd glances. I strode to the bar, lined with mostly humans and a peppering of *minori* fae, most looking worse for the wear. The standard for 99% of the towns outside of the capital.

The barmaid, a middle-aged, broad-shouldered human who looked like she knew how to handle herself, arrived. Her Ouvelleet accent thick as syrup as she shouted to be heard over the music.

"Are you after a room or just here for the music?"

"No, thank you. Just here to have a drink—

"All I've got left is our fae wine," she nodded toward the musicians, "They tend to draw a thirsty crowd."

"That's fine. Thank you."

I turned in my seat, trying to casually peek at the musicians I couldn't quite make out through the crowd of dancing and writhing bodies. Admittedly, the music was infectious. The beat of the leather-skinned drums had my hips yearning to move; the melody of the strings, my body eager to sway.

I slid several coppers across the counter to the barmaid as she passed me the fae wine. Her brows lifted in appreciation, and she gave me a respectful nod before returning to her other patrons.

Sipping my wine, a surprisingly pleasant blend of tropical flavors but was balanced with a dryness that made it refreshing and not too sweet, my eyes studied the patrons nearest me... Looking for the drunkest ones so they wouldn't recall and alert anyone to my interrogative questioning regarding Nakoa Solanis, the hybrid male I'd come to kill.

My gaze settled on a young male, dancing with the slightly sloppy movements of someone who'd been drinking heavily. If it weren't for his dancing, he'd be wildly attractive.

The band's music slowed, and I let my body begin to sway in sync with the seductive melody curling through the air. I could practically feel each note caressing my skin.

No wonder this place is so crowded.

There was something about the music that compelled you to dance. *It beckoned your soul.*

I weaved and danced my way through the crowd, eventually making my way in front of the drunk male. He was only a few inches taller than my five foot eight inches but was far broader, stocky with muscle. When his rich brown eyes finally met mine through his shaggy light brown hair, his lips parted in surprise briefly before he managed a surprisingly dashing smile that belied his youth. His sweet, earnest, excitable energy.

And I prayed to *Akash* this male wasn't Nakoa. He seemed entirely too sweet to kill. I could only hope that the male Zurie had sent me to kill was the scum of Atratus. They often were, thankfully, but on occasion... They weren't. And those were the ones that haunted me.

The distinct scent of the forest - crisp mountain air, soil and fallen leaves, mixed with a particularly warm, earthy, sweetness... like fig, filled my nose.

Lykos.

The only *wielders* that remained so richly scented of the wilderness, no matter their surroundings, were the ones who had a lykos form. Unlike a wolf, the Lykos' wolf form was giant. They were closer to the size of a horse.

My relief was palpable. This male was a Lykos and not one trying to glamor himself.

CHAPTER
NINE
NAKOA

My eyes had been shut, as they usually were, as I drifted within my mind in that place of in-between that allowed me to dance along the veil separating this world from the next. It enabled me to commune with the divine in a thoughts-without-words way. Distantly, something began to pervade my mind... My soul. Still keeping the rhythm and melody with my *olana kah'hei - my chosen family -* playing beside me, my eyes opened. Scanning the crowd for whatever or whoever had drawn me out of my reverie. The crowd was entirely too dense, however.

In the same moment, an entirely new yet inherently familiar scent reached me... Night blooming rose. My nostrils flared as I breathed deeply, trying to detect every note of this salivating scent of citrus.

I continued to play, fervor increasing, as if rising to challenge whoever had seemingly pulled my soul back into its body. A flash of sable hair, olive skin, and a dark emerald dress stirred something inside me, like a great beast awakening for the first time in millennia. My eyes tracked the creature as a predator would its prey. My hunger increased with each passing moment until recognition settled on my chest like a fucking boulder.

No.

No. No. No.

Not her.

Despite the dread of destiny working through my body in painful knots, I found my eyes were securely locked onto the creature, entirely unable to look away. Without thought, I found my song shifting into something seductive and filled with longing. It was a wholly new song, and thanks to the expertise of my *olana kah'hei* they fell in seamlessly.

My vision flashed in and out of the present like a light flickering on and off until it settled briefly.

The searing pain of a blade dragging across my throat. Blood sprayed across my female's front. I dropped to one knee, clutching my throat.

I felt a grin twisting across my face and my eyes darkening to black. My words little more than a rasp.

"Look how beautiful you are, covered in my blood."

The vision was ripped away, replaced by the cosmos blossoming and withering before me... I barely managed to keep the music going and pulled at the only thread tethering me to this world.

Her.

The present reality returned. Her body sang harmoniously to the music I was playing but could now only distantly hear. My heart pounded a frantic rhythm as I tried to steady myself.

Was my own soulbound destined to be the end of me?

I'd experienced far worse than a cut throat and survived.

As much as my rational mind repelled me from her... I couldn't tear my eyes away. I couldn't sever the cord that I knew tethered my soul to hers. And despite the alarms wailing their warning and that violent premonition, my eyes tracked her like a predator silently stalking its prey.

I held my breath as she moved with a mesmerizing feline grace.

As if that thread I pulled to draw myself back to reality had also drawn her towards me, she danced closer and closer to the stage...

Until she stopped short.

In front of Roderick.

One of my brothers - not by blood but by something more - gifted him with a seductive smile through heavy-lidded eyes.

Possessiveness - the type I had never truly experienced until now - burned within me.

Until now, I'd considered myself an incredibly patient and reasonable male. Never the jealous type with previous females. Over the years, I'd managed to hone an unwavering sense of security and strength. Never truly felt attached to anyone or anything, with very little exception: my mother and my *olana kah'hei*. Many considered me aloof, but I felt that was reductive. The very nature of this realm was change.

And despite my love for my brother, in that moment, I felt rather murderous.

Roderick, of course, looked at her as though he'd just won a lottery. She leaned forward, whispering something in his ear before her lithe body moved closer against him as they began to dance *together*, and his hand *caressed* the small of her back. My eyes narrowed, fury burning, as I watched his pinky and ring finger roam lower as though reaching towards her ample backside.

For the first time in more years than I could remember, my bow stuttered against the strings of my instrument, causing it to shriek out an unholy note. My playing stopped abruptly, my *olana kah'hei* halting their own performance as they threw shocked looks my way that I could only see through my peripheral vision.

My gaze was locked onto this she-devil, who had not even noticed me. How was it possible that she had this effect on me, and yet she hadn't even batted an eye in my direction. The gods were indeed playing some kind of cruel joke on me.

Finally, her gaze lifted to mine as my eyes bore holes through her. Wary and distrustful, her jaw tightened. She rose defiantly at my glare that a lesser male or female would crumple beneath. And I was blessed in witnessing a flash of the beast awakening within her.

Roderick gave me a strange look, eyes bouncing between us as I addressed the crowd, and he wisely backed away from her.

"I must offer my sincerest apologies for the abrupt ending of our performance, but there is an *urgent* matter I must tend to."

CHAPTER
TEN

MAREINA

The crowd cried their protest as the male, currently staring daggers at me, placed his fiddle in its case, hopped off the stage, and, for some reason, made a beeline straight to me. Something stuttered in my chest as all my senses came alive at the sight of him despite the dull throb in my shoulders. Although the fact he looked furious had my hackles rising.

The male beside me sighed, suddenly looking bored. "Were you trying to make him jealous or something?"

"I beg your pardon?" I reared back indignantly. His attention, however, was focused solely on the male barrelling through the crowd that wordlessly parted for him.

"Apologies, brother- I didn't realize she was one of yours."

My jaw clenched painfully as I ground out my response, shoving his shoulder so he would finally acknowledge me.

"Do you have a fucking death wish?"

Calm down. Too obvious. And unwarranted.

The male reared back as he took me in with new eyes.

The performer finally arrived, towering over the both of us. His broad, muscled shoulders took up far more space than he deserved.

"And I have absolutely no idea who *this* even is," I added, trying to sound a little calmer. And a little more sane.

The performer responded by parting his perfectly formed cupid's bow lips to reveal a slightly unhinged, though no less dazzling, grin made lopsided by the faint scar that ran through the left side of his upper lip as he took another step towards me. The male looked menacing at worst. Begrudgingly and sinfully handsome at best. And something within me seemed to recognize him.

Perhaps it was one twisted soul recognizing another.

I didn't like it. It was like looking into a mirror.

And suddenly coming face to face with it was... deeply unsettling.

Like magnetic repulsion.

"Are you sure about that, *lohane thili?*"

My eyes narrowed to slits. Without conscious thought, my fist found its way to the front of his shirt and tugged his face closer towards me, lest I make a scene by raising my voice to be heard over the crowd.

You are insane. Stop acting like a lunatic. You have a job to do.

While I'd always been prone to losing my temper, never in all my years working for Zurie had I lost my composure so quickly. Especially not when completing one of her tasks.

Instead of being affronted, the male leaned in eagerly, grin widening, revealing his sharp fangs as if to spur me on. And it worked.

"I don't know what a *lohane thili* is, but I suggest you show me some respect before I introduce your balls to a dull, jagged blade."

The male gave an appreciative and thoughtful hum as though I'd said something wildly endearing. His friend's brows leapt before swiftly dissolving into the crowd. Wisely leaving the crazy people to their madness.

The performer's large hand curled over mine, swallowing it whole, and I swear electricity sparked where our skin touched.

"You beautiful, vicious creature... You say that as if it's a deterrent?"

My lip curled, no longer having the time or energy to invest in this male. I snatched my hand back before turning to stride away.

His hand gripped me around the bicep with firm but surprising gentleness.

"Wait—

I glared at the hand he'd laid on me, my eyes slowly rising to meet his as a low growl escaped me. He released me instantly, raising his hands in surrender. He bowed slightly and slowly stepped backwards to give me my space. As one would a cornered, feral animal.

"Don't leave...," he continued, "I apologize for my impulsive behaviour. The last thing I would want to do is offend you."

I found myself hesitating and my anger diminishing. Something whispered in the back of my mind.

He might lead you to Nakoa.

Admittedly, the male before me was remarkably pleasing to look at... Not beautiful in the way of perfection... But in a darkly intimidating, rough around the edges way. His dark brown hair was a tumbled mess of thick waves that reached for the black arches of his eyebrows. One of which had a thick scar that ran through it. Thick, long, black eyelashes framed his dark umber eyes, reminding me of rich volcanic soil.

Potentially even delicate in the past, his nose had the distinct look of having been broken many times before. His lips were full, and another considerable scar ran through them, from the apple of his high cheekbone to his chin. His jaw was hard and covered in closely shaved scruff.

His broad frame commanded attention with wide sculpted shoulders. His chest visible despite the billowy linen shirt that failed to hide it. The laces at the front worn loose and untied, gifting anyone near eye level with his chest- like me, for example- with a delicious sliver of tan, scarred, and tattooed skin.

Dark, fitted trousers were tied low on his narrow hips and hugged long, muscular thighs. Knee high boots were snug against thickly muscled calves.

He smelled distinctly of that specific scent that hung heavy in the air before a thunderous rain... Ozone... As if he spent a lot of time in the clouds.

Something deep within me buried long ago, seemed to shift and rise and peek its eyes open.

Gross.

"Have one drink with me..."

Before I could think better of it, I gave a subtle nod, and he ushered me towards the bar, where we joined a long line.

"May I have your name?" He asked with sudden politeness. Entirely contrasted the intensity he was studying me with. His gaze felt like it was stripping me naked, baring all the most deeply hidden parts of myself. It made me wary.

"Mareina."

I don't know why I'd given him my real name. I *never* gave any of Zurie's targets my real name. But it had slipped out without a conscious thought.

His dark brows pinched, still studying me in that intrusive way. *"Mareina...,"* he repeated thoughtfully, savoring its flavor.

"And yours?"

His lips tilted upwards with surprising warmth.

"Nakoa."

My breathing stilled, though I managed to effectively disguise it. His ears were pointed, like the fae, and if it weren't for the magic oozing off of him from beneath his glamor, I'd have assumed he was just that. However, I could very clearly *scent* and *feel* that there was something else... Something *more*. Zurie had said he was half-human, half-fae, but... that felt... *wrong*. My senses were significantly more acute than most others. Of what, outside fae, I couldn't be sure... The glamor was the best I'd ever seen. Even *I* couldn't see what lay behind it.

More often than not, I found glamors glaringly false. It was like looking at someone through a lens that constantly blurred and shifted. Gifting me with a headache if my eyes lingered for too long.

But Nakoa's was crystal clear. I could simply *feel* that it was there. And that the bulk of his magic was hiding behind it... Like an enormous dam holding back the deluge of a rushing river.

Neither of us uttered the standard, banal pleasantries, such as 'pleasure to meet you'. Instead, his hand embraced mine for longer than what could be deemed unintentional. That lingering touch caused a knee-jerk reaction in me that had me snatching back my hand, fisting it at my side to push the sensation away. His brow dipped, softening his features briefly as though in understanding... Like he could read me like a book. And it made me want to run in the other fucking direction.

Thankfully, he mentioned nothing of it.

"You're not from here..."

"No... Bastrina."

"Your family is from there?" He asked, eyes searching mine as if he were digging around for something I wasn't sure existed.

"No..."

"... No?"

"My father is originally from Hades... My mother was from *Sangui Reinum.*"

Blood Realm. Where the sanguinity originated, though many had sought exile here...

Nakoa's brows leapt. "Fascinating..."

I hadn't told many people that. Only Malekai and Seline... Unease twisted inside me that I'd revealed it to this stranger.

"And where are they now?"

I shook my head. "My mother left us shortly after I was born- don't bother asking me where she is because I have no idea- and my father is in the capital. We aren't close."

Nakoa frowned, gradually nodding.

"And yours?"

"My mother lives halfway between here and Vyssini. My father died when she was pregnant with me... I have a handful of other relatives in Spriga but... No one that I'm close with... But that unsavory lot over there..." Nakoa nodded in the direction of a group of males, including the one I'd nearly assaulted and one female. "They're my family more than anyone other than my mother."

My heart squeezed in time with the twitch of my lips when, as one, their eyes that had been locked on us darted like pinballs in different directions as they tried to feign innocence.

"They seem... rather invested in your personal life."

He chuckled warmly, affection in his eyes as his gaze lingered on them for a moment longer.

"Yes... We're all a bit nosy when it comes to one another's business."

Guilt twisted in my gut.

This male, however unhinged, *would be missed.*

I cleared my throat, trying to push the thought away. Nakoa seemed to sense my sudden discomfort and changed the subject.

"What brings you to Ouvelleete?"

He piqued a brow as though encouraging me to elaborate.

"Just travelling back home from visiting the sea..."

His brows leapt at this.

"And you're... Alone."

My eyes narrowed again in distrust.

"Yes. And?"

"It's rather dangerous to travel alone through the wilds—

I snorted my laughter.

"What?" He pressed, his smile wavering with uncertainty.

I huffed a laugh. My voice turned dramatic with mock innocence.

"It's *soooo* dangerous travelling through the wilds, all by my lonesome... Is this where you suggest I spend the evening with you, kind sir? Lest any bandits or other unseemly *wielders* take advantage of a lonely maiden traveller?"

Nakoa burst into laughter. The sound gravelly and warm.

"Darling, I'd sooner think you a murderer than a maiden..."

His dark eyes twinkled with mirth as I tried to mask just how right he was.

"If anything, I'd be worried about *you* taking advantage of them... But I would be greatly pleased to spend the evening with you. No intimacy expected."

Well. I wasn't entirely sure what to say to *that.*

He actually seemed sincere about that last bit. Something squirmed uncomfortably inside me.

Mercifully, the cue cleared, and we reached the bar, where a bartender already had two drinks waiting for us. I gratefully took mine, thanking him as I brought the burgundy liquid to my lips.

Nakoa gave him an appreciative nod, sliding several coins - far more than any wine was worth - across the wooden bar top to the bartender.

That, too, served to increase my discomfort. Was this male... Dare I say... *decent?*

Gods.

Zurie would probably want him dead for that reason alone. However, I couldn't help but wonder what the *actual* reason was.

I found no small amount of irony in the fact that if he knew who I actually was... He would have attempted to kill me on sight. He was clearly a Kahlohani warrior. Their signature geometric patterns wove and whirled across his wrist, up his forearms, and bled onto his chest if the peek of flesh I could see through the V of his collar was anything to go by.

I was all too familiar with them, considering I had slaughtered countless Kahlohani soldiers during the war... The guilt of which festered in me like a gangrenous fucking wound... Not that it would make a difference to him.

By merely standing in his presence, something seemed to be rousing awake within my chest.

I wanted to bury it.

A devilish grin lifted a corner of my mouth, and it further coaxed that thing waking within me.

I wanted desperately to run in the other direction. Duty was the only thing that kept my feet planted in front of him.

The male chuckled, brows furrowing as if in disbelief despite the appreciative grin spreading across his scarred face.

"Look, even if you don't necessarily *need* any protection... I would still like to extend the invitation to you... My chosen family and I," he said, nodding in the direction of a group of males and one female who were rather openly watching us, "... will be leaving for Vyssini tomorrow... We aren't travelling all the way to Bastrina, but at least we could escort you safely most of the way..."

ELEVEN

NAKOA

I felt the tiniest pang of guilt at my lie. Although I had spent a lifetime swearing that I would run in the other direction the second I'd laid eyes on this female, I suddenly found myself incapable of letting us part ways. I had zero intention of allowing this female to leave us when we arrived in Vyssini to bring our ill-gotten gains that we had just procured this very evening to the unofficial headquarters of The Uprising... The Uprising that I had been leading for the last two years.

No one outside my *olana kah'hei* knew that fact, lest I put an even bigger target on my back. I just needed to persuade Mareina to hold off a day or two while I convinced Mareina to stay with us without having to force her hand.

My eyes flicked towards my chosen family, still lingering in the distant corner of the tavern. As if spurred by my words, they snaked through the crowd and disappeared beyond the exit. I knew that my *olana kah'hei* wouldn't be pleased having some strange female join us... But once I confided she was my *soulbound,* they'd be ecstatic. She'd been featured in my very own personal fucking reoccurring nightmare.

And everything about this female exuded just that.

She was every single glorious, broken piece of bloodied perfection that I could have dared to imagine.

As much as I hated to admit it to myself, she had no choice in the matter, really... There was no way in fuck I was going to let her travel to Bastrina alone to potentially be attacked by *Akash* knew what foul creatures would try to take advantage of her, even if she could defend herself.

But most of all, I already knew Mareina was mine, through and through. I could *feel* it. My Knowingness had been whispering confirmations since the moment I'd spotted her in the crowd.

She is the key to strengthening your power.

She was the one that I had seen in this prophetic nightmare I knew to be a premonition. I had told myself for the last hundred years since the premonition had started that I would run as fast I fucking could in the other direction as soon as I saw her.

All the resistance I'd had at one day coming face-to-face with her evaporated. Replaced with this overwhelming sensation that she was *mine*. It burned through me as though I would explode with rage if I didn't claim her.

Which, admittedly, was a wildly inappropriate thing to do with a complete stranger, so I was trying my best to tamp it down and appear normal when I was actually the furthest thing from it.

The only kink in my plan to convince her to stay with me was... Well, she didn't entirely seem wooed by my charms. Though I knew that was at least partly due to the glamoring of my magic. Something that I did to draw less attention to myself. Despite being half-fae and half-human, my true form could be considered... mildly alarming.

It was as if there was a beast within her whispering to my own... *soulbound* and reuniting for the first time after having been separated, and the two were merely catching up... The newly awakened beast within me listening and utterly enraptured as hers wove its tale. One not so different from my own. Of heartbreak, horror, and death... So very much death.

I couldn't exactly *hear* the words, but... I could *feel* her. My heart clenched in equal parts sadness and awe as all that she was funnelled into me by my Knowingness - one of my gifts.

Something that felt entirely separate from myself, like a separate consciousness altogether, my Knowingness could read people, things... Situations. An instantaneous transfer of information and energy that I could decipher. All that was required was to stand in their presence.

I studied her, trying my best to at least appear normal as my mind processed all of the information flowing into me from her. Images flashed, sounds, feelings... It washed over me with such potency I was amazed my knees didn't buckle. I had never experienced a *Knowing* so profoundly before. Usually, it was just the essentials... My magic always seemed to decide for itself what was 'essential'.

Things like:

Is this person trustworthy?

Are they lying?

Should we rob them blind?

Would the world be better off if we killed them?

'*We*' obviously referring to my *olana kah'hei* and me.

Things that were necessary in our line of work... Which consisted of robbing and looting from those who possessed... shall we say... Ill-gotten goods. Or, more transparently...

Extraordinarily wealthy individuals who had made their fortunes via the exploitation of others.

Then... We shaved a nice hefty chunk off the spoils to keep for ourselves before anonymously distributing the remainder among those in need. Because the *Akash* knew that Queen Zurie didn't give a shit about any of us and wouldn't dream of robbing anyone of their suffering.

This is also what was currently funding The Uprising.

Not only had Queen Zurie and her army slaughtered nearly all of my people - the Kahlohani - but she had overtaken our islands and enslaved the poor souls who had unwittingly chosen to remain. After exploiting the mainland of Atratus for the first 447 years of her reign, the last remaining place in the entirety of Atratus where *aetra* could be grown was the Kahlohani Islands. And without *aetra*, she would likely be rendered powerless and poor.

Guised as providing the sole resource that would provide even the weakest of wielders access to a deep well of magic, she had inspired nearly an entire kingdom to fight for her.

Though now, it seemed the tables were turning. For the last few years, my *olana kah'hei* and I had been growing an opposition to rise against her again, and it hadn't proven too difficult a task.

For nearly 500 years, she'd had 90 percent of Atratus living in poverty. A fact that inspired both my rage and heartbreak. I knew it meant to live in poverty. Exiled after we'd lost the war, I'd found myself destitute until I'd literally *stolen* my wealth from the very ones who'd taken it from me. Though I didn't necessarily consider Atratusians *my* people, I knew their plight, and I would wish it on no one but the ones who had forced it upon them.

Such as Zurie.

To add insult to injury, the mass majority of the Atratusians living in destitution because of her had also been the ones who had fought *for* her. All in vain under her guise of making *aetra* accessible to all because *aetra* equals power, and power equals wealth.

The only caveat she failed to mention was that to purchase *aetra,* you had to already possess wealth.

Which still left the mass majority of her people in poverty.

Once we gained enough support, we would overthrow her so that I could reclaim the Kahlohani Islands. Liberate the Kahlohani people she had enslaved. Give back our exiled people their home.

Purge the land of Zurie's exploitation that was destroying our land and sea.

The dream that had haunted me for nearly my entire life began to replay distantly in my mind as my eyes consumed Mareina.

King, my Knowingness whispered, *You are destined to be King.*

Anxiety knotted in my chest. I promptly swallowed back. I tried to visualize a future with *her* in which there wouldn't be yet another war despite my efforts to prevent it, as my vision foretold. One in which she didn't loathe the very sight of me. One in which I didn't transform into what appeared to be a hellish monstrosity.

And it was like trying to lift a boulder from the sea floor.

Fuck off, I growled back to my Knowingness.

Unease settled in my gut as flashes of the premonition returned to me.

Why? Why does it have to be that way? I seethed internally as I plastered a lopsided grin on my face. One that I knew females *always* found disarmingly charming.

Instead of being wooed by it, Mareina stood in front of me, eyes warily narrowed, studying me as though I were a puzzle made up of entirely mismatching pieces.

If she only knew.

She seemed to be deliberating internally as she took a pretty sip of her drink with a daintiness that surprised me. The way she'd held my gaze and parted her lips to bring the glass to her mouth had my cock twitching and blessedly snuffing out the premonition, trying to thrust itself into my mind.

"And what, exactly, is bringing you to Vyssini?"

"Business."

An unamused brow piqued with suspicion at my deliberately vague response.

"So... Will you allow us to accompany you?" I pressed.

She shrugged a bare shoulder. Her dress was long-sleeved but left her neck, shoulders, and the tops of her full breasts exposed. The sight was mouth-watering, and it took considerable effort not to lean in and bite, kiss, and lick every inch of her exposed flesh.

"I'm generally not inclined to go anywhere with strange males."

I couldn't help the devilish grin curling my lips and had to bite my undeniably lascivious retort.

"I'm relieved to hear it... But I would ask you to consider that it is truly for your safety... I'm actually surprised you made it all the way to the sea by yourself unscathed. As you know, not everyone you encounter on your way has your well-being in mind."

She merely hummed in amusement.

"And I suppose you do?"

"Actually, yes."

Mostly.

She rolled her eyes, finally breaking my gaze, and took another sip of her drink. Something about her energy turned hard and bitter. My chest tightened in response with a bizarre mixture of compassion and rage against all those who had harmed her. It was becoming unsettling how strong my Knowingness with her was.

With her, I could feel the sensation of all the pain caused by her long-buried past sinking its talons into her, dulled only by time. It took everything within me not to pull her into my arms and swear to her in my blood that I would do everything in my power to protect her.

Before I could think better of it, I found myself leaning into her and slipping my hand over her wrist where it rested on the bar top. Electricity tingled, sending a delicious current through me that had my heart thumping. Her gaze snapped back to mine in a way that, all too briefly, had her looking like a startled doe.

"Would you like me to swear it in blood?"

She reared back slightly, brow furrowed in disbelief, as her eyes searched mine for the truth of my words. Her delicate throat worked on a swallow.

"That won't be necessary..."

"Are you staying at the inn?"

"... No."

Such opportunity...

Now, do I dare risk being stabbed?

"... Do you need a place to stay the night?"

Her brows lifted, something unreadable shuttering her gaze, but to my surprise... She didn't seem entirely opposed to the idea.

Yes, yes, yes, little fox... Come fall into my trap.

CHAPTER

TWELVE

MAREINA

"I hadn't actually planned on staying the night in Ouvelleet."

Because as soon as I kill you, I'm going to head straight back to Bastrina.

"... But, I'm not entirely opposed to spending some time with you."

Nakoa's trained, neutral expression was commendable. So much so, it had my lips quirking with excitement.

Let's see how neutral your expression is when I drain you of every drop of your blood.

Something in my gut twisted at the thought... I'd managed to suppress the reality of the situation until I reminded myself of the harsh reality. And I didn't have anger clouding my mind.

He's doing more good for the realm than you ever have.

His lips finally twitched in response. "How generous of you..."

I drew in a steady breath, trying to mask the fact that I wanted nothing more than to collapse in despair.

"Well, in that case, I'm not one for crowds... Shall we leave?"

Nakoa's brows lifted in surprise at my boldness before his eyes narrowed briefly with suspicion.

99

"I would love nothing more..."

There was a certain warmth and disarming sincerity in his words. And made my despair in what I knew I had to do all the greater. I turned to lead the way through the crowd just as the smell of smoke reached my nose. I halted, exchanging a glance with Nakoa as his nostrils flared. No one else had seemed to notice yet.

I turned towards the exit, flicking a glance back at Nakoa before darting through the crowd.

We burst through the front entrance to find a crowd filling the streets, gaping up at a lone house in the distance that was half consumed in flames.

Anger sank its talons into me. Surely, at least a few of these people could do *something* to help.

"Does no one here wield water?" I roared over the crowd.

"Not when it's been burned from the air, ya cunt!" A male hissed in my direction.

I growled, shoving my way through the crowd towards Chihiro, not bothering to see if Nakoa would follow.

Please don't, I prayed silently.

Untying Chihiro swiftly, I mounted him, spurring him toward the flames. The sound of galloping hooves behind me had my head jerking to find Nakoa right behind me.

It took long minutes to arrive at the house. It was three stories, and the fire had already consumed the bottom half. The soil around the shabby, dilapidated house was completely barren... A clear answer as to why no one in town had been concerned with the fire spreading.

I leapt off Chihiro just as an elderly human female and two small children rushed towards me. "My husband! Please!"

My gaze fell to the bottom half of the home.

Fuck.

The elderly woman's pleas and the children's wailing faded into the background as I dread settled in my gut.

I could *will* a barrier around me, but if there was anything that could tear it down quicker than fire, I hadn't discovered it. And even if I could keep it up in the flames, it would do nothing to suppress the heat. I would be cooked alive.

An elderly man appeared in a window on the third floor, looking as though he were struggling to open it.

I didn't miss the irony of the fact that I'd spent my entire career killing people, and yet, I was probably about to die saving a single human.

A fair enough way to pay a shred of penance before I died.

Is this what the Pharalaki had been following me around for?

Was it a sign that I would die soon?

Just as I moved to race forward, Nakoa's hand gripped my arm.

"Mareina, there's no way... You'll die with him if you go in there."

The words were laughable. Little did he know that not only did I wish for death daily but that he would be sparing his own if I did.

"Either you join me, or you get out of my way."

Ripping my arm out of his hold, I approached the house, *willing* a barrier around me.

I push-kicked the fiery door open. Outside winds rushed in, whispering its mal-intent. The flames bade its command, roaring higher.

As if *Akash* herself had laid the path, somehow, the stairs were *mostly* intact. I rushed forward, Nakoa right behind me. The second-floor landing was almost entirely devoured. A heavy wood beam split and collapsed in the center that I used as a lily pad to leap to the second set of stairs. Nakoa, right behind me, was barely visible through the smoke surrounding his own barrier.

My booted foot plunged through a step just before the third-floor landing, causing part of it to cave in. Nakoa leapt forward, yanking me up with him onto a slightly more secure part of the landing.

We both tumbled forward into the hallway. It had yet to be touched by flames but was bound to collapse into the lower levels at any moment. I kicked open the first door to find the elderly man already unconscious on the floor, perhaps even dead, from the smoke.

I could have laughed. Was this Mors' way of mocking me? Not even in dying would I be able to find some sort of redemption?

I rushed forward, curling his frail body into my arms and my barrier. Nakoa waited at the doorway, tension carving his face as I swiftly joined him, and we raced down the hallway to return to the stairs landing, which was now little more than fiery splinters.

Nakoa swore behind me. "This place is going to—"

An ominous crack rent the air as fractured webs split the walls. Nakoa's arms lashed out as he leapt backwards, towing both me and the unconscious human against his chest just before the entire staircase gave way. A support beam from above us gave way, along with a portion of the roof, threatening to crush us beneath it. Before it could, Nakoa caught it above his head. The fire roared around us, and our barriers threatened to give way.

"The window. Quickly," he growled, straining from beneath the weight of the beam and the parts of the roof it was attached to.

Guilt weighed like a fucking boulder in my gut as a fire, one that had nothing to do with the one threatening to devour us, tore through something in the center of my chest. I was supposed to kill this male. So why the hell did I feel so viscerally averse to the idea of leaving him here to die?

"Mareina!"

I forced myself to move down the hallway and back into the bedroom, hesitating briefly at the sight of Nakoa bearing the weight of a fucking roof.

Gods damn it.

I tore the sheets off the bed, tying them together, and then around the male's chest and shoved the windows open. I looked down to see his wife and their wards, surely too young to be their own children, looking up at us with hopeful, wide, watery eyes. I propped his body precariously on the edge of the window and began lowering him to the ground. I knew the sheet likely wouldn't reach the entire way to the ground, but that was just too damn bad. The male would survive a few falling a few feet.

Nakoa, however, probably wouldn't survive being crushed by a house and consumed by a fire... And Zurie *had* demanded I bring her his body.

The elderly male's body hit the ground with a discomforting thud, and I rushed back to Nakoa, now bent on one knee and rushed to his side, kneeling beside him to alleviate some of the weight. His dark eyes widened with shock.

"Do you have a death wish, *lohane thili?*" He ground out.

"More than you know."

As if *Akash,* or perhaps *Mors*, had heard my prayers, the floor caved in, and Nakoa and I plummeted through the second floor and landed in the center of what may have once been a kitchen. Flames consumed us, our disintegrating barriers.

Nakoa and I wheezed, scrambling to our feet. Our eyes locked with a door only a handful of feet away. We hobbled toward it on mending bones. He threw the weight of his body against it, and it gave way instantly.

My broken ankle decided to give away at that precise moment, and I went tumbling to the ground beside him.

"*Reckless... Reckless, female,*" he rasped between coughs.

Some strange emotion worked through me...

"I'm sorry... For making you risk your life."

"I would do it again in a heartbeat, Mareina."

THIRTEEN

MAREINA

Beside me, Nakao rode on the largest horse I'd ever seen. Though it suited him, considering he appeared only a couple inches shorter than Malekai's six foot eight inches. Nakoa's horse, Pumpkin- or as he affectionately pronounced it, "*Punkin*", had a darkest umber coat and black mane that even I found enviable. The hide of her legs flashed with long black fur, referred to as 'feathering', below the knee.

When we'd returned from the fire, he'd baby talked to her and given her and Chihiro several apples before we'd left. Pushing away the warmth of watching him do so was a painful thing.

Among a number of other things I was entirely unwilling to examine, I felt indebted to this male that I was supposed to murder.

We'd laid on the ground in silence, watching that house burn to the ground from a safe distance away as our bodies healed. Nakoa had not only ensured they had a room at the inn for the next several weeks paid for, but he *willed* a considerable sack of coins into his hand and given it to the woman before we left. The act had made my heart squeeze, and my gut clench with preemptive remorse.

This was a good male.

As we rode closer and closer to The Sentient Forest, civilization seemed to disappear entirely. The woods were thick, and I could feel just how alive, aware, and observant it was... Watching us as we road on the lone path that tread through the dense trees that filtered out all but the barest slivers of moonlight. Tiny lights zipped, floated, flew, and flickered throughout. *Sprites.* Never lingering in one spot or getting close enough to ever be able to make out any discernible attributes aside from the glow they emanated in the night.

That pressure between my shoulder blades pinched tight and ached as anxiety for what I knew I had to do sank its claws deeper into me the closer we drew to his home. The few people we'd passed along the hour-long journey had all greeted Nakoa affectionately and with warmth. And for no other reason than the fact that I was there beside him, they'd even offered me warm, though curious, smiles. It was a foreign sensation to be greeted in such a way. Everyone in Bastrina was, naturally, stand-offish with me at best.

I was still lost in thought when the wood suddenly gave way to a clearing where moonlight illuminated a large cabin and a beautifully laid garden. A tree adorned in long moss with a trunk nearly as wide as Chihiro was long. It had a couch-like swing hanging in front of a large pond where groups of sprites danced on the cool summer breeze.

Something in my chest twisted painfully at the realization I'd never be able to come back here. It looked and felt like such a haven of...

Peace.

I wanted this. A haven. Peace... A family like this male had culti-vated for himself despite having no one but his mother.

My heart gave a painful thump as my thoughts drifted to Malekai, but Nakoa's impending doom drew me right back to the present.

He seemed to be nothing like Zurie's other targets.

Mildly arrogant, maybe...

An outlier? Clearly.

Deranged? Probably/Kinda.

But *bad?* No.

When someone had sinister intentions, it oozed off them. They radiated it. And they certainly didn't have such a large group of friends and family vested in their lives.

For the most part, when Zurie sent me to *take care of someone,* most of them were *starkly* among the dregs of society. And it wasn't far-fetched to imagine that they deserved to meet such a sudden and violent end.

The touch of Nakoa's gaze pulled me out of my head to find him patiently watching me with an unreadable expression. When I finally turned to look at his ash and soot-streaked face, a corner of his mouth tilted in a soft smile. Something seemed to pull tight between us as if trying to draw me closer to him, and I quickly shoved it back.

He grinned wryly, eyes twinkling with a hint of pride.

"Home sweet home."

FOURTEEN

NAKOA

S he belonged here. She was quite literally the woman of my nightmares - *ahem* - dreams. All the previous dread I'd carried since I'd begun having these often violent and rarely endearing premonitions of her evaporated further with each moment I spent beside her. Trying to deny the tether anchoring my soul to hers would be like trying to deny my body food and water.

The sight of her sitting on Chihiro and simply staring out at my home with such tremendous longing written all over her face made my heart swell to bursting. Only further intensifying at the sight of her undeniable beauty. She lacked a certain feminine softness found in conventional beauty... There was a certain harshness to her features... An expression and demeanor I could clearly imagine being a deterrent to lesser males.

My gaze dropped from her profile, luminous in the moonlight despite the sooty streaks. I followed the line of her full lips... the generous swell of her breasts beneath her dress...

Another vision bled into the present, drowning out my present reality.

An identical silhouette of the moonlight illuminating Mareina's profile. Dressed in a long silk robe, standing in front of the window that has a panoramic view of Bastrina. Her face turns to meet my gaze. Her green eyes glow brighter than I've ever seen, but within them, I see no love. I see... Sadness.

The vision disappeared, leaving nothing behind but a sore fucking ache in my chest. And questions that no one can answer. Not even my Knowingness.

The vision left a thick, sticky emotion in my throat that I refused to let ruin the present moment.

Mareina, at my stare, gave me a questioning look.

I cleared my throat like it might clear my mind and emotions, trying to make myself seem normal.

"Yeah... You just look... Beautiful."

Not even remotely a lie.

Her brows leapt before burrowing with skepticism.

"Even covered in soot," I add over my shoulder, turning towards my house.

I heaved a sigh as I finally dismounted Pumpkin, removing her saddle and reins and setting them on the porch railing.

"Thank you, *Punkin*..." I pressed my forehead against hers, giving her thick neck a pat before she turned and strode off to graze. I didn't need to keep her in the stable on temperate nights like this. Thanks to my magic, any creatures who would wish her any harm stayed *far* away. She also knew better than to wander in The Sentient Forest, which was its own kind of fortress of protection around my lands and home. Very few beings were allowed to enter *and* live...

"You don't have a stable?"

I turned to face Mareina, praying that the hardened length in my trousers had softened enough to not be visible in the moonlight, but considering her sanguinati sight, I wouldn't be surprised if she could.

"I do, but in this weather, they're safe to roam."

Mareina hesitated, eyes scanning the hills and dark forest that surrounded us.

"Don't worry, I have wards up."

She piqued a brow.

"Wards?"

"Yes, wards," I affirmed, approaching Chihiro to unsaddle him.

"Do you need *aetra* to maintain it?"

My hackles raised the question. *Never* would I take that gods-forsaken plant. I didn't need it. I already had more power than I knew what to do with. It was constantly churning and ready to burst out of me.

"No. Never," I managed, perhaps sounding a little more dour than intended.

Her delicately arched brows drew together, eyes roaming over me as if it would reveal how I could do such a thing. It was unusual for someone to be able to maintain constant wards... But I attributed that to my mother, who was an exceedingly formidable human witch, and my father, who... I knew nothing about it. Only that he was fae.

Silence followed as I set Chihiro's tack down on the rail beside mine and made my way up the steps. The sound of claws scraping against my front door cut through the silence. I *willed* the front door open as my two loyal beasts, Peanut and Bellona, flung themselves towards me, and I knelt to embrace them.

"Yes! Oh my goodness, my sweet babies! Did you miss Daddy? I missed you both *so* much. Did you behave while I was gone? I know you did, my angels. Wanna meet our new friend?"

I stood, wiping their slobber off my neck and hands, to introduce Mareina. Her deep green eyes widened as Peanut, quite the opposite in size, galloped towards her. On all fours, she was hip height and all muscle, wrinkly skin and floppy ears. And while her parents were former beasts of war - a breed explicitly used to assist soldiers in battle to tear their enemies apart limb from limb- she had a gentle and sweet temperament that could rival any puppy.

Bellona, on the other hand, could be described succinctly as *tiny but mighty*. She was a ferocious little thing with an asymmetrical maw, teeth that jutted out at bizarre angles, and a half-gnawed-off ear. I'd found her in an alley digging for scraps. She'd nearly bit my face off, but... Much like Mareina, I knew I would win her over. All she needed was time and a gentle, loving hand. And I'd always had a soft spot for wounded, vicious things.

My heart just about leapt out of my chest to throw itself at Mareina as she knelt to greet Peanut, wholly appreciative of her kisses and unconcerned with her slobber... And when she *smiled,* I knew I'd give my left testicle if it would inspire that smile again.

Bellona approached her warily, stretching her little neck out to sniff her before huffing loudly and turning back towards me.

"Peanut, let her inside. She's tired," I called, patting my hip as I turned toward the house. Peanut promptly turned, galloping towards me. Bellona, however, stood her ground at the front door, peering at her through slitted eyes.

"Don't mind, Bellona. She's just wary of strangers but is loyal as they come... She'll warm up to you."

She stepped inside behind me, eyes lingering on the painting of Kahlohan in battle - the famed warrior and, later, King of the Kahlohani Islands who had led the *agrios* to victory against the so-called *axios* so many thousands of years ago.

Agrios. Savage.

Axios. Worthy.

Agrios was a formerly used term that referred to anyone who wasn't fae.

Without his efforts, the fae would have exterminated all others. I wouldn't be here, Mareina wouldn't be here...

Being a sanguinati, I could imagine she shared my appreciation.

"A fascinating history he had, no?" She said, her gaze still fixed to the painting. Indeed, he did. It was said that the male had come from nothing. Risen through the ranks, seemingly, out of nowhere to somehow miraculously turn the tides of the war, despite being outnumbered. It was something I could relate to deeply. Except for the winning the war part...

"Inspiring," I murmured, feeling a familiar stab of pain at the reminder of just how thoroughly we had lost against Zurie and her army. Mareina's brows furrowed at my sudden change in demeanour but, thankfully, chose not to investigate.

I gave her a tour of my home while she followed me silently, radiating that sentiment of longing. It made me wonder where *she* lived. My home wasn't extravagant by any means, but it was cozy and eclectic and had been built with love by my hands.

She'd come here under the pretence of us sleeping together, but I had *zero* intention of following through. The female was already at least mildly averse to me despite my efforts. No matter how much possessiveness I felt towards her, and how much every molecule in my body was burning with desire to fuck her until every male before me was wiped from her mind... I knew that if I gave into this so soon, it would be one less reason for her to stay. I needed to drive her mindless with need for me. What better way to do that but with angst?

Less selfishly and begrudgingly, I could intuitively discern that she would appreciate having the option of her own space... And if I was going to convince her to remain at my side, I would also need to gain her trust...

"The guest bedroom has doors that lead out to the porch if that'll help you sleep better in a strange home..."

Surprise lit her features, followed by a suspicious dip in her brow, but she said nothing more than, "Thank you... Again... For earlier, and... hosting me for the evening."

"It was a remarkable thing you did earlier... If not unforgivably careless for your own life..."

Mareina's gaze dipped to the floor briefly, drawing in a long breath.

I shifted uncomfortably on my feet. On our short journey here, her energy had become increasingly... *stressed,* and my Knowingness and intuition confirmed it had nothing to do with the *fiery* event earlier.

And I felt keenly compelled to fix it. Some innate part of me, though I barely knew her, ached to give her a reason to smile.

Before I could think better of it, I stepped close to her, my eyes searching hers.

"You wanna tell me what's wrong, *lohane thili?*"

Lohane thili. Soulbound.

Her expression remained unreadable, though I couldn't help but notice her delicate throat work on a swallow.

"Even if I did, it would change nothing."

"You're certain? Perhaps I can help."

She hesitated for a moment before breaking my gaze.

"There are some occasions in life where we have no choice."

I shook my head, daring to reach out and gently wrap my fingers around her arm.

"We always have a choice... And if there's anything I can do to resolve the problem itself, I will do everything within my power to help you regardless."

Her brow furrowed, face almost twisting in a scowl.

"Why?" She asked bitterly. "You have nothing to gain from it. You have no idea who I am. I could be here to rob you blind for all you know. Why would you want to help me?"

My mouth twitched at the irony of her words.

"Firstly, I absolutely have something to gain from it. Your peace. Your trust. Your affection. And most of all, your heart - in case that wasn't clearly my intention already. Secondly, if you are here to rob me, you can save yourself the trouble... You need but only ask, and I would happily give you everything I have and more."

Mareina's brows pinched. Her expression hardened.

"Words are like dandelion fluff. Here one moment and gone the next at the faintest breeze..."

I had to bite back the response I felt, trying to claw its way up my throat. The fact that she was my *poa hanei*. But I knew I needed to water it down, at least. Mareina had a wall that wouldn't even allow her *soulbound* to pass without having proven loyalty.

"I... Because I feel like I know you... And I know that I *need* to make sure you're ok... As strange as that may sound."

While the tension in the air was palpable... Much to my dismay, there was nothing even remotely sexual about it. I had at least hoped to taste her lips and caress her tongue... Touch those ample curves hidden beneath her leathers. Tease her and give her something to pine over.

She studied me, and the scowl gradually replaced with a sigh.

"I would enjoy taking a bath before..."

"No pressure... If you need to sleep afterwards, that's fine too..."

Her brow tensed with wariness as though surprised I'd give up the opportunity to fuck her. I gave one last attempt to lighten the mood, letting a devilish grin curl the corner of my mouth.

"We'll have plenty of time on the journey to Vyssini to become better acquainted..."

She studied me for a moment longer, again entirely unaffected by my charms.

I'm not sure I'd ever had this effect on women before... That is to say... None at all...

"My bedroom is just across from yours if you need anything."

Moments later, in my bedroom, I stared down at the gold and jewels we'd looted from some decadent, debauched *Lord* in Hallofrin, a mining town a few days from Ouvelleete. He'd been a horrible cunt that employed indentured servants and was notorious for withholding their wages and sexually exploiting the females who worked for him.

I often experienced guilt for my lack of hesitance or remorse when I ended their lives. Perhaps they one day could have found redemption and done greater things... But... That was rarely the case, if ever... And I couldn't help but feel a twisted satisfaction because I knew in my heart of hearts... That they fucking deserved it.

I had experienced too much oppression. Had been forced to live in exile on this *Akash*-forsaken continent in poverty for too long because of people like him. *And fucking Zurie.*

When I'd first begun looting from the Lords of Atratus, I'd been alone. The first Lord I'd targeted, I'd followed him home from a tavern. He'd initially drawn my attention because he'd gotten aggressive with two of the females from the local brothel. Dressed in finery, he'd climbed into a gilded carriage. It had been entirely on impulse that I'd followed him home and discovered that he was just as aggressive with his wife. I'm sure if I'd allowed him to live longer, I would have seen that he was equally so with his servants, whose hardship was carved into every line of their gaunt faces.

When I found his head in my hands, I knew that I couldn't subject his wife and the people he employed to the poverty that would surely follow with no Lord to support them. Especially if I was going to be alleviating his liquid assets. It was only then that I'd consciously realized it would make me no better than the Lord I'd murdered if I hoarded his wealth to myself.

Since then, my *olana kah'hei* and I would pay ourselves a portion of this, Pomona would distribute a portion to the late Lord's *employees*, and for the last couple of years, we'd begun reserving a remaining third to fund The Uprising.

We used these proceeds to house a number of our members. In addition to training and facilitating *operations* similar to the ones we'd just conducted. We also used it to purchase weaponry, among other necessities. It had been two years, and it finally felt like we'd been progressing. Unfortunately, that came at a price: Zurie's attention and, thusly, her wrath. Thankfully, all of us had vowed our secrecy and discretion in blood to eliminate any chances of our actions being traced back to anyone beyond any individuals who might have garnered suspicion, whether by family, friends, etc., that might feel inclined to report them.

Zurie had a rather handsome reward system for those willing to rat out anyone suspected of being a member of The Uprising. Often paying them a fortnight's salary to do so. And anytime the reports became too numerous, the town was often *purged.* Her favored method of exacting her revenge and quelling any Uprising members was to have their heads mounted on pikes in the offending town's square. Both methods are equally effective at stifling our ranks.

Eventually, we would have the numbers and the weapons to form a coup and put Zurie's head on a fucking pike outside her own palace.

All without the help of fucking aetra.

And finally, I would liberate my kinsmen and their forced exile. Liberate the Kahlohani Islands of Zurie's scourge and her mass production and control of *aetra.* Outside of its magic-enhancing abilities, I would be more than tempted to eradicate it if it weren't for its numerous and imperative medicinal uses for *wielders* slight in their prowess.

All of Atratus would be free of her oppression. We could *all* live in peace and be allowed to flourish.

It had been *the* dream since I was little, and I realized that living in terror, genocide, and impending war wasn't natural or necessary.

The only hitches in my visions of grandeur were that, according to my visions, war would befall us no matter how I tried to prevent it, and the female sleeping in my guest bedroom was destined to despise me... The last of which I couldn't fucking fathom why.

My skin prickles from the sudden wave of magic as another vision drowns out the present.

Zurie's blood gurgles from her mouth as she's impaled on a sword and lifted over a foot off the ground.

Her words are unintelligible, but I can feel what she's trying to say.

"He will never forgive you."

The vision pans out slightly to reveal that Mareina is the one who has overcome Zurie.

My heart beats furiously in my chest as I watch with held breath.

The vision was ripped away, and I blinked down at the gold and jewels still sitting at my feet.

But... How?

I shake my head in disbelief... My *lohane thili...*

Pride and fear, in equal measure, fill my chest.

The vision plagues me for the rest of the evening as I divided the gold and jewels for my *olana kah'hei,* The Uprising, and what Pomona would distribute later tonight while the heinous Lord's servants and mine workers slept none-the-wiser and would wake up to a hefty, life-changing sum.

Finally, I allowed myself to sink into my copper bathtub as fleeting images of the premonition returned to me that I promptly rejected by stroking my cock for nearly an hour. The effort proved to do almost nothing to quell the *need* for my *poa hanei* burning through my veins like fire.

Even then, I knew that I would accept the fate of that premonition if it meant that I could have her.

She doesn't even like *you...*

Was I destined to have a Queen that despised me?

It would be no less than you deserved.

I groaned, battling my warring thoughts.

By the time I crawled into bed, I tossed and turned- my worries alternating between what the future held and Mareina. *For Mareina.* My *soulbound* was indeed fierce, but... I would never have fathomed her capable of killing Zurie...

My heart had twisted into some strange, painful knot.

I couldn't tell her this was her destiny, but... I needed to speak with her.

And to further enflame matters, I'd taken so long bathing and working my dick into a chafe that it was now too late to invite

Mareina for a cup of herbal tea or something equally innocuous that would give me an excuse to do so.

Even though I'd only known her for mere hours, I knew that my *charm*, or even the fact that we were *soulbound*, would convince her to stay with me once we reached Vyssini. Every fucking kind word, gesture, or expression of concern was what with cynicism and distrust.

Who had wounded this creature?

My Knowingness had shown me many things - violent things - but it hadn't given me any discernible details. Instead of giving me answers, it left me with more questions. And fucking anxiety.

I knew what I had to do, especially after seeing that she was how we overcame Zurie.

She'll hate your it, my Knowingness whispered.

Fuck.

Fate could truly be a wicked thing.

As I stared up at the ceiling, begging *Akash* to help me sleep, a familiar magic drifted over to me. I heaved a great sigh of relief at the welcome distraction, pointing to the neatly divided mountain of riches sitting in the corner of the room.

"The loot's just there," I murmured as I absently pointed in its direction.

Pomona had a rare gift that enabled her to *fold* through space and time. *Without* the aid of *aetra*. Out of principle and loyalty to me, none of my *olana kah-hei* took *aetra*. And thankfully, they were all powerful enough in their own ways to not need it. They had strengthened and honed their gifts, in addition to being naturally formidable. Like Roderick, when in his gigantic wolf form, was one of the largest Lykos males I'd ever seen.

Though Pomona had limitations in her ability to *fold*. A limit as to how far she could travel, and she could only ever travel alone or with inanimate objects. From what she'd told me, she'd only tried once to fold with another person... And they'd merely... disappeared entirely, never to be found again.

That person had been her brother.

She'd only been 19. A few short years before I'd met her.

It was a scar, a guilt, that weighed heavily on her despite her perennially effusive love, warmth, and lightheartedness.

"Who is she?"

Pomona's question held no hint of jealousy. Only curiosity. She was like a little sister to me. I'd killed her abusive father, who was another wealthy lord, during a raid twenty years ago. Long before we'd started The Uprising. And in all our years together, she had never seen me behave with a female like I had with Mareina.

I sat up in bed as she strode over to lean against the windowsill beside my bed. Her unruly, fiery, red hair glowed like a bloody halo from the moons illuminating the window.

"I...," I hesitated, wondering if I should tell her already. My Knowingness firmly replied with a resolute *yes*.

"She's ... the female from that fucking nightmare.*"*

Pomona's smirk split into a grin. Her Reilandish accent thick and lilting.

"Your *leath-anama*? Are you serious?"

Leath-anama. The Reilandish term for *soul-halve*.

I groaned in response and massaged my brow with my thumb and forefinger, feeling a little helpless and disoriented.

"Like a fucking hole in the head."

She hummed thoughtfully. "Ya know... I had a feeling."

"Yes, well... She's utterly unaffected by me."

Pomona chuckled as though pleased by my plight. "About time you met a female who was... Shouldn't she feel it, too, though? You're absolutely certain she's your *leath anama?*"

"About as certain as I am of my own name... My Knowingness won't shut up about her, and...," I gestured helplessly at my diaphragm as though that would clarify things, "This *thing*... It's relentless and all-consuming. It *burns.*"

Pomona's huffed a laugh. "Sounds vaguely familiar..."

Pomona was one of the few I'd met who had found their *soul-*

bound. Who just happened to be the Orisha male part of my *olana kah'hei,* Famei.

"I'm beginning to feel like I'll lose my mind if I don't claim her soon."

Pomona made a gagging sound, feigning disgust at the idea of me *claiming.* "Gross... That is *not* an image I want in my mind... But that does sound about right... That's how it was when I tried to deny mine and Famei's bond."

"How long you were able to resist it?"

Pomona's mouth twisted in a wry grin. "Maybe... 12 hours?"

I gave a pitiful chuckle. "I can't imagine Mareina will give in after only 12 hours."

"I'm sure the glamor has something to do with that."

I nodded my agreement. "To some extent, probably."

"So remove it. Reveal your true form."

My chest tightened with anxiety. "Bad idea."

The few females I'd been in relationships with over the years had never appreciated my true form. Because they cared for me, they might have tried to pretend otherwise, but... Their initial reactions had been... A little humbling, to put it mildly. And I couldn't blame them. I looked uncannily similar to something that could have been birthed in a hell realm.

"Maybe it's time to... As your *leath-anama,* I'm sure she's got a kink for every single one of your qualities. I bet she's secretly dying to lick every one of those pretty scars."

I huffed a mirthless laugh. "I'm pretty sure she'd rather cut her tongue on a rusted bread knife."

"I've offered to escort her tomorrow. That *we* escort her tomorrow."

Pomona's brows leapt again.

"What? Where? And what about Vyssini?"

"Back to Bastrina, but I have no intention of letting her leave us once we arrive in Vyssini. She'll stay."

"*Letting* her leave?"

"Yes..."

"Does she even have a choice in the matter?"

"She's my fucking *soulbound*. Neither of us do."

She chuckled. "I doubt she'll share, much less appreciate, your sentiment."

"So what's your plan? We head to Vyssini with her... And then what?"

"I convince her to stay with me."

"And if she remains unconvinced?"

"She *will* be convinced... but in the *impossible* scenario she isn't... I'll just..."

Pomona's brows leapt. "You'll just what?"

"I'll fucking tie her up if I have to. She'll thank me for it eventually."

Pomona gave me a pitiful look, shaking her head.

"You are... unhinged."

"We already know this. But I have some redeeming qualities, no?"

Pomona sighed.

"Aye. That you do, brother. I'm just having a hard time imagining her actually recognizing them if you've gagged and bound her."

"I didn't say anything about gagging her," I mumbled as that exact image flashed in my mind, making my cock twitch.

Pomona simply shook her head with pity.

"It's not as if I can very well explain any of this to her. She'll think I'm deranged or just trying to take advantage of her. The female has trust issues."

"Ah, ok, so kidnapping her will resolve that."

The scowl on my face deepened.

"Well, I'm all ears if you have any better suggestions."

Pomona exhaled heavily.

"Just be honest with her. She might be feeling the same way you are. And you'd never know because you think simply *talking* to her is too *crazy,*" she went on, tone still dripping with sarcasm, "so the solution is surely to kidnap her... If you lose more than an eye in the process, I can't promise not to laugh."

She strode over from the window, giving me a quick pat on the shoulder. "I'll warn the boys so they can brace themselves."

Pomona folded away, leaving me no room to argue.

I groaned, sagging back into the bed.

Well, fuck.

FIFTEEN

MAREINA

"... *S* *o the solution is surely to kidnap her... If you lose more than an eye in the process, I can't promise not to laugh.*"

My heart pounded its betrayal against my ribcage. The pain in my shoulders so intense it had my jaw clenching.

You barely know the male... Why would you expect anything less?

I cursed at myself internally for having so foolishly thought he might actually have been a *decent* fucking male. That this tangible thing I felt between us, pulling me to him, was... *real.* That I would be killing someone who would be not only missed but perhaps even deserved to be in this world. Someone who might make it a better place simply by having been a part of it.

As I'd laid in that bath, trying to talk myself into doing it... It had given me a visceral, painful reaction that stole my breath away. Just imagining following through with it for the last several hours since we'd arrived had made me feel like I was suffocating.

Now, whatever wavering doubt I'd had in carrying out Zurie's task was gone. I willed my blade into my hand, reaching for the door handle, ready to burst through and do it the satisfying way. Until I'd heard *her* words, whoever *she* was, I'd planned on... Feeling things out on our journey to Vyssini. I hadn't been planning on *not* killing him...

Now, on the other hand, I was *more* than fucking ready.

I'd all but forgotten it... I hesitated for a few more moments before finally deciding that it was a risk I was willing to take. Surely, if the Miroslav wanted me dead... All he had to do was *will* it so. The memory of watching hundreds, if not thousands, of soldiers at a time dropping to the ground the moment he stepped on the battlefield was something that haunted me to this day. There was nothing brutal or gory about it. It had been silent and swift. He would simply *fold* onto the battlefield, *will* their collective deaths, and in less than a breath later, he would be gone again. Only a great silence following in his wake.

Releasing the door handle, I willed the vial into my hand, studying the seemingly innocuous pale blue fluid in it for a few fleeting moments before finally flicking off the cork and downing its contents.

Grip tightening on my blade, I took a deep breath before gently swinging open the door as I willed an opaque barrier into place to keep his dogs out. My heart gave a painful clench at the thought they would no longer have a father. Perhaps I could take them with me...

The sight of Nakoa merely sitting up in bed, breath held and studying me intently as I approached the bed almost made me laugh. Surprise flickered as though he thought I'd decided to join him in his sheets.

Until I allowed my blade to come into view... Whether or not they actually deserved it, I *usually* gave Zurie's targets a fighting chance.

He merely piqued his brow at me as though I were dressed as a clown and not as the murderer I was, in my fighting leathers, only served to further fan the flames of my--

My vision suddenly swayed in time with the whirl of my equilibrium.

What the fuck?

I felt like the floor had shifted into an undulating wave.

The vial.

Oh, my gods.

I was going to fucking *murder* Miroslav. Right after I murdered this lying, conniving, opportunistic, arrogant—

Bright spots dotted my vision as drowsiness, unlike anything I'd ever experienced, consumed me. My limbs grew heavy and leaden and muscles began to loosen, my knees to buckle.

Faster than a human eye could see, Nakoa leapt towards me, prying the blade from my hand with ease, and caught me just as my knees buckled out from underneath me.

"*Mareina...* What in the fuck—

Panic seared my veins as I was drug further beneath a hungry wave of dizziness and disorientation.

OH MY GODS.

This was it... He'd somehow tricked me. This is how I was going to die.

I summoned the last dregs of my energy and muscle control, *willing* my blade back into my hand and thrust it into his chest.

Or at least attempted to.

I'd failed to pierce his chest plate, and instead, the blade had gone no further than the thick bulk of his pectoral.

Nakoa's brow merely lifted in surprise briefly at where I'd stabbed him, not even flinching, and began to chuckle.

As if he weren't even remotely surprised.

The sound grew deep and distorted, as did his words, before I fell entirely unconscious.

"My beautiful little nightmare..."

CHAPTER
SIXTEEN
MAREINA

S till burrowed deeply in sleep's warm embrace, the sensation of something beautiful blossomed in my chest, like the soft petals of a fragrant rose, stirring the thick haze of my mind. Vaguely, I began to recognize the weight of a large hand pressed against my belly.

The heat radiating from a broad chest pressed against my back... and that of a deliciously thick erection along my core caused my hips to writhe gently against it.

Oh gods, yes. Malekai.

The hand on my stomach shifted to grip my hip, thrusting softly against my movements.

A deep, husky voice murmured against my shoulder, nipping, licking, and biting in a way that instantly sent my toes curling and my core flooding with need... But this voice wasn't the smooth, velvety baritone of Malekai... This was gravel and whiskey and—

"Mmmmmm, lohane thili..."

Recognition and awareness washed over me, making my eyes burst open as adrenaline flooded my body and memories flooded my mind. Followed by panic and rage.

Nakoa's long, heavily muscled arm tucked me tightly against him, groaning.

"Please, just a little longer..."

Kidnap her.

I rolled to mount him, eager to strangle him with my bare hands, only to discover that they were bound, along with my ankles. Because of this, he easily pinned me beneath him. The hard length of him straining against his pyjama trousers as he sat atop me and pinned my bound hands to my chest.

Fury swelled and rose within me like a fiery tsunami. I called upon my magic to *will* the bindings away, only for it to remain just out of grasp. My voice became an otherworldly growl, fangs lengthening.

"What have you done?"

Nakoa exhaled heavily, annoyance written all over his face.

"Prevented you from doing something you'd regret."

My voice dropped to something inhuman and guttural.

"I'm going to rip you apart with my teeth until you beg me for death."

Nakoa rolled over, climbing out of bed.

"What do you remember of last night?"

"Enough to know that you're a fucking lying, conniving —

His abrupt, deep belly laugh cut me off.

The flames of my rage rose... Tempered with begrudging gratitude at the fact that Nakoa apparently had the decency to not take advantage of me in such an uninhibited state.

"That is *hilarious* coming from the she-devil that sauntered into my bedroom wielding a dagger. Was the only reason you accepted my invitation happen to be so you could murder me in my sleep? And who gave you grá root potion?"

Nakoa shook his head, scrubbing a palm over his face as he waited for my response.

Miroslav. That wretched bastard.

Had it been an accident? Miroslav wasn't the type who fell prey to *accidents*... Was he hoping that I would just get myself killed? But how was it he had known my dream...

He can read minds, you idiot.

I couldn't fathom why, in all the god's names, he would plan such a thing... Unless this really was just all entertainment for him. As an Orisha, living for many thousands of years, perhaps he had grown so detached and bored with *everything* that he could only seek fulfilment in the manipulation and suffering of others... But all under the guise of creating some kind of revolution?

None of it made sense.

If that was his way of trying to get me killed without raising any eyebrows, that would be pretty fucking elaborate.

Oh, gods... Was he testing my loyalty? Had he even planned it with Zurie?

I also obviously had no *reasonable* response to Nakoa's line of questioning. I didn't even have fully formed answers of my own.

My mind whirled, trying to come up with even a vaguely believable lie. But lying had never been my strong suit, and the male was going to die anyway. So what did it matter if he knew I was sent to kill him? If not me, then by someone else. It would change nothing.

"You've clearly made an enemy of the wrong person."

Nakoa gave me a blank look before bursting into a throaty laugh.

"You're gonna have to narrow it down for me, *maha mo'ina li'ili.*"

My little nightmare.

A growl escaped me. Of course, he had so many enemies that more than one of them wanted him dead.

"I work for Queen Zurie as her Royal Irae."

CHAPTER
SEVENTEEN
NAKOA

Queen Zurie? What in the actual fuck?

Every one of The Uprising's members had been sworn to secrecy in a blood vow. There was no way she could have discovered such a thing. And it's not like the Lords who ended up dead in our raids would talk to her beyond the grave. Though that seemed more likely a reason than the former...

But even more importantly—

This female before me that, without a shadow of a doubt, was my *soulbound* was The Royal Irae for the person I hated most in the realm. She was basically her fucking glorified henchwoman.

A mirthless laugh began to bubble up at the twisted irony of it.

My little nightmare, indeed.

Her features contorted as she watched my laughter grow, gradually dying as anger and hurt twisted in my gut - at whom I wasn't even sure.

Akash? The gods?

I should have fucking run the moment I'd laid eyes on her.

But I'd been helpless to that, too.

If it was anyone other than my *soulbound,* I'd fucking end them here and now. Do the realm a favor and and wipe her from it.

Because of her, you will be King.

I growled internally at the reminder.

It was unimaginably cruel to imagine that my *soulbound* would be among my worst enemies. Mareina had likely even already killed some of the members of The Uprising.

No, my Knowingness swiftly replied, making a tiny portion of my anger less vehement.

"Did you fight in the war?"

Her mouth thinned, already knowing that we may very well have fought on the same battlefields.

A vision flashed before me in the fleeting second of her hesitation.

Mareina drives her sword so fiercely into the gut of a Kahlohani warrior that his large body is lifted from the ground.

Ice flooded my veins in the wake of the fleeting image.

"Yes."

The vision, along with that singular word, were like knives twisting in my gut. I released her like I'd been burned by the mere touch of her.

My voice came out a growl.

"*Stay.*"

Her lip curled at being spoken to like a fucking dog, but it's not like she had much choice in the matter.

I stood, pacing beside the bed.

After having witnessed two visions of her committing such extraordinary acts of violence, paired with the fact she was Zurie's Irae, suddenly made my vision of her killing Zurie like such a simple solution. Perhaps we wouldn't even *need* The Uprising to accomplish the task. The future was within reach. The throne was just a breath away from my grasp.

Perhaps her being the Irae was a *gift.*

Still, this female had killed my countrymen. Likely even my

friends and family. It was a wonder we hadn't crossed paths before, considering the Kahlohani Army hadn't exactly been massive. There had only been maybe 60,000 us against Zurie's 120,000. Despite that, we had been so close to winning. Until Miroslav, Zurie's personal seer had appeared. We had all but been exterminated and forced to surrender. Though, by some miracle, many of my loved ones had survived. Though they had long passed now. No thanks to Mareina's efforts.

I was furious; this *was the female I had been haunted by all these years.*

And she was clearly loyal to Zurie. How in *Akash's* name would I convince her to betray her Queen.

The vision where I became King and liberated my people from Zurie's oppression and exile, liberated the Kahlohani Islands of the fae scourge that had enslaved the few Kahlohani that remained and had exploited the land and sea so they could grow and harvest *aetra*. Where I created peace and prosperity for all of Atratus. Where I claimed and vowed myself to my precious *lohane thili*.

And the fucking nightmare where our hatred for one another burned the tether between us, where violence ensued, and my true form shifted into something even more demonic looking than what it already was. The same form that I already had to keep disguised by a constant glamor because it was already too *different. Too terrifying.*

Too... *much.*

And yet, I was powerless to turn away.

It was such a bizarre contrast to imagine that the female who had slaughtered my soldiers in droves was the same one who would readily dive into a burning building to save a singular human's life.

Most wielders wouldn't have bothered, human or not. The remaining few who might have been willing to help would have consoled themselves with the fact that he was elderly *and* human. Not worth saving because he would have only had a few fleeting years left to live anyway.

I conveniently shoved aside the knowledge so I could fuel my justified rage.

I wanted to destroy something.

No.

I wanted to fucking kill this female.

It's what she deserved.

The distinct and tangible sensation of a tether connecting us, body and soul, flared to life, *burning* at the thought.

Every second I'd spent in this female's presence... That tether between Mareina and me wound tighter and tighter as though it was trying to *drag* me to her. Just as every passing second with her, that feeling of *rightness* grew with increasing fervor and began to blossom into something more... something that caused a painful, and now no longer welcome, ache in my chest.

How fucking twisted was fate that my Queen would also be my enemy?

I needed her out of my sight before I did something regrettable.

I bent over the bed, roughly taking Mareina's bound body into my hands and tossing her over my shoulder.

In all the years I'd possessed these particular binds, not a single *wielder* had managed to escape them. I silently thanked my Knowingness for urging me to bind her. It had pained me to do so at the time, but now, with the bitterness poisoning my need for her, I found no small amount of twisted satisfaction in it.

Thankfully, I'd also had the sense to feed Peanut and Bellona and send them out in the fields to keep Chihiro and Pumpkin company. Otherwise, it would be complete mayhem here.

"Where are you taking me?"

"To your new prison."

She growled viciously as she tore a chunk of flesh from my back and slammed her bound fists into my kidney. The missing chunk of flesh, I could handle. The blow to my right kidney, however, had my right knee buckling.

I tossed her onto the bed only for her to lunge for my throat, snapping her fangs at me gain, gifting me with another wound - this one on my cheek. I barely caught her by the jaw as I allowed my own fangs to lengthen - fangs that I knew were even more deadly looking than hers as I removed the glamor from my eyes for them to return to their pitch-black color.

Instead of the fear I'd hoped to inspire, her gaze only hardened, and the sight of her licking my blood from her lips had my traitorous cock thickening in my trousers.

"I can bite too, Mareina, so unless you'd like a few more scars and some blood loss, it would be wise for you to calm the fuck down. And right now, I would love nothing more than to make you suffer, *maha mo'ina li'ili."*

My little nightmare.

She didn't bother replying verbally.

Faster than I could anticipate, Mareina's bound arms lashed out, uppercutting me with both closed fists so hard I saw fucking stars. My head snapped back with a crack, my consciousness nearly fleeing me, and she was on top of me before I could even recover. We landed on the hardwood floor with a loud thud, and instinctively, before she tore my fucking throat out, my open palm connected with her face with a loud *smack*.

She hit the ground so hard it even took me by surprise. How she remained conscious was beyond me.

The action had only stoked her fury. She lunged at me again. This time, I was ready for her. She seethed as I gripped her throat and again pinned her beneath me. Blood trickled from her head into her eyes from the laceration on the side of her head where she'd hit the ground.

The sight of both her blood and being helplessly bound beneath me brewed a twisted melange of satisfaction, guilt, and arousal. A bizarre and wholly unfamiliar need nearly consumed me. The need to sink my fangs into her and *mark* her.

"I fucking hate you," she growled before lobbing a wad of bloody spit at my face that landed directly on the apple of my scarred cheek.

A chuckle of dark delight swelled at my little nightmare's boldness.

And her naiveté.

Her character judgment was woefully deficient if she'd deemed me sane enough to be offended by the act. With my free hand, I wiped at the saliva sliding a trail down my face, bringing it to my mouth, and hummed my satisfaction.

"Mmmmmmm... *Fucking delicious.*"

Her breath caught, and the unmistakable scent of her arousal curled through the air. It smelled like her but... *richer,* like night-blooming roses. Her delicate scent starkly contrasted the wretched creature I was coming to know.

I promptly pushed away the arousal stirring low in my gut in an attempt to clear my head.

"I need you to answer a few questions, and if you're a good girl, maybe I'll reward you."

Her scowl hardened.

"Fuck you."

A bitter laugh burst from me before I leaned in and whispered in her ear, indulging myself in just *one* more lungful of her scent.

"Mareina, I wouldn't stick my dick in that wretched fucking cunt of yours if you fucking begged me to."

Liar, some heinous voice inside me whispered that I dutifully ignored.

I'd expected... No, *hoped* to wound her with my words, but again, she seemed... entirely unfazed by them. She merely gave a mirthless chuckle.

"So kidnapping is where you draw the line?"

I didn't bother answering her question. I needed to know *which* of my endeavors Zurie had rooted out so that I could warn my *olana kah'hei* and potentially The Uprising members.

"Why did Zurie send you to me?"

She remained silent. *Fine.* I didn't need her words. I'd read her like a fucking book regardless.

"If she sent you after me, that means Zurie either found out that my *olana kah'hei* and I are the reason all those Lords and Ladies who've been disappearing or ending up dead. The ones who have been helping the *minori.*"

Lessers. As degrading as it sounded, it was merely the term for the less magically inclined of the wielders, who were often forced into either becoming indentured servants or taking low-paying jobs that required manual labor. Even though Zurie had inspired them all to help her win the war with the promise of making *aetra* affordable and accessible to them. *Lies.*

Mareina's expression revealed nothing. This was likely what had led Zurie to me.

A smug grin curled my lips in anticipation as I proceeded. And in finding no small amount of satisfaction in the fact that my very life-style and career choice since the war had ended was no doubt every-thing this female and Zurie had fought against and failed to thwart.

How would I ever convince her to betray Zurie?

"*Or* she found out I'm the leader of The Uprising."

Mareina's jaw dropped. And some victorious feeling swelled within me as I waited for heinous insults and threats to spill from her lips - the same ones I'd heard that Orisha cunt glued to Zurie's hip spout at every public forum.

Miroslav.

None came. She only studied me with... *awe.*

"Aren't you going to say something like... How did you so eloquently put it earlier?... *You're going to rip me apart with your teeth until I beg you for death?*"

She took a deep breath, eyes dipping to some distant, unfocused point. Based on her expression, you'd think I'd just proven to her we were living in a simulation. She absently tortured her lips with her teeth before finally replying.

"Well, whatever your plans for me, they're irrelevant. I don't have any information for you to torture out of me if that's what you were hoping. Soon enough, it'll be Zurie you're begging for death from."

The fight seemed to have drained out of her at my news. I shifted off of her to lean back against the wall.

"My plans for you are entirely relevant to Zurie, I'm afraid..."

Somehow I would make her loyal to me. So loyal she would kill her Queen.

That finally drew her attention back to mine, eyes narrowing.

"However, logic warrants my discretion... Despite the fact you're Zurie's Irae, and I should have already killed you..."

"If you plan to use me against her, you'll be sorely disappointed. Zurie cares about as much for my life as you do."

Her words struck an odious cord in me... Surprisingly pained by the idea that Mareina was nothing more than a weapon for Zurie to wield. Not that it was surprising.

"You might be surprised to learn that I am *personally* invested in your life."

Her lip curled as she sat up, making my senses prick in warning.

"And why would that be? Do you plan to sell me off as someone's bed slave for a handsome sum to fund your *endeavors*?"

The idea tore a harsh laugh from my throat.

"*Mo'ina li'ili,* I wouldn't wish that fate upon even my greatest enemies... But the idea has merit. Reason and *fate* would have it that I keep you as my own bed slave. You are my *soulbound,* after all."

Her jaw dropped, and her eyes rounded so wide it was almost comical. She remained silent for several moments, searching for the truth in my words...

Finally.

A response.

So I stood and removed the glamor shielding my true form and my magic, and thusly any wavering doubt.

CHAPTER

EIGHTEEN

MAREINA

T craned my head up to where Nakoa had risen; the entirety of
Nakoa's eyes bled to black. Into what I could only describe as
twin pools of midnight glittering beneath the moonlight.

The air around him rippled as his magic unfurled and crashed
over me like a tsunami, swallowing me whole... The energy around
him hummed and vibrated, making every molecule stand in awe...

Something like... *Recognition*... had my lips parting as he quite
literally *stole my breath*.

That *thing* that seemed to bind us flared and throbbed so deeply
it stole my breath. Swiftly burning away any doubt that I'd had
against his declaration that I was his *soulbound*.

A pair of dark umber wings emerged from behind him and
spread wide, the span of which stretched from one side of the room
to the other. A long, thick tail reached towards me and curled itself
around my ankle. My eyes dipped to it, and thanks to that traitorous
tether, my heart fluttered at the gesture. I thoroughly extinguished
the sensation.

Nakoa frowned at the appendage, and as though it were a guilty
pup, it retreated, coiling around his thickly muscled thigh.

An icy dread seeped into my veins.

Not at his form.

No, his form was... Admittedly, breathtaking. Despite my hatred for this male, simply taking him in had caused a certain heat to blossom low within me that I refused to acknowledge.

The dread I felt was the fact that I was impossibly destined to be with this *Akash*-forsaken male.

We both remained silent for several too long, tense moments as he stared down at me, looking not unlike some dark, avenging, fallen *Seraphi*.

Nakoa's grin broadened into something cruel as if he enjoyed the look of shocked horror on my face.

Finally, he grinned in a way that didn't reach his eyes.

Was that vulnerability?

"Is my form truly that horrifying, *lohane thili?*"

I snapped my jaw shut, drawing in a deep breath, slowly shaking my head. My gaze drifted out of the window through which brilliant sunlight shone. Harsh and mocking to the contrast of this *nightmare*.

"No..."

Surprise flickered on his features.

No, your form is not horrifying.

No, I will not acknowledge that you are my soulbound.

No, I will not succumb to this fate.

No.

No.

No.

No.

NO.

Though, I couldn't quite muster the energy to say any of that aloud at the moment.

Instead, I simply laid back down. Curled up in the fetal position on the floor and stared out of the window of my latest prison.

After a few moments, the sound of his footsteps receded, stopping short in the doorway.

"The room is warded. Not that you have the means to, but if you try to escape, I will know, and you will be punished."

The door shut quietly, followed by the sound of his own door across the hall slamming shut.

Silence rang, heavy and oppressive.

My eyes burned in warning of the watery deluge to come.

CHAPTER

NINETEEN

NAKOA

"No."

I'd felt the truth in her response before she'd even spoken it. She *liked* my form. Through our tether, standing so close to her, I'd felt that curl of pleasure in her belly as if it were my own.

When I'd revealed my form, I'd expected her to cower in fear, like every other person to whom I'd shown my true form.

Pomona's words from the previous night echoed in my mind...

'I'm sure she's got a kink for every single one of your qualities.'

My heart pounded a furious beat as I paced restlessly in my room.

My plan to terrify her by revealing my form had backfired because not only had it intensified the bond for her between us by lifting my glamor but for me as well.

My skin itched as though stretched too tight over the shuddering muscles of my body with the need to claim her.

I *willed* my pyjama trousers away and stood beneath the shower, praying the hot water would help soothe this beast within me. Instead, with each passing moment, my need for her only increased.

Fuck.

I growled angrily, finally resorting to stroking my cock that was heavy and throbbing with neglect. I tried desperately to visualize previous lovers, but each time I did, their faces would linger for all of a second before they morphed into Mareina's. I hadn't seen her naked, yet, somehow, I could conjure with perfect clarity the dusky hue of her nipples that my tongue salivated to taste and tease. The glistening of her pretty pink pussy. How it would clench around and grip my cock as it stretched her and demanded her channel to accommodate me. How she would moan and writhe beneath me as I made her submit to me.

My cock pulsed ropes of my cum down the drain, and I watched, feeling a little of my willpower to resist her go with it.

Gods damn it.

I'm going to lose my mind at this rate, I thought to myself as I stepped out onto the porch with Peanut and Bellona, waiting for my mother. She always took care of them when I had to leave town.

"She's fucking wretched, isn't she?" I grumbled to Peanut sourly, brushing her fur as we sat on the porch swing. Bellona, having already been brushed, laid curled up in my lap.

Bellona huffed her agreement as Peanut turned her head, licking my hands and forearms. She'd love a toad if it so much as looked in her direction.

My gaze caught on Pumpkin as she moseyed along a nearby hill, grazing on wildflowers and grass as I sighed absently.

"Hatred and denial are not becoming of you, *ku'kāne.*"

Ku'kāne. My son.

Peanut and Bellona promptly leapt up and rushed toward my mother, clamouring off of the swing to shower my mother with affection.

I turned to find her walking towards the steps. She looked as

140

though she were only in her fifties despite being nearly triple that, thanks to all her magic and potions. She had long silvery salt and pepper hair and dark blue eyes, delicate and ethereal features... Unlike me. I'd taken after my father, apparently.

"*Why?*"

She remained silent for a few moments, knowing exactly what I was referring to.

Why is she *my soulbound?*

Why does it have to be my greatest enemy?

Why does it have to be someone I should *hate?*

"Everyone and everything in this life is a teacher, my love. Just as I have helped teach you how to survive and thrive in this world, you have taught me a great many things. *Like patience.*"

My gaze bounced to hers to find a grin curling her lips.

"There is a reason why *Akash* would guide *the fates* to weave your souls together. Why *Akash* would choose the both of you, together, to lead Atratus into a new era of peace... Against all odds."

I remained silent for several moments as I mulled over the wisdom in her words... My mother's abilities to scry through time and place were unlike any I'd ever witnessed before. I'd always assumed it was what had lent me my Knowingness.

She'd probably witnessed Mareina's entrance into my life long before it had ever actually come to pass.

"I imagine you're already aware of the fact that she's the Royal Irae? That she fought in the war for Zurie... That she *personally* contributed to the genocide of our people..."

My mother heaved a heavy, sad sigh, cuddling Bellona in her arms as she smiled knowingly and turned her gaze towards me.

"She also risked her life to save a human...," I added reluctantly.

"I'm not surprised, darling... The Well has shown me *so* much more. She's a valiant female when given the opportunity."

Internally, I deliberated whether or not to tell my mother about my vision of Mareina... That she was the key to obtaining the throne...

She was probably already well aware and would just replay in a way that left me with more questions than answers.

I grumbled something unintelligible as my gaze drifted back towards Pumpkin and Chihiro, munching on wildflowers side-by-side.

"Are you familiar with the story of the warrior and the wolf?"

"... No."

"Well... As you know, sometime during The Fae War, there was *the great divide*. What is now Atratus was then *Agrios* and *Axios*. Agrios was deemed wild and untamed, reserved for those who were considered demons - which simply meant anyone who wasn't fae. Axios was for those who were considered cultured and refined. And anyone who wasn't fae was exiled to Agrios under threat of execution. As the war progressed, Agriosian lands became more and more encroached upon, and their population began to dwindle.

"One of the most famed Axiosian warriors, Lysander, was the one leading them. By some stroke of fate, Lysander managed to kill the General of the Agriosian army but failed to escape before he was captured and tortured by a few of the General's soldiers.

During Lysander's time in captivity, his torture further cemented his heinous prejudice against the Agriosian people that he had been taught to hate. Taught an extremist ideology that anyone who wasn't fae was 'innately wicked' and that they needed to be exterminated for the greater good.

One day, Lysander managed to kill his captors and escape. However, he had been so thoroughly injured during his captivity that he failed to make it past what is now called 'The Sentient Forest'..."

My mother's lips quirked as her eyes darted back to mine before she continued.

"Lysander, as he ran, found a number of native predators after him... By some miracle, he survived relatively unscathed, except for a broken ankle. And due to being so thoroughly malnourished, he no longer could heal as a normal fae would.

"Knowing that any cry for help would either be answered by more hungry predators or the torture that he had just escaped, he finally succumbed to the idea that his time had come. Night descended, and he waited for the next predator to come along and devour him. He had even begun to welcome it. And it did. In the form of a wolf... However, instead of killing him, the wolf brought him food."

I can't help the incredulous look on my face, making my mother chuckle.

"Is this a true story or just some witchy parable?"

My mother's chuckle increased, almost with glee.

"Oh, it's a very real story... One you'll soon recognize, my darling."

I heaved a heavy sigh, leaning back in resignation.

"And day after day, the wolf came bringing him meat or berries, whatever it could find. It even dragged his body to a river to bathe and drink. The wolf remained by his side to protect him from other predators.

"And each night, he would tell the wolf stories about his life, his aspirations, his dreams. How he had come from a *fae* family and risen so high in the Axiosian Army's ranks that now he could take care of his mother and sisters, who had previously been sold by their father to a *high fae* family as indentured servants. How he dreamed of one day ending the indentured servitude that was still prominent in Axios. How he dreamed of having a wife and children. How he actually hated war and wished to bring an end to all wars. How he longed for peace.

"Eventually, Lysander finally recovered from his injuries and malnourishment enough to walk and begin gradually making the rest of the journey back to Axios. When he tried to leave and bring the wolf with him, it refused. Lysander attempted to force the wolf, at which point, the wolf transformed... Into a female."

My brows dipped impatiently, waiting for her to elaborate.

"Initially, he was shocked and felt betrayed that she had taken so long to reveal herself, though he knew it was because she feared he would murder her if he knew she was a 'lowly' lykos.

But this *wolf* had saved his life. Protected him, fed him, even defended him against the hungry creatures of the forest. Stayed at his side most of every day and even through the nights. He had grown to love this wolf for the loyal companion it had become.

Lysander longed to go home to the safety of Axios. Where he knew she would be killed."

"When he asked her why she didn't kill him, she admitted that she'd wanted to. Desperately. But when she realized how wounded he was, she couldn't bring herself to kill someone so defenseless. Every day, she brought him food and swore to herself she would kill him as soon as he could properly defend himself, but every night, when he told her his stories, her heart would soften towards him. Each time she protected and defended him, she swore to herself that it was only so that she could have the satisfaction of killing him herself..."

My mother grew silent, a wistful smile on her face as she stared into the distance.

"And...?"

She heaves a sigh, drawing her gaze back to mine.

"*And*, they fell in love. They were *lohane thili*... Several months later, after coming to know her, and eventually her people, he turned the tides for them and led them to victory in The Fae War."

My brow furrowed deeper as I scoured my memory banks.

"But... Wait... Kahlohan was the one who led them to victory..."

Her smile grew ear to ear.

"Indeed, he did. But before he was Kahlohan, he was Lysander. The lykos was his wife, Akela."

My jaw dropped.

"I'm sorry... *What?*"

She chuckled. "So many millennia later, everyone likes to forget Khalohan's origin..."

"How have I never heard about this?"

"Well... It doesn't exactly serve anyone's narrative. Nor inspire a warrior's bloodlust, does it?"

I reeled. Just when I thought my mind couldn't possibly be any more blown.

I'd always idolized Kahlohan. He won the war against the fae and saved... his *adopted* people. *My people.*

"So you see, *ku'kāne*..... No one is beyond redemption."

I couldn't help the frown carving its way onto my face.

"Gods damn it," I grumbled, more to myself than anyone else.

My mother reached over and rubbed my shoulder.

"What's the matter, darling? Did you think that hating your own *poa hanei* would somehow solve all your problems?"

Soulmate.

I released a dramatic groan, palming my face in my hands. She only chuckled again, rubbing my back and making Bellona growl with neglect.

My logical mind also reminded me that my father was fae. *I* was half-fae. Something I'd always kind of resented.

"What was my father like again?"

The question took my mother aback. Taking her off guard was something that rarely occurred. She often knew what was coming long before it happened. She took a deep breath, exhaling as she seemed to formulate an answer.

"He was... A powerful male. Kind. Quick to overwhelm with emotion. And naive..."

I had heard most of these things before. I always asked to be reminded that he was a good male and not like the other fae I'd come across or held power over Atratus. The last part, however, I hadn't known.

"Naive?" I asked, surprised.

She chuckled sadly. "Yes. Naive. He was very trusting. Often took people who didn't deserve it for their word. Put his trust in people. When he found himself betrayed, he seemed to go through cycles of grief. Sadness. Resentment... Anger. He had a rather fiery temper. He generally erred on the side of compassion but could be prone to... detonation...," she chuckled a little wistfully, "He could burn whole cities down with his rage."

I heaved a sigh, lingering in the weight that pressed on my chest at his absence. My mother studied me for a moment, reading me like a book and therefore changing the subject.

"Don't worry... Your journey to Vyssini will change things with Mareina... The sooner you can forgive her, the easier it will be, and the sooner we can get this show on the road."

I gave her a bored look. Somehow, she *always* succeeded in leaving me with more questions than answers.

"You sure you can't spare us the trouble of having to ride the two days it takes to reach you?"

Her lips quirked up in a knowing grin. "I am, indeed."

I shook my head, scrubbing another hand down my face.

"You'll be glad for it," she promised, grinning mischievously as she strode away.

The sound of Peanut's and Bellona's nails against the wood of the porch disappeared, and a certain silence rang in the air. I didn't have to look behind me to know they'd already left— via portal.

TWENTY

T ime went by at a glacial pace as I watched from where I laid on the floor, the light of day brightening with the noonday sun as my hope darkened. During which, I found my thoughts oscillating between two things. Two people, rather.

Malekai... And *Nakoa.*

Talons of regret sank in deep at the thought of never seeing Malekai again.

Would he come for me?

I knew the answer was *abso-fucking-lutely.*

But Zurie had given me five days... And unless Nakoa planned on leaving me here to rot, we would be leaving for...

My breath caught.

Vyssini.

If... If Nakoa brought me with them to Vyssini, I could escape. And then I would have not only Malekai's protection but an army of 30 soldiers to shield me from Nakoa's wrath...

Though it didn't solve the problem of being bound to the male by my very soul.

The sound of footsteps coming back down the hall pricked my

ears and renewed the thumping of my heart. Both in dread and, admittedly, excitement.

Gods, I'm unhinged.

I quickly stood, my entire right side numb, and hopped my way over to the bed. I'd be damned if I'd let him see me lying in a puddle of my own tears. As if I'd been so easily defeated. I swiped at my mussed-up hair and perched on the side of the bed.

Fuck, what I would give for a bath. For the reprieve of hot water.

I couldn't exactly *will* my clothes away... And being forced to wear wet leather was a special kind of torture all its own. I seriously doubted Nakoa would take any compassion on me to dry them.

The door swung open behind, Nakoa's presence hovering there for a few silent moments. When he said nothing, I twisted to look at him. He'd glamored himself again, stifling his magic from me and hiding his true form. I ignored the pang of disappointment I felt at it.

My voice came out harsh and cutting.

"Yes?"

His came out gruff and... Sullen?

"You need to feed, no?"

My fangs ached with the desire to taste his blood, and the tether between us practically writhed with demand.

I managed to shake my head. "I just fed last night."

Nakoa strode into the room to stand in front of me. His expression grim.

"We will leave for Vyssini soon. You will need your strength."

As if that settled it, he brought the underside of his forearm to his mouth and bit into the thick, muscled flesh. The scent of his blood nearly consumed me, thick with the scent of the earth, a hint of sweetness like amber, and something else I couldn't quite place my finger on but smelled familiar nonetheless.

His blood trickled onto the floor with a steady *drip, drip, drip* like the ticking of long seconds as I forced myself to remain still.

"I will force you if I have to. I will not have you slowing us down."

He growled, stepping forward and thrusting his arm closer to my mouth. I reared back.

His brow hardened as though offended.

"I'm not going to hit you..."

"That's not what I'm worried about."

"Is it the venom's effects you're concerned with? Is there some lover waiting for you back in Bastrina?"

I looked up to meet his gaze and found myself momentarily mesmerized by the blackening of his eyes. His voice dropped to a low growl as he squatted in front of me, bringing his face to eye level with mine. *Was he jealous?*

"Is there actually someone back home pining over that blackened heart of yours?"

I didn't respond. I wasn't about to give Malekai another enemy.

A sinister grin split Nakoa's face as he swiftly pinned me beneath him. Pinning my arms above my head. Fighting against him was a useless endeavor. His head dipped to my neck, inhaling deeply.

"I don't smell a male on you..."

His hardening length pressed against the front of my fighting leathers.

"But even if you do, you'll never see him again. *You're mine.*"

"I will never *be yours,"* I rasped, my vision beginning to sway.

Something hard and punishing coiled around my waist. My eyes dipped to find his *tail.*

His fangs sank into the flesh of his free arm more viciously than the first time, making blood splatter onto my face from above before he pressed the bleeding wound against my lips.

I managed to resist for all of a singular fucking heartbeat before my fangs tore into his flesh like a beast starved. Arousal burst through me, hot and swift as my venom and his blood flowed. A crooked, satisfied grin that curled one corner of his scarred mouth. The tether between us pulled tighter, and need *burned* through me, causing a whimper to escape as I swallowed gulp after gulp of his blood.

"I can smell your desire, Mareina... Are you desperate to feel the pounding thrusts of my cock?"

Nakoa's length was already firmly against clit through our clothes as he ground against me. A moan tore from my throat. Smug male satisfaction seeped onto his features.

No.

I would *not* give him this.

Thankfully, Malekai had made me feel, and I was able to force my mouth away from his arm. I spat a mouthful of his own blood on his face.

"*Never,*" I hissed.

Nakoa chuckled, licking his lips and wiping the blood from his face with his free palm. His other hand and tail still pinning me to the bed.

"Is that so? I bet if I touched your pussy it would be soaking fucking wet."

He didn't wait for the moment it would have taken me to deny it. He simply willed away the trousers of my fighting leathers and thrust his fingers through my slick folds. A cry tore from my throat as I attempted to wrench my hips away from him, but his tail had me so firmly pinned beneath him that my efforts only served to thrust my hips against his hand.

"*Get your fucking hands off me, or I swear to the gods—*

Nakoa's hand came down with a firm slap that landed directly on my clit, drawing a humiliating whimper from me. He held his hand aloft to examine the slickness glistening from his fingers, even spreading his index and middle finger to see the clear fluid of my arousal stretch and drip between his fingers. Hot-faced shame and fury burned my cheeks as he gave a cruel chuckle.

"You swear to the gods what? *You'll cum?*" He hummed his pleasure before dragging his fingers against his tongue and licking them clean. My core clenched in response, my arousal burning brighter. "See how much you need me, *mo'ina li'ili?*"

My breaths came in shallow pants as he brought his hand back down to my pussy and slid his fingers through my slick mess again, dipping into my core before returning to circle around my clit. I cried out, my hips thrusting of their own volition.

"*Stop,*" I begged.

I didn't want this. I wished with every ounce of my fucking being that it was Malekai touching me like this, and I cursed myself that I had, for all these years, let fear stand in the way of my happiness.

All that time, it had stood right there in front of me.

Waiting.

"Are you sure?" Nakoa asked with surprising gentleness as he continued to tease and work my clit.

I forced the word out.

"Yes..."

His hand withdrew, and my utterly disloyal body wept in response.

Nakoa rose, leaving me bare from the waist down. His arousal shone thick and insistent through the linen trousers he wore, a large wet patch staining the pant leg where I could make out the outline of his crown. He unbuttoned his trousers, making my panic spike.

"What're you doing?"

A wicked smirk tilted his lips. "Painting you with my fucking cum."

The pulse in my clit throbbed painfully even as my heart threw itself against the cage of my ribs as if it could escape. Nakoa's gaze remained fixed on me as he pulled his cock free - long, thick, and significantly darker than the deep bronze of his body. Plump veins branched towards its dark, broad crown.

Pre-cum dribbled from the tip onto the floor as his hand palmed the tip to coat his length with it before he began to stroke it. My breath caught, momentarily mesmerized by the sight.

Oh fuck.

I forced my eyes shut, wanting to roll over and face the other way, but then I'd only be pointing my ass and bare pussy in his direction.

"Open your eyes, Mareina. I want the image of me cumming all over you, marking my fucking territory, burned into your mind."

Obscene wet sounds filled my ears like a taunt. I squeezed my eyes shut tighter, jaw clenching so hard it ached.

"I am *not* yours."

In the next moment, something coiled tight around my throat, making my eyes burst open. *Nakoa's tail.*

Nakoa stood mere inches away from me, staring down at me as his strokes became punishing.

"*Liar.* If I have to haunt you every fucking day, like you've done to me, so help me, *Akash,* my name will be the only name on your tongue when you writhe with pleasure."

Amidst the lust burning through me, confusion rose. *Haunted him?*

Before I could formulate a coherent response, a growl tore from Nakoa's throat, followed by hot, thick ropes of cum that landed on my chest, neck, and mouth.

Shock and anger speared through me, coiling my muscles tight. I twisted and kicked out with both legs at Nakoa's stomach. He *barely* managed to leap out of the way with his cock still in his hand as he began to laugh.

"That was close, little demon."

His eyes took me in, still pantless on the bed as I laid there, legs dangling off the bed. "Admittedly, you do make a beautiful canvas..."

He *willed* away his clothes and lunged forward, gripping me by my hips and tossing me over his shoulder, causing his fucking spunk to slide into my eyes. I growled, swiftly wiping it away with my bound wrists. At the same moment, cool air replaced my top.

"*What are you doing?*" I hissed, trying to writhe out of his hold.

His large hand came down hard in a searing *smack* that made my pussy clench. "Behave. You're getting a bath. Unless you'd prefer to travel covered in my cum... The idea has merit."

CHAPTER
TWENTY-ONE

NAKOA

Mareina grew silent as I climbed down the steps into the large bath, only realizing then that the tiles lining it - that *I'd* chosen - matched the rich emerald green of her eyes. It made me want to tear them out.

The tiles, not her eyes.

Resistance is an exercise in futility, my Knowingness whispered to me.

My chest tightened, knowing that the words were true. I set her down in waist-high water, and when I stepped back, the sight stole my fucking breath. No matter how much I hated to fucking admit it, she was beautiful.

The way she managed to hold her head high, despite her face being so beautifully decorated with my cum. Her green eyes roved over me through long black lashes. High cheekbones proudly boasting the glistening pearls I'd gifted her. Full, cupid's bow lips poised in something between stoicism and what almost looked like a pout.

The sight alone nearly had my hatred for her buckling out from underneath me.

Her dark hair draped over her full breasts, her nipples dusky and pert, just as I'd imagined them - were hard points in the cool air. Her waist tapered slightly before the flair of her generous hips gave way to bare me a glimpse of her smooth pussy. Her legs were long and muscled with a layer of feminine softness that had my fangs aching with the need to sink them into her flesh.

Another vision bleeds over the present.

Mareina nude, and without my binds, standing in this exact position in a thermal spring in a cave.

The vision is gone, and the present returns so fast that if I wasn't so desensitized to it, I'd question if I'd actually seen it all.

Her still-wandering gaze was like a caress, making my cock harden all over again. It was impossible to hide with the top half of my cock jutting up out of the water.

Not that I cared. I enjoyed her looking. I wanted her lustful mind filled with thoughts of only me.

"Zurie will hunt you down. And when I don't return, she will just send ten more to replace me," she murmured, snapping me back to the present, "And thirty more after that. She will send an entire army after you until you're dead."

"Well, she'll just have to die then, won't she? I've got an entire army ready to greet her."

Mareina huffed a pitying laugh. "Prideful foolishness. Good. It'll just bring me my freedom that much sooner."

I stepped in close to her, gripping her by the back of her head and pulling it down to bare her throat to me.

"You will *never* be free of me. I welcome any soldier brave enough to meet their death to so much as breathe in your direction. And if you ever try to escape me? Well, I can promise you there are worse fates than death."

Mareina's laughter began softly, gradually rising into something maddened.

"Then you would be dooming yourself to just as miserable a fate... Permit me the gracious opportunity to correct what appears to be a misunderstanding: *I* am absolutely fucking deranged and will find a superb amount of joy tearing your limbs from your bone-fucking-dry corpse as soon as I drain you of your blood the moment I get the chance. And *oh*, there *will* come a chance. There's a reason Zurie hired me as her Irae. And I can assure you, it wasn't merely based on tenure and skill."

Despite the resentment and hatred towards her past deeds simmering beneath the surface, her words only had my resistance to buckling further.

Outside of her being perhaps my *second-greatest* immortal enemy...

She was fucking perfection.

Her ferocity made me burn in the most beautiful way.

I stared down into her eyes, practically sparking with her rage and desperate for me to ignite her fuse.

The dark fury inside her sang a siren song to my own as my Knowingness whispered to me.

You are two halves of the same soul. Hating her would be like hating yourself. Your power and your redemption can only be found in her.

Those words stilled me to my very core. The truth in them. A truth that I wasn't yet quite ready to hear. My Knowingness urged me to reach out and...

I gripped her wrists in mine, releasing the glamor on my magic but keeping it tamped down on my form, with the exception of my tail that coiled around her waist.

My vision swam, fading to black, as visions of her past played before my eyes. My own rage burned through me just as much as the heartbreak that had my blood running cold.

Memories poured into me... Her, as a child, held in the arms of another young girl as she wept over her absent mother.

Images of male patrons soliciting Mareina's attention, and being beaten when she didn't humor them... Or worse.

Mareina trembling in the fetal position in blood-stained sheets, or curled beneath a shower as blood trickled from between her legs.

The most beautiful voice I'd ever heard came from her as she sang before numerous audiences at the Erosyan Temple.

Mareina thieving and sleeping in the streets, fighting off predators.

Joining Zurie's army.

Falling in love with a female who later died in Mareina's arms.

Scene after gut-wrenching scene of Mareina having to watch her comrades slaughtered. At times even having to put them out of their misery.

A dark blonde male with golden skin and eyes the same luminous color of the Kahlohani Sea clutching her against his chest as she wept. Both of them covered in blood.

I watched, filled with an overwhelming love - her love - for him, as they saved one another's lives time after time.

In a dizzying, wholly overwhelming and rapid succession, I felt each and every emotion that she experienced in each of those moments.

"Please. Stop."

I released my grip on her arm as if I'd been burned. Her emotions that had flooded me drew back like a waning tide at the same moment the bathing room around us returned. Those twin emerald seas, framed by thick dark lashes, glittered and swelled with emotion. Tears threatening to escape, I watched her delicate throat work on a rough swallow.

The breath I'd been holding punched from my lungs.

"Oh god..."

My chest tightened to the point of pain. Mareina's gaze fell from mine, taking my heart with it.

Oh fuck...

The *suffering* she had been through. It was like each and every pivotal moment of her life had been stacked in order ascending order and speared through my consciousness to arrive at the resulting female in front of me.

Truly, monsters are made, not born.

And I wanted every crooked, broken piece of her. It was no coincidence that they aligned perfectly with each shattered piece of me.

I desperately tried to harden my heart again to her, reminding myself of who exactly she was. She'd had choices. Just as each of us did. And she'd chosen wrong.

You'd have chosen no differently, my Knowingness reminded me.

I tried to wear a stoic mask to conceal just how rocked I was by what had just happened. Not only the fact I'd *experienced* her memories and what she'd endured at the hands of others but now... Much of the anger and resentment I'd had for her was already slipping away, like blood down a drain.

CHAPTER

TWENTY-TWO

MAREINA

My breaths shuddered out of me slow and steady as I gradually managed to quell and *re-bury* my emotion. Nakoa's energy had shifted dramatically since he'd witnessed my... origins. His hatred for me was no longer scalding and vicious... Instead, it had been reduced perhaps to a simmering resentment. And he'd hardly looked at me since he handed me a soapy washcloth to bathe myself with. He now stood in front of me, gaze averted as he quickly bathed.

I couldn't help but dart glances at his glistening muscles, shifting with each movement. Guilt churned my stomach at the thought of Malekai even though I'd always kept a solid boundary in place, but...

If he wasn't on his way to Vyssini, he'd probably be sating his lusts at Satia Fama even now, I quickly reminded myself.

Still, I forced myself to look away as I made quick work of scrubbing myself, paying particular attention to the cum that had dried to my face. Frustration and fury fisted my chest.

How the fuck was I going to get out of this?

Currently, I was bound. My magic was suppressed. The only

chance I had at escape would be if I convinced him to unbind me because *hopping* my way to freedom didn't seem like a viable option.

And the only way I could gain his trust, which... *now*... now that he seemed to have softened slightly towards me after having witnessed a great many of the *events* that had sculpted me into the female I am now... It seemed a little more of a possibility.

But how?

It would take us at least three or four days to reach Vyssini...

Even with his mere *simmering resentment,* it still seemed highly unlikely that I could gain his trust by then, but... Just as I'd learned throughout the course of my career as Zurie's Irae....

Lust could make fools of even kings.

CHAPTER
TWENTY-THREE

NAKOA

Bathing beside Mareina had been a quick, silent endeavor. Albeit painful. I'd experienced what one could only consider was the worst the emotional spectrum had to offer and now it had left me with a tremor in my hands.

Rage at those who had dared to violate her. *My soulbound.*

Grief at all the loved ones she had lost.

Guilt... Her own for all the atrocities she had committed, and mine for how I had treated her.

Shame... Both her own and mine for how I had treated her.

And lastly...

Jealousy.

Because *who the fuck* was that blonde fae fucker?

He saved her life. You owe him gratitude.

I promptly shoved that little fact away.

That was the male she loved. The one who was no doubt waiting for her to return.

I stifled the anger, tightening my muscles. Despite all my lingering *resentment* towards her, I needed her trust...

Her *affection.*

I needed her to fulfill the bond with me.

And, most of all, kill Zurie.

Claiming her body *physically* was only one aspect of that. I need her to swear *the soulbound's vow* to me.

Only then would my power... *our power*... reach its zenith.

Because even if and when Mareina killed Zurie, there would be repercussions. Zurie had a whole court of formidable individuals who would try to seize the throne and use her army against us. Each time *olana kah'hei* and I conducted a raid on one of them, it was merely a matter of days before a new one would pop up to replace them. If I had any hope of eliminating Zurie's entire court *and* overcoming Zurie's Army with the help of The Uprising... I would need it.

Preparing for our departure, my hands on Pumpkin's saddle still as what starts out as a dull hum in the background increases until it reaches a deafening volume, and I realize it is the sound of thousands of soldiers tearing a battle cry through the air.

The vision takes over slowly. My wings pound the air above thousands of soldiers dressed in dark green and umber armor. In the present, I am silent, but in the vision, I hear the roar of my own voice crying out to them.

"They will suffer the wrath of Atratus for daring to take what is ours!"

The soldiers raise their swords as another impassioned roar rents the air.

The vision abruptly left. The hairs on the back of my neck stood on end. Hands still frozen on where they'd gripped the buckle of Pumpkin's saddle.

"Are you ok?" Mareina asked. I could feel her keen eyes on my back.

I cleared my throat, trying to center myself. "Yeah, sorry... Sometimes..."

I turned to where she stood behind me, waiting while I'd been preparing Pumpkin and Chihiro for our journey. My gaze catches on a dark, shadowy figure looming at the edges of the forest. Fear, a rather foreign sensation to me, grips my chest tight and chilling. It disappears through the trees, leaving behind a deeply unsettling feeling.

Not to mention... Nothing and no-one should be able to get past my wards...

Mareina's voice calls me back to the present.

"Hello?"

I return my gaze to her, shaking my head as if it will rid me of the dread now churning my gut.

"Never mind."

Maybe I was just seeing things... Since my reoccurring premonition had begun, I'd become plagued with a great many other visions. They'd never even had the courtesy to wait until I was asleep. They would overcome me at any given moment, bending my reality into something that contained both present and future, or occasionally past. I might be in mid-conversation with a stranger and suddenly double over in pain because, in my vision, I'm being stabbed on a battlefield.

That actually happened once. The female I'd been trying to charm into my bed hadn't been terribly understanding when I'd tried to explain myself out of my sudden reaction, face contorting with anger as I growled my fury at her and *not* at the male in my dreams.

Now, the concern in Mareina's expression had shifted to wariness. She hadn't said a word until then. Not since I'd glimpsed into her memories. Such a thing had never happened before. I could only assume it was due to the combination of both my Knowingness and the intangible tether connecting our souls.

My mother's words and her story of Kahlohan's origin had been set on a perpetual loop in my mind, alongside images of Mareina's tortured past. Each pass further dissipated my anger and resentment towards her. After all, I had killed more of her comrades than I'd dared to count. And somehow, she didn't seem to hold an ounce of animosity towards me for it.

My *olana kah'hei* weren't yet aware of who exactly she was yet...

Only Lokus and Rayne had fought in The Atratusian War, having both come from Selcarim as Kahlohani allies, but I imagined they would have far fewer qualms about it because it wasn't their people that had all been exterminated, nor their land decimated.

I mounted Pumpkin, and a sharp gasp escaped her when I suddenly reached down and swung her into my arms before settling her in a side saddle position in front of me. Entirely unwilling to risk the consequences of unbinding her ankles if I were to let her ride standard.

"Why can't I ride Chihiro?"

I chuckled dryly in an attempt to alleviate the tense silence that had hung like a dead weight between us. Cradling her between my thighs, I gripped the reins in one hand and pulled her firmly against me. My head dipped to caress her neck with my nose...

The first of many silent apologies I already knew were destined to come.

A shiver worked its way through her body before she went ramrod straight.

"Is that what you want, Mareina? For me to chase you and hunt you down like my prey?... I'm more than happy to oblige you, but I can't promise I'll be able to control myself when I catch you. And I know you're not ready for what would happen next."

She seemed to deliberate something if the feathering of her jaw was anything to go by. To my surprise, her body gradually relaxed against mine.

"And what exactly would that be? *If* you were to catch me."

I had to suppress my groan. My arm instinctively curled tighter around her, pressing her harder against me as I leaned into the crook of her neck, my lips grazing the sensitive skin. I'd sworn aloud mere hours ago that I wouldn't give her the pleasure of my cock, but... My resolve in that was dissolving like sugar in boiling water.

"*When* I caught you, I'd pin you to the fucking ground and claim that needy little cunt of yours. I'd mark you in a way that would leave you branded so that everyone would know you belong to me.

I'd fill you with my seed so that everyone in your vicinity would smell me on you and know to stay away lest I rip their fucking throats out."

The idea alone had anger burning through my veins. I urged Pumpkin forward, jolting Mareina against me. Her luscious ass now firmly bouncing against my already throbbing cock just as the scent of her arousal curled through the air, making a modicum of my control snap.

My fangs lengthened, and a deep, familiar ache began to radiate from my back as my wings and tail yearned to be unfurled. She hissed, her body going rigid against me as I grazed my fangs along her neck, locking her in place.

"You mark me and swear the fucking *gods* I will slit your throat," she hissed.

I hummed a chuckle from around my mouthful of her flesh as my Knowingness whispered to me.

I released the hold on my glamor, my wings and tail immediately bursting forth, making Mareina gasp. My tail promptly coiled itself around her waist, holding her in place as I sank my fangs into her throat. A cry tore from her throat. One of both pleasure and pain.

"*I fucking hate you,*" she intoned in an otherworldly voice that had my hairs rising.

Guilt, sharp and sudden, speared through me.

She truly hadn't wanted my mark.

But the deep, rich, velvety taste of her was already spilling down my throat, and I was beyond stopping at this point. My error laid not only in the fact that I had done this against her will but now that I had gotten my first gulp of her blood... I knew I would crave it for the rest of my days.

Why did it have to be her?

Never had I claimed another female in this way. Nor had any desire to. This was purely instinctual, and everything screamed its *rightness* as loudly as the wretchedness of it.

With the venom now pumping through her veins, a soft moan

spilled from her throat. One of unmistakable pleasure. I willed myself to calm, taking in deep breaths, trying to maintain my grip on the singular thread of my sanity.

Her blood continued trickling into my mouth as my eyes travelled down the length of her front, where I could see the aching points of her nipples from beneath the fabric of the dress she'd worn the night before.

Her breaths turned to pants, and her chest expanded as though straining for my touch. I caressed up the curve of her heavy bosom to its turgid peak, clearly begging for my attention. I tugged down one side of the bust of her dress, exposing her breast that gave a mouth-watering jiggle at the action. My palm grazed over the hardened, dark pink tip before teasing it back and forth with my thumb.

"*Oh, fuck...,*" she cried out softly, nails digging into my forearm barred around her waist as her hips gave a mindless thrust against the saddle and, incidentally, my cock from where it was still being strangled by the left fucking pant leg of my trousers. The pinching discomfort from that alone tethered me slightly back to reality.

I heaved a sigh through my nose, forcing myself to release her. I licked and sucked away the few drops of blood escaping from the rapidly healing wound, though I magicked it so that a scar would remain. I knew she might not be entirely appreciative of it just yet, but that was just *too fucking bad.*

"You belong to me, Mareina," I growled near her ear, my words coming out harsher than I intended.

She craned her neck up to look at me. Her gaze belying her hatred for me.

"*Only one male has the right to claim me. And it isn't fucking you.*"

Now that she knew I'd seen her lover, she had no reason to try and cover up the fact. Jealousy and anger burned through me, but I buried it beneath a malevolent grin.

"Lie like that again... You'd look fucking gorgeous with a gag."

Her eyes narrowed at me briefly before she struck and sank her fangs into me, only to rip out a chunk of my flesh.

I grunted at the searing pain, expecting her to spit it out, but instead, she swallowed it along with a strip of my linen shirt.

This female is a fucking animal.

It only served to broaden my grin and intensify my arousal.

I chuckled, looking down at the gaping, shredded wound on my right pectoral.

"Yet again, you've completely misjudged me. Violence is my love language, *maha mo'ina li'ili.*"

She seethed, holding my gaze as my blood dripped down her chin. The sight alone had my resolve against her crumbling further; gods damn her.

Her eyes narrowed, dipping to the cloth in my fist.

"You wouldn't fucking da—

Faster than she could track, especially with the binds suppressing her magic, I gripped the ends of the cloth with both hands and firmly tugged it against her mouth until her jaws opened. She screamed in protest through the gag, nails digging into the flesh of my arms as I tied it securely.

"*Shhhh.* You wouldn't wanna fall off Pumpkin and hurt yourself now, do you?"

Unintelligible expletives hurtled out of her as I finished tying the gag and barred my arm against her waist, her legs draped over my thigh.

"When you decide to be a good girl again, I'll happily remove it."

The last of the sun's pink and purple rays shone over the horizon as we drew near the meeting point where my *olana kah'hei* and I would begin our journey.

Mareina was still wearing the gag, but the idea of anyone having the privilege of witnessing her vulnerability outside of me set my blood aflame with rage. Not to mention, her jaw would be sore by now.

I reached up for the gag, making her body go rigid as I leaned down to speak softly against her cheek.

"If you're a sweet girl, I'll remove the gag."

She held my gaze, a growl escaping her. Perhaps *sweet* was a little too optimistic at this point.

"I promise I'll reward you."

The scent of her arousal reached me.

Fuck, she was perfect.

The fact that without the bond - the tether and its demands - my vicious creature would have no such feelings was the only thing that kept me from dragging her off Pumpkin and rutting her like an animal in the forest.

Perhaps I should use it to my advantage. There's no way she'd have the strength to resist. And then you both will have the power to conquer Zurie, and you can put your hatred of another in the past.

I felt a pang of guilt at the slight manipulation as I traced my mouth over her jaw and to the sensitive flesh of her neck. Slowly slipping my hand over her thigh, I waited to see if she would protest. Her heart quickened further as her body tensed.

And ever so slightly, she *sweetly* parted her thighs. Edging her over the last several hours had weakened her fortitude against me. The idea made me grin as I growled my pleasure, sliding my hand between her legs and grazing her undergarment to discover they were fucking *soaked*.

Gently, I pulled aside the fabric and stroked one finger through her warm, wet folds. The action drew a needy sigh from her that made my chest ache and my cock throb. My voice dropped to a husk.

"*So fucking ready, aren't you?*"

I dipped a fingertip into her entrance before drawing it up to circle her clit. Her hips bucked their approval as another soft whimper escaped her.

I glanced around briefly at the expanse of the forest surrounding us to doubly ensure we were alone before *willing* a barrier around us and drawing the skirt of her dress up around her waist. The sight of her parted thighs and delicate pink folds, glistening with need, stole my fucking breath. My movements slowed as I found myself staring in awe, gaze locked on the most beautiful pussy I'd ever laid eyes on.

She stared up at me with pleading eyes as her hips writhed. Combined with the soft whimpers muffled by her gag... My heart squeezed painfully tight at the realization... *She's submitting to me.*

However briefly.

She'd probably try to kill me again before the day's end.

My plan was to gain her trust so she would fulfill our bond...

But this...

A tingle of fear worked its way up my spine.

She will bring you to your knees, my Knowingness whispered.

I could have sworn I detected a hint of smugness. I should have heeded it as a warning, but I was already powerless to stop.

"Look how well you're behaving, *lohane thili,*" I hummed, my self-control waning by the millisecond. "Do you want me to make you cum?"

She nodded, holding my gaze longingly as I pulled down the bust of her dress, her lush nipples pebbling instantly against the cool breeze.

"Fuck, Mareina," I hissed, taking in all her vulnerable glory and bared body just for me.

Braced by my arm around her back, she responded by drawing her heels up to rest on the top of my thigh, allowing her bent knees to fall to the side. I groaned at the sight.

"Such a good girl, aren't you?"

She nodded gently, holding my gaze with those wide, supplicating eyes. A deep purr began to resonate from my chest, and her eyes widened in surprise at the vibration that radiated from my purr all the way down from my chest to my tail.

She gave a cry of pleasure as my tail unwound itself and began to caress her slit before thrusting in and curving perfectly to rub against that sensitive spot inside her as her walls spasmed and clamped down firmly as if to trap it there. My fingertips painted the peaks of her nipples with her own juices before I drew my still-drenched finger to my mouth to taste her.

I watched her in awe, committing every detail to memory, as I sucked on my cheeks and allowed a ball of spit to drip down to her clit before returning my middle and ring finger to her little pink pearl, painting circles around it with gradually increasing pressure.

Her legs began to shake as her hips writhed in counter to the thrusts of my tail.

I removed my fingers, earning myself a cry of protest, to tug her gag down.

"Tell me who you belong to," I purred.

Her breath caught, eyes widening and her mouth clamping shut.

I *tsked*, stilling the movements of my tail.

Her face instantly hardened, and her legs smacked closed with my tail still inside her as her bound hands tugged her dress down.

"I can just as easily make myself cum, you manipulative fu—

I yanked the gag back into her mouth, drawing my tail out of her only for the traitorous appendage to tenderly coil itself around her waist as if in apology.

Frustration burned through me as she straightened in my arms, trying to not touch any part of me.

Well, that wouldn't do it all now, would it.

My arms clamped tightly around her, dragging her body back against mine to growl in her ear.

"Deny it all you want, mo'ina li'ili. It doesn't make it any less true."

The sensation of my *olana kah'hei's* magic in the distance had my hackles rising. More than one of the twisted fuckers would enjoy the sight of her being gagged and bound. Not to mention...

You need to gain her trust, my Knowingness whispered.

And having her gagged in front of them wasn't going to do me any favors.

I willed away the gag and fixed my glamor back in place.

They had all seen my true form. I just preferred to keep everyone else from seeing them as we travelled. Wings and tails were relatively rare. It would be something that would make us all easily identifiable. Like this, we all could almost pass for being human. Except for Famei. He was an Orisha. A *horned* Orisha.

Even without the horns, it would have been obvious. Obvious that he was something... *other.*

"*Heeeyyyyyy!*" Roderick called out in greeting, mischief in his tone, "Fancy seeing you here."

There was a look of compassion on his face as he met Mareina's gaze after having dipped to the bindings on her wrists and ankles.

"Mareina, I believe you've already met Roderick...," I gestured with my hand holding the reins, "Pomona's the redhead over there with the staring problem. She advised me *not* to bind you, but we both know I'd be dead right now if I hadn't. Famei, here is our gentle giant. I'd recommend being extra nice to him because he's the *chef*... *Prince* Lokus," I emphasized, making Lokus roll his eyes, "known more often than not to be a dickhole with a death wish, isn't nearly as mean as he looks. He's mostly all bark and no bite. Among us, anyway. With everyone else, though, he does have remarkable follow through... And he also just happens to be the best swordsman in all of Atratus... Rayne, on the other hand, has little need for swords despite his affinity for them...He's often accompanied by a few... *friends.* The incorporeal kind. And if that wasn't enough to boast about, he's got just about the prettiest mug I've ever seen on a male, but he makes up for it with his sourpuss personality."

Rayne rolled his eyes as he tried to hide his grin and gave her a silent nod of acknowledgement before turning his horse to begin our journey.

Pomona shook her head at me, wearing an annoyed smirk before her gaze settled on Mareina, offering her an apologetic smile. "If you'd like me to tie him up and gag him for you, you just let me know."

I couldn't help but notice the appreciative smile curling a corner of Mareina's mouth.

"What's with the binds?" Lokus butted in, ever the shit-stirrer, as he narrowed his bright green eyes at her, even though I was certain he knew the answer. Pomona, no doubt, having already informed them of the little addition to our crew.

His question earned me Mareina's glare, and it gave me a twist of glee despite his intentions.

"Just a bit of insurance for the time being, *your highness.*"

He abhorred it when I addressed him like the royal he was. The Seventh son to the King of Selcarim himself, Razael.

Pomona rolled her eyes and rode off to join Rayne.

"It was a valid question, ya cunt," Lokus huffed.

"One I'm sure Pomona already gave you the fucking answer to."

CHAPTER

TWENTY-FOUR

MAREINA

You're playing with fire, Mareina.

Despite my hatred for this male, there was a growing soul-deep ache for Nakoa physically, emotionally, spiritually... And every time he let his glamor down, the need intensified 1,000 fold.

And I did *hate* him

He'd fucking *marked* me.

I wanted to fucking weep.

What would Malekai say?

Would he even want me anymore?

I bit back my tears, settling further into my resolve to carry out my plan.

Lure him in... Stoke the flames of his lust, and perhaps even gain his trust... And then you will be free.

The only problem with this plan is that the tether between us wound impossibly tighter each time I opened myself to him... And now I was beginning to wonder if my plan was... flawed.

Not to mention...

I hadn't had sex in *years*. I had originally been absolutely certain that having sex with him wouldn't even be a remote temptation.

He'd... fucked me with his *tail*. And due to this wretched fucking tether inspired a lust comparable to that of venom, I'd *wanted* him to.

When he'd been caressing me, the tether between us had radiated and hummed with tremendous force. The demand of the bond was a visceral thing so visceral, it brooked no argument. No doubt.

If I had previously had any lingering hopes that he *wasn't* my *anim gemla* - the sanguinati term for *soulbound* - they had been utterly obliterated now.

Even now, my heart had pounded a steady beat with the effort to smother this deeply unsettling feeling.

I needed to fucking speak with Miroslav. For some reason, he was protecting Nakoa. Why else would he fucking drug me unconscious to prevent me from killing Nakoa? Or was he trying to protect me by not murdering my own mate?

Either possibility was equally shocking.

And why wouldn't he just tell me he was my *soulbound*... instead of going about it so underhandedly?

Because you wouldn't have listened. He knows you love Malekai.

Not to mention, Miroslav probably wanted me to suffer in at least *some way*.

Even if I wanted to be with this wretched bastard - which I absolutely *didn't* - how in *Akash's* name would we escape Zurie's wrath?

She was waiting for me to bring her his *corpse*.

As if sensing the turbulence of my thoughts, Nakoa leaned in, nuzzling his nose gingerly against my neck, which was... as unsettling as it was disarming.

Nakoa chuckled as if he could read my thoughts. His cock firmly pressed against my behind and thigh, where it was trapped by the fabric of his trousers.

"You may not *want* to want me, but it doesn't change the fact that you *need* me. That you *ache* for me. Just as I do for you. Soon enough, I'll get you to bloom for me, little rose."

Anxiety churned in my gut, knowing his words to be true, and that deep ache between my shoulders burned.

I couldn't help but huff a mirthless laugh.

"A rose with far too many thorns."

I felt Nakoa's lips spread against my neck in a grin.

"Oh, *maha mo'ina li'ili...* Your thorns are my favorite part."

Something like a shudder worked through my heart as if he had just chiselled away another chunk of the stone protecting it... Despite the fact that something about his words had me recalling Zurie's own when she'd made Malekai bleed to coax out his fangs.

For hours after that, my mind had twisted itself into an incomprehensible labyrinth of thought and possibilities. None of which gave me any sense of peace.

I'd long given up trying to sit up straight so that I wouldn't have to torture myself by leaning into Nakoa as we rode. Sitting at this awkward angle while trying to maintain a modicum of distance between us had proven exhausting. My buttocks and lower back were *on fire*. To further exasperate matters, even though I'd grown accustomed to sleep deprivation, the swaying of the horse and the blanket of darkness surrounding us was lulling me to sleep despite the chatter and laughter of Nakoa and his *olana kah'hei.*

Eventually, my willpower lost the battle against exhaustion, and I'd succumbed to the temptation of Nakoa's thickly muscled arms. Something he'd rewarded me with by pressing a terrifyingly tender kiss to the top of my head. I fell into a deep sleep, cradled in his embrace, and had yet again found myself in the twinkling darkness of my reoccurring...

That quiet voice that made every molecule in my body tremble beneath its power whispered, roared, and sang within my mind:

"O ziton irini feri polemon, al o kaloumenos 'O Vasiléfs mou' synaxi. Protá dio emisfaíria tou auto olo én genisete, ke tote panta pesite."

"The one who seeks peace will bring war, but it is the one you call, 'My King', who will unite. If two halves of the same whole become one, all your kingdoms will fall."

The dream ended abruptly at the sound of Nakoa's deep voice, magnified by his chest pressing against my ear.

My heartbeat galloped at having been snapped out of it... The words echoing in my mind...

My King.

Unease worked its way through me like creeping vines.

"We're setting up camp, maha loha," Nakoa murmured softly against that sensitive spot just beneath my ear. Nakoa's arms still had me tucked firmly against his chest, his powerful thighs cradling my backside as I lay curled in his cocoon of warmth. I hadn't slept so deeply in... Well, outside of the *grá root's assistance* the previous night, longer than I could remember.

At my silence, Nakoa looked down at me, brow furrowing as he took in my paled expression.

"... Strange dreams?"

My throat worked on a rough swallow.

"How long was I asleep?" I rasped, quickly wiping the drool from my face that had created a wet spot in the centre of Nakoa's shirt, hoping he wouldn't notice.

"5 hours or so," he replied, tilting his head down to discover the darkened spot.

"Oh darling, you left me a present! How sweet," he teased in a surprisingly lighthearted tone that had my eyes narrowing. "I shall never wash this shirt again."

He quirked a black, perfectly arched brow at me, voice dropping low. "Do you prefer my cruelty then?"

"I *prefer* honesty... You being nice makes me feel like you're just trying to manipulate me."

Nakoa chuckled. "Hmmm... Well, if you want me to be completely transparent, I'm torn between either burning the shirt because I should hate you or keeping it and never washing it so I can always have some part of you with me."

Well... I had no idea how I was supposed to feel about that.

Before I could formulate a coherent response, Pumpkin drew to a stop, and Nakoa dismounted, leaving me alone with my warring thoughts for several moments until he tugged me down into his arms to carry me where the camp was already mostly erected.

My eyes drifted to Famei's dark, broad, *horned* form. I almost did a double-take at the sight of them. He must have had them glamoured previously. Without the two spiralling, lethal-looking horns that jutted out of the top of his head through the short, tight curls of dark hair, he stood even taller than Nakoa, though his form was more lithe. The horns, however, easily added an extra foot and a half. With his back turned to us, he sprinkled a few seeds into the ground before hovering his hands over the soil. A few moments later, the flora grew lush and bursting with ripe flowers, fruit, and vegetables in a matter of seconds.

My lips parted in awe.

Nakoa had mentioned he was Orisha, which was made obvious simply by looking at him. Most Orisha were preternaturally tall and hewn with lissome muscle that gave them a certain grace, but it was their eyes that screamed *other*. Unlike Miroslav's silvery iridescent irises that were nearly as pale as the whites of his eyes, Famei's eyes *glowed* like the pale yellow and orange of a flame.

Nakoa *willed* a chair into existence in front of us before setting me down on it and leaving me so he could help finish setting up camp - which, from as far as I could see - was pretty extravagant. I'd assumed we'd be roughing it - sleeping on bed rolls, bared to the elements.

A streak of heavily muscled, pale skin snagged my attention through the trees. Roderick stood in the thick of the forest, stripping away his clothes. I felt only a tiny bit of guilt that I didn't bother to give him any privacy as he undid his belt and stepped out of his trousers to liberate a surprisingly *large* cock, despite it being flaccid.

My brows leapt.

Good for him.

As if reading my thoughts, his eyes lifted to mine, and heat rose to my cheeks. A knowing smile quirked his lips, but he seemed entirely nonplussed. Lykos were notoriously liberal when it came to nudity.

It was the work of fleeting moments before he fully shifted into his wolf form - a wolf form larger than any other I'd ever seen. He took off in a blur of grey and white fur, disappearing into the dark forest.

Nakoa appeared out of his tent, a stringed instrument in his hand and sat down beside me. Familiar fingers began to pluck and strum a harmony that almost instantly had this ache in my chest intensifying. Within moments, the beauty of it even had the hairs on the back of my neck rising.

Everything within me yearned, cried, to sing... But I felt like that part of me had been so cut off after everything that had transpired when I sang in front of an audience. No matter how small.

Emotion clogged my throat, and I had to force my gaze away, attention returning to the campfire as Pomona sidled beside Famei. He turned to stare down at her, grinning a mile wide, with nothing but love and adoration in his gaze. That look alone, despite not being directed at me... Nearly stole my breath away.

I wanted that.

And I just needed to fucking escape so I could return to Malekai. My regret weighed like a damn boulder thrown into the sea because now... I couldn't help but feel like it was too late.

My longing for him was just as overwhelming as this godsforsaken tether binding me to Nakoa.

Famei plucked a branch boasting delicate teardrop-shaped white and periwinkle-colored blossoms and offered it to her. A smile leapt across her face as she inhaled their fragrance before standing on her tip-toes and pressing a lingering kiss to his full mouth.

"I love you more than life itself," she whispered softly in a casual and sweet manner.

Famei cupped her cheeks in his long hands and pressed kisses to her forehead, nose, and mouth. It was only then that I noticed the distinct, glowing, *soulbound* marks weaving around their hands and wrists like a glove.

"You alone are the only reason I still breathe," he murmured reverently.

Emotion swelled in her eyes, but she breathed it away, pressing a quick kiss to his lips before turning to find me openly staring at them. While perhaps a little melodramatic, especially for one such as me... The earnestness in their words, the tenderness and love in their gaze... I'd never, in all my life, witnessed such a tender display of love.

My cheeks flushed with guilt and embarrassment as my gaze darted to the bonfire.

Pomona strode toward me, grinning warmly, and plopped down beside me.

"I'm sorry... I didn't mean to stare... I just... I don't think I've ever witnessed anything quite like that."

She tilted her head to study me, her smile dimming.

"I'm sorry to hear that. And you have nothing to apologize for. I stared at you for most of our journey here."

Surprised by her candidness, my eyes lifted to hers. Before I could respond, she placed the branch of blossoms into my hand.

"Ereni flowers... They're my favorite. They're said to ward off dark spirits and energy. Bring peace and calm to those who keep them near and breathe their scent."

I hesitated, my gaze flicking briefly to Famei. "But didn't he just give them to you?"

"He gives them to me every time we stop for camp. And there's plenty more. Keep them with you. We're happy to have you... *I'm* happy to have you," she whispered the last part, leaning forward into my ear, "You're Nakoa's *leath-anama*. His soul-half."

My breathing stilled. "He told you this?"

She grinned, her vibrant red curls bouncing. "I have a sense about these things... but he confirmed it," she chirped, tipping her head at Nakoa and grinning. Nakoa's fingers stilled against his instrument briefly, gaze searching my reaction before he wordlessly returned to his music.

Pomona stood before I could say anything more.

"Resisting only painfully prolongs the inevitable," she added, her eyes wandering back to Famei, "I found that out myself the hard way..."

I wondered what the story of their union had been as I brought the branch to my nose, filling it with the ereni blossom's divine and delicate floral fragrance. Pomona walked off, disappearing inside the tent just as Famei turned towards a cauldron that he *willed* into existence between us. Boasting a variety of exotic, freshly picked vegetables in his hands, he set to work as his gaze darted upwards to find me watching him. A smile curved his full mouth, bright and luminous against his dark skin that seemed to have a glow all its own. His accent was thick, his voice a warm baritone.

"Hungry? I'm going to make a traditional *Yatól* stew. Simple and quick but delicious and nourishing."

My stomach grumbled in response before my mouth could, making Famei's grin widen. Gentle giant, indeed. Similar to Roderick, he radiated warmth and kindness. So much so that he was unintentionally, disarmingly charming. It made it hard for me to imagine him doing anything other than nurturing those around him. Though I knew better than to assume such a thing.

"Do you mind if it's spicy? I find that *Yatól* dishes aren't quite the same without it."

"I *love* spicy food."

I tucked the petite ereni branch into the blouse of my dress as Famei set his vegetables down in a pot before turning back towards his miraculous garden and picking off a large, otherworldly-looking purple and yellow fruit. As he neared, its sweet, tangy, and floral scent had saliva pooling in my mouth.

"Here, you can snack on this while you wait," he said, carving off a large piece of its tender flesh, dripping juices at my feet.

"Thank you."

I plucked the piece from his fingers and popped the whole thing into my mouth. Its flavour - sweet, creamy, tangy, and floral - exploded on my tongue, causing me to groan.

I laughed both in surprise and complete awe. "*Oh my gods.* I've never tasted anything so divine."

Famei beamed all the brighter, popping a juicy piece into his mouth before carving me a few more and slipping the large seed at its center into a pouch that hung on the side of his hip. "This fruit is called *bujera*. It grows only in the mountains of *Yatól*, in the densest parts of the forest. It is my favorite."

"I'm moving to *Yatól* now," I joked, wiping juice from my face as I chewed.

Nakoa's strumming was instantly cut short, eyes narrowing in my direction.

Famei's laughter was warm and unrestrained, causing a pang of longing to spear through me... I could probably count on one hand the occasions I'd laughed so freely in the last... however many years.

Each of those occasions with Malekai.

Roderick, still in his lykos wolf form, appeared from between the trees and dropped a full-grown deer at Famei's feet, who rewarded him with an affectionate side-pat.

Roderick padded over and, to my surprise, plopped down directly in front of me and placed his enormous head in my lap. His nose nudged my hand, only stopping when I finally began to run my hand over his head and ears.

Akash, his fur is like silk.

Roderick's eyes slipped shut and I swear he grinned.

Nakoa's gaze dropped at the sight of Roderick's lykos head resting in my lap. His eyes narrowed at him before flicking up to mine.

Famei chuckled, rescuing me from his accusatory glare.

"How do you feel about that, brother? Perhaps she will find a good Orisha male who will be more than happy to remove those binds for her," he taunted Nakoa with deceptively innocent mirth filling his bright eyes.

Nakoa's gaze burned into me with an intense but unreadable expression on his face.

"If she wishes for someone's death, she need only ask."

"You can't be serious," I huffed.

Nakoa, carrying me in his arms, hummed his pleasure at my protest. Again, it was a lighthearted sound... Making me wonder, if we weren't each other's greatest enemies if this is what he would be like. Lighthearted and playful...

He strode into his canvas tent, a large but singular pallet of furs lying in the center of it.

"What's the matter, princess? I don't mind how loudly you snore."

"I do *not* snore."

"You did last night. Softly... It was... heinously adorable."

My throat suddenly became dry, scowling in response just as Nakoa plopped me down on the pallet of furs. The tiny ereni branch stabbed at my breast with the movement. I withdrew it, taking in its intoxicating fragrance.

"Will you keep this somewhere safe for me?" I asked begrudgingly.

Nakoa piqued an eyebrow.

"Pomona gave it to me."

Nakoa studied me for a moment as though surprised by my request. After a few moments, he finally took the branch from me, sniffing the blossoms before *willing* it away.

"Pomona is the peacekeeper of our group and one of the kindest people I've ever known. Only paralleled by her mate, Famei... I think you and Pomona could grow to be close friends... Despite the hatred between us."

He punctuated his words by giving me a devilish smirk and a *wink.*

Tension tightened in my chest...

How dare he be so fucking charming.

I only managed to conjure a mild disgust as I chose to remain silent.

As if trying to disarm me completely, Nakoa tugged his shirt off, baring his truly mouthwatering form. Bronze skin peppered with scars and covered in tattoos covered thick ropes of muscle. A curl of heat blossomed in my traitorous body just as Nakoa looked up from where he was unbuckling his belt to find my eyes *locked* onto him. A smug grin curled his scarred mouth.

My scowl deepened even as my cheeks flushed.

"You disgust me," I lied, my tone flat and not even remotely convincing.

Lying had never been my strong suit.

My lie only served to broaden his grin as he breathed a wistful sigh. *"I can tell, lohane thili.* The scent you give off when you are is utterly mouthwatering... I shall have to ensure that you are... constantly *disgusted."*

I seethed silently, refusing to give him the satisfaction of my submission by lowering my gaze. He knew what he was doing. It would have been easier for him to simply *will* some pyjamas over his *disgustingly* magnificent body. Instead, he chose to deliberately taunt me with this strip tease.

My breath caught when he slid his trousers beyond his brawny thighs, giving room for that long, thick, dark bronze and *fully erect* length to liberate itself from its confines. He hummed his pleasure, eyes half-lidded.

"I can feel the weight of your gaze like a physical touch, *mo'ina li'ili...*"

The tension between us tightened, dry throat working on a rough swallow. It was either hold his stare and provoke him... or silently admit defeat by finally averting my gaze.

My gaze shifted to a paisley whorl on the rug that lined the floor of the tent as I desperately tried to stifle this need coiling within my core and promptly clamped my legs together.

Fucking soulbound demands.

Though it did nothing to mask the scent of my arousal already perfuming the air.

Nakoa's nostrils flared again as he emitted a low growl, the whites of his eyes bleeding into black. The sight should have been off-putting, at the least... It was a trait I'd only ever read about in various species of wielders. Instead, it only further beckoned me to him. To my soul, it seemed.

"You've been teased so much today, little mate... You must be half-mindless with need for me by now..." He husked in a voice that made my pussy clench with desire.

"Fuck off. I can't help it that this cursed bond demands things my heart and mind reject."

"Whether or not you're not ready to admit it, we need each other, Mareina. It is the way of the *soulbound,* and there's no denying it, no matter how hard we try. There is a reason why *we* are *fated.* And I choose to have faith in *Akash's* omniscience... I will try my best to forgive you your sins... *Wretched as they are...* I only ask that you forgive me, mine..."

My jaw remained tightly clenched as I attempted, in futility, to create a rebuttal.

Nakoa took his now cock in his hands and stroked over it slowly. Once, twice, and then brought his tight fist around the head and squeezed. The viscous, clear fluid of his pre-cum dripped from him, reaching for the ground. I had to stifle the whimper crawling up my throat.

"Besides... How could I ever hope to resist that pretty little cunt of yours, knowing how drenched she is for me. I can smell her sweetness from here... And it's driving me fucking *insane.*"

I could only watch, breath held, as Nakoa stepped closer to the bed until his cock was only inches from my face where he stood near the edge of the bed, staring down at me, looking like some dark god.

My mouth, quite literally, began to salivate at the sight of him, and I couldn't bring myself to look away.

Malekai. You love Malekai, I chided myself.

And how the fuck am I going to escape and return to Malekai?

Trust. Gain Nakoa's trust.

My heart pounded its fear, frustration, and... admittedly, lust... As I internally warred with myself whether or not to dive off the edge of this cliff... The desperate, twisting, writhing need that *demanded* I let Nakoa claim me roared within me to... that I fulfill this fucking bond - pleaded with me to give in. But my heart, my mind, and the part of my soul that was very much *not* bound to him *wailed* its protest.

And my logic told me that continuing to resist and spew my hatred towards him would only keep me in these binds. And if I had any hope of escape, I had to get him to free me of them.

Nakoa's hand began to stroke steadily over his cock. He seemed to be both devouring me with his gaze *and* witnessing my internal debate.

"You don't have to decide it all now, Mareina. Why don't you let me take care of you? Then perhaps you will be better capable of making rational decisions."

Not even having realized my lips had parted, as if they were readying to say *yes,* I snapped my jaw shut, stifling the answer I caught, ready to spill from my lips.

Nakoa's hand began to stroke in earnest, earning wet sounds from the pre-cum now coating him as he continued to try and shove me past my line of indecision.

"... For me to suckle at that pretty clit of yours as I teased your entrance with my tail... Would you like that? I'd make you gush so I could drink every last fucking drop. And then, and only then, would I take my own pleasure. Spread those sweet thighs, the soft little lips of your cunt, and slide my cock inside you. Stretch you and fill you...

Caressing your clit as I stroked slowly inside of you while your tight channel adjusted to my size."

His breath became ragged as his strokes became harder, faster.

"I would tease you and fuck you until the only word you remembered was my name..."

He growled, slowing the pace of his strokes as if to edge himself, his eyes holding my gaze all the while. My fingers clutched the furs beneath me...

"Lay down, Mareina... *Now.*"

Arousal staggered through me, fangs throbbing and mouth salivating. Twice, only hours ago, he'd brought me to the edge of orgasm, and it seemed my body had *not* forgotten.

He growled at my indecision despite the need pulsing through my body. I yelped as Nakoa's tail swept my legs out from under me and laid me on my back. Shock filled me as my clothing was *willed* away. I couldn't do this... As much as I craved it, I couldn't—

"Nakoa, no—

"Shut the fuck up and give me this fucking pussy," he growled, kneeling in from of me, taking the binds around my ankles in his hands and lifting my legs until my knees were bent on either side of my breasts.

A cry tore from my lips as Nakoa's mouth came down on me like a male suffering starvation. His tongue dove through my folds, licking up all my wetness as though it were his sole source of sustenance before his lips wrapped around the throbbing bud of my clit and *sucked.*

My back arched, and I cried out, my bound hands reaching down to grip his hair as though it would prevent me from lifting off the furs entirely. His purr returned, radiating into his mouth. Just when I thought it couldn't possibly get any more intense, his tail teased my core. The vibration of his purr rippled through his it as it caressed my entrance before sliding gently inside me, stretching me. The appendage was thick and smooth, its tip rounded.

Between Nakoa's lips, tongue, and tail, I thought my mind and body would shatter so completely that I would never be able to recover. The broken pieces of me scattered, never to be reformed the same as before.

"Are you thoroughly *disgusted,* little nightmare?'

My legs were shaking as I dared a glance down at where he looked up at me as he continued to devour me like a fucking feast, a wolfish grin tilting his lips. Something terrifying tugged at my heart... That tether between us.

I was so *disgusted* I could barely fucking speak. Each part of my sentence punctuated by a moan, cry, writhing, or of my hips.

"I have... ugh!... never... been more... "

My breaths came in short pants as I forced the rest of my words out...

"... disgusted... oh fuck!"

Writhe.

"In my..."

Thrust.

"... Entire..."

Writhe.

"Fucking..."

Thrust.

"... Life."

A deep groan rose to join his throaty chuckle and the obscene wet noises accompanying his vigorous and *thorough* ministrations.

"Mmmmm... Good girl..."

Pleased by his words, my core clenched around his tail. After all of the pent-up frustration and arousal that had built all day, my orgasm built rapidly and mercilessly.

"I still fucking... hate... you."

Another husky, self-assured chuckle as his lips sucked my clit and then released it with a soft *pop.*

"So long as you know who this pussy belongs to."

As if to prove his point, Nakoa's mouth returned to its core with intensified fervor; his free hand came up to tease my nipples, and it was my undoing. Fluid rushed from my core, causing the thrusting of his tail within me to make embarrassing squelching sounds. Nakoa growled his pleasure as he continued to devour me.

"Mmmmmm... Gods, yes. So fucking delicious, lohane thili."

My hips bucked against him in a silent plea for mercy, to which he acquiesced.

Nakoa's efforts eased, gently suckling and teasing my clit between broad, firm passes of his tongue to clean up the evidence of my orgasm.

Oh.

My.

Fuck.

That was... quite possibly absolutely the best orgasm of my entire life.

Not that I would *dare* tell him that.

Nakoa gave a deep hum of pleasure as he rose and stretched out on the palate of furs.

As the haze of lust began to lift, the realization of what had happened began to settle. My bound hands reached up to cover my breasts, but his tail smacked away my hand.

"Don't you fucking dare," Nakoa snarled as his tail curled around my torso, dragging me onto my side and against his broad chest.

The candles in the tent went out, and I felt the furs being drawn over our bodies.

I laid there, glued in place on the pallet of furs, as dread settled low in my belly. Three wars waged in my mind and my heart.

Clutched in the safety of his solid arms as though I was some... *Cherished* thing. I had spent a lifetime craving this. And part of me - the bond - swooned and swelled with the rightness of this. *Of him.*

Another part of me raged against it. *Recoiled.* The idea and physical sensation of being touched by anyone but Malekai felt so fucking wrong.

And now that I felt like the opportunity to be with him had been smashed within the tight, merciless fist of this bond... Regret weighed like an anchor in a blackened trench beneath the sea.

Away from the precious, life-giving breath to fill my lungs and the light of day to nourish my soul.

All because of *fear* and my own deeply buried self-loathing... That I didn't deserve that kind of happiness.

So now here I was, trapped in a prison of brawny, unforgiving arms that threatened to tear me apart and rob me of the fragments of my heart that had survived because of one male alone... *Malekai*.

But *I had* to gain this male's trust so that he would free me.

The knowledge birthed a whole new fear, swelling and cresting like a tide being sucked back by unseen forces beneath the deep before reaching a terminal height that threatened to crush me beneath its weight. Drag me under and force its way into my lungs and every cell of my body.

And lastly... Could I kill him? Zurie wouldn't accept failure. She'd demanded I bring his dead body to her. As desperate as I was to escape him... As much as I resented him... This male was the other half of my soul. I didn't know enough about the laws of the *soulbound* to know for certain what the consequences would be, but...

A sickening sense of foreboding filled me every time I tried to imagine myself walking those harrowed steps to Nakoa's death - and returning to Zurie... To just continue on that well-worn, dead-end path that I now clearly recognized was the entrance to a tomb of my own fucking making...

The idea of killing Nakoa... *And* returning to my old life...

It felt like grazing the hem of death's cloak... snagging his lethal attention and beckoning him closer, a whispered promise of oblivion on his lips.

Panic tightened my throat, coupled with the crushing weight of a fear that I was certain would cause my sternum to buckle.

Where the fuck was Miroslav?

He had questions to fucking answer!

And here I was, bound and kidnapped. Surely, that could be considered 'harm' and went against his vow.

"I can *feel* your internal battle as if you were carving me up with your sword, Mareina. Let it go. At least for now. Let us sleep. We have a long day tomorrow."

At my silence, Nakoa began to caress my hair. The tender action suddenly had my eyes stinging with unshed tears. Even though he was my enemy, it took everything within me to not turn in his arms and bury my face in the comforting, muscled wall of his chest to weep.

As if reading my mind, he turned me over and tilted my chin up with his thumb before cupping my face, holding my gaze to witness the tears streaming down my cheeks. He watched their descent, as if mezmerised by the sight, before wiping them away with his thumbs.

"How about we make a bargain, hm?"

The tension in my body went rigid again.

"How about during the day and the evening you can hate me all you want, and we can burn one another with all the ire we can muster for one another as much as we desire... But at night... *Here*... Whether it's in *our* bed or a pallet of furs on the forest floor... Where it's only us, and the space between us is reduced to this blissful barrier of flesh - the only thing that separates my soul from yours - let us seek solace in one another as we are meant to..."

The only sound between us was our sound of quiet, shared breaths and my now parched throat swallowing back another rising tidal wave of fear and emotion.

"*Please...*"

I couldn't bring myself to speak... Even if a part of me - that part of me that I knew belonged to him but refused to give - *yearned* for me to say *yes*.

Though he could no doubt feel it through our tether, with my bare chest grazing his with each inhale.

His face lowered gradually to mine as if giving me the opportunity to stop him. It was the flicker of vulnerability and... *hope* on his face that prevented me from denying him.

His lips softly grazed mine... Tentative... Searching... *Hopeful...*

My heart fluttered like a hummingbird caught in the winds of a storm...

He gave a palpable groan, and his hand slid from my jaw to the nape of my neck, where he fisted a handful of my hair. His tongue swept against the seam of my lips in a silent question. The tether between us ached for me to give in, even as anxiety wound through my stomach that *this wasn't Malekai.*

The tether burned brighter, making my breath catch.

You have to gain his trust.

I gave in, caressing my tongue against his and taking his bottom lip between my teeth, biting hard enough to draw blood.

Out of frustration and helplessness.

His groan turned into a growl that had my wetness blooming anew as I licked away the evidence of the tiny wound. The taste of his blood only spurred me on.

He ground his hips against mine, and the sensation of his thick cock slicing a vertical trail across my abdomen had me pulling back. His eyes searched mine for a moment in understanding before he pressed his forehead against mine.

"Thank you...," he murmured so softly I wasn't sure I'd heard him correctly.

"For what?"

"For giving me hope."

My heart pounded a new, equally thumping beat that had nothing to do with arousal.

Nakoa pressed one last kiss to my lips before curling his arms around me as he wove our legs together.

"Sleep, *lohane thili.*"

Oh, gods...

I was well and truly fucked.

I could take his fire and his hatred. It would only further cement my walls.

But this?

This tenderness?

This tenderness I'd longed for the entirety of my 120 years in this realm... I would be powerless against it.

TWENTY-FIVE

NAKOA

For the second night in a row, I'd slept deeper than I ever had because my mate was in my arms. The guilt at the realization of that left me feeling like my stomach was trying to digest gravel. It was a betrayal. This woman had slaughtered thousands of my fellow soldiers... Had played a heavy hand in wiping out the majority of our population. Destroying and exploiting our lands.

I'd forced myself to approach her with tender touches and kisses in the hopes of gaining her trust. All the while assuaging my guilt by telling myself it was so that I could reclaim my home for my people. Liberate us all from exile.

And instead, I'd felt my own resolve in maintaining my hatred towards her dissolving like a fucking sand castle on the shore.

And it was fucking terrifying.

My mother's story of Lysander, now more famously known as Kahlohan, and Akela's story kept inconveniently pushing at the forefront of my mind every time I tried to steel my emotions and my heart against her.

You have tortured and killed more of her comrades than you count, my Knowingness spat at me.

I willfully ignored the reminder.

And that look...

The way she had looked up at me... Like she had never before experienced such intimacy and tenderness... That, too, ate me up inside because as much as I loathed to admit it... My soul ached to give that to her.

It also made me wonder what in the fuck was the nature of her relationship with that blonde fae I couldn't stand the fucking sight of.

Another inconvenient truth that my Knowingness had thrust upon me, coupled with the history lesson in relation to her *origins*... I knew that Mareina had long been dying to liberate herself from the oppression of Zurie's tasks. She could be... an invaluable ally... If I'd only allow her to be... She was destined to be my Queen... Another fact made me sick to my fucking stomach.

While Mareina remained sleeping soundly in my tent... I'd spent the morning explaining the truth of the situation and the aforementioned details to my *olana kah'hei*. I'd expected far more pushback from them. The only one who seemed, at least openly, resentful was Lokus. Which came as no surprise. Though the fact that she was my *lohane thili* had him biting his tongue. That and the fact I'd threatened him bodily harm if he spoke against her. If anyone was going to make her atone for her sins, it would be me and no one else. Thankfully, he left without argument or incident and set off ahead of us to scout the road we'd be travelling for bandits.

"This is getting pretty old, pretty fast," Mareina growled, holding her bounds hands up as I set her atop Pumpkin. I stepped into the stirrup and swung my opposite leg over Pumpkin's back, settling behind the wretched female who was glaring daggers at me.

I couldn't suppress the grin that quirked my lips, taking a twisted pleasure in her frustration and helplessness against me. Readjusting my cock currently being strangled in the pant leg of my trousers, I hummed my pleasure at the memory of her submitting to me... Gagged, bound, and staring pleadingly into my eyes as I gingerly pleasured her pretty little pussy.

"I easily could have torn your throat out last night, and I didn't. I think we can move beyond this without having to fear your life."

"It's not my life I'm fearful of losing, Mareina. It's *you*."

She reared back, studying me warily.

"What am I missing? Tell me the truth. I can see it lingering there in the shadows behind your insidious fucking eyes... And don't try me with some bullshit about us being *soulbound*. It's more than that."

I willed my face into a mask of neutrality even if her words struck so close to home it nearly toppled over.

'*You know you can't tell her,*" my mother's words echoed in my mind...

If I told Mareina about my premonitions before they came to fruition... She'd definitely run in the opposite direction. And I needed her to fulfill our bond so that I would wield a power not even Zurie's army could resist.

The *lie* slid from lips as smoothly as butter against a blade...

"One day, I will earn your trust, Mareina... Along with every other part of you that is mine to claim."

I spurred Pumpkin into action as if to punctuate the closing of this conversation.

Instead, her eyes narrowed with further distrust.

Fuck.

Any other female would have swooned...

Just when I thought I'd had her figured out, thinking all I had to do was use a bit of tenderness to coax open the petals of my thorny little rose for her to blossom for me...

"I want a separate tent... I have no desire to be subjected to your manipulations. If you can't give your me the courtesy of truth, then there will *never* be any part of me available for you to claim, no matter what pretty words and soft touches you try to coax me with."

Her words were like a bucket of ice-cold water straight to the face.

"And actually, on that note, if you refuse to let me ride Chihiro, I would ask that you let me ride with someone else. If you wish to have *any* hope of gaining my cooperation in whatever fucking scheme you're working at, you *will*."

A melange of hurt, anger, and frustration split my face into a cold smile.

"No."

I was shocked my skin didn't burst into flames from the burn of her fury.

"*Well*, in that case... I hope you enjoy sleeping with one eye fucking open."

The threat in her words made my cock twitch. I beamed wide, and when her eyes flicked briefly to my lengthening fangs, it filled me with a dark satisfaction. My voice dropped to a husk.

"If you want me to gag you again, darling, all you have to do was ask." Her pupils flared as her breath caught, surely recalling with vivid clarity of the last occasion she'd submitted to me.

Her eyes darted briefly to my *olana kah'hei,* save Lokus, who was about an hour ahead. She remained quiet, though her anger poured off her in waves.

Pomona's disappointed look in her eyes as she stared at me took a little of the wind out of my sails. Famei, the most considerate and boundary-respecting one of us, kept his face forward in a courteous effort to at least *pretend* he wasn't listening.

Rayne and Roderick, however, didn't bother. Rayne watched keenly, though his expression was as unreadable as ever. Roderick, however, was flat-out scowling at me. The soft spot he seems to have for my little nightmare grates against my skin like fucking barbed wire.

CHAPTER

TWENTY-SIX

NAKOA

F or the first few hours of our journey, Mareina and I didn't
speak. I'd been lost in either my thoughts or the ever-
increasing visions... Which had grown to become disorienting and overwhelming. Several of which revealed moments
during this future war I was desperately going to try and prevent.

And how the fuck does one go about preventing something they
can't even predict how or when it will happen.

And while the last thing I wanted was another war, if that's what
it would take to overthrow Zurie and free my people and our lands,
then so be it.

To further inflame matters, the constant ache in my chest due to
our wounded and unfulfilled bond was bringing me to a whole new
level of *unhinged.*

Mareina's words - despite the sense of doom they should have
inspired - were like taking a gulp of fresh air after being dragged
beneath the surface of a tumultuous sea.

"Zurie expects me to the day after tomorrow. What will you do
when she sends mercenaries after us?"

My Knowingness filled me with an unwavering determination

and certainty.

"Exactly what I've been doing. Building The Uprising."

She looked up at me in disbelief. Just another vision stamped itself onto my present reality.

Mareina standing at a glowing river's edge, The River Oblivion. A field of tall grass and poppy flowers behind her. Two of Mors' famed Pharalaki hover at her sides. A mournful look sits heavily on her face.

The vision cuts away all at once, leaving me staring down at *present reality Mariena.*

Terror creeps over my senses... Terror I can't accept.

There's no way...

Why would she be in Avernus?

The Underworld.

Does she die killing Zurie?

I'd had countless premonitions of Mareina for over a hundred years before I met her. So many of which hadn't even yet come to pass. It was entirely possible this one wouldn't take place for hundreds more.

The realization lets me exhale a breath I hadn't realized I'd even been holding.

Mareina's brow pinches. "Are you OK?"

Her eyes searched mine and forced the thought and a deeply unsettling sensation with me.

"Yes. Fine."

She gives me a strange look but blessedly doesn't push the matter.

"And you have an army large enough to match her *tens of thousands?*"

"We are well on our way..."

Not that I will need to rely on it once we can fulfill this fucking bond.

"You could let me go back, and I'll tell her I couldn't find you."

Despite the lack of conviction in her voice, a traitorous and entirely unwanted pain flared in my chest at the words she *didn't* speak. She mentioned nothing about even returning.

Which was precisely why she was still bound.

I dropped my glamor. Her sharp intake of breath at the sensation of our souls being utterly inextricably bound was a balm to my soul. Our tether was even stronger since last night. The mating instinct winding that unbreakable tether between us tighter and tighter until we collided.

"You *do* know. You're just as powerless to this as I am. The sooner you come to accept that, the sooner we can enjoy our lives together."

The words tasted bitter. A gut-churning melange of truth, help-lessness, and betrayal.

I watched her expression carefully as the faint echoing of words from my Knowingness returned to me... *Resistance is an exercise in futility.*

Maybe I should unbind her.

That alone may earn me her trust.

Hope, thickly twined with anxiety, knotted in my chest...

Another brief vision bleeds in - a sweet relief from the previous one.

Mareina and I standing in front of one another, bloody palms clasped together, as took our vows in front of a priestess.

The vision, though fleeting, burned into my mind's eye like a beacon of hope.

There was absolutely no way of gauging how long it would take before a vision came to fruition. Perhaps the previous vision of Mareina standing in *Avernus, Mors' underworld,* wouldn't take place for centuries.

I couldn't hinge my decisions upon what might not occur for hundreds of years...

Though it seemed entirely impossible that Mareina and I would be taking our *soulbound* vows any sooner considering her hatred for me was palpable but... I'd learned long ago that no matter the odds, it could all change in a fleeting moment.

My rational mind continued to try and reason as to how this might actually work. If I let her go under the pretence of... *compas-*

198

sion and my own trust in *her*... If she ran... A dark pleasure curled through me at the idea. My grip on her tightened as my cock twitched at the idea of getting to chase my little nightmare... Not to mention it might give her the opportunity to see for herself just how all-consuming the demand of the bond was...

Especially, with an unfulfilled bond... From the moment we met, trying to resist was like trying to douse a forest fire with a cup of water.

"She *will* come for us."

The words spilled from my lips as a new sort of betrayal that settled on my chest ...

"Let them come, *lohane thili*. There is no world in which you can be taken from me. And do not take my words for prideful foolishness. It is my Knowingness that tells this truth. And it has never, in all my years, been wrong. Zurie will soon have her day of reckoning."

While my words were absolutely true... I'd wielded them with the purpose of manipulating my own *soulbound* into trusting me rather than as words of love and reassurance... As they should have been.

Guilt and his all too familiar *friend,* shame, drifted out from the shadows of my mind and into the spotlight. Trying to shove them away was like trying to shove *smoke.*

Mareina remained silent, her gaze locked on mine. Her expression hard, yet unreadable, as if she were intensely focused on finding some lost piece to a puzzle.

Just as she'd opened her mouth to reply, my Knowingness prickled at the back of my neck. My gaze shifted, passing over the forest surrounding us. Gradually, the scent of a bonfire wafted towards me. My jaw snapped shut as my heart began to pound in my chest.

"Dakrun," I growled, turning my head toward Pomona and Famei who were riding closest behind us. *Bandits.*

Famei gave me a sharp nod before sliding off his still-walking horse. His form shifted, bones painfully and rapidly shifting, snapping, and growing until the form of an enormous gryphon promptly broke into a sprint and leapt into the air. The slap of his mighty wings caused a gust of wind that had me instinctively shielding Mareina's eyes from the dirt and debris it rustled off the trail.

Mareina looked up at me, mirroring my own surprise.

"Sweet Gods...," Mareina breathed.

Gryphons were an exceedingly rare thing that most believed were either extinct or mythical.

"Where is he going?"

"To check the area for—

My Knowingness speared through me.

Protect.

On instinct alone, I curled my body over Mareina's just as an arrow found its home in my shoulder where her throat had been exposed the moment before.

A grunt escaped me as it pierced through flesh and bone.

"Nakoa!" Mareina cried just before Pumpkin reared back, nearly knocking us off her, and took off at a gallop. I gripped Mareina tighter against me with my uninjured arm, Pumpkin towards the forest cover nearby. I twisted to look behind me and found Pomona, Lokus, and Rayne, still astride their galloping horses, heading in the opposite direction towards the bandits.

"Take these Akash-forsaken binds off me!" Mareina yelled over the wind and pounding hoofbeats.

The swift *thunks* of arrows narrowly missing us and being buried into the tree trunks beside us were like the sounds of dangerous seconds ticking by.

Indecision warred within me at whether or not I should follow through with my idea...

"Why? So you can kill me? Run away from me the second I piss you off?"

"So I can help you, you fucking fool!"

Too busy gritting my teeth against the pain radiating in my shoulder, I didn't bother responding as I steered Pumpkin into the forest. I'd attempted to *will* the arrow away, but it was, unsurprisingly, warded from anyone being able to do so. It would have to be removed *manually*.

I needed to help my *olana kah'hei*. Although, together, I knew that whoever they came face to face with would meet Mors himself shortly after. And I was entirely unwilling to ride with her helplessly bound in my arms and didn't dare risk one of the bandits taking off with her.

Mareina gripped me by the collar of my shirt with both hands, yanking me down to meet the severity of her gaze.

"Let me help you."

I took her in, shock stilling my breath as her glorious green eyes *glowed*... Just as they had in my earlier visions.

As her words settled, I realized I *wanted* to witness her being set free in all her bloody glory. Just as deeply as I felt the need to protect her.

I pulled on Pumpkin's reigns until her gallop halted. My heart pounded a furious beat in time with Mareina's.

I slid off Pumpkin, towing Mareina in one arm with me. We hit the ground less gracefully than intended, making the air whoosh from her lungs from where my arm was firmly banded around her waist.

After releasing my grip on her, I dared a glance down at my shoulder. It hadn't pierced through the other side of my chest so that we could cut off the arrowhead and pull the shaft cleanly through.

In other words, *this was going to fucking hurt.*

"I need you to remove it."

Mareina's scowl tightened, briefly giving me a look of apology that told me she knew exactly how painful this would be.

She lifted her bound wrists, waiting for me to remove the binds.

My chest fisted with anxiety.

My Knowingness remained silent.

Do I dare let fate run its course?

CHAPTER

TWENTY-SEVEN

MAREINA

I could see the tension radiating through Nakoa's body at the thought of freeing me. I watched as his eyes briefly slipped shut, offering a silent prayer to *Akash*. When his eyes opened again, the binds around my wrists and ankles vanished.

Tension wound tightly between us as my window of opportunity to escape cracked open.

Nakoa's throat worked on a swallow, holding my gaze before he turned to offer me his back. My eyes dipped to the large dagger sheathed at his side, the handle angled towards me as if beckoning me to reach for it. With my speed, and now my magic returned to me, there was no way Nakoa would be capable of stopping me. I could kill him now and escape. Long, tense seconds passed as I held my breath- my window of opportunity quickly closing.

It wasn't too late to return to the palace...

My gut twisted at the idea.

But what other choice do I have?

And Malekai would be there... I wouldn't have Zurie and her army after me for committing treason. It was the clear, *logical* choice.

The tether between us was doused in tar and set afire, demanding I abandon the idea.

No. I couldn't be with him. I would *not* exchange one master for another. He was only using me for some unseen end.

Nakoa's voice came gently, cutting off my tumultuous train of thoughts. His words, the perfect affirmation.

"Do it swiftly."

Eyes locked still to the blade at his hip, the whisper of cloth snapped my gaze to where he was peering down at me over his shoulder, a smirk tilting his full lips.

"Well?"

He's fucking baiting me...

An oily unease seeped into my veins.

Why would he be doing this? It was too easy...

I didn't bother moving swiftly as I drew the blade from its holster and pressed the blade against the flesh of his neck.

"Good girl, *lohane thili.* Now do what Zurie sent you here to do."

Anger and frustration swelled within me.

Regardless of his manipulations, I fucking *needed* to do this.

I *had* to do this.

"All your problems will be solved, Mareina. Just do it."

Despite the bitter grin tilting his perfect lips, something like heartbreak briefly shuddered his gaze. Keeping the blade pressed against the flesh of his neck, I shifted to stand in front of him.

Do it, Mareina.

In that final second, which seemed to stretch beyond time, the air left my lungs as I watched my door to freedom begin to close.

He opened his mouth to speak. Before his words could form, I dragged the blade across his throat. Blood sprayed across my front. He dropped to one knee, clutching his throat.

This beast that had awakened within me roared its fury in time with the blinding pain that tore through our tether.

A twisted grin spread across his face as his black eyes met mine.

His words came out a half-whisper.

"Look how beautiful you are covered in my blood."

Tears swelled in my eyes at the sight of him, making his grin spread wider. Despite all the pain and blood loss, he still managed that look of smug male satisfaction.

"See how you need me?"

My words came out forced. A guttural and cracked whisper.

"Fuck you."

"Not until you beg me."

Nakoa swayed, catching himself with one hand on the ground.

My heart pounded furiously in my heart knowing it would take more than this to kill him. Nakoa forced himself upright.

I steeled myself, taking a small step to close the distance between us.

He stared up at me like a boy in love, clearly far more deranged than I'd given him credit for.

I pressed the blade just to the right of his sternum where I could *feel* his heart pounding.

Alarm bells went off in my mind just as the command escaped my lips, pulled from me directly that unfathomable thing between us.

"Lift your glamor," I whispered.

All at once, his magic poured over me, and the rest of his features shifted. His glorious wings unfurled, his fangs descended, and his tail immediately curled around my leg.

"Sorry... He has a mind of his own."

My heart squeezed at the action but he removed his tail, which only proved to make my heart ache at its absence... And just like that, I slammed the door to my freedom shut. Nakoa watched, knowing clearly what he'd witnessed, too.

My lungs, too filled with both relief and despair to breathe properly.

"I understand a future beside me might seem bleak right now, but... If it brings you any consolation... There will come a day that you no longer have to fight or wield a sword to survive because of it... I know that... you have grown weary of it."

Little did he know just how desperately I craved such a future. To be able to trade my sword in for... gardening and forest-dwelling... Seaside walks, and lots of books.

And love.

Most of all, love.

With Malekai.

Gods, I fucking burned to return to him. Just to be wrapped in his arms.

Nakoa's bronzed skin had grown pallid due to blood loss and likely our fraying tether. Remarkably, his neck was already halfway healed as I pressed the blade against his chest above his heart, a bead of blood blossoming. However, I found myself roaring in frustration before finally returning to his back, where the arrow was buried.

"You're going to be weakened from blood loss," I said, my voice a hollow shell.

"You almost sound dismayed at the idea."

"And you sound even less concerned than I am."

"It's not the first time I've been shot with an arrow, or fought with far graver injuries. Though, I can proudly say you're the only one who's ever managed to slit my throat."

I scowled, knowing what I needed to do if he was going to go fight a horde of bandits.

"Wreckless male."

Nakoa let out a grunt in time with the sickening sound of tearing flesh as I firmly yanked the arrow from his shoulder. An inch-wide hole gaped, followed by a steady gush of blood. I quickly sunk my fangs into the flesh at the underside of my forearm before pressing it to his mouth. Nakoa reared back in surprise for a moment.

"Hurry up."

Nakoa responded by gripping my forearm and holding it to his parted lips.

As he dragged in the first gulp, a low groan escaped him followed by a doubling of his efforts. My heart began to pound in my ears nearly as intensely as the throbbing, tingling pleasure started to build in my core.

Despite the arousal rising within me... I felt entirely numb to it... My mind and my emotions seemed to be drifting away from it. Observing and distant, my heart laid in torn, bleeding chunks on the ground at the idea I'd just thrown away my chance at freedom. The opportunity to escape and untether myself from the male who hated me and only wished to use me. That chance to run back to Malekai. Zurie be damned.

Nakoa had undoubtedly had enough by now after several gulps in. The gaping wound in his back was nothing more than an actively fading pink scar- but he was still drinking me in. The sound of his deep, rough groans between each swallow told me just how *not* numb he felt.

My eyes slid back to Nakoa's, now entirely black and locked onto me.

Even through his haze, he must have seen the stark despair of my expression because a moment later, he pulled back, grabbing me by the throat. I growled defiantly, his face hovering only inches from mine.

"Hold onto me, *lohane thili.*"

With my blood still coating his mouth, he swept me into his arms, and before I could react, his wings gave thunderous beats, lifting us into the air. I jerked back, watching the ground grow further and further away from our feet.

Oh fuck.

That snapped me of my daze.

My grip on him tightened so fiercely he grunted out a chuckle, voice lowering but becoming surprisingly tender. His gaze lowered to meet mine so I could feel the gravitas of his words. He spoke of so much more than just carrying me through the sky.

"I've got you. I can carry us both - I only need you to let me."

My throat tightened at his words, though I refused to be swayed by them. *Time* would reveal all. My heartbeat pounded frantically as we ascended over 100 feet in the air, simultaneously stealing the breath from my lungs. Pumpkin, little more than a speck beneath us, I could barely distinguish the barrier he'd willed around her.

So, he is capable of tenderness.

I imagined he didn't wish to risk her life unnecessarily by forcing her into whatever it was we were about to face with these bandits. If she was shot with an arrow, or otherwise wounded, she didn't have the healing abilities we had to heal.

Nakoa clutched me tightly to his chest and nuzzled my neck, taking my scent deeply.

Nakoa's wings pounded a furious rhythm through the air before we nosedived toward the ground, making me bury my face in his chest on instinct.

Heights had always been a weakness of mine.

Nakoa suddenly reared up and sent a tickling *whoosh* through my guts as we plummeted towards the ground. The scent of blood filled my nose. My gums throbbed and ached, fangs descending.

I dared a glance down in the fleeting seconds it took to descend, taking in the scene rushing towards us. There had to be at least 30 of them here.

Rayne and his shadowy beasts worked as a trio with graceful and vicious efficiency. Lokus wielded two swords severing through torso and limb with unparalleled effortlessness in a way that made it look like a dance. A performance. Famei, no longer in his griffon form, stood in place, looking not unlike an orchestra conductor, summoning roots from the ground that speared through, strangled, and tore apart bandits before they even came within 10 feet of him.

Pomona, usually disarmingly sweet and earnest, was apparently a fucking acrobat. She worked in tandem with a spear. Leaping, flipping, and spinning as she *folded* from one victim to the next, impaling them on a 6-foot spear with a double-edged blade that took up the last foot of its length - cutting clean through them.

In his lykos wolf form, Roderick devoured and tore through

bandits like a lion would a rabbit, snatching a bandit off the ground, tossing him high, and catching him 12 feet from the ground in mid-air to swallow him whole.

I unfurled from Nakoa's arms the moment our feet hit the ground at the edge of the battle. In the same instant, half a dozen males and females rushed forward before suddenly dropping to their knees clutching their throats as if they couldn't breathe.

Nakoa *willed* his broadsword into his hands and I watched as some surreal sense of déjà vu washed over me. The bandits before him struggled as he arched his sword through the air, and heads began to roll...

Something cracked in my chest as a thousand versions of myself on that dais in Zurie's enormous outdoor amphitheater performing executions passed before my eyes.

Oh gods.

A new set of bandits rushed towards Nakoa, snapping me out of my flashback. Terror shot bolts of electricity into my limbs at the sight of the male moving to drive his sword into Nakoa's back. With a speed unable to be witnessed by the human eye, I lunged forward and carved through the first of him and the ones following him.

At the next onslaught, I *willed* away my broadsword so that, at last, I could *feed*. My fangs pierced through flesh and tendon, like a scythe through wheat.

With each of them, I gulped down their blood in only a handful of gulps. My fingertips began to throb with a new sensation, and I glanced down, dropping a freshly drained corpse to the ground, to discover a set of lethal-looking black claws now protruding from my nail beds.

What in the fuck?

Power pulsed through my veins and everything around me seemed to slow down. I watched with awe and confusion as more bandits leapt towards me, blades and arrows raised, moving like through sludge. It seemed a wholly unfair advantage.

An entirely *new* advantage.

Despite this extraordinary gift, I had no idea how to control.

Time suddenly leapt back to normal, forcing me to dodge the new onslaught, twisting and gripping a female that I swiftly yanked flush against me and tore out her throat. I caught the next male rushing me by surprise as I willed my blade to return. The whites of his eyes stretched wide with shock as he impaled himself in his attempt to swing his own blade in a downward arch that left his diaphragm wide open for me.

Time pulsed in and out of normalcy, and I began to shift in a swift rhythm guided solely by instinct through each of the bandits until I was quite literally drenched in blood.

My eyes caught on an arrow sailing towards Pomona mid-leap and drew it out of thin air just before it sunk into her exposed throat.

Time leapt again and even as I continued to fly through the motions of nullifying those attacking us, my mind became distant. Everyone was distracted...

Escape, an unfamiliar voice whispered in my mind.

Perhaps I didn't have to kill Nakoa to do so...

Don't throw it away again, the voice urged me.

With surprisingly little effort, my claws pierced the chest of a remarkably large fae male, and I found my hand grasping his still-beating heart. Time slowed again as I brought it to my mouth. Its beat, nearly as loud as mine, echoed in time with that voice in my mind.

Go.

Go.

Go.

I'd already proven to myself *and Nakoa* that I wouldn't be able to kill him. But what were my options? Even outside of my selfish desperation to be free of him, if I were to stay, we would be chased by Zurie and her army to the ends of Atratus. *Nakoa* would be hunted. And fleeing Atratus for one of the other continents Hades, Ishra, or Maimyō mo Qì... Well, that promised all sorts of life-threatening danger.

CHIARA FORESTIERI

I could return to Bastrina and tell Zurie that his body had been reduced to ash during our battle, trapped in a burning building... Or perhaps taken away by a river... Sure, they all sounded a little far-fetched, but... She couldn't read minds. And clearly Miroslav didn't want him dead for some reason. Perhaps he would be willing to corroborate my story.

Guilt stabbed my chest as surely as Nakoa's blade had pierced the male before him.

This creature that paced restlessly inside me roared in protest as my logical mind tried to run through potential scenarios.

Zurie would be relentless in her pursuit of him if she thought that he was still alive. He was the leader of The Uprising, after all. Which is why I imagined she wanted him dead in the first place. And when she found out that *I* was with him, her efforts would double in her and her army's merciless hunt for us.

And Malekai...

Gods, Malekai...

It would surely be him she sent until she found someone to replace me as her Irae. And as ruthless as Malekai was... I knew his loyalty would be to me. Not only would Zurie be after Nakoa *and* me... Malekai would become her target as well.

I knew I would have to face Zurie's wrath returning to her without his body. Still, perhaps Miroslav would corroborate my story if I told her his body had been lost to a fire... If not... At least The Uprising wouldn't lose its leader, and Malekai would remain in Zurie's good graces. They would both live.

My eyes caught on Nakoa battling his way through the other side of the camp. He moved with an awe-inspiring, lethal grace that I'd only ever witnessed when I'd seen Malekai working his way across a battlefield.

There were very few bandits left. Nakoa and his *olana kah'hei* would undoubtedly come out victorious. And almost entirely unscathed.

I would not shut this window of opportunity on myself again.

Power electrified my veins as I sped through the forest, *willing* away the blood coating my body lest I leave any more of a scent trail for Nakoa to follow than I already would with my natural scent.

Bitterness clawed at the tattered remains of my heart as the realization hit me.

I had found my *soulbound,* a rare gift from *Akash.* For as long as my soul had silently yearned for such a thing, it was only fair that we were fated to be enemies. I had committed far too many sins to deserve such happiness. Destroyed too many families to find such priceless unity.

But how could my life have gone any differently?

Should I have remained in the streets?

Or remained at the Erosyan temple? To remain a victim?

The fact that I had Malekai... was a gift I may not deserve, but I refused to take it for granted.

Katadamna kaza.

CHAPTER
TWENTY-EIGHT
NAKOA

She left.

Within moments of killing the last of the bandits, a crushing sense of absence had settled on my chest like a fucking anvil. Mareina's magic, the palpably sweet yet fierce sensation of her life force energy... Had vanished like fucking smoke on the wind.

At first, I'd panicked, half expecting to turn and find her body prone and lifeless on the ground behind me.

Despite how much I despised my *soulbound,* relief filled me as I realized she'd merely tried to escape me... Just as a dark, twisted, sickened part of me had secretly hoped.

Wicked excitement electrified my veins, luring out a dark chuckle. Lokus looked over at me, piquing an eyebrow, as he cleaned off his twin blades. Both of us dripping in our enemies' blood. The rest of our *olana kah'hei* were busy searching the campground to loot any spoils.

"I can't determine whether or not you're actually pleased that your *soulbound* seems to have abandoned you."

Before I could reply, Pomona cleared her throat behind me.

"Koa... You might wanna come look at this."

Lokus and I exchanged a worried glance as we followed Pomona through the bandit's camp to a storage caravan with barred windows. Roderick, still in his lykos form, paced restlessly in front of it with blood still dripping from his grey and white fur. My ears perked at the sound of a furiously beating heart. Pomona pulled open the caravan door for the acrid stench of fear to crash over me.

My senses had become increasingly acute since I'd awoken with Mareina the previous day. And after the adrenaline rush of our little altercation and my drink of her blood, my strength, endurance, and magic had doubled.

I followed Pomona up the caravan's steps to find Rayne kneeling at the back beside a...

A *mimicryx.*

My breathing stilled at the sight of her.

They'd all been *exterminated* at the beginning of the war. Or so I thought. Deemed by Zurie too dangerous to let live when they, in their entirety, refused to join her war efforts. They could shift forms as effortlessly as I could *will* clothes on and off my body. Disguise themselves, their scents, their voices as other people with unerring accuracy.

My lips parted as I recognized the fucking *gift* that was so graciously kneeling before me.

Kismet, my Knowingness whispered.

A series of visions flashed before me, one right after the other.

Mareina stands in a white marble crypt, Zurie impaled on her sword.

Mareina and a blonde fae male laugh together as he draws near and caresses her cheek.

My chest heaves as I stand in front of a pyre of burning bodies on a battlefield. The scent of burning flesh is cloying, and it feels as though I'm already there.

A crone's gnarled hand presses a blade to my throat as she hovers above my face from where I lay wounded on a cot. Her voice is raspy and deep.

Her words feel like oil slicking over water as she spews them through a maw of blackened teeth.

"The blood of a Nephilim will do nicely."

The vision is ripped away like a curtain in front of a window. The glare of reality is both a relief because I'm not there and terrifying because I know it's only a matter of time before I am.

Now, with the mimicryx in front of me, it made Mareina's likelihood of killing Zurie and coming out unscathed and my *olana kah'hei* and I quelling her army that much more fathomable.

While my *olana kah'hei* is used to the effect these visions have on me.

The mimicryx was staring up at me with a look of wariness. She's gagged, bound, and already wearing a palladium collar to suppress her magic chained to a bolt on the floor. Her face hardened with anger and defiance despite the fear that poured off her in waves.

Whoever these bandits were, they hadn't been kind to her. She was filthy, her clothes torn and bloodstained, even though she bore no visible wounds. Thankfully, palladium collars didn't suppress the self-healing element of one's magic. I knew from personal experience.

I'd read that palladium was a metallic element from The Aeternian Realm. Supposedly, it had originally been used to oppress slaves. Frequently injured but always needing their strength and vigor, the palladium allowed them to still heal but kept the rest of their magic just out of reach.

The mimicryx's white, silvery hair was stringy and matted in parts. Dark circles rang her dark purple eyes. Blood streaked her lilac skin and hair. Two thick curling horns rose from the top of her head, only one of which ended in a wicked point. The other had been bluntly cut clean off at the half.

My chest gave a sympathetic twist. Not only had she survived being hunted down by Zurie's army, and likely *my soulbound*, but she had clearly suffered at the hands of these bandits and gods-knew-who or what else. Used and manipulated for her gifts and mutilated one of her horns when she tried to refuse.

It was well known that the horns of any being possessing them were a point of pride and beauty. A broken horn was seen as a sign of weakness and brought tremendous shame.

I couldn't help but notice the fire burning in Rayne's eyes as he looked up at me. Not directed at me but at the sight of her suffering.

I tried to soften my voice as best I could, as though speaking to a frightened, wounded animal.

"I have no desire or intention of bringing you harm..."

Her jaw flexed as she bit into the cloth of her gag that Rayne was untying.

"You cannot imagine how many times I've heard that," she spat, stretching her jaw and licking her lips before a scowl quickly hardened what were otherwise soft, delicate features.

She seemed surprised when Rayne removed the chains binding her at the wrists and ankles. She rose to shaky feet, trying to pull at her torn clothing to adequately cover her mostly exposed body.

Rayne promptly *willed* his cloak into his hands, draping it over her shoulders. The sight of her expression hardening further with distrust reminded me of Mareina.

And the fact that *my little nightmare* was getting further and further away with each passing second.

A thrill went through me in anticipation of hunting her down. Nearly bursting at the seams to do so, but first...

I nodded at the mimicryx in understanding.

"I'm sorry to hear that. Genuinely."

She scowled impatiently, rubbing her sore wrists.

"But?"

Admittedly, a tiny pang of guilt went through me. Indeed, I did have my own ends to meet. Though it would ultimately be in her best interests.

All of our best interests.

"Do you have a home to return to?"

Her brows pinched tightly, almost sneering. Even though Mareina was likely one of Zurie's soldiers who'd hunted her down and killed many of her loved ones. Yet they had an extraordinary amount in common. Both from tragic, haunting pasts and hardened to distrust at even a gentle hand or a kind word.

"No," she answered flatly.

Judging by the possessive energy radiating from Rayne, he certainly wouldn't mind if she joined our family. The rest of them would likely welcome her as well. Especially if my Knowingness was correct in what it whispered to me about her and Rayne.

"I'd like to make you an offer—

"Pass."

Rayne reached to remove her collar, making her flinch when his skin touched hers. Their eyes met, and her lips parted briefly before her jaw snapped shut again. Rayne hesitated briefly before pulling the collar free from her throat with a tap of his magic. Her eyes slipped shut briefly as she rubbed her neck, her gifts no doubt coursing through as they returned. My heart swelled with empathy.

I know that feeling.

Her eyes narrowed with suspicion, alighting between each of us. Still, her expression had softened when we'd returned her magic to her.

"Being alone will make you vulnerable... I'd like to invite you to stay with us."

She knew better than anyone just how true my words were. It would only be a matter of time before she was caught again.

"And who are you exactly?"

I introduced myself, gesturing towards each of my *olana kah'hei*, taking the liberty to do the same for them.

"And you?"

She studied me warily for several moments.

"Vesper... And what exactly do you gain from this?"

"Another family member..."

She gave a derisive snort. "And what does this *offer* entail?"

I took a deep breath... I obviously hadn't had a chance to speak with my *olana kah'hei* about it yet, but... We didn't have any other options.

"While we do need your help with something... We will take care of you and reward you handsomely. And after all is resolved, should you wish to stay with us, you will become part of our family. We all live... outside the bounds of normal society..."

I reached out with a question to my Knowingness.

I thanked *Akash* it gave me the response I'd hoped for.

"... We are... members of The Uprising. Founding members..."

Her expression shifted subtly, and her interest suddenly piqued.

"... We're loyal to the death and take care of one another, and it would be no different for you..."

Vesper held my gaze for several moments before shifting to Lokus, Famei, Pomona, and Rayne... Where her gaze lingered for several tense beats.

"Sounds a little too good to be true... I imagine this favor is something that entails a bit of masquerading..."

A grin tipped up the corner of my mouth.

"A bit..."

"And whom, may I ask, would I be impersonating?"

"Me... Or my corpse, rather... And the Queen."

Rayne's gaze snapped to mine, jaw flexing, already having sussed out where I was going with this.

Vesper huffed a laugh in disbelief.

"What?"

"Don't worry, you don't have to be entombed or anything. And you'll be accompanied—

Vesper waved her hand dismissively, heaving a great sigh.

"Look, before we get into the dramatics and minutiae of this *favor*... I need to fucking eat and drink something. Does anyone have any food or water?"

Rayne *willed* a flask into his hand, offering it to her. Her lilac cheeks darkened as she murmured a nearly inaudible thank you and proceeded to guzzle the entire thing whilst Rayne finally spoke for the first time today, making our brows lift.

"Famei... Would you be so kind?" He rumbled, his voice hoarse from disuse.

"Gladly," Famei nodded in reply before returning outside the carriage.

"We'll stay here tonight... I have to... Run an errand, but I'll be back by morning... You're in good hands. If you need anything, speak with Rayne."

Rayne's eyes widened almost imperceptibly and leapt to meet mine. For the first time in the century we'd known each other, I could factually say this was the first fucking time I'd ever seen Rayne Umbraborne blush.

My lips pressed together in a meager attempt to stifle a grin.

"Pomona, would you *fold* and fetch Pumpkin for me? She's just inside the forest on the other side of the road we were travelling..."

"Good luck with your *errand*," she snickered before disappearing.

Lokus gave me a knowing smirk as my blood roared with excitement.

My conniving little nightmare was going to fucking pay.

CHAPTER
TWENTY-NINE

MAREINA

I ran for miles through The Sentient Forest, not daring to travel on the open road, even if it was far less dangerous. Only stopping when I reached a river that promised to be treacherous to cross if its tumultuous current and jutting, sharp boulders were anything to go by.

Fuck.

I had no idea how potent Nakoa's sense of smell was... Generally, a fae's sense of smell was greatly heightened compared to a human's, but...

Would he be able to smell my scent lingering in the forest?

How good was he at tracking?

Should I risk the river to mask my scent and avoid leaving footsteps?

Intuition told me the answer to all of these questions was yes.

Fuck me.

The sun was setting, and I knew I would need to find cover soon lest I attract one of the innumerable apex predators or the few rogue entities that roamed this forest at night.

My heart thumped a steady pounding beat as I worked up the courage to leap. I knew that, worst case scenario, I wouldn't *die* from it... But there was a whole lot that laid between the space of life and death, and pain was pain, no matter how immortal. And being repeatedly smashed against boulders by a torrential current until you were washed up on a shore *Akash* knew where and waited for your broken bones to heal would be fucking excruciating. It would also make me incredibly vulnerable. And if someone came upon me... Well... There were a great many things they could do, most of which ended in death.

How was I supposed to defend myself if all my bones were shattered? It would likely take me hours to fully heal from something like that.

It was entirely too late to curse myself for not thinking this through. I'd faced insane odds serving in the war, on numerous battlefields, and even after as Zurie's Irae...

But I'd been raised in a city. I only had the most basic of survival skills when it came to enduring *the wild*. Nature had always been something that I'd stood in awe of from a healthy and escapable distance.

A low, inhuman growl sounded behind me, raising the hair on my arms and neck. I turned to find a pair of large glowing yellow eyes and a row of razor-sharp teeth belonging to a rather hungry-looking *cor na tir* only a few meters away, which basically looked like a giant cat mated with a horse-sized dragon. Drool dripped from its jagged maw- each fang the length of my forearm.

River, it is.

I leapt forward at the same moment as the *cor na tir*. One of its giant paws lashed out. The tips of its claws only grazed me, but that still meant I now had three gaping wounds shredding the entire span of my back.

Rushing ice-cold water swallowed me in one giant gulp, lungs and limbs burning, and I could only pray that it would be kind enough to spit me out whole. Within moments, the river *rudely* revealed that wouldn't be the case by slamming me into a jagged, broken tree branch that punctured my side before it snapped off, still embedded in my flesh as the current took me away.

My lungs burned with the need for air, and I managed to break the surface for only a fleeting moment, gasping, before it pulled me back under and promptly smashed me into a boulder.

It didn't take long before consciousness began to flee me.

Followed by a dizzying swell of gratitude, fear, guilt, and remorse. At least I wouldn't have to endure *all* of this. In those last moments, still capable of forming thoughts, I wished so badly that I could feel Malekai's arms embrace me. Press my cheek to his chest and revel in the sound of his beating heart that seemed to beat a loving rhythm just for me.

That I could somehow hold him and freeze, or slow time like it had earlier so I could finally rest in his arms. Hide there forever, safe and warm, so I wouldn't have to fight any longer.

For the first 20-plus years of my life, I'd been a victim. And I'd spent the last 90 years ensuring that I was no longer vulnerable by turning others into victims. Either way, I had always been at war with everyone and everything around me except Malekai. Even my own *soulbound*.

As everything finally went dark, I sent a prayer to Akash that he would be ok. That he knew how much I loved him. And a small, distant part of me wished that... Perhaps things between Nakoa and I could have been different.

CHAPTER

THIRTY

MAREINA

Some indeterminable amount of time later, my consciousness wavered distantly. Though I recognized no sense of self or reality - it felt as though every bone in my body had been shattered. A rasping, rattling, wet noise filled my ears, rousing more of my consciousness enough until I realized the sound was coming from *me*, and a scorching pain radiating from my side reached the surface of my mind. My lung was punctured. Alarm bells distantly went off in my mind as several hands gripped each of my limbs. Unfathomable pain tore from my throat, now raw from coughing up more water than any pair of lungs could ever possibly hold. I tried to open my eyes, but I realized I couldn't. They were swollen shut, likely from my face being smashed into countless boulders.

My consciousness dissipated again until my equilibrium soared and whirled like a spinning top, likely from a severe concussion, as those rough hands lifted me, and my ass came down hard into a chair. It felt like electricity scorched every nerve ending in my body, muscles spasming as my broken and torn body conformed to the seat that I could only slump forward in. Consciousness nearly escaped me again, but the sensation of coarse rope came around each of my ankles as my hands, sending more wailing bells of alarm to go off in my mind.

The sound of several unfamiliar voices murmuring in aggressive tones had my head spinning further, gradually settling like motes of dust as I felt the unmistakable and excruciating sensation of my body knitting itself together.

I dared to feel a tiny glimmer of hope at the speed with which my body was healing... My mind began to settle, and eventually, I could make sense of the noise around me, picking up on their words.

"... *She's The Royal Irae...*"

"... *We should send her back in pieces... Send a message to Zurie.*"

"... *Embolden The Uprising.*"

Reality began to settle on me like a boulder.

Perhaps I should have taken my chances with the *cor na tir*.

And fuck, if it didn't hurt that these males were part of Nakoa's Uprising.

Would he condone such a thing if I weren't his soulbound?

I couldn't answer that for sure... And I couldn't blame him if he would...

"She's healing pretty fast... We need to get a palladium collar on her before she's conscious again..."

Heavy footsteps rushed away, and I held my breath, waiting to see what they'd do next.

The curve of a finger drew up the side of my fighting leathers, around the curve of my breast. Rage boiled within me, incidentally helping to block out a tiny bit of the physical pain.

"She's prettier than I remember... Even if she is a little banged up."

One of the males chuckled.

"I vote we have some fun with her..."

My heart stalled in my chest before it began to pound so loudly it echoed in my ears.

"Heard she grew up at The Erosyan Temple... I bet she knows how to properly please a male."

My heart kicked up, pounding in both fury and dread.

No.

Never again.

In unison, three rough hums of pleasure sounded beside me in agreement.

Another chuckle sounded, followed by the scrape of metal against stone. In the next moment, icy water sloshed over me, forcing me to take a sharp, gasping breath that renewed a fit of coughing and the searing agony in my side.

Having healed enough to open my eyes, my vision swam as three males stood before me. Two fae and one sanguinati. All three were built with lean muscle - *too lean*- and had a hungry look in their eyes. Their clothes looked worn, their hair unkempt. I would have said it looked like they'd seen better days, but they probably hadn't.

And I knew that I had something to do with it.

The sanguinati, fangs already descended, bent forward, curling a finger beneath my chin to lift my head up, sending more pain shooting through my spine. Blessedly, it was not nearly as bad as it had been only minutes ago.

"Hello, traitor," he purred, a malevolent glint in his pale blue eyes.

I gave a mirthless, bleary chuckle. He wasn't wrong. Zurie had oppressed the sanguinati more than most species of wielders. She ruled, blinded by fear and greed- anyone potentially more powerful than her felt the brunt of her wrath. Though she'd needed us during the war and had bribed us with the chance to escape poverty by joining her revered army. And many of those who didn't, she executed.

"Hello," I grinned, fangs lengthening.

His confidence and twisted grin faltered as he recognized the predator within me rising to the surface. The sound of rushing footsteps came from behind me just as I lunged forward, ropes snapping, and dove for his throat just as a collar came around my neck and yanked me backwards, slamming me to the ground.

The sanguinati's face poured blood as his lips thinned, bringing a hand to his shredded cheek. The collar around my neck pulled tight, dragging me backwards against the grimy stone floor, and fear speared through me when I attempted to *will* it away, and my magic remained just out of grasp.

"Put her in the fucking shackles," the sanguinati snapped at the men beside me. I twisted around to jump to my feet, but before I could, the palladium collar around my neck - connected to a thick chain - yanked hard again, slamming me back to the ground and driving that gods-forsaken branch deeper into my side. My throat opened with a gasp from the mind-numbing pain as I was rendered powerless to the explosive coughs wracking my body, blood splattering on the grey stone floor in front of me. The chain connected to the collar lifted, pulled taut through a metal hook fixed to the stone ceiling, dragging me *up, up, up* with it.

My hands gripped at the collar, wringing my neck before they attempted to force them back down to shackle my wrists. I kicked out with my legs at the fae male, crushing my wrists with his grip and sending him flying into a wall. The sound of his ribs cracking would have been deeply satisfying if it weren't for the animalistic fury burning through me.

The all-too-familiar sensation of a blade cutting through flesh and bone had a cry tearing through my throat. Or at least attempting to. Instead, it was merely the sound of gurgled blood that came out.

My body sagged, and their hands came around my wrists and ankles again, shackling them. The shackles at my wrists were affixed to the ceiling, taking off most of the pressure around my neck, whilst the shackles around my ankles were bolted to the stone floor.

The sanguinati, who appeared to be their leader, approached me. The wound on his cheek was now reduced to a gash.

"You fucking cunt," he spat. His open palm came down on my face, so hard stars burst through my vision. "You're going to pay for that."

He *willed* a blade into his hand, pointing it at the center of my chest; his confidence and malevolent delight returned in full force now that I was effectively restrained and choking on my own blood.

As the sanguinati examined me, strung up before him, he noticed the inch-thick branch jutting from my side and wiggled it. My blood splattered his face as I continued hacking and choking. He licked his lips clean of my bloody spittle.

"Delicious... but distracting."

Without warning, the sanguinati gripped the stub of the branch jutting out from just beneath my ribs and yanked it out.

He watched me with a blank expression as he waited for my body's violent attempts to clear my lungs of blood to cease as they healed.

When I could finally breathe again, mere minutes later, he gave a sadistic chuckle. "Hmmm... Where should I begin?"

His eyes travelled up and down the length of my body for several moments, like he was trying to decide which cut of meat he preferred.

"Or should I say *we?*" He added smugly.

The males around us chuckled.

My face remained impassive as a familiar numbness returned that had nothing to do with my current state of blood loss and everything to do with the trauma I'd experienced at the hands of males in my youth.

The sanguinati's hand settled at my breasts before he slowly drew the blade through the front of my fighting leathers. The two panels parted, freeing my breasts. My stomach churned at the sight of his pupils dilating and the scent of his arousal. I fucking *wished* that I would vomit on him.

Instead, my body trembled fruitlessly as it grew cold with a familiar resignation that most anyone who had ever been rendered utterly powerless knew intimately.

After all I've done, perhaps this is what I deserve.

My eyes slid shut at the thought, and the sanguinati gave

another throaty chuckle. My heart was pounding so loudly in my chest that it muffled his words.

"Ah, ah, ahhh...," he warned, pressing into the bottom of my jaw with his dagger, "You either cooperate and keep your eyes open and watch, or I cut your eyelids off and force you."

My eyes gradually opened to meet his as cold fingers cupped one of my breasts and gave it a hefty jiggle before pinching my nipple.

"These look like a *lovely* place to start."

He breathed in deep as he brought his face down to one of my breasts. His tongue slithered out to give my nipple a teasing lick that made me want to fucking impale myself on a blade just so I wouldn't have to endure this.

My jaw clenched furiously, my heart fighting so hard against my ribs as though it might actually have a chance of escape.

Not again. Not again. Not again.

Please just kill me now.

Not again.

His grin widened at the sight of tears swelling in my eyes.

"None of that, pet... You don't get to cry. How many people have *you* slaughtered despite the tears in their eyes, hm? I bet you've lost count."

Admittedly, the male's logic was faultless.

The sanguinati groaned, burying his face in my breasts as his hands came around to grip my ass and pull my body flush against his. The other fae males watched on in rapt silence. The scent of their arousal cloying. His fangs pressed in slowly against my breast as though he were savoring every sick moment of this, groaning loudly in the back of his throat as they sank in and he began to drink. He ground his hips against me, his cock along with it. Adrenaline pounded through me, blessedly and instantly, dissolving any effects his venom would have had on me.

Tears slipped down my cheek as I strained against the wrought iron shackles in futility.

The sanguinati suddenly reared back, tearing at the laces of my fighting leather trousers. "I'm going to fuck you raw," he promised hoarsely.

He yanked my trousers down to mid-thigh - as far as they would go with the way I was shackled - and promptly began to unbuckle his own. A long, thin, veiny cock sprang free that he gave a few presumptive pumps. I squeezed my eyes shut as bile crawled up my throat.

As if summoned by my plea for forgiveness, the sound of metal groaning drew our attention to the door on the opposite end of the room.

The sanguinati swiftly tucked himself away as he cursed and began to bark orders to his comrades, who all drew their swords. The sanguinati *willed* a broadsword into his hands and levelled it at my throat as they waited for whatever was about to come barrelling through that door.

Hope burst, sharp and potent, as I felt a fierce tug in my chest just before the iron door went flying off the hinges, crushing the male nearest beneath it.

A towering dark figure stood in the door frame as thunder cracked and lightning illuminated the torrential sky behind him.

THIRTY-ONE

NAKOA

My wings held me aloft a turbulent river where Mareina's night-blooming rose scent abruptly disappeared. The sun had already halfway set, and in less than an hour, The Sentient Forest was consumed by darkness.

How the fuck did she even make it this far?

Sanguinati were fast, but this... It had only been perhaps a twenty-minute head start that I'd given her.

She is not as she seems. Her power strengthens, my Knowingness had whispered.

United, your power will be indomitable.

Its words didn't surprise me... My power had increased exponentially since Mareina and I had met. We would be unstoppable once we'd fulfilled our bond.

I searched my Knowingness for guidance as to where Mareina had gone.

Follow the river.

Obviously, I'd snarled back inwardly at its vague reply.

The scent of ozone had drifted to me, and I'd turned to discover dark storm clouds looming in the distance.

Fuck...

Fuck.

Fuck.

Fuck.

My wings pounded through the air, propelling me forward, flying just above the tree line, as my eyes scanned the river and everything in its vicinity.

Mile after mile passed, my anxiety soaring higher than I ever had as Mareina remained nowhere to be found. By the time the sun finally finished its descent and Atratus' moons illuminated the sky, I was on the verge of full-blown panic - tremors and all.

Despite how much I detested this female.

When I passed the fifth town, I considered doubling back to see if somehow, too gripped by panic, I'd missed her, but my Knowingness urged me on.

Scents of all kinds reached me - hundreds of them - yet none of them *hers.*

Thunder rumbled as dense, ominous clouds blotted out the moons above. I could only *pray* I wouldn't be among the things the approaching lightning chose to strike.

With a silent prayer on the tip of my tongue to *Akash* and all the gods that served her, I resorted to begging.

Please. Please let me find my soulbound.

Guilt weighed heavily on my winged shoulders that I'd spent our only days together spewing hatred at her and trying to manipulate her.

The pace of my wings slowed as if urged by some unknowable guidance. I lowered and continued beyond a small marina where the river's mouth gaped, and the current slowed.

Finally, hope flared like an explosion in my chest in time with a flicker of life through our tether. Mareina's scent reached out to me like a beckoning hand. I dove, landing on the landing bay of the riverbank so hard it cracked the cobblestones.

The scent of her blood in the air had my blood turning to ice. Only thawed by my fiery rage.

The skies began to weep as I sprinted down road after road until I found myself in a filthy alleyway replete with refuse and scurrying rats. The skies chose that precise moment to open up, turning the rain into a deluge and stealing the last of her scent.

Muffled by the pounding storm, my ears pricked at the sound of voices... There were too many of them, and still, none of them belonged to Mareina.

Pulling at our tether again drew me towards a dark set of stairs towards the end of the alley. Several males stood beneath an over-hang that kept them out of the rain. The group of them did a double take at the sight of me stalking towards them.

As much as I wanted to relish in the satisfaction of ending them with fist and blade, I knew I didn't have the time. Mareina didn't have the time. I *willed* my magic forward to take hold of the blood in their veins. I increased the pressure in every vessel and organ in their bodies until blood wept from every orifice. It was the work of a moment for them to collapse dead.

I descended the steps to the basement door, reaching out with my senses, feeling each of their heartbeats, including Mareina's, which beat a furious pace. My magic poured from me, and the iron door in front of me groaned, denting and caving in as I pressed onto it with intensifying gravity.

Shouts rose up on the other side. The moment the door's bolt warped, I push kicked it open. The hinges flew, sending the iron surface flying across the room, crushing a male beneath it on the floor.

And now...

Rage and horror, unlike anything I'd ever experienced, consumed me as my mind registered the sight of Mareina hanging in shackles, her precious body bared to the males surrounding her. One of the males, a sanguinati, levelled a broadsword at her neck.

I recognized him. These males were a part of my Uprising... How many of its members participated or idly allowed such unforgivable behaviour?

"I'll remove her head from—

The male's words cut off abruptly as I *willed* the air from their lungs. Their brains barely had time to register that they were suffocating before I sped into the room, cleaving my blade through each of their bodies so swiftly it was a blur.

I rushed to Mareina's side, *willing* away the shackles and palladium collar from her body and clutching her in my arms.

My hands shook as she crumpled against me. Relief at her scent still being unsullied washed over me so fiercely my knees nearly buckled.

"Mareina," I croaked, burying my face in her neck and deeply taking in her scent to assure myself she was here.

That she was alive.

Her only response was the sob that wracked her body.

Cradling her tightly against my chest, I walked out of that *Akash*-forsaken basement into the pouring rain as I *willed* that building to burn to the fucking ground.

THIRTY-TWO

MAREINA

An orange glow illuminated the town, now far behind us, from where Nakoa had set that building ablaze.

I felt an urge to tell him that the males who had taken me were a part of his Uprising but I couldn't muster the energy just yet.

My body trembled in his arms as my thoughts sunk back into my haunted past, both recent and distant. Nakoa clutched me harder against him, pressing a kiss to my forehead.

"I'm here, lohane thili. I will always be here."

Despite our animosities, his words soothed my tremors in mere moments.

I silently wept tears of gratitude that I was in Nakoa's arms. Held protectively against his chest as he walked - waiting for the monsoon to calm before he could fly again, lest we get struck by lightning - for what felt like an hour in the pouring rain. He'd put a barrier around us, but I'd asked him for the rain. I needed to feel the rain. To feel it wash away the touch of the males in that basement. Cleanse me of the memory, the fear, the heartbreak.

By the time we arrived at the next village, I'd fallen asleep in his arms. The sound of minstrels playing music in the distance roused me. I opened my eyes to find us approaching a large inn that sat alone at the edge of the road amidst undulating hills where the silhouettes of hoofed animals could be seen in the distance, illuminated by the moons' light now that the storm clouds had cleared.

A sign hung above the inn's hitching post that read *The Gorgon's Haven Inn & Tavern*. A few of its patrons stumbled out, singing and laughing as we approached, holding the door open for us.

"You can put me down now...," I offered, not wanting to attract more attention than necessary.

Nakoa merely growled in reply, clutching me tighter against his chest. A sound that I now found a deep comfort in.

Nakoa approached the tavern's bar, unconcerned with the odd glances thrown our way. The music, soft and poignant, boasted a human female's voice. Clear and crisp as a bell rang, she sang lyrics that sounded like a spell.

A tapestry woven with threads of pain,
Let love's redemption begin to reign.
The burdens of yore laid to rest.

Through the echoes of thunder, secrets unfold,
A tale of courage, of a love untold.
A guardian in the pouring rain,
Carrying through joy and pain.

In the embrace, a sanctuary found,
Love's tender grace on sacred ground.
Through the shadows, a forbidden chance.

Forgiveness blooms in the rain-soaked night,
Healing whispers and ginger touches,

Making love and taking flight.
Past sins washed away in the heart's cascade,
In the warmth of love, where all fears fade.

Nakoa turned us to face the singer and her minstrels boasting stringed instruments: a mandolin, lute, and harp. The entire audience, only a handful of people - an orc, a dryad, a few elven, and a fae...

A sensation of rightness settled over me, and I know Nakoa felt it too, as if the stars had aligned, and this was precisely where we were supposed to be.

Along with a sensation of deep longing that I had buried away a century ago.

The desire to sing.

It had been years since I had sung for anyone... A sense of... Knowingness filled me that I would survive this.

And that one day, I might be able to finally put away my sword and sing.

A female with dark green skin and long braids that I quickly realized were snakes appeared beside us dressed in a chiton, looking surprisingly elegant, considering we were in the middle of nowhere.

Her voice was deep and soothing and, somehow, *familiar*... Though I knew not from where.

"Are you in need of lodging?"

"Yes, please... Can we also have a bathing tub and hot water sent in, please?" Nakoa asked for us.

She gave us a warm smile. "The baths here are thermal. We have one in every room... Would you like me to send in dinner?"

"Yes, thank you."

The gorgon gestured for us to follow. She seemed to glide away as we trailed behind her. Something felt blessedly different and yet vaguely familiar about this place.

The room was simple but elegant and warm. A large, fluffy pallet of furs sat on a dais in the center of the room, just in front of a fireplace which flared to life the moment we entered. Steam curled from the surface of a large thermal bath at the corner of the room. Candles, bathing oils, and soaps lined the edge, along with a set of linen towels.

"There's an enchanted bell beside your bed if you require... *anything* else." She gave us a pointed, knowing look as though she knew some secret we'd yet to discover.

Nakoa and I thanked her, feeling a little taken aback by her and her tavern. As soon as the door shut behind her, two covered trays of food appeared on a small table against the wall.

"Bath or bed?" Nakoa asked.

"Bath, please."

I *willed* away my shredded fighting leathers, and Nakoa his a moment later, just before descending the steps into the thermal bath. As soon as he sat back on the stone seat beneath the water, dual groans left our throats. Every rigid muscle in our bodies relaxed.

A long silence passed between us; only the sound of the crackling fire filled the room. I'd spent the last few hours with my face buried in his chest, and now that it wasn't... I mourned its absence.

After what I had just survived, thanks to *him*, I would allow myself this comfort. The comfort of my *soulbound*. No matter how brief it was destined to last.

I took a deep breath, trying to ease the pang of nervousness before I shifted in Nakoa's arms to straddle his lap, keeping my face buried in his neck.

The tether between us throbbed painfully, and I felt some innate need to soothe it... And to show Nakoa with more than words, I was grateful he set aside his hatred for me to come find me. Even though I'd abandoned him. That he'd risked his life to save me.

I reached for the soap, lathering it in my hands before massaging it into his scalp. A metaphorical olive branch to declare a truce.

Peace.

A soft groan left him as his eyes slipped shut. Though his brow remained pinched. After rinsing his hair, he opened his eyes to watch as I lathered the loofah and scrub his body. Nakoa's head tilted back, something wounded evident in his gaze.

"Thank you, Nakoa...," I murmured gently.

He studied me silently for a few moments before he straightened, removing the soap and loofah from my hands to pull me against him as he drew in a shuddering breath. His tail snaked around my waist, curling tight.

"Mareina, I—

Nakoa took in another shuddering breath to quell his emotion before continuing.

"... Words cannot describe the terror I felt when I realized that something might have happened to you."

Emotion seared my eyes, and I bit my cheek so hard I bled in my attempt to keep my voice steady.

"And when I saw you--

Nakoa's grip on me tightened, his fingers digging in so firmly it would leave bruises. Arms trembling with barely held restraint.

"For a moment, I thought that... That they had—

I pulled back, cradling his head in my hands so I could hold his gaze. Reassure him.

"They didn't... They didn't get a chance to because you came for me."

Nakoa's brow pinched, his jaw working furiously as his glittering tears finally spilled.

"I will always come for you, Mareina. I will always be there to save you. Whether you wanted me to or not, I would crawl on hands and knees through the fires and chasms of every hell to save you."

My gaze scoured his, searching for the veracity in his words. Though I couldn't help but doubt... If it was merely because the bond compelled him to or because of his machinations. If those were the sole reasons... Something in my already withered heart wilted at the idea.

"I want you to tell me the truth, Nakoa... I know you desire and care for me because the bond demands it, but I also can *feel* there is something else. Some other end to meet..."

I could see the indecision warring behind his eyes. The petals of my heart that had begun to blossom curled shut.

A wave of emotion crested like the swell of a tidal wave threatening obliteration. Is that why he'd saved me? Because of some fucking bond we had no choice but to submit to, and whatever other manipulations he'd been hiding from me?

The reckless, wounded, savage part of me lamented that he had even come. That he hadn't just left me there to die. Just when I thought that perhaps that...

A growl tore from my lips as I drew myself away and out of the bathing pool. Water sloshed, and Nakoa's tail drug me back in to fall back into his arms.

"Mareina—

I stood, shoving him back so fiercely his big body stumbled, bouncing off the side of the bathing pool.

"Thank you, Nakoa. You've done your *soulbound* duty. Now allow me to liberate you from any further obligation. I will give you *one* opportunity. *One.* To be honest with me and tell me what the fuck it is you want with me outside of whatever gods-forsaken uncontrollable *urges* this cursed bond demands."

Nakoa opened his mouth to speak, but I cut him off by pressing my blade to his throat as I pressed in close to him.

"Truth, Nakoa Solanis. The *full* truth, or I swear to *Akash* I won't waste another opportunity to carve your fucking heart from your chest."

Nakoa searched my gaze for a moment, his features hardening.

"The bond. I need the bond fulfilled, so we both have enough power to overcome Zurie and her army. My visions have shown me repeatedly that *you* are to be the one to kill Zurie."

Icy shock doused me like a bucket of cold water.

Even though a part of me had already suspected... intuitively *known*... that it would be something like this... It didn't soften the blow. The words were like a knife slamming to the hilt in some already wounded, fleshy part of me.

Of course.

This is what you deserve, that familiar, guilt-riddled, insidious part of me whispered.

A defeated breath left me as I let my head sag to his chest, and I removed the blade from his throat.

His sharp grunt of pain twisted into a growl as I plunged my blade into the meat of his thigh.

"The only reason my blade is in your leg and not in your heart is because you saved my life. Consider the debt repaid. And do *not* follow me."

Nakoa's tail coiled impossibly tight around my waist.

"Remove your tail or I cut it off," I seethed, yanking the blade from his thigh.

He gave a maniacal laugh. "If you think a little mutilation would deter me, you're sorely mistaken."

Despite his words, his hand lashed out, snatching my wrist before I could make good on my word.

"Mareina, please... Just listen to me."

His tail uncoiled from around me, raising his hands pleadingly.

"To what? More lies? More manipulation?"

"You and I both know you don't wanna go back to being Zurie's pawn..."

The words were like his own blade, twisting in a century-old wound.

That was an inevitable truth that I had no idea how to acknowledge.

Something had irrevocably changed in me. And willing stepping into her shackles was... Not an option. With or without Nakoa's corpse, she would hunt me down if I didn't return to her. I'd be on the run for the rest of my life, and she would continue destroying Atratus and its people.

I wanted her dead nearly as much as I wanted to get back to Malekai.

Nakoa could no doubt *feel* my turmoil through our tether.

"Join me, Mareina..."

"Join you, how?"

"Help me overthrow Zurie. Join The Uprising. Fulfill the bond... *We will not fail.* I have seen it. My visions are never wrong."

Miroslav... This is what he had seen.

That strange voice... That inner Knowing whispered its confirmation to me, urging me forward on this path beside Nakoa. The idea of being shackled to this male *forever* was fucking soul-crushing.

Which is worse? Zurie or Nakoa?

I scowled at the answer.

A tiny spark of hope flickered... Nakoa hated me... Perhaps after... *if* we succeeded... Perhaps he would let me go. Perhaps after the bond was fulfilled, we wouldn't be so consumed by this *need*.

"*If* I join you... After I kill Zurie... You will let me go."

Nakoa's face slackened briefly before hardening, and his familiar, mocking cruelty returned.

"You can try to run as far as your heart can take you, but no one will ever be able to fill that longing you have for me in your soul. Not even your pretty fae warrior."

CHAPTER

THIRTY-THREE

NAKOA

Mareina's lips parted in shock before her features hardened into something that promised violence... Faster than she could conjure a venomous response, I closed the distance between us, fisting her hair in my hand. Her entire *being* was an all-consuming force that beckoned me. Demanded me to claim her. The bond demanded it. As if her soul was seeking a way to return to mine, its other half.

"I have spent a lifetime *haunted* by you. *Aching* for you no matter how I tried to run from you. No matter how many pretty faces or cunts I tried to lose myself in, I could never free myself from you. And now that I've finally tasted you, I wouldn't want it any other way. So hate me as much as you want, *lohane thili,* but I will *never* let you go."

Rage and anguish mingled in the shadows of her gaze.

I'd felt the pain tear through her chest when I admitted my manipulation...And now I could sense that pain mingling with fury. Standing this close to her, I could feel it as though it were my own.

The hairs on the back of my neck rose as a vision of the future seeped onto the canvas of the present.

Mareina's gaze hardened. Her wet, nude form standing in the bathing

241

pool momentarily shifted to dry and clothed in a darkest red silk dress. The bathing pool was replaced with a large bedroom, and a flaming hearth behind her cast her in a dark shadow. Her voice, both present and future, layered one over the other. The effect served to double its vehemence and the violence it promised. Her eyes glowed with menace.

"You will let me go, or you will wish for death."

My grip on her hair loosened as my anger evaporated along with the vision. Swiftly replaced by a hollow feeling in my gut.

I managed a sad, mirthless laugh. "I have no doubt, *maha mo'ina li'ili.*"

She reared back in confusion.

Shit. She had only spoken those words in the future.

I was... Losing my grip on reality.

I cleared my throat, shaking my head as I stepped back from her. "Nothing... Just..."

I looked up to find understanding had already dawned on her face. I didn't bother finishing the sentence.

The sudden look of compassion on her face just about broke me. She knew I was losing my mind.

Before I could say more, she turned and hauled herself out of the bathing pool with feline grace. Wariness had my muscles tightening as if readying for another chase.

"Where are you going?"

She didn't bother looking back as she *willed* her body dry. My cock, along with every other part of me, ached at the sight of her. Lush and soft yet firm in all the right places.

"I have a feeling our host can officiate our vows."

Despite how many times it had happened, it never failed to shock me when my visions began to unfold into reality. Her words were laced with grim resignation, but the tension in my body still slackened. My heart leapt. Both at my own selfish need - the ever-increasing desire for *her* - *and* my endeavor to overthrow Zurie and liberate the Kahlohani Islands and its people.

Mareina *willed* her fighting leathers over her body before she reached for the bell beside the bed.

"*Well?*" She asked impatiently, scowling at my nude form, still submerged in the pool.

I leapt out of the water, sloshing water all over the floor, and stood in front of her, dried and dressed in a matter of moments, staring down at her with an intensifying heat that she refused to surrender to.

The hours I'd spent walking in the rain, Mareina clutched tightly in my arms against me, praising *Akash* that Mareina was safe and had been relatively unharmed, had done little to assuage the tension in my mind and my body - my soul - at just how closely I'd come to losing her... Least of all, because of my endeavors. It was in those moments that I'd finally allowed myself to admit that she was the most essential thing in the realm to me and a vital part of my existence.

Whether that was because the bond demanded it, I didn't actually care. Just because my blood demanded oxygen didn't make me question my gratitude for air.

I'd been gifted first-hand with witnessing her capacity for self-lessness when she rescued that human male. And I'd come to know her fire, passion, strength, and tenacity... Even her softness and vulnerability... How far she'd come despite the adversity I'd *experienced* in her memories... My heart swelled at the very idea of her. Not a single female in Atratus could make a better Queen.

And now that she was safe and at my side, where she fucking belonged, I refused to waste another moment of it. I may have had ends to meet, a Kingdom to conquer, but... Despite everything I resented about her past... I couldn't fathom a more perfect person to do it beside.

Her expression almost always remained hardened and utterly closed off to the world... But in fleeting moments, I had witnessed her softness and openness. Her *vulnerability* in the sweetest and most delicate way that told me I would burn the fucking world down to protect this female. This battle-hardened warrior turned assassin and executioner that had suffered at the hands of so much violence it was a wonder that she had survived. I would do anything to get her to be open and vulnerable with me again.

Mareina's body went rigid as I clutched her to my chest as though she were the most fragile and precious thing in all of existence.

And, *to me,* she absolutely, unequivocally was.

"One day, Mareina... One day, you'll be glad for this bond."

She closed her eyes, features tightening as she appeared to steel herself. Heaving a sigh, she rang the bell. The gorgon appeared in our room within moments, wearing a heavy grey-ish, silvery cape over her chiton.

She unfurled herself from my arms, turning to face our host.

"Would it be possible for you to witness our vows? I'm happy to pay whatever fee you'd be willing to accept."

The gorgon gave us an enigmatic smile that made me wonder just who the hells exactly she was... Perhaps she knew my mother?

"It would be my honor."

She extended her hands to us as if to *fold* us, and a flutter of anticipation went through me.

After accepting her hands, we found ourselves standing in an open-air shrine. Mine and Mareina's eyes widened as we took in our surroundings. High on a mountain's peak, enormous stone pillars stretched towards the cloudless night sky, surrounded by a dense forest. Glowing orbs I briefly mistook for faelight emerged from the forest until I realized they were something else entirely.

"They, too, would like to bear witness," the gorgon said softly as we gaped in awe.

"Who's *they?*"

"The *Seraphi Ousia...* They are the fragments of resting *Seraphi* spirits... When angelic deities such as these go to sleep, sometimes for millennia, parts of their souls wander the realms, drifting until they find a... a certain energy source."

My brows knit, studying these seemingly benign amorphous

whorling wisps of light... The harder I looked, the more my eyes finally focused, finding what appeared to be whorls of cosmos and stars around them.

Little was known about the *Seraphi*. 'Seraphi' being a broader term for beings and deities who had come from one of the higher realms, dimensions accessible only by them and those who exceeded their... *evolution*. The only *Seraphi* I'd heard of who had come to Atratus were the *Nephilim* and *Archestratim*.

"An energy source? As in, they feed off of our energy?"

The gorgon chuckled. "Not in the way you think... Just as a flame is not diminished by sharing its fire, it only grows."

As if in affirmation, the *Seraphi Ousia* drifted closer, surrounding us. Immense energy swelled within me, making the very core of my being tremble at its gravitas... Both soothing and familiar yet new, awe-inspiring, and wholly intimidating.

"*Who are you?*"

The gorgon gave us a pitying look as she replied in a gentle tone.

"My name is Phaedra... But you're asking the wrong question, Mareina. What you should be asking is who *you* are... Who your *soul-bound* is. Though these are not answers for me to tell. I apologize."

My arm curled around Mareina's waist to draw her against me as I caught the wavering in her voice.

"*Do you know my mother?*"

Phaedra tilted her head.

"Those who you think are your parents are not of your blood..."

Mareina went so still in my arms, I worried for a fleeting moment she'd turned to stone.

"Your parents are not in this world," she added before her eyes settled on me. She seemed as though she had something more to say but remained silent. Before I could ask her what I could *feel* was on the tip of her tongue, Mareina interjected.

"Not in this world? As in... Dead?"

"Your parents are ageless beings."

"*... What?*"

245

"You will find out soon enough."

"Where are they?"

Phaedra shook her head. "That I cannot say."

"As in, you don't know? Or *won't* say?"

Phaedra's expression turned fierce.

"As I in a *cannot* say. One, I am not omniscient. Two, as a guardian of fate, I am vowed by my blood and magic to not reveal it," she said, heaving a great sigh to calm herself, "All that I *can* do is help guide those whose fate crosses my own by leading them toward the path of the greatest good. That is *all.*"

What was before a gentle breeze rose into an urgent gust of wind, and the *Seraphi Ousia,* entirely undisturbed by it, continued drifting closer to us until some of them *touched* us. All at once, I was transported to...

A distant place engulfed in darkness but filled with drifting *Seraphi Ousia.*

What I initially thought was a brilliant light - perhaps a distant star - radiating behind me, I realized was the light radiating *from* me, and Mariena, who floated beside me, was engulfed in what I could only describe as divine fire. Her form was terrifying in its beauty. Even if I felt like it was the only form of her's I'd ever known. One composed of divine fire and an immense gravity that I could only describe as a love overwhelming in its power.

Despite these new forms, a sense of peace and rightness came over me as if in realization of, '*Oh, this is what we are*'... Beings of divine love and wrath and fire...

However, I also recognized that these forms were merely part of a greater whole. And if Mareina's expression was anything to go by, it was clear that she recognized it too.

The world began to shift in front of us, catapulting us through space, though we experienced no physical sense of acceleration or velocity. Soon, we were travelling through countless realms ranging from those consumed by violence and suffering to those filled with peace and indescribable beauty.

Eventually, we arrived in a place where a female with four enormous wings led thousands of soldiers to battle. Flames consumed them as a dragon, larger than any creature I'd ever seen, swooped in from above.

A thunderous voice filled my mind as we watched the scene unfold.

"Mi lanthonéti, lei mortatum ei aeternitate m*a skhimata dothate. Letare coi me, Vitum Guardatore. Guarda lei oi buscora thanatou."*

"Born between realms, she is eternity given form. Her home is with me, The Guardian of Life. Guard her or find your death."

Something felt intensely threatening about those words, but time and place shifted once more before I could give it more thought. Mareina and I arrived in a place I could only assume was Zurie's palace. I found myself staring down at two crowns. One gold, the other silver. Both glowing with the power they radiated.

There was a sharp tug on my naval and, as if being sucked backwards by a vacuum, I landed *heavily* back into my physical body. Mareina and I found ourselves standing, again, face-to-face with Phaedra in the open-air shrine.

I glanced down at Mareina to see the lower half of her face slackened with shock while her brow remained tight with disbelief.

"Do you understand now?" She asked, her face tense with gravitas.

A deep laugh bubbled up within me.

"Understand? I've never had so many questions in my entire fucking life."

Phaedra's brow pinched scornfully at my cursing in such a holy place in the company of so many divine beings, *Seraphi Ousia.*

"You and Mareina are here for a greater purpose beyond Atratus. Beyond you being King," she growled fervently, eyes dipping to Mareina, "And you being Queen... I have no control nor certainty over what you were shown. If the *Seraphi Ousia* didn't reveal everything to you, I'm afraid it's not meant for you to know yet."

I couldn't help but chuckle at the absurdly immense weight that rested on both our shoulders. "Right, so... unleash Death and just hope for the best... Seems a little risky."

Phaedra's brow leapt as though I'd just made another absurd observation. "You both agreed to this before you came to this realm. You might not remember it because of the veil between realms that obscures all that came before and beyond your arrival, but the fact that you both *chose* this, *chose* one another, remains the same."

My brows pinched so hard it made my head throb, and judging by Mareina's expression, she felt similarly.

I'd read numerous religious texts that spoke of *divine contracts* and *soul agreements,* but... I suddenly didn't have the energy to ask questions. Not that Phaedra would answer any of our questions anyway. Truly, this female must know my mother. If she didn't have snakes for hair, I'd be forced to assume they were sisters, considering they both hoarded all the most illuminating knowledge for themselves and left the rest of us in darkness.

However, there was one certainty... And it had a familiar anxiety twisted my gut.

War.

I'd agreed to wage a war.

Or perhaps was forced into one...

I wasn't sure which was worse.

Fighting in one was more than enough, and the entirety of the Kahlohani people had nearly died because of it.

Mareina had seen the crowns in our shared vision... How would she feel about being Queen? *How would she feel about having to fight in another war?*

All I'd ever dreamed of was reclaiming the Kahlohani Islands. But in order to do so, I needed to claim all of Atratus. Which came with a *bone-crushing* amount of responsibility to protect my islands and prevent another war. Yet somehow, war, according to my visions, was *still* inevitable.

THIRTY-FOUR

MAREINA

I felt numb in most ways... As I often did when it came to life-altering consequences... But as I waded through my emotions and thoughts... I couldn't find shock among them. Even in regards to my parents... The female I assumed was my mother hadn't even participated as my foster mother. The male, who I'd assumed was my biological father, well... We'd never been particularly close. He'd tried his best, and for that, I was grateful. I didn't hold his mistakes and shortcomings against him. Gods knew I had too many of my own to do such a thing. I loved him, but... We hadn't spoken in so many years I'd stopped counting them.

Ageless beings.

What the hell does that even mean?

I didn't have the time or energy to dwell on it.

Though the image of Nakoa in a winged form engulfed in divine fire was now seared into my mind... And well, it only added to my suspicions that who his parents were was also highly debatable.

And despite all of the premonitions I'd had since I'd entered adolescence over a hundred years ago... Hearing that voice, beckoning me to release it, *Death*... Proving to me that it wasn't just some insane dream... Made it all a little too real. Too imminent. It had always been something that I could question and hovered in the distance...

Now, I was supposed to bind myself to a male I despised and was hellbent on using me to conquer a Kingdom.

Right one cue, Phaedra *willed* a gilded box with intricate designs boasting jewels and a thick set of runes into her hands. She opened it to reveal a glittering, golden dagger resting within its darkest blue velvet-lined confines. Clearly a thing for ceremony and not battle. Glowing runes trailed down the length of its handle, hilt, tang, and blade.

My heart pounded like a war drum in my chest.

It felt like fate was sealing off any other routes towards a different path as Nakoa grasped the dagger from the gilded box and began his vow first as he drew the blade across his palm. Shock rolled through me as I witnessed the emotion swelling in his glistening eyes. Nakoa's magic, darkness and a deep gold wove through the air before following his blood that spilled and trickled to the ground between us.

"Mareina Kalini, my heart, my body, and my soul are yours in this life and all our lives to come - as a token of my love and eternal gratitude to both you and Akash, I offer my blood, my magic, and my vow to always protect you, provide for you, honor you, and love you throughout all our days to come. In joy and tribulation alike, I shall stand by your side."

My heart stalled in my chest. Some terrible alarm went off within me, screaming at me to not make such a vow even as everything in my soul and this bond demanded that I do. It almost felt like I was watching from a distance, somewhere outside my body, as Nakoa passed me the blade. His eyes bore through me as I squeezed the dagger's hilt tightly to steady myself.

My eyes caught on several shadowy, hooded figures beyond the shrine at the forest's edge in the distance. Icy fear punched through me briefly.

Oh gods. Of course, the moment I go to take my vows - what is supposed *to be one of the happiest days of my life - is the day that Mors'* *Pharalaki come to reap my soul.*

But in the next moment, they slink back into the shadows.

Disappearing.

How much longer did I have left to live?

Surely, this was an omen.

Oh, well... This vow would be fucking meaningless if I was about to die *anyway.*

The rationalization gave me the bravery to finally draw the blade across my palm and speak my vow.

Nakoa Solanis, in honor of Akash and her omniscient wisdom, I vow *with my blood and my magic to help you rule justly so we may protect the* *realm and bring peace and prosperity to all its people.*

My magic manifested as darkest red, glowing bright against the hovering *Seraphi Ousia,* bearing witness as it whirled around us before descending to join my blood and Nakoa's on the ground beneath our feet.

Nakoa's expression hardened in understanding before a hint of that cruel grin returned with grim determination. Nakoa pulled me hard against him, taking me by surprise when I raised my palm to meet Nakoa's, weaving our fingers together. Our blood continued to trickle between us as our magic whirled around us and between the floating *Seraphi Ousia* that appeared to have stilled entirely. The breeze picked up again, circling us forcefully as if pushing us together. Nakoa leaned close, whispering in my ear.

"You already belong to me - mind, body, and soul - but I will *have* *your vow Mareina. Even if I must spend the rest of my days punishing you* *to get it."*

Dread and anger, in equal measure, curled through me like claws seeking flesh. Before I could respond, Phaedra's voice cut through the wind like the blade, our flesh. With each passing word, a piercing golden light rose from beneath our palms where mine and Nakoa's hands were intertwined. As Phaedra spoke, that golden light slid over our hands and wove around our wrists and fingers in an intricate design, boasting runes in a language I had only seen on the pythos in my dreams.

"May you serve one another for the benefit of Atratus. May you be one other's strength, allies in every battle, solace in every storm, the light in each other's darkness, and a source of joy in each moment. By the power of Akash and all the gods who serve her, I, Phaedra Borealis, bless this union and their fated destiny. So mote it be."

The light settled beneath our skin... And *disappeared.*

My brows pinched as confusion twisted into unease and sank like a boulder in my belly. Nakoa's markings that only moments ago were elaborate, bright and vivid travelling over his forearm, wrist, and hand had vanished entirely.

As did mine...

I quickly drew up my sleeves, and the sight of what lay marked on the inside of my right forearm had that icy fear trickling back into my veins.

The gold had darkened into black. Instead of beautiful and elaborate whirls and runes like Nakoa's had been before they faded, now all that remained was...

An inverted torch with wings.

The symbol for Mors.

The God of Death.

The words *"Invenitum Thanaratou"* scrawling, letter-by-letter, *beneath it.*

This was it... All this had been for nothing.

Surely, I would die very soon.

I was fucking *marked* for it.

Had been stalked by Mors' *Pharalaki* for *years.*

I didn't know what these words meant, though they sounded identical to the ancient language in my dreams, but the mark itself was foreboding enough.

"What have you done?" She whispered in horror, nails digging into my arm.

I was in such shock I could only gape at her like a fish out of water.

Nakoa growled viciously, snatching her wrist in a crushing grip that made her yelp in pain as she released me.

"Get your fucking hands off her."

A sudden cry tore from my throat as the familiar ache that had always sat at the back of my shoulder blades pierced through me like twin broadswords. A searing pain that *burned* like hellfire. Bones cracked, and my knees buckled.

Nakoa caught me in his arms before I hit the ground. My vision went white from the blinding pain, followed by a wholly *unfamiliar* weight that settled on my back. I ground my teeth against the pain before forcing my gaze to Nakoa's. His face was illuminated with a golden light, jaw slackened, and eyes wide with awe.

"Wings," he breathed.

My fingers sank into his shoulders, and I ground my teeth in pain while the worst of the pain gradually subsided. I gasped for breath like I'd been held underwater. Warmth and wetness seeped into my palms, and when I could finally open my eyes, I realized that my trim fingernails, while not even long or sharp, had still pierced his skin from gripping him so fiercely. He scarcely seemed to notice, his gaze fixed on what had sprouted from my back.

"Oh, Mareina... They're beautiful," he breathed.

The pain in my shoulders gradually faded to a dull, throbbing ache that was, while impossible to ignore entirely, no longer mind-numbing.

Nakoa helped me right myself and maintained his grip on my hands as if he knew just as much as I did that I would likely topple over from the tremendous weight hanging between my shoulders.

I craned my neck to look over my shoulder, instinctively *stretching my wings.*

All four of them.

Holy fuck.

The action caused another searing pain to whiten my vision, and I had to reach out and clutch onto Nakoa.

Each wing was long as I was tall. Feathers such a deep black they seemed to absorb the light instead of reflecting it.

Phaedra had gone sheet white.

Her gaze frantically bounced between us, shaking her head.

"This is... Wrong... *All wrong...*"

Before we could reply, she gripped our arms, and darkness consumed us.

CHAPTER

THIRTY-FIVE

NAKOA

P haedra *folded* us directly back to our room and left without another word. Mareina crawled onto the bed face down and winced at the sight of all the blood drenching her fighting leathers from where her *four* wings had burst out of her back. They were perhaps the most beautiful thing I'd ever seen... Though I'd never seen such a thing in real life. Only in sculptures, paintings, and religious texts...

And it made the possibility of who the hell Mareina's birth parents could be all the more intriguing. Unfortunately, now was not the time to try and find out. Nor could my mind bother to focus on that fact. I stared down at my hands in disbelief. They were gone... My *soulbound* marks. They'd been there one moment, breathtakingly beautiful, and then gone the next.

Anger fisted my chest. Mareina hadn't given me a true vow. She'd only given a vow to help me rule our Kingdom. Nothing more. The bond was still unfulfilled. My eyes shifted from where I was scowling down at my hands to where Mareina was sprawled out on the bed.

Blood drenched her back from where her wings had burst from

her back. Her wings trembled as if still throbbing in pain. The sight softened my anger. And the fact that Mors' had marked her.

The memory of my vision of Mareina standing in the underworld beside the *Pharalaki* returned.

Please, Akash... No. How could I rule this Kingdom without my lohane thili.?

Guilt twisted in my gut at how much I had manipulated her...

Still, I shoved it away. I would not regret doing whatever it took to liberate my people.

I knelt beside the bed where Mareina's head was facing. Her face pale with shock and exhaustion.

I forced my voice into something neutral.

"How are you feeling?"

Her throat worked as her eyes shifted to mine. Her voice was dry and hollow.

"Like a new woman."

I could only manage a frown.

"I can... go down to the tavern and see if they have any ice?"

Mareina gave a scant shake of her head.

"Let's not push our luck. I half expected her to throw us out of here."

So did I.

I conceded by sitting on the floor, leaning my back against the nightstand.

My chest and our tether ached. Admittedly, not only was I angry because she was jeopardizing our success... But I was wounded. She had rejected me when I'd vowed my life to her. Or at least tried to. Though I begrudgingly understood why, it didn't make it hurt any less.

I had no idea what the symbol or words marking her skin meant other than recognizing the symbol of Death. *Mors.* The words written beneath were in a language I didn't recognize.

"Do you know what the inscriptions on your marks mean?"

Another slight shake of her head.

"I'm sorry I fucked it up…"

Despite the pain that tore through it, a rough, mirthless laugh erupted from my chest. How wrong she was. It wasn't *her* that had messed it up. It was *me*. If I hadn't been so ruthless and cruel to her… Perhaps she would have given me her vow. Maybe I would even *deserve* it.

A better male would have been able to admit that. I didn't even have to push the realization away because fear promptly took its place.

Fear that everything I had spent my life working for would be snatched away.

And soon after, my anger returned.

"Oh, don't worry, *maha mo'ina li'ili*… You might be marked by The God of Death himself, but that suits our needs just fine because anyone or anything that stands in our way will be sent straight to him."

CHAPTER

THIRTY-SIX

MAREINA

For hours, I'd laid in bed tossing and turning. By the time I did manage to finally fall asleep, I'd been welcomed by nightmares depicting so much death that even as desensitized as I'd become to it, it had driven out the contents of my stomach.

So after enduring hours of that, it had been rather befitting that the following morning, I'd awoken feeling very much like death.

Phaedra herself had been nowhere to be found, and I'd been as glad for it as I was to leave.

Waiting outside the tavern whilst Nakoa took care of our bill, my gaze fixed on the horizon as I tried to breathe away the tension drawing my body taut. We would return to his *olana kah'hei*... to then head towards his mother's, Vysinni, and then Bastrina.

My plan to escape Nakoa would apparently have to be... postponed for the time being. At least until we killed Zurie and overtook the throne. I had vowed to help him rule Atratus, but I'd promised nothing about committing my heart or my body to him. Perhaps I could help him achieve his dream of living out a peaceful existence in the Kahlohani Islands, just as he'd always dreamed.

Yet again, my mind drifted to Malekai, which only served to intensify the ache in my chest. Had he arrived in Vyssini yet? I couldn't help but feel like I was knowingly walking us all into a trap. One in which Malekai could even be harmed...

Should I warn Nakoa?

How could I warn Malekai?

Nakoa's voice snapped me out of my thoughts. Could he sense my turmoil?

"How do they feel?"

I twisted to find him examining my wings and extended them wide.

"Much better. Awkward, but not painful."

I could hear the frown in Nakoa's voice as he rubbed at my leathers near where the bone had burst out of my back and punctured my top.

"There's blood all over your back still."

I shrugged, now a sluggish and uncomfortable movement.

What difference did it make?

I felt a swift pass of his magic against me, presumably cleaning the blood off himself. Nakoa rounded on me to look down into my face. His expression was surprisingly neutral, considering I'd basically ruined his hope of reaching full power *and* our soulbond vows. He opened his mouth to say something but seemed to wrestle with it for a moment before he finally settled on, "Do you think you're ready to try flying? If not, I can just carry you."

My stomach gave a nervous lurch. Heights had never been my strong suit, but I forced the words out anyway. "The sooner, the better, I imagine."

Nakoa's brow pinched before his gaze darted to the roof of the inn.

"Try stretching them and giving them a few flaps, then we'll practice taking off and landing from the roof."

I nodded, taking a deep breath to steel myself against my nerves.

My wings shot out, one of them banging into one of the hitching post poles. *"Ow, fuck!"*

Nakoa gave a warm belly laugh that, despite the pain that had caused it, alleviated the heavy tension in the air. He gently grabbed my shoulders and eased me out of the vicinity of hard objects. The tenderness in his touch made my traitorous heart squeeze, but I promptly stifled it.

"If you wanted me to carry you the whole way again so badly, you need only ask. No need to go breaking any wings," he teased.

My brow furrowed.

"Why are you being so nice?"

Chest heaving, he smirked a little bitterly. "Am I that predictable?"

My glare should have reduced him to a husk.

"Well, considering the shit storm that was yesterday... Maybe we could *try* to enjoy the day while it's still peaceful," he gestured flippantly towards the marks on my arms, "Since we're are all about to die, apparently."

I gave a noncommittal grunt.

"And, you are particularly breathtaking with your wings out..."

I rolled my eyes, ignoring his charming words and gave my wings a heavy flap. I squealed in terror as it launched me a foot off the ground and sent my stomach leaping. Nakoa howled with laughter as he caught me around the waist.

"Easy there," he purred, "Gently..."

My heart thudded a frantic beat in my chest as I tried to breathe away my fear... And the effect his words were having on me. Still holding onto my waist, he took a step back.

"I've got you."

My hands fisted his biceps as I tried to make my wings give a gentle flap. My heels lifted off the ground, and I came back down, steady on my feet.

"Good girl... Again."

Two more gentle flaps held me aloft in the air. A sultry grin split Nakoa's face.

"*Akash almighty...* You look like some avenging goddess sent from the heavens."

I forced myself not to preen at the compliment. My wings gave a few more flaps that lifted me another foot in the air and sent my nails digging into his flesh.

"*Or hells,* according to Phaedra."

He hummed thoughtfully. "I'd follow you to either."

There was a tense silence, and I cleared my throat as if it might alleviate it. Nakoa's fingers gave my waist a squeeze.

"You wanna try making it up to the roof?"

My eyes darted to the roof, only about twelve feet from the ground, but it still had my stomach giving a phantom leap.

"Oh, Gods..."

Nakoa dropped his glamor, wings stretching wide, and took my hands in his.

"We'll go together. It'll only take a few steady flaps. When your feet are a foot or two above the edge of the roof, just lean forward. I'll go first and will be right there to catch you, ok?"

Gradually, I managed a nod, pushing down any efforts this bond made towards putting any faith in his words. Nakoa's eyes searched mine for a moment, hesitating.

"Do you know what *lohane thili* means?" He murmured softly.

I shook my head.

"It's Kahlohani for *soulbound.*"

"... But you've been calling me that since we met."

A soft, sad smile tilted a corner of his mouth.

"I knew from the moment I saw you in the distance of that crowd. With or without the gifts the bond endows us with, I would have taken you. I want you for *you,* Mareina. That has never changed. And... I am sorry that my actions have led you to believe otherwise."

The weight of his attention... His affection... was too much for my shields to bear at this moment. I forced myself to take a step back.

"Let's see what these things can do, shall we?"

Nakoa hesitated for a heavy moment before acquiescing with a grin and giving his wings a singular, powerful beat that had him landing gracefully on the roof in under a second flat.

I scowled up at him. "Show off."

Nakoa's head tipped back with laughter.

My heartbeat throbbed so loudly I could feel it in my eardrums. My wings gave a heavy flap that launched me into the air like a rocket, and I screamed louder than ever before as I went sailing far above the rooftop. Fear had me locking up and the ground rushing towards me.

Strong arms caught me around my waist and scooped up my legs.

"I've got you, I've got you," Nakoa soothed, murmuring against my neck as we hovered in the air above the inn's roof.

My breath came in sharp, quick pants, and my nails dug into Nakoa's shoulders like the claws of a cat resisting a bath.

"Please... No more. No more," I begged.

Nakoa chuckled, clutching me to his chest. My adrenaline was pumping hard.

"Shhhh. It's ok, Mareina. I've got you. Don't worry."

THIRTY-SEVEN

MAREINA

It took no less than 20 minutes for my heartbeat to steady after our flight practice. I'd also kept my head safely buried in Nakoa's broad chest for the duration. I told myself it was *purely* out of my fear of heights.

Not at all because the feel of his thickly muscled chest and his scent filling my nostrils were tremendously comforting...

"You ok, *lohane thili?*"

My heart pinched at the endearment now that I knew what it meant.

It's not an endearment. It's factually what you are. It means nothing. Nothing but a whole lot of trouble, I chided myself.

"If by *'ok'*, you mean *'traumatized'* - then yes. Thoroughly."

Nakoa chuckled. "You know, for such a battle-hardened warrior, you're awfully skittish when it comes to heights."

"Yes, well... Thankfully, most battles take place firmly planted on the ground."

Nakoa hummed thoughtfully. "I'd bet good money that once you learn how to fly properly, I won't be able to keep you out of the sky."

I shook my head, not even able to consider that at this moment...

And drifted back to the previous day's events, all at once stealing away the comfort and joy in this moment.

"... There's something I need to tell you... About yesterday."

Nakoa's fingers dug into me as if trying to tamp down his reaction to the memory.

"The males you rescued me from... They were a part of your Uprising."

Nakoa's voice dropped to a growl. "I know... Forgive me."

I reared back, still forcing my gaze away from the ground far too many hundreds of feet below us.

"It's not your fault that they—

"It *is* my fault. It is my fault that I have not been a more shrewd judge of character towards those I allowed to join its ranks."

I shook my head. That was too much responsibility for any one person to bear.

"Nakoa... *How?* How would you be able to determine such a thing?"

"My Knowingness. If I had only thought to ask. I'd only had them swear their loyalty - no matter their character - for the sake of numbers. And I selfishly ignored the implications of that."

"You can't help the fact that someone who might be loyal and valiant on the battlefield might be absolute scum the second they step off it."

I had witnessed this firsthand. Males and females who had won awards of valour during the war, I'd also witnessed committing unspeakable acts. My thoughts drifted briefly back to Galvor, the burly fae warrior and guard who had protected me, in a genuinely selfless act, on the battlefield on a singular occasion but had decided to hang it over my head for the last 70 years in an attempt to lure me into his bed.

If the war had taught me anything, it was that no one was ever completely good or completely evil.

And based on Nakoa's silence, he knew it too.

"It's not your fault, Nakoa... You know just as well as I do that those same males would have done exactly the same thing even if they weren't part of The Uprising."

Nakoa remained silent as the truth of my words sunk in. Having fought in the war himself, I had no doubt that he had witnessed his fellow warriors committing abominable acts. I couldn't help but wonder if he had known the males that had raped and killed Malekai's mother.

My thoughts began to drift back towards my own violent past *before* joining Zurie's army... None of the males that had forced themselves on me had been in Zurie's army...

I felt Nakoa's body tense further, likely sensing where my thoughts had drifted, being this close to him. I cleared my throat, trying to redirect our thoughts and emotions.

"Where is everyone anyway? They stayed at that horde's camp?"

Nakoa grunted in affirmation.

"I feel like maybe... I should glamor my wings... I don't think I have the energy to explain. Not that I would know where to begin anyway."

Nakoa frowned. "I don't like the idea of you having to mask yourself... I've been doing it my entire life... My *olana kah'hei* are the *only* ones who I trust with my true form... If there was anyone you could trust, it would be them... Not to mention... Your wings are far too beautiful to hide away when it's not absolutely necessary..."

I dared a peak up from his chest to find a soft grin curling a corner of his mouth, gaze fixed on the horizon until it dipped to meet mine.

"It would bring me tremendous joy for you to be comfortable enough not to glamor yourself around them... I can explain as best I can to them for you... But the decision is yours."

I nodded gradually, deciding to take this small leap of faith. I'd avoided attention whenever and wherever possible, confining myself to the shadows since I'd left the Erosyan Temple. And it had left me feeling alone and isolated. Malekai had been my only reprieve from that, and even so... I hadn't confided in him about most of my aspirations, longings, or past.

"Ok... I'll trust you in this."

Nakoa's lips parted for a moment as he took in my open expression before a grin overtook his face, and he pressed his lips to my forehead.

"Thank you, *lohane thili*," he murmured against my skin.

"Though in public, I imagine..."

"Yes, it would be wise to conceal your wings to prevent drawing too much attention..."

"Are you able to glamor them?"

I nodded distantly, thoughts wandering back to his chosen family as we neared the camp.

"Do you think they'll be upset with me for leaving?"

"Not at all. You had every reason to. They understand."

Silence stretched for a few moments as we soared, and I found myself finally able to appreciate the beauty and the peace to be found so high above everything.

"We kept one, by the way..."

Kept one?

"*One what?* One of the bandits?"

"A prisoner of theirs, technically."

"... There's a reason you haven't freed them..."

Not a question but a bitter realization.

"She *is* free... She just doesn't have anywhere to go. And she needs protection. But yes, there is something that I hope she will agree to so the Queen doesn't put a price on your head for treason."

I craned my neck to finally look up at him as the world below continued to pass by beneath us.

"... *What?*"

"We've found a *mimicryx*," he replied smugly.

My face slackened in shock.

"But... I thought they were... gone."

And I had been one of a handful who had made sure of that.

266

Guilt and shame twisted in my gut.

"Zurie missed a few apparently..."

During the war, she ordered that all Mimicryx be executed for not siding with her. Deemed too great a threat to be allowed to live.

My mouth hung open as I realized why he would want to use the mimicryx... *Gods.*

The smell of blood grew stronger as we neared the horde's camp. When we finally descended, I couldn't help but notice that not a corpse remained in sight.

"Where'd all the dead go?"

Nakoa cleared his throat as though surprised by the question.

"Rayne's shadowy friends have a rather *large* appetite."

My brows leapt towards my hairline just as my stomach swooped before Nakoa landed gracefully near a campfire where Famei was making breakfast and the rest of Nakoa's *olana kah'hei* sat sipping cups of coffee. Among them was the mimicryx, and I couldn't help but notice Rayne hovering nearby, watching her.

My wings shook themselves out, taking me slightly by surprise, like some kind of innate reflex. I turned to find everyone, with the exception of Rayne, with varying degrees of surprise on their faces.

"Have you had wings this whole time?" Lokus asked.

It was an entirely legitimate question... Nakoa kept his glamored almost always.

My spine went rigid, bracing myself for the explanation I would have to give.

"No..."

Nakoa curled a fortifying arm around my waist, our wings effortlessly sliding one over the other as though perfectly suited puzzle pieces.

Lokus' brows merely rose impossibly further. "Huh." And then proceeded to snatch a bit of fruit from a bowl near Famei.

Pomona gave me an encouraging smile. "Cool."

Nakoa looked down at me to gift me a smug grin before he

turned to the mimicryx whose eyes were currently dancing keenly between us.

"So what exactly is it that you need me to do? And does it benefit The Uprising?"

"Zurie has requested that my *dead* body be brought to her."

The mimicryx huffed a laugh in disbelief in the same moment Rayne scowled silently at Nakoa.

"You expect *me* to willingly be tossed into Zurie's lair?"

"*Zurie* will be dead," he replied pointedly, "And as I mentioned before... You will not be alone."

Nakoa proceeded to explain his plan to Vesper and the rest of us. I found myself only distantly observing as I tried to visualize each step of the way. Each potential outcome of every move. All the bravado and reassurance I'd gained during my and Nakoa's ceremony evaporated into thin air. Apparently, I was endowed with the task of killing the Queen myself.

That wasn't what I found upsetting, no. What had sent my gut churning was the fact that Nakoa didn't hesitate for even a moment to think perhaps he wouldn't wish to find me in that kind of imminent danger... Not that I thought that I would be incapable of succeeding in the task, especially with the element of surprise... And it was true that the plan he'd concocted was by far the simplest and most efficient.

If I succeeded, Zurie would be dead, and not a single person would know other than Vesper. At least until we were ready. Which would need to be shortly after, but still...

There would be no guards or her army to deal with until Vesper could take on the Queen's form after her death and announce Nakoa King...

There would be consequences sure but....

Logic and rationality repeated these facts in my mind to soothe my viscerally lacerated heart.

It didn't work.

Instead, it left me feeling... expendable.

"You know the castle well?" He asked me, jerking me out of my thoughts.

Steeling myself against my emotions, I managed a nod.

"... Like the back of my hand."

"Is there a... discreet entrance you could bring us in through? In case you need... backup."

"... There's a distant tunnel entrance in the forest that's hidden but left unguarded. There are wards in place that make it impossible to find unless you've been brought there before. I can let you in through there before Vesper, and I go through the front."

The group of us silently deliberated.

Akash almighty... Could that actually work?

Even without the bond being fulfilled, my power had heightened considerably... Not to mention... I couldn't help but wonder if there was some *gift* that I hadn't yet discovered linked with my mark that tied me to Mors in *some* way... Perhaps I would need to pay a visit to one of his temples. The idea alone had a shudder wracking my body.

A new voice, echoing Nakoa's Knowingness, silently reassured me. The knots in my gut eased slightly despite the tense weight of Vesper's gaze.

She knew.

She must... Mustn't she?

Had I hunted her or her family down?

The guilt at the mere possibility had caused a slight tremor in my hands.

Vesper's own hand drifted to the severed horn on the right side of her head.

"Will it grow back?" Nakoa asked gently.

She remained silent for a few moments, and my heart clenched at the sight of the sudden glistening in her eyes, her voice hushed.

"No."

Vesper's head turned towards the ground as a tear slipped down her cheek.

I couldn't help but notice Rayne's pained expression before he reached out his hand, and the broken half of Vesper's horn appeared in his hand as he knelt beside her. His voice was inaudible to everyone but her and, incidentally, me...

"Where I'm from, our scars are a great source of pride because it means we were strong enough to survive. Beauty is not diminished by our scars but enhanced."

Well damn, Rayne. Look at you.

I was shocked her undergarments didn't burst into flames right then and there.

Vesper slowly lifted her tear-filled eyes to meet his; something silent and tangible exchanged between them. *Soulbound,* that Knowingness pressed upon me.

Nakoa's eyes found mine, and a soft, knowing smile curled a corner of his mouth. He drew my hand, the one marked by our vows, to his lips and pressed a kiss to it, making my heart flutter with both fear and... perhaps a blossom of affection.

Vesper's expression turned thoughtful as she made a noncommittal grunt. "I'll need *her* help with something first."

My heart just about stopped dead in my chest for a brief moment before I steeled myself.

She *did* know. And now she was probably going to try and exact her revenge.

Which means one of us would end up dead.

One of us, or more specifically, *her.*

As much guilt plagued me, this is *not* where my life would end.

I nodded at her before looking up at Nakoa, feeling guilty already.

So much for his plan.

Nakoa gave me a baffled look that, very clearly and wordlessly, stated, '*Do you really think so little of me?*' before returning his attention to Vesper, studying her for several long moments as though he were having some sort of internal discussion. Perhaps with his Knowingness, considering our earlier discussion.

"... Swear your loyalty in blood, and you're welcome to ask her for as much of her time as she's willing to give."

Vesper's expression hardened to a scowl.

"I've lost count of the number of times that I have been manipulated, bound, leashed, caged, and exploited. I reached the conclusion a long time ago that I would, in fact, rather die than be exploited and manipulated again... If I decide to help you, it's because I want to. Not because I'm bound by my very life force to do so."

Nakoa gave her a sympathetic look. "I imagine your journey has been a painful one, but that doesn't change the fact that we don't know you, and we need to be able to trust you. Every single person here has sworn their loyalty by blood and magic... Just as every member of The Uprising has. If you intend on becoming a part of our family and thusly... helping to bring Zurie's reign to an end... Then, no exceptions will be made for you. I will not risk the well-being of my *soulbound* or my *olana kah'hei* because you have been betrayed by others. You're welcome to leave if this is not something you can concede with."

Vesper remained silent for a few moments before her gaze passed over each one of us as she spoke.

"... And shall I, in turn, have all of *your* loyalty?"

CHAPTER
THIRTY-EIGHT

NAKOA

"Indeed, you shall," I promised, lips quirking.

Vesper heaved a sigh to accompany the waning of her resistance.

"I have two conditions."

I shrugged, not having to feign nonchalance. If she did this for us, it would certainly streamline our efforts to overthrow Zurie, and if she chose to stay with us, which I imagined she would, considering she probably no longer had any living relatives, she would become one of us.

"Anything for family."

She huffed, shaking her head. "We'll see about that."

Nodding with no small amount of confidence, my Knowingness told me she would remain.

"As I'm sure you may realize, there are very few of us that survived the war."

My eyes drifted to Mareina, whose expression revealed absolutely nothing. I had no doubt she had played a significant part in their genocide, and I couldn't help but worry that Vesper recognized her and would attempt to exact her revenge. Even if it would be an exercise in futility for her. The last thing Mareina needed was more violence wrought against her or more blood on her hands.

"I want you to help me find a mimicryx male."

I could practically feel the growl Rayne was suppressing in his throat. His dark *friends* seeped into existence beside him, their vapors whirling and tumultuous though their luminous eyes remained fixed on Vesper. My Knowingness had confirmed that she was Rayne's mate. I couldn't help but wonder if his shadow beasts were her mates too... What a fascinating event their *joinings* would be... If such a thing were possible. They certainly had a consciousness all their own. I'd witnessed their individuality and independence of Rayne on too many occasions to take their silence for granted.

"A male?" I asked, though I already knew the answer, "A brother or cousin of yours?"

"No. I need a male so that we can prevent the extinction of my people."

I studied her for a moment, training my expression to be thoughtful as my gaze slipped momentarily to Rayne. His jaw was clenched, and the hole he seemed to be intent on searing into the side of Vesper's face finally lifted as his gaze fell to the ground.

Poor male.

I inwardly cursed.

Fuck.

'Anything for family.' ... Gods, I was an idiot.

"And if we can't find anyone? Surely you've tried already?"

"Of course, I have... But my powers are limited. And this one," she nodded at Mareina, "just happens to know the most powerful Seer in all of Atratus."

So she did recognize her... All the more reason to make her swear her loyalty.

Miroslav. A slew of emotions went through me at the name. He'd slaughtered thousands of my countrymen.

And his own, I reminded myself.

And yet... He had saved my life. *Twice.*

United me with my soulbound.

My Knowingness whispered to me that there were other things he had done that I wasn't even aware of, but it remained silent when I pressed it to elaborate.

"I see..."

"And when he tells me where a suitable male is, you all will take me to him. And I will take you up on your offer to become a part of your... chosen family. Along with my future partner."

Ooph.

In my peripheral vision, I could see Rayne was already mounting his horse.

Vesper's eyes trailed him as he rode off, her expression tense but determined.

"Ahla'toa?" Vesper pressed, speaking Kahlohani to me.

Agreed?

Very few people knew my language, and it made me wonder where she had learned it, no matter how little. Who had taught her? Did I know them? It was possible. Not many of us remained. Though by some miracle, much of my Mother's family and closest friends had survived.

And our people were not quite on the cusp of extinction like hers.

My heart sank, feeling as though I were betraying Rayne, but I didn't need to reach out to my Knowingness to confirm that things wouldn't quite go as she envisioned. It would be a temporary thing, this endeavor to find a mimicryx male. She couldn't resist her *soulbound* any more than she could resist breathing air.

"Ahlei." Agreed.

THIRTY-NINE

NAKOA

Mareina offered Vesper her horse for the time being, incidentally endowing me with the gift of being able to still hold Mareina's body firmly against mine. Since we'd left, her body had been... Particularly rigid.

"We will succeed, *lohane thili*. My Knowingness tells me this. It is never wrong."

Several moments passed, and eventually, I thought she wouldn't respond.

"... And if we succeed? You're truly ready to be a King?"

The stark whites of a male's eyes broaden in recognition of his rapidly approaching death and the sword I've buried in his belly. He's dressed in silver and grey armor bearing an insignia I've never seen before. A bloody grin parts his lips on his last words.

"What we do in this realm follows us into the next, Demon King... What will you tell her then, I wonder?"

I wiped my face absently at the phantom spittle from the soldier's mouth. Though the vision had faded, it left a deeply unsettling gnawing sensation in my bones. It was also the first time I'd heard that moniker... *Demon King*... It only further served to increase my unease. I knew my *transformation* was on the horizon, but... I wasn't exactly looking forward to it. I was already different enough with my tail, wings, and black eyes... I didn't even have the capacity to wonder about who '*her*' could be.

And the visions, as of late, had increased in frequency... Before Mareina, I'd perhaps receive one or two a week... Now, it had become one or two a day... The threads between past, present, and future... The very fabric of reality that wove my consciousness and sanity into place was...Fraying, to say the least.

At my silence, Mareina twisted in her seat as she continued. "I can assure you there isn't a soul on her council that..."

Her words drifted as she took in my paled expression.

"Are you alright?"

My slackened jaw snapped shut, and I straightened, slipping my mask of sanity back into place.

What was she asking? My mind grasped at the wisps of recent memory, trying to recall her question...

Ready to be King...

"... I am prepared to do whatever it takes to liberate the Kahlo-hani Islands so we can return home as a free people. Ruling Atratus to prevent another war over *aetra* is one of those things. I'd never had any desire to rule over Atratus until that became clear to me during the war. Unfortunately, whoever rules Atratus will want to monopo-lize control over *aetra* harvesting and distribution, and because it can only be grown on the Kahlohani Islands... It would only be a short matter of time for history to repeat itself. Since I was a boy and started having that premonition, I have known that I am destined to be King... And *you, lohane thili,* are at my side. So I believe the more appropriate question is *when* we succeed... Are *you* ready to become *Queen*?"

Mareina stared into the distance, heaving a great sigh, and through our tether, I could feel the palpable weight of it.

"I have no desire to be shackled to that kind of responsibility, but it seems fate has herded me onto a path that only leads in one direction. And I do not feel worthy of such a role... I can't imagine I ever will... But I have made a vow to help you rule... And I don't know anyone outside of your *olana kah'hei* who wouldn't exploit the role simply for its wealth and power... So, yes, I am as ready as I'll ever be. And in doing so, I will do my best to serve that role, and thus our people, justice. To give them what I never had."

"... And what is that?"

"*Hope.*"

A staggering melange of both pride and sadness swelled in my chest for my *soulbound.* I bowed my head and pressed a kiss to the crown of her head, my tail appearing to coil around her waist as fervently as my arms held her against me.

"Do you know how I *know,* even without my Knowingness to confirm it, that you will be the best Queen Atratus has ever seen?"

Her breathing stilled as if taken aback by my words.

"Because you know what it is to suffer. You know poverty. You know war. You know violence. You know oppression. And yet you remain unbroken. Instead of bowing beneath the weight of adversity, you became *strong.* You are powerful. And despite all this, instead of becoming cruel, you are compassionate. I know you are haunted by the deeds of your past, deeds enacted on Zurie's behalf, but you are not remorseless. You did not lose your conscience or become desensitized. Through that, you have learned the many ways in which Zurie has *erred.* And now... because of all of this violence and suffering... You will not be blinded by your power like so many others before you were. You *will* bring peace and prosperity to Atratus, Mareina."

My hand slid up Mareina's throat to draw her gaze to mine so she could see the gravitas of my words written on my face.

"*We* will bring peace and prosperity to Atratus, *lohane thili.*"

* * *

When we arrived in the first small town after passing through the Wildlands a few hours after the sun had descended beyond the horizon. I'd watched as Mareina's face tightened at the sprawling poverty before us. I hadn't been to Bastrina in many years, but I couldn't imagine that it had changed much. For the most part, Bastrina was a haven of wealth. While there were poorer areas and slums, they were few and far between and, thus, easily ignored.

This wasteland, however, *Toluna,* was one of the best examples of just how little Zurie cared for her people. The land and surrounding mountains, nearly barren and over-farmed, were riddled with mines and quarries. The town laid in the center of a small valley between two mountains. Despite how much industry and export the town provided, the town was bleak at best.

Nearly all of the homes and businesses were made with the grey stone from the mountain. The roads were all made of dirt and mud, with little to no trees or *life* to be seen for miles, with the exception of its people, who all seemed to have a hungry, desperate look in their eyes that set my teeth on edge.

Thankfully, we passed straight through and made our way a few hours outside of it to a small village, *Darporr,* the one nearest my mother's. It was quaint by comparison, though still quite poor, with thatched-roof houses and dense forests. Its people were mainly fairy folk, dwarves, orcs, dryads, and a number of other mountain and forest-dwelling peoples.

I watched as Mareina tipped her head up to the towering blood-wood trees surrounding us, her eyes nearly identical to the deep green hue of their thick, needle-like leaves. They were the tallest trees in all of Atratus and had sap the color of blood, hence their name, which was said to have healing properties.

"There's something you should know... I'm sorry I didn't tell you sooner... I... I didn't know what to do...," Mareina said quietly, out of earshot of my *olana kah'hei.* "Zurie is sending some of her men to Vyssini to hunt down members of The Uprising. They'll likely arrive around the same time we do."

A little more of my resentment towards her dissolved as my heart swelled with no small amount of gratitude. By confiding this information, Mareina would be saving the lives of at least two dozen males and females that were absolutely imperative to the success of The Uprising. I could only pray that they weren't dishonorable like the ones that had captured Mareina...

Holding her tightly against me and squeezing, I returned my nose to her neck, nuzzling her affectionately. Her throat worked on a swallow, and her heartbeat doubled.

"Thank you for telling me... You've saved lives because of it."

FORTY

MAREINA

"I t's just there," Nakoa murmured in my ear. I'd just begun to fall asleep and realized I'd drifted to sleep against him again. Both of his long, thickly muscled arms held me against him and my head was leaning against his chest. I straightened, making Nakoa give a soft growl of displeasure.

All I could make out in front of us was the steep incline of a mountain with a layer of trees peppering it. Behind us, his *olana kah'hei* trailed behind.

"Where?"

Nakoa lifted his arm, holding the reins, and pointed toward the densest copse of trees. "She keeps the entrance glamored, but it's just behind there."

Twilight had given way to the blanket of night as we arrived, crickets chirping. Nakoa dismounted Pumpkin to then lift me off her, cradling my waist between his strong hands. Despite my efforts to suppress it, the action made my heart flutter.

Nakoa's hold on me lingered for a moment as he studied me in the pale moonlight, his face inches from mine.

"Thank you," he offered, voice warm and gravelly.

Shifting on my feet, I nervously licked my lips. His eyes tracked the movement, bleeding black briefly. So intimately being the sole focus of his attention was as disarming as it was nerve-wracking. I cleared my throat as though it would dissipate the tension between us.

"For what?"

"Just letting me touch you and hold you... That alone makes my heart feel full."

My vision snagged on Roderick, dismounting and practically skipping towards the cliff wall. A welcome relief to the sensation of the tether being pulled taut between us. I'd have thought that fulfilling the bond would have alleviated some of that tension, but it hadn't. It only made it that much stronger. I couldn't help but intuitively feel as if it were the tether pulling at me and demanding that I give up everything that I still held back from him... Like my heart.

Both a plea and a demand, it wouldn't settle for anything less than *everything*.

When my eyes return to Nakoa's, his face has gone pale, and he seems to stare *through* me. As if his mind is elsewhere...

"Darling, you're just in time for dinner," a velvety female voice chirped to him. Nakoa blinked, giving a subtle shake of his head before he tried to give me an encouraging smile before his gaze lifted to his mother -

The tall woman with bronzed skin and silver salt-and-pepper hair standing in a doorway of a jagged cliff face of the mountain dressed in pastel and dark blues. Her arms opened wide and Roderick practically leapt as he swooped her up in his arms, squeezing her tight. She gave a throaty, fully-belly laugh in a way that would have sounded maniacal if it wasn't for the sheer joy and warmth it radiated. I couldn't help but smile watching them. In all my years, I had ever seen such exuberant affection.

"*Mommy,*" Roderick sighed.

"My sweet boy," she replied affectionately, petting his hair as she beamed from ear to ear, eyes closed.

I glanced to Nakoa. "Is that really his mother?"

"Basically," Nakoa smirked, chuckling as he pulled me in her direction. "... Roderick's parents were both killed during the war. She took him in when he was little. Thought he was a wolf pup at first glance. Found him rooting around in the garbage outside a tavern in Darrporr," he added quietly.

My brows leapt even as my heart gave a painful twang of empathy. The rest of Nakoa's *olana kah'hei* approached his mother, eagerly embracing her before entering her cliffside home.

When everyone had ventured inside, her eyes landed on us. Her broad grin fading slightly as emotion seemed to swell in her breast, eyes darting between the two of us before they very clearly dropped to our arms as if searching for our *soulbound* marks. Her brow pinched at the sight of their absence, though she said nothing. My arms were, thankfully, covered by the sleeves of my fighting leather, and she didn't seem too concerned that my hands were bare of them.

"Mother, this is Mareina. Mareina, this is my mother, Leilani."

I stepped out from the arm Nakoa had wrapped around my waist, extending my hand towards her and bowing slightly. "It's lovely to meet you."

"I'm so happy you're here, sweetheart," she said softly, taking my hand in both of hers and pulling me into her arms. Energy, soothing and filled with love, seeped into me at the contact. My body immediately relaxed, and the knot I hadn't even realized was in my chest loosened.

"Thank you for hosting us, as usual... Have you begun cooking already?" Nakoa asked.

Leilani gave him an admonishing smirk as she stepped aside, ushering us in.

"Well, it's about damn time you came to visit me, finally."

I turned to look back and find Pumpkin and Chihiro grazing alongside the other horses.

"Don't worry, they won't wander too far. There's a ward," she added, patting me on the shoulder as Nakoa pulled me inside behind him.

Staring in awe, I gazed around at the floor to ceiling windows that looked out on the forest and mountains surrounding her home. Nakoa had mentioned his mother was a formidable witch but for her to have enough magic to keep a place this big under a constant glamor, have magic left over to live freely, *and* as a human... I couldn't help but be a little floored.

"Why don't you work on dinner with everyone while I give my new daughter a tour, darling?" Leilani asked.

Nakoa glanced between the two of us for a moment, a question in his eyes. I squeezed his hand in affirmation.

"Before you do, I need to discuss something with you..."

Leilani's brow pinched with worry.

"Mareina gave me some alarming news that Zurie is sending some of her army to hunt down and quell members of The Uprising. Would you be able to portal me to warn them?"

Leilani gave a swift nod. "Yes, certainly..."

Leilani gave me an apologetic look before she stepped a few feet away and began murmuring ancient words, and the curved window of a portal began to appear.

Instantly, my heart spiked with fear for Nakoa's safety *and* Malekai's.

"Let me go with you," I blurted, unsure if he intended to go without me.

"I'll be back in a matter of minutes," he whispered against my neck, curling a tendril of my hair around his finger before turning to his mother.

My panic rose swift and cutting now feeling as though maybe my earlier anxiety had been an intuitive warning. For not only Nakoa's safety but for Malekai's.

The portal widened, towering above our heads, revealing a homely kitchen with lots of stained wood and brass fixtures.

"Wait, Nakoa—

Nakoa stepped through with his mother and glanced back at me, his brow pinched, eyes searching mine with something like suspicion, just as it closed.

Could he tell I was worried about another male?

Probably.

My heart thudded a frantic beat as panic rose.

Pomona appeared beside me wearing an encouraging smile.

"Don't worry, love. He'll be back before you know it... If that male is anything, it's determined, and I can already tell that nothing would keep him away from you. Not even Zurie's army."

I frowned. I couldn't help but feel her words were foolish. What was one male against thirty if that was how many Malekai had brought with him. I also couldn't help but worry for Malekai... If they came toe-to-toe... I wasn't entirely sure who would win.

Fear speared through me at the idea... Malekai and I had saved one another's lives more than I could count. He had *always* been there for me. I could only pray that somehow their paths wouldn't cross.

Pomona chuckled as if reading my thoughts. Though she only knew half of them. "His power is unlike any other's."

I nodded, gulping audibly.

"I know..."

I was grateful for it but also terrified of what it might mean for Malekai and now I felt like a traitor for not having warned either of them... But who's to say it wouldn't have sent Nakoa in search of Malekai just to eliminate the competition? If I told Nakoa, would his Knowingness reveal Malekai's, not at all platonic, love for me. Would it show him visions of all the tender moments Malekai and I had held one another. The countless moments things between us had so very nearly become something... *more?* Would his Knowingness tell him just how badly I'd *wanted* to give in but had been too afraid?

While it was long before Nakoa and I had ever met... I'm not sure that he would be reasonable enough in the heat of the moment to take that fact into consideration...

Pomona's brow furrowed as she tried, and failed, to read my conflicted emotions. I took a deep breath... and a leap of faith.

"I just... Some of those soldiers are good people."

Pomona frowned, gradually nodding in understanding.

"Are some of them good friends of yours?"

I nodded, the knot in my chest winding impossibly tight. So much so that I felt like something inside me would fucking break.

"One in particular..."

"I'm so sorry...," Pomona offered softly as she pulled me into her arms. It only served to heighten my panic. I felt like I was going to jump out of my skin.

"What's his name?" She whispered so softly in my ear it gave me pause. It would have been inaudible to anyone but a sanguinati.

Tears swelled, and my throat seemed to close... If Nakoa and his mother found them on the road to Vyssini...

Had I just doomed Malekai to death?

"...Malekai Theikos."

"What does he look like?"

My breath caught, and hope burst through me, bright and over-whelming.

Oh gods... This angel of a female...

"He's the General of Zurie's army... Blonde, tall, built like a warrior... *fae.*"

She pulled back to quirk a brow at me.

"Is he uh.... A former flame of yours?"

"No... He's... My closest friend and ally."

"And that's all? You never had any feelings beyond... friendship? I'm just asking because I imagined Nakoa won't be inclined to show mercy to a male he feels would challenge him."

"Our relationship has always been platonic but... He would like it to be something more."

Pomona scrubbed a hand down her face. *"Akash...* Let's pray they haven't reached the city yet... I'll check the outskirts for any signs of a camp... And if I find him, what would you have me do? I doubt your

285

friend will be keen to turn his soldiers around at the drop of a dime. Not to mention what Zurie would do when she finds out..."

"You can't take me with you?"

She shook her head. "Unfortunately, my power to *fold* has limitations."

My mind raced... What could I say with only a few words that would get him to betray Zurie and abandon his task...

"Tell Malekai I said, 'Leave Vyssini so we can watch the world burn. *Katadamna kaza.*'"

Her brows lifted in surprise. "... Alright... I'll do my best."

"Thank you, Pomona. Words can't express my gratitude."

She gave a nonchalant shrug. "You're the one who just saved about two dozen of The Uprising's most influential members, outside of us. It's the least I could do. And if it spares us all some bloodshed, then even better."

I couldn't help but worry for her now... Throwing herself into one of Zurie's army camps. Even if she could *fold* out of it in the blink of an eye.

"Be careful, please..."

Pomona gave me an appreciative smile and a wink. "Piece of pie, love... But perhaps we should just keep this between us for now, yeah? If Famei asks where I went, just tell him I went to the bathroom."

She turned and disappeared down the hallway. I found myself watching her back, sending a silent prayer that they *all* would be ok.

I returned to the kitchen where the rest of Nakoa's *olana kah'hei* were. All were blessedly distracted, pouring themselves drinks, except Vesper, whose gaze was fixed on me as I made my way over.

Wearing a mask of stoic neutrality, I sat beside Vesper at the kitchen island's bar top. Her brows pinched that I'd dared to do such a thing. Granted, it was perhaps bold, considering I'd spent an entire year hunting her people down and... killing them. My stomach twisted into a knot of guilt and shame. The person I was then versus the person I had now become was genuinely staggering. Then, I'd still been willfully ignoring how utterly morally corrupt my actions in service to Zurie had been. I'd been more like Malekai in my ability to pretend that what we were doing was just. That anyone and anything who threatened the crown must be eliminated to preserve the peace of Atratus lest another *Great Divide,* and the violence preceding it, befall us.

According to history, and those who had survived it and still lived among us, before The Great Divide, Atratus was a lawless place. Tension between *wielders* had been higher than ever, and violence was a constant normalcy even in the smallest villages. Raids were frequent, and death in the streets even more so. *Aetra* was unregulated, which Zurie claims was part of the Atratusian downfall, and made the violence occurring all the more devastating. Though I highly suspected that was a falsity.

But in this moment, my mind was too preoccupied with its concern over Nakoa, Malekai, and Pomona. Each pounding beat of my heart was like the ticking of painfully long seconds. I couldn't help but feel like I'd doomed all of them. Nakoa by telling him of Zurie and her soldiers infiltrating Vyssini, and in turn, Malekai... And now Pomona.

Roderick sidled up next to me, two glasses of amber liquid in his hands, and pushed one towards me. "You look like you could use this..."

I took it gratefully, lifting it to cheers him. "Thank you..." The rest of his *olana kah'hei* turned towards me raising their glasses. Everyone except Vesper that is, who remained nearly as stoic as I was.

Famei gave me a beaming grin. "To Nakoa's *soulbound,* Mareina... And thusly, *our* peace."

Famei, Lokus, and Roderick chuckled as they took healthy swigs of their drinks. Even Rayne gave a slight grin.

I felt like a traitor as I plastered on a small smile and raised my glass.

Hah. If they only knew.

I could barely swallow back the tiny sip I'd taken. All the while, Vesper openly stared at me like she could fucking see through me, and I was about to snap because of it. Rayne must have sensed the tension between us because he leaned in, dragging away her attention, and whispered something in her ear that I was too distracted to hear.

Lokus and Famei worked as a pair on the dinner preparations as Roderick lingered beside me. His nostrils flared, and a look of concern tensed his features.

Fucking lykos sense of smell.

He leaned towards me to speak discreetly. "Everything ok? You smell kinda stressed."

"Just a little worried about Nakoa..."

Roderick studied me intently as though he could clearly see there was something more that I wasn't saying.

"About him going to warn The Uprising members?"

I nodded, consciously relaxing my body language to the *opposite* of what I was feeling.

"Is there... Something specific that we should be worried about?"

My gaze met his, and I witnessed his own trepidation blossoming.

And thank *Akash,* in that moment, Nakoa and his mother reappeared. My sigh of relief audible. Roderick and I turned to face them. Famei and Lokus only glancing briefly as they cooked.

"What'd Val say?" Roderick asked. His relief also palpable as his eyes returned to mine with a question still in them.

Nakoa gave a casual shrug as he strode towards me. "That he would alert everyone and had seen no sign whatsoever of Zurie's soldiers...." His arm curled around my waist, and the relief that went through my body, both at his arrival and at the news, was difficult to hide. "Told you I would be right back... Were you really so worried just for me?"

His question was just as probing as his gaze.

Intuitively, I imagined a fog shielding my mind and the tether between us before I replied.

"As I confided earlier... I'm afraid you'll be taken from me... And I... There are decent soldiers in Zurie's army... No matter how disillusioned. I can't help but feel some modicum of guilt at their inevitable deaths..."

A half-truth.

Nakoa's eyes narrowed as though he could sense there was something more I wasn't saying, but he decided to let it go after a moment.

"I appreciate your concern, *lohane thili...*"

His eyes lingered on mine, and I visualized that dense fog shielding my mind, my emotions thickening... Finally his gaze shifted to back to his *olana kah'hei.* I had to force back my exhale of relief.

Now, I only had to worry about Pomona... How long would it take her to relay the message... I knew Malekai would question where I was and what was happening... Would she tell him about Nakoa?

Malekai and I had never been romantic outside of the way we held each other, or how he pressed lingering kisses to my forehead... Or the way he frequently declared his desire to be with me, and the extents to which he was willing to go to take care of and protect me... Or how I've always pined to just finally give in. *Katadamna kaza.*

My stomach churned.

Malekai would be fucking gutted.

"Val said he wanted to discuss a few things when we arrive tomorrow... I didn't mention our plan to infiltrate Zurie's palace without them. Thanks to Mareina and Vesper, I think it's no longer necessary and is a far less *messy* alternative. Not to mention more discreet... I also mentioned to him that, going forward, I want our members to be more thoroughly vetted..." His eyes returned to mine pointedly.

The clearing of a throat sounded, and I twisted to find Pomona striding towards us without a hair out of place and a grin parting her rosebud lips.

Oh, thank fuck.

I could have wept with relief.

"I think there'd be some merit in that. A lot of those fuckers are awfully crass," she chirped as she began cleaning up the food scraps peppered all over the counter from Famei and Lokus' preparation.

Lokus chuckled, throwing a grape at her which she, somehow, caught with her mouth and chomped brightly. *Still not meeting my eyes.*

"Yeah, maybe you should teach them some manners."

Pomona laughed, her eyes nonchalantly sliding to mine and giving me a wink. Famei leaned towards her to snag a kiss. "Where'd you run off to, hm?" He asked quietly. She beamed brightly, pressing a *lingering* kiss to his lips. I watched as Famei set down the knife and melanzane he'd been chopping and pulled her against him, hands gripping tightly.

Sly female.

"Just the bathroom... Wanna hurry up in here?"

Famei gave her a heavy lidded gaze, ember eyes glowing, his earlier question long forgotten.

"Hurry up what?" He asked feigning confusion before turning to Lokus. "You got this, brother." Lokus smirked, shaking his head, but good-naturedly continued his tasks without complaint.

Leilani's hands slipped over mine and Nakoa's shoulders.

"Why don't you do something productive so I can have a chance to get to know my new daughter?"

Nakoa's gaze fell to mine as if to ask permission. Despite having several urgent questions for Pomona, I grinned, finally allowing myself to heave a sigh of relief that everyone had lived to see another day.

FORTY-ONE

MAREINA

"I'm so grateful they found each other," Leilani said lightly. Some secret seemed to twinkle in her eyes as she spoke. As though Nakoa wasn't still burning a hole in my back with his gaze as she slipped her arm around mine and led me through her cavernous home.

"Yes... Family is such a gift. Blood or no."

Leilani smiled in agreement. "Indeed, it is. The bond between the family you choose versus the family you're born with can often be greater... Much like yours and Malekai's."

My breathing stilled as my gaze hardened and met hers.

"Don't worry. I know my son will earn your loyalty eventually."

Something about her words made my hackles rise, but... Could I blame her?

"I would appreciate it greatly if you wouldn't scry or peer into my life."

Leilani chuckled. "I have about as much control over that as I do the wind. Which is to say, none at all. I cannot help what The Well shows me."

"... The Well?"

She nodded, patting my arm again. "You can have a look for yourself. It's just down the hall."

A silence ensued between us that made tension fist in my chest.

"Do you have any blood relatives that made it over from the Kahlohani Islands?"

Leilani studied me momentarily, and I couldn't help the guilt that knotted up inside me.

Was she wondering the same thing as me? Had I killed any of her loved ones?

I hadn't ever gone as far south as the Kahlohani Islands, but I had battled their warriors when they came to the mainland to prevent us from reaching them. Though it had been an exercise in futility, thanks to Miroslav.

As if sensing my guilt, she rubbed my arm with unmistakable reassurance.

"I do, thankfully..."

Relief audibly whooshed out of me.

"We still lost many loved ones," she added gently, "But I do not blame you, Mareina. Just as I do not blame the blade when it cuts me but the one who wields it. You have merely been Zurie's instrument of death. Thankfully, you and my son are in the process of great awakening, and because of that, Atratus will also face great change."

My brow furrowed, steps stilling in the long hallway. The entire place appeared to be carved parallel into the mountain so that each cavernous room, all decorated with wood, candles, elaborate tapestries, and furs, had floor-to-ceiling windows.

How much did she already know? Nakoa had told me she was a witch with tremendous powers of divination... And she indeed appeared less than half her age.

"Have you seen what happens when we reach Zurie?"

She studied me for a moment, her expression unreadable.

"I have. As has Miroslav... There are many paths... Many potentialities... Many paths leading to the same desired result - the result that stands in the best interest of us all. Let us pray this will be the path you take."

Her mouth quirked in a tiny, mischievous smile.

My lips parted in shock.

Miroslav.

My mind reeled.

Leilani chuckled, pulling me along.

"I believe The Well will help clarify things..."

At the end of the long hallway, we reached a set of dark wooden doors boasting intricately carved designs and runes. Magic radiated from it, making every hair on my body stand on end.

My footsteps slowed as we approached, and Leilani came to a stop, gently laying her hand on my arm.

"I have a scrying well... I don't know what exactly it will show you, but it has been made clear to me that it is necessary..."

The magic emanating from that room felt as if it were causing every molecule in my body to vibrate and hum in a way that both warned me, yet called to me like a moth to the flame.

"What you're experiencing right now will calm once you're inside."

"Is it a ward?"

"Not quite... But... It gives tests to us all. It is different for each person."

"Is it your magic?"

Leilani chuckled, shaking her head. "Heaven's no... But it's why I made my home here. To better guard it. Protect it."

I could feel the magic radiating from the door beckoning me forward, only serving to make me want to dig my heels further in.

At my hesitation, Leilani slipped her arm around mine, gently tugging me towards the door.

"Come. You will not be harmed."

Leilani whispered in an unfamiliar language beneath her breath, and an unseen hand parted the doors in front of us.

As we stepped in, I gasped, discovering the ceiling was nothing short of palatial... It rose at least a hundred feet above us with gigantic Stalactites stretching like deadly, jagged sickles towards their towering stalagmite counterparts. I stared in awe as I realized that they were not merely made of stone and mineral deposits but crystal.

Within my mind, I heard a faint echo of the voice from my dreams.

"O ziton irini feri polemon, al o kaloumenos 'O Vasiléfs mou' synaxi. Protá dio emisfaíria tou auto olo én genisete, ke tote panta pesite."

"The one who seeks peace will bring war, but it is the one you call, 'My King', who will unite. If two halves of the same whole become one, all your kingdoms will fall."

"Mi lanthonéti, oti kei mortatum ei aeternitate ma skhimata dothate. Essita me, Vitum Guardatore, na evrīs tin oikisí sou."

"Born between realms, forget not that you are eternity given form. You are never alone. Seek me, the Guardian of Life, to find your home."

A wave of overwhelming... *kismet* washed over me.

Nakoa's mother was part of this. Just as Miroslav was.

How?

From within my mind's eye, a dizzying sensation overtook me as the perspective of my life's events, from birth to present, radically shifting. I stumbled, and Leilani's hands, with surprising strength, gripped my arms to support me.

Leilani's voice distantly registered as a great power that seemed to sink into my very DNA. The glamor shielding my wings since we'd begun travelling fell. My wings shot out as though bursting free of shackles. Leilani leapt back to prevent herself from being knocked over by them, gazing in awe.

"You've already begun to shift," she affirmed with no small amount of awe.

Words escaped me as what felt like the hand of destiny reached into my soul and pulled taut the cord connecting all the events of my life, finally aligning them so they hung in unwavering linearity, revealing how even the smallest of events had been an imperative part of the journey that had led me here, to this moment.

The images I'd been shown in Phaedra's shrine passed before my eyes. Tears spilled from my cheeks as I watched again in awe.

A talon of fear scraped sent my heart galloping as this destiny opened up before me and beckoned me towards a path I would never have chosen.

Something is still missing, some internal internal voice warned me. An image from my dreams returned to my mind.

"Where is the pythos?" I asked, barely above a whisper as I tried to steady myself.

"Pythos? I don't know anything about a pythos..."

I searched her gaze, and she gave me an apologetic look.

"What is its significance?"

"I... I don't know yet."

"That is often the case with visions initially. Though, eventually, it will be revealed. Don't worry."

Leilani nodded in understanding as she slipped her hand into mine and walked me to a darkened corner with a rather large, perfectly circular, gaping hole in the floor.

As we neared, I realized it was not a hole but a well. The water within reached precisely the edge of the cave floor, making it look like it could have been a pane of glass. Instead of reflecting the dim faelight that flickered behind us, it seemed to absorb it.

A rectangular floor pillow, nearly as long as a bed, lay beside the stone cave floor, surrounded by more crystalline stalagmites. Leilani led me on a narrow path between them before gently pulling me down to join her on the pillow.

Leilani began to chant in that ancient language. The placid water of The Well shuddered and began to ripple until her words quieted. I stared, waiting for something to happen, and just when I began to grow unsure, I noticed a tiny pinprick of light at the bottom of the seemingly bottomless well.

My enhanced sanguinati sight strained to understand what I was seeing. The pinprick of light gradually grew and spread across The Well like beams of light until it filled the entirety of The Well. Shining an iridescent white so bright that I had to shield my eyes. When the light dimmed, and I looked back into The Well, I saw...

Myself.

As if by some unknowable force pulling me, I leaned forward on my hands and knees. The cave around me, Leilani included, disappeared, and I suddenly found myself standing in...

Queen Zurie's bedroom...

Zurie lay on her bed in a pool of blood that framed her hips with the covers pulled back. Her ordinarily perfect, unruffled appearance and indifferent demeanor were gone. In its place are sweat, tears, and blood.

So much blood.

And a tiny infant lay nursing on her breast.

My breath caught... The dark umber wings, the dark hair, the dark golden skin...

Nakoa.

My legs nearly buckled as shock rang through me like the toll of a giant church bell. This fearsome and captivating male at his origin, tiny and innocent, and vulnerable... Still unburdened by the world's heavy, merciless hand. And his mother, this ruthless queen who could surely drown many lifetimes over in all the blood she, or those working on her behalf, had spilled. Myself included.

Zurie looked up, panic spearing straight through me as she stared directly at me. I gasped as someone suddenly walked straight through me towards her. A midwife carrying a bowl of clean water.

The midwife dipped a cloth and began cleaning her sweaty brow.

Zurie swatted her away.

"Go get Miroslav," she demanded hoarsely.

The midwife pulled the cloth away, twisting it anxiously.

"... Your majesty, you should rest while the child is calm."

"*Go. Get. Him,*" Zurie demanded in a formidable tone, her magic seeping out of her like a poison taking hold of its victim.

The midwife went rigid, turning immediately on her heel and rushing out of the room.

Miroslav appeared only moments later, and for the first time in all the many years I'd known him, something like tension shuddered his gaze.

"Your majesty... How is the babe? How are you feeling?"

Zurie's nostrils flared as her jaw hardened in an attempt to stifle the deluge of emotion flooding her eyes. Never, in the entirety of the century I had spent serving this female, had I ever seen her express emotion outside of anger or malevolent glee.

"*Why* must you always ask questions you already know the answers to?" She croaked, voice cracking with emotion.

Some deeply rooted knot of dread twisted in my gut and my chest to the point where I could scarcely breathe.

Miroslav remained silent, his gaze fixed on the child on her breast before Zurie regained a modicum of her composure.

"He is as you saw him in your vision? You are sure this is the one who would destroy me and my kingdom?"

Miroslav's throat worked on a swallow, his impassive mask cracking ever so slightly as his eyes flicked from the babe to Zurie.

"Yes, Your Highness."

Zurie's jaw clenched furiously as though she would burst as her tears began to spill freely.

"Take him," she hissed through gritted teeth, voice cracking again. Even as her arms seemed to clutch baby Nakoa tighter against her bare chest.

Miroslav hesitated for a moment before Zurie snapped.

"I said take him!" She cried. The babe started, kicking in her arms as it released a stuttering wail, choking out his sobs.

Miroslav moved, quickly taking baby Nakoa, still nude from

being birthed, and curled his arms around him, cradling him against his chest with surprising tenderness.

Zurie tore her gaze away, covering her bared breasts still leaking with milk before clasping her now empty, trembling hands together with barely restrained emotion. Her voice was scarcely audible.

"Make it swift and painless."

Miroslav hesitated for only a moment before he dipped his head, *folding* away with the child, as Zurie roared her fury - tendrils of her magic exploded from her like a detonated bomb.

Just as her magic consumed me, the queen's room disappeared, instantly replaced by... Palm trees and thunderous waves crashed on a rocky shore in the nearby distance. Dark, billowing rain clouds loomed above, heavily pregnant and threatening to burst. Harsh winds tore through the land. Baby Nakoa's wail came from behind me, and I turned to discover Miroslav still clutching him protectively against his chest as he stood at the front door of a small hut that sat amongst a dozen others.

As though he could see me beyond time and space, his gaze lifted to mine, hard and filled with pain. My heart stuttered in my chest, and I opened my mouth to speak, but he gave a subtle shake of his head and turned, opening the front door to reveal Leilani. Her hair, no longer streaked with white but a lustrous jet black. Her figure, full instead of lithe. I rushed towards the door as they spoke, unable to catch their words, only reaching it just as it shut. I attempted to push it open, and though I could still see my hands in front of me, they went straight through.

I passed through the closed threshold to find Miroslav standing close to Leilani as they spoke Kahlohani in hushed tones. Miroslav carefully handed her Baby Nakoa. Leilani's face crumpled, tears streaking her cheeks, as she began to sing softly in a voice that wavered under the weight of her emotion as she gently rocked him against her chest.

As shock waned and reality began to settle on me, my own tears began their descent. Unable to bear the anguish, my restless eyes settled on Miroslav's face... Marred with unmistakable heartbreak and longing.

I took in the scene... The fullness of Leilani's face and figure... The bassinet and basket beside the bed were filled with tiny dresses and a rosy pink blanket. My throat worked on a rough swallow, stifling the sob clawing its way up my throat.

Nakoa's cries quickly quietened to whimpers as she soothed him and finally sat on her bed. When she pulled a tie at the shoulder of her long dress, exposing her breast, heavy with milk, his whimpers were silenced as she brought it to his mouth, and he began to nurse. She watched him, her tears still relentless.

Miroslav sat beside her, his face tight with emotion as he curled his arm around her, pressed a kiss to her temple, and closed his eyes. Tears began to slip down his own cheeks. Too overcome with emotion, he was forced to hang his head in his hands as he leaned, elbows on knees. His shoulders began to shake as he silently wept.

Despite being unable to speak Kahlohani, each word they spoke, The Well, again, seemed to whisper its meaning in my mind wordlessly.

Leilani's lips trembled as her voice, barely above a whisper, cracked.

"It's not fair that she's not here too."

Miroslav's hand slipped over her knee and squeezed.

"No. It's not," he managed hoarsely.

Soul-crushing grief welled up inside me.

"I feel as though nothing will ever heal this sadness, Miroslav..."

"I know, *lohane thili*... I know."

Miroslav took a deep breath, his body stilling before he spread out on the bed beside her where she laid, taking her face in his hands and pressing a soft, lingering kiss to her lips, Nakoa still nursing at her breast.

"Loha au iiāna 'oe i kēia poa me'ka hopona, poa hanei," he whispered.

I love you in this life and the next, soul mate.

"*And I, you,*" she returned softly.

Their watery emotion continued to pour. The only sounds in the room were the soft suckling of Baby Nakoa and the distant rolling thunder. After several painful moments, Miroslav spoke.

"... You cannot stay here much longer. It's not safe. Come back to the mainland with me. You don't have to stay in Bastrina..."

"We have time... I will not abandon my people. And Nakoa is not safe close to the capital..."

"Yes, but Mareina is there; their magic and life forces are stronger when they're near one another. And you know that it is clear in my visions that Nakoa is *from* there. He will need to be a part of that place, those people, know their ways in order to lead..."

The room faded until I found myself blinking down at the glassy surface of The Well. Its previously bright surface, dark. Present day Leilani sat beside me, her eyes lifting to mine.

"*Oh my gods...,*" I breathed, chest tight with overwhelming emotion.

"What were you shown, darling?" Leilani asked as she leaned closer to me, searching my eyes as if they could verbalize everything I'd just witnessed.

Fat tears sprang to my eyes, promptly diving over the dam of my eyelids as I drew my hand to my mouth to stifle a sob.

Oh, Nakoa.

And Leilani... Miroslav... I couldn't even begin to fathom what they had been through.

"He doesn't know, does he?" I whispered, trying to hold back a sob.

Leilani's eyes slid shut briefly, a soft frown creasing her lips. She didn't speak for several moments as though trying to work through something before finally looking back up at me, something firm in her gaze.

"You cannot tell him, Mareina... *Promise me.* Or it could change the course of... *Everything.*"

FORTY-TWO

NAKOA

T he visit my mother and I took to Vyssini had been brief but efficient. And thanks to Mareina, lives would be saved. I'd warned one of the few leading members who actually knew my identity, and he'd set off to warn the others. Afterwards, we'd portalled to the city's outskirts but had found no sign of Zurie's soldiers.

"Any news from Val?" Roderick asked.

"Only that our numbers are steadily increasing... And that he has a male on the inside."

Their jaws collectively dropped.

"... What do you mean on the inside? Like... Inside, inside? Inside the palace? Or someone in her army?"

I shrugged. "He couldn't say... Said his secrecy was sworn in blood. Just that it's someone who he... we... can trust."

My brothers and sister grew silent for several moments.

"Well, that's... Promising. Perhaps we should include Val so we can gain access to his contact. Would be a significant advantage to have another one of Zurie's own to get us inside the palace."

"How do we know he's not a mole?"

"Get him to swear his fealty."

"Val said he doesn't even have a way to contact him... Said that he has to wait to hear from him first."

Lokus grunted thoughtfully. "Highly suspect..."

"Indeed. Another reason I didn't tell him about our plan to infiltrate Zurie's palace."

"He *is* normally a rather good judge of character."

I gave a noncommittal grunt. As accurate as Lokus' words may be...

After several moments of thoughtful silence, Lokus finally picked up a bottle of amber liquid and poured refills into our glasses.

"To Zurie being reduced to fucking ash and you," Lokus said proudly, "Becoming fucking King."

King.

You and your soulbound are destined to liberate all *of Atratus,* my Knowingness whispered.

All I'd ever wanted was for me and my people to no longer live oppressed in exile on this twisted fucking continent. To liberate the Kahlohani Islands of the fae that now plagued its land and seas, and live in fucking peace... And while I wanted that for *everyone*... And I was viciously pursuing the crown... Sometimes, insecurity still gripped me.

Who was I to lead an entire Kingdom?

I was a broken warrior who had lost a war and had been reduced to little more than a thief and a murderer.

Sometimes, I really wondered who was planning all of this...

Akash?

Moirai, the three-faced goddess of fate?

Rayne, Lokus, and Roderick raised their glasses as Vesper watched, looking mildly intrigued.

After a moment's hesitation, I raised mine.

"To Zurie's death and all the peace it will bring."

Lokus pinned me with a knowing gaze as if he'd seen right through me.

302

"You are the harbinger of peace, brother... To the only King Atratus has ever known that has a vision beyond his own greed and power. To a King who has a vision for freedom. For peace. For unity. For a Kingdom in which *everyone* can flourish... Long live the King."

"*Long live the King!*" The rest of them echoed exuberantly.

* * *

More than an hour later, after Mareina had gone with my mother to tour her home and *still* hadn't returned, I'd grown anxious. After some initial discussion with my *olana kah'hei* regarding my discussion with Val regarding Zurie's attempts to quell the uprising, my *olana kah'hei* had resumed talking and joking around merrily as Famei and Pomona finished preparing the rest of our feast after their little rendezvous.

Rayne hovered near Vesper, who seemed to have momentarily given up trying to ignore his existence. Rayne, for the first time since we'd met during the war, was openly grinning with the female as she chuckled. It was a startling sight. The male, if anything, was dour. Roderick and Lokus were chatting away, following Famei and Pomona's orders. And here I was, simply staring, practically grinding my molars into dust at the thought of whatever my mother might be telling Mareina or what The Well was showing her.

Gods. Had they fallen in The Well?

I smirked to myself, imagining Mareina soaking wet and scowling.

"Oy," Lokus huffed, "You wanna help out, or are you just gonna mope around until your fanged princess returns?"

As if on cue, the oven dinged.

"Sorry," I mumbled, reaching in the drawer for the oven mitts and an apron, earning odd glances from the group.

Quickly tying on the apron and donning the mitts, I pulled out the roasted pheasants adorned in various vegetables and stuffings, all their juices sizzling in the ceramic oven dish, and slid them onto the wooden kitchen island.

Pomona approached, handing me a glass of amber liquid as I began cutting up portions of pheasant.

"You alright there, lover boy?"

I huffed a chuckle, taking a grateful sip. "Thank you... And yeah, they're just taking a while. Can't help but wonder what horror stories my mother might be telling her and incidentally putting her off me."

"She's your *leath-anama,* Koa. She could tell her all about your escapades, and it wouldn't deter her. And it's not like she's a saint either..."

I huffed a mirthless laugh. "She's *already* deterred."

Pomona frowned, but before she could respond, the sound of soft footsteps drew my gaze to where my mother stood.

Without Mareina.

Her face was flushed with emotion that made anxiety knot in my gut.

"Darling, would you mind joining us in the study?" My mother asked gently.

I looked back briefly to Pomona and her grim expression, giving her a pointed look before turning to follow my mother, who led me down the hall to her study.

Mareina stood beside a chair as though too anxious to sit. Her face was reddened and puffy from crying. All previous thoughts emptied from my mind as dread curled in my gut.

My throat worked on a rough swallow, struggling to force out a question I wasn't certain I wanted to know the answer to.

"What's wrong?"

Even my Knowingness seemed to have grown silent, further spiking my anxiety.

Tears slipped from Mareina's face as she made her way towards me. The wind left my lungs in a grunt with the force of her hug.

I caught her around the waist and wound my arms around her, feeling some of the tension in my body dissipate at the contact.

"She showed you The Well..." I asked, already knowing the answer even without my Knowingness.

Mareina's head nodded against where it was buried against my chest.

My eyes flicked up to my mother's as the words left my mouth, her body going rigid. "Can you tell me what you saw..."

This, too, was a question I already knew the answer to. My mother had had The Well since I could remember, and I could count on one hand the number of times she was allowed to share what had been revealed to her.

Mareina shook her head, still buried against me, her arms squeezing tighter.

"Can you at least tell me if one of us has some kind of terminal disease?"

Mareina huffed a sorry laugh.

She finally pulled back, making my heart squeeze at the sight of her watery appearance. As the Queen's fearsome Royal Irae, I couldn't imagine anyone else got to see her like this... Emotional, vulnerable, caring...

I took her face between my hands and looked down into her eyes.

"*Hey there...,*" I murmured gently, "Whatever you were shown, we'll get through it together... Ok?"

The surprise on her face was apparent at my words but dissolved into a small, determined smile that tilted her lips as she nodded.

My mother cleared her throat. "Our guest has arrived," she announced as though she had some kind of telepathic doorbell. She turned, striding towards the door. My mother stepped outside briefly, leaving the door only slightly ajar. My eyes locked on their joined hands as she tugged a tall male inside. He was even taller than me but half as broad with ebony skin and silvery eyes. Objectively speaking, I could recognize that he was a remarkably handsome male, if not a little unsettling in his stoic, otherworldly features.

Features I could never forget, although it had been over 70 years since I had seen him. Fury had my jaw working and my grip on Mareina tightening.

My mother's smile was nervous as she spoke, her hand still clasped in her guest's.

"Darling, I'd like you to meet Miroslav..."

I reached for my Knowingness, which finally seemed to spark back to life. What I suddenly felt radiating from this male nearly took my breath away. I felt... *love.* So much love- and something like... *Relief* shuddered from him. My lips parted in shock as I *felt* the tether between them...

Nā Poa Hanei.

Soul mates.

Miroslav strode towards me, his long legs eating up the distance between us in two steps, to offer me his hand.

"It's an honor to finally formerly meet you. I've... Heard so much."

Disbelief warred within me, my eyes gradually drifting from Miroslav to my mother, who looked up at me with pleading eyes. Clutching Mareina to me, my eyes flicked momentarily to the offered hand, and I took a step back as though it were a weapon.

My mother stepped forward, wrapping her own arm protectively around his waist. "I'd planned on telling you before he arrived, but I didn't imagine Mareina and I would be so long—

"Do you know who this male is? *What he's done?*"

My mother took a deep, calming breath. "Yes, I do, Nakoa. He's not who you think he is. And *we* owe this male everything. He's my *poa hanei...*"

My gut churned at the confirmation. *Miroslav had spared my life on more than one occasion.* It was much clearer now as to why. He was my mother's mate. He obviously hadn't killed me because of her. And it was likely the exact reason why my aunts, uncles, and cousins had escaped and remained safely in Spriga, on the southern coast of Atratus, to this day.

I shook my head, still unable to fully grasp the fact that my

306

mother's *mate* was this brutal murderer who had killed thousands with nothing more than a thought—

Mareina's hands gripped my shirt, yanking my gaze back to hers, tears still spilling as she shook her head at me.

"Nakoa... *If you knew...*"

My brow furrowed, and my heart pounded in my chest. Whatever The Well had shown her must have involved him to some degree. I reached for my Knowingness for some semblance of guidance.

It's because of him you're alive...

My mind reeled at those words... He had been the one to give Marina the *grá root* to prevent her from assassinating me... My Knowingness seemed to linger, something telling me there was more to it than that, but I was still too shocked to figure out what it meant.

Mareina's face tightened almost painfully with the expression of whatever it was that she was trying not to burst with. Whatever The Well had shown her, I imagined.

Miroslav's baritone voice was grave yet gentle.

"Please know that all I have done was to protect your mother. And thus, this kingdom... I will not claim to be a *good* male. I have committed sickening crimes, and I would do it all over again if it meant your mother was safe. I would ask that you do not assume I am not haunted by these things. You can rest assured that my day of reckoning will come, and I will welcome it because it means you, your mother, and Mareina will be safe...

"*A me ka 'olana kahai a lo... Ua 'ikei 'ya a ua hikei mahka mea a lo e koa mo'ah puna 'ana a 'oei yaku.*"

And all of your chosen family... All that you have dreamt, and more will come to pass.

Shellshocked, I could only stare as my Knowingness pressed upon me the truth of his words.

Gradually, I managed a distant nod, my own voice sounding foreign to my ears.

"Right..."

Several quiet moments passed before my mother spoke.

"I understand it will take some time to adjust to this news, but... Once you arrive at the palace, I'll be there to assist."

It came as no surprise to me that he was already aware of our plan. Between his gifts and my mother's, they were nigh omniscient. I was wary of even my own relief that he was supposedly on *our* side.

We studied each other briefly, and I couldn't help but wonder if the tactics my mother had taught me to shield my mind had ultimately come from him.

"Miroslav and I will be waiting for you in the kitchen... If you'd join us as soon as you're ready, it would bring me immense joy to have us all in one room together for the first time in..."

My mother's words drifted off, catching herself, but I was reeling too wildly to pay it any mind. She cleared her throat before finishing her sentence.

"Take your time, *maha loha.*"

My love.

In my peripheral vision, I saw Mareina offer my mother an apologetic smile, and my mother reached out to squeeze her hand appreciatively.

What the fuck in Akash's name am I missing?

The second Miroslav and my mother left, shutting the door behind her, I fixed my gaze on Mareina.

"What were you shown? And what does *Miroslav* have to do with it?"

Mareina drew a deep, steadying breath as the tear in her forest green eyes renewed.

"Nakoa... If I tell you, I fear it will alter the course of things. And it didn't show me the future. It showed me... *The past.*"

My brows furrowed in confusion. *My past?* What did Miroslav have to do with *my* past? I'd only ever encountered the male once...

Mareina shook her head in resignation.

"I probably shouldn't tell you this, but I can't imagine it would change anything other than perhaps that it might bring you a little more peace about Miroslav being your mother's mate... But... It wasn't just during the war that he spared you your life or because he gave me the *grá root.*"

My brows leapt at the confirmation. Mareina raised her hand as she shook her head.

"I can't say anything more... I'm sorry."

Much to my surprise, dinner passed by jovially for the most part. There was unmistakable wariness and tension from my *olana kah'hei,* but after Miroslav illuminated us to the fact that he was fully supportive of any and all efforts made against Zurie, had spared my life on multiple occasions, and would actively be working behind the scenes to misdirect her so that our efforts would be successful eased their tension enough for us to have an enjoyable meal together.

To say the least, my mind was fucking *blown.*

All eyes had been drawn to me when discussions of future Uprising efforts - like our trip to Vyssini - came up, which shortly shifted to the basics of our plan to overthrow Zurie. My mother and Miroslav had listened as though they had already heard me say it 1,000 times.

"You'll need more than just The Uprising to swear their fealty to you once you're King," Miroslav added lightly.

My gut gave a foreboding churn.

"Are you speaking in terms of general practicality or something specific from your visions?"

"Both."

My frustration flickered. Apparently, my mother wasn't the only one leaving me out of the loop.

"Anything that I'm privy to?"

Miroslav and my mother's eyes met in a wordless exchange.

"There will always be outside threats. Ishra, Hades, and Maimyō mo Qì are only days away by boat. There are also other realms to consider. Just as Zurie's ancestors arrived and colonized these lands, another more advanced race of beings could arrive at any time. None of this is new information to you."

"... No, it is not, but surely, if you have visions of such a thing, it would be wise to make us aware of them so that we may prepare accordingly, no?"

Miroslav appeared entirely nonplussed. "Surely."

I narrowed my eyes at his nonchalance. My mother, recognizing that my temper was wearing thin, shifted in her seat uncomfortably.

"I have to say, not that I would readily trust you with the role, but I'm rather surprised you're not interested in taking Zurie's place on the throne, considering you're clearly the most eligible after all your years of service as Royal Advisor and Seer... Accompanied with your formidable powers, No one could challenge you."

Miroslav gave us a frustratingly understated, enigmatic smile that was painfully similar to the one my mother deferred to when I was asking something only she had the answer to.

"Despite the fact that I have no desire to bear that burden, before Zurie hired me, she made me swear a blood vow that *I* would never attempt to take her throne, become King, or harm her."

I lifted my brows, urging him to elaborate.

"That's a rather fine line you're dancing on with that last one, Miroslav."

He gave me a tight smile.

"I would die a thousand deaths if it meant protecting your mother. What is one death if it saves both her and the realm?"

My heart stalled in my chest... *Oh gods.*

My eyes dipped to my mother leaning further into his side as though needing to hold onto him to prevent such a thing from happening. As much disdain as I might personally hold for the male... I would never wish the pain that comes from losing one's *soulbound* on my mother.

"When?"

"That all depends on you."

My jaw dropped.

"What?"

"On how much you and Mareina require my intervention when it comes to overthrowing Zurie..."

Right. So, no pressure.

FORTY-THREE

MAREINA

My appetite dried up after finding out that if Nakoa and I couldn't overpower Zurie ourselves, Miroslav would be forced to step in, and he would die because of it...

That male I had hated for nearly a century had done so much to protect his mate, Nakoa, their family, and all of Atratus... Potentially the entire Bellorum Realm if what he previously implied was accurate...

A grim resolve rooted deep inside me as I sat there, unable to listen to anything more during dinner. Whatever happened when we infiltrated Zurie's palace, we would *not* rely on Miroslav.

Thankfully, that Knowingness that had lent itself to me since Nakoa and I had begun bonding, despite how fractured, bolstered my resolve and my confidence...

My magic had been steadily increasing since we'd met. Since attempting to fulfill our bond, I could feel it roiling through me like tumultuous, crashing waves in a caged sea.

I glanced down at my hands, now clasped in my lap, as conversation continued to find dark red tendrils seeping from them... My breath caught, and I *willed* them to retreat, lest anyone notice.

This is new.

His gaze snapped to mine, having noticed some shift or felt my shock through the tether. Brow furrowed in question, his eyes scored over me.

I'd always been able to *will* things to and from places, sense things, and had a strength and speed that rivalled even the largest of males, thanks to my magic... But having a physical manifestation of it was entirely new.

Still lost in thought after excusing ourselves from dinner, the second Nakoa and I rounded the corner, he took me by surprise by leaning down and sweeping me off my feet.

"What're you doing?"

"Do I need to remind you again of our nightly bargain?"

My chest squeezed with tension, even as the tether between us burned with demand. I knew he felt things for me, but I was reasonably certain it was only because of the bond forcing him. Which was in addition to the fact that he was *using* me to meet his own ends. I felt like little more than a chess piece on the board for him.

Cradling me in his arms as if I were his bride, he marched us down the hallway until we arrived at one of the numerous doors that swung open and closed by some invisible hand.

Nakoa set me down on the bed, arms bracketing my body as he searched my eyes.

My chest tightened. Despite Nakoa's past... I still felt this boulder of distrust between us. Not to mention the resentment I felt at him for having no qualms about risking my life to kill Zurie.

That was, of course, in addition to the anvil of guilt that I was supposed to be murdering his birth mother without him being made the wiser. I had promised Leilani that I wouldn't tell him... I had been in such shock that it seemed like a rational thing to do, but the longer I sat with it... The more unsettled about it I became.

Would he still want her dead? She had, after all, *ordered* his death moments after giving birth to him. Surely, he wouldn't want her to live...

Even so, it didn't change the fact that it would be... a *heinous* transgression to not at least make him aware.

Leilani's words echoed in my mind.

"... It could change the course of... Everything."

Fuck.

"Nakoa... I..."

His brows drew together, jaw hardening as if preparing himself for the sting of rejection. The confession sat on the tip of my tongue...

But I swallowed it back, replacing it with another truth.

"I don't want intimacy between us just because we're forced into it by this bond..."

Nakoa hesitated, hovering over me for a few moments longer before he shifted to sit on the edge of the bed, giving me his back.

The tether between us burned, and some gods-forsaken emotion clogged my throat.

I was tired

So fucking tired.

I had spent my entire life fighting to survive, and the *one* person I was supposed to be able to trust and find respite in... Was the one I felt like I could trust least of all because he didn't *want* me. He simply *needed* me. Trusting him with any piece of me only ensured more heartbreak.

Having been very much alone for virtually the entirety of my formative years and for the mass majority of my adulthood, I longed for intimacy and trust with another like it was a gaping wound in my chest that could only be healed by the tenderness of another. Malekai was the only person who had ever allowed in enough to heal the wound that I, until now, thought had scarred over.

Now, it was like he had completely carved that wound anew... Revealing, however briefly, what it could be like to open yourself up to another... But how could I ever find that with someone who was unwillingly shackled to me and despised my very existence?

Regardless, I felt a deeply rooted sense of determination to see this through. It was time for Zurie's reign to end. And I had every intention of fulfilling my vow to help him rule this Kingdom. Even if it wasn't in the way a King and Queen would typically rule...

I recognized that this whole thing was so much greater than us... Miroslav's earlier mention of potential threats from Ishra, Hades, Maimyō mo Qì, and the realms beyond... Gave me a profoundly unsettling and ominous sensation that weighed heavily in the pit of my stomach... And somehow, I couldn't help but feel it was tied to who or *what* was connected to those dreams... and the pythos...

So that the world may be born anew...

Those words echoed in my mind from my dream...

What if killing Zurie was only the beginning and not the end?

Phaedra had already warned us that all of this extended far beyond Atratus...

The sound of a bath tap turning on snapped me out of my downward spiral. I looked up to find Nakoa striding towards the opposite side of the room, where a large copper tub sat. He willed his clothes away, baring the sight of his perfectly sculpted backside. The tether between us pulled painfully tight at the distance between us. Not physically but emotionally... It felt like a chasm that held only a single fraying rope to connect us.

How much longer could I endure this?

Something needed to change.

We might not *love* each other... We certainly had our differences... But that didn't mean we needed to be enemies.

I heaved a deep, fortifying sigh as I steeled myself for what I was about to do. Eventually, I forced myself to sit up and make my way towards Nakoa. His handsome, scarred face set in an expression that someone who wasn't tethered to him might assume was neutral or indifferent... but I could very clearly *feel* what laid behind that mask. Turmoil. Pain. Longing. Frustration.

It took several moments before his gaze finally lifted to mine.

"Do you mind if I join you?"

Surprise flickered in his eyes briefly. "By all means."

I willed away my clothes, and I didn't miss the way his eyes flared briefly before he forced his gaze away. The water was just on the cusp of being too hot, which meant it was utterly perfect as I sank beneath the water on the other end of the tub. A groan I hadn't realized needed to be released was dragged out of me. Our legs puzzled together, and I couldn't deny the rightness and relief the sensation gave me.

Just as I'd finally managed to piece together some words I thought might be a constructive way to begin, Nakoa broke the silence.

"I'm sorry, Mareina... I won't lie and say that *part* of my actions aren't driven by my need to overthrow Zurie. That everything I've done and said wasn't, *in part*, an attempt influenced by that... But there is *more*... And I have tried to fight against it. I don't want to anymore. I just want you. I want what we could have. *Between us.*"

His words returned that aching sensation to my chest, tight and heavy. As reassuring as he might have intended them to be...

"But is it just the bond? If it weren't for the bond, you would have killed me... Much less chosen me to be your fated mate."

Nakoa held my gaze, jaw clenching.

"I wasn't lying when I said that I was certain you would be the best Queen Atratus has ever known..."

I huffed a sad laugh, unable to look him in the face any longer as tears swelled in my eyes. *Again.*

Fuck, what I wouldn't give to be in Malekai's arms right now.

"That has nothing to do with it."

"That has *everything* to do with it."

I shook my head. "Let's pretend for a moment that The Kahlohani Islands didn't need liberating. That your people weren't living in squalor and exile... That you didn't need to become King. You didn't need a Queen to rule beside you. You could live your life freely and as you pleased. And we weren't *soulbound.* Would you still want *me?*"

He looked shocked by the question. With every passing moment,

I sank deeper into the tub and into my despair. His silence had said enough.

"... I don't know, Mareina..."

The fact his admission was not surprising did nothing to soften the blow of his indecision... Perhaps it was what I deserved. For all that I had done, all the suffering I had inflicted on others... Why would he have willingly chosen me?

"Would you have chosen *me* if things had been different? If we hadn't been enemies. And..." His jaw flexed with anger. "If you weren't pining over the male I've seen you with in my visions."

Despite the hurt, I considered his question, and my mind slid back to the Nakoa I had met before he knew who I was to Zurie.

Before he realized I was his enemy.

And that Nakoa... The one who could inspire my soul by strumming his fingers on an instrument, wearing dark charisma decorated in scars, and actively spent his days liberating people from indentured servitude and gifting them riches he had stolen from the same masters that had exploited them...

The Nakoa that hadn't taken advantage of me despite my vulnerable state when I'd taken *grá root*. The male who had laughed readily opened his home to me without trying to lure me into his bed... The one who could play my body like an instrument he'd spent a lifetime mastering...

Lamenting *that* Nakoa...

It hurt too badly to dwell on it and left me feeling that much more alone.

Unable to hold my tears back, I dunked my head underwater and quickly began scrubbing my scalp and body. All the while, Nakoa watched me with a penetrative gaze.

When I finally rose, grabbing the muslin towel and robe folded on a stool beside the tub, I could actually *hear* the pounding of Nakoa's heartbeat. His hand lashed out, gripping my calf before I could fully step out of the tub.

Meeting his gaze, I steeled myself with another deep breath.

"When I think of the male I met before you realized I was someone you should hate... Then... Yes. I would."

His lips parted in shock. I yanked my leg free, stepping out of the tub.

"But the male that has used and manipulated me every step of the way. The one that is so easily prepared to sacrifice me to Zurie to meet his ends... The one who fails to see beyond my flaws... No. I want nothing to do with him."

Forcing myself not to give up and give him my back, just for us to have more of the same, I attempted the most optimistic tone I could manage. Instead, it came out sounding like a sad resignation.

"We don't have to be enemies. Why don't we just... Call a truce? I plan to honor my vow to the best of my abilities in helping you over-throw Zurie and bringing peace to Atratus. If we can find peace between one another, it'll make our endeavors that much easier."

CHAPTER
FORTY-FOUR
NAKOA

As if my own subconscious wanted to punish me for being such a fucking *hypocrite*, my sleep had been riddled with nightmares that consisted of reliving twisted flashbacks of every soldier in Zurie's army that I'd tortured and killed. Soldiers who had begged me to spare them their lives because they had families to return to...

I found myself lying in bed beside Mareina, who, although laid only half a foot away, curled on the side of the bed, felt about a million miles away.

Everything within me ached to reach out and pull her against me for no other purpose than to feel her close to me.

Was it simply the bond?

Past set aside, my mind conjured up everything about Mareina that I had grown to appreciate... Her strength, her resilience, her bravery, her selflessness... My mind returned to the human she had rescued only days ago, though it felt far longer.

Fuck, I was such a godsdamned idiot.

It was obvious there was so much to love about her... And I had become so blinded by my lifelong desire to kill Zurie and reclaim The

Kahlohani Islands that... Perhaps I'd lost sight of what would make all the suffering and sacrifice worth it.

Anguish and guilt clawed and gnawed at my chest...

Kingdom aside, how could I have been so blind as to not recognize how fucking perfect she was for me?

What other female could challenge me and force me to face my demons as she did? What other female could better inspire me to become a male worthy of ruling a Kingdom? Could coax out a tenderness and softness within me that I hadn't even known existed?

Just as I mustered up the courage to wake her and risk her wrath, my heart kicked up at the sound of a voice calling to me from my mother's cave. The same voice that had haunted my dreams but had now made its way into my waking life.

As though pulled by some unseen thread, I silently rose from the bed and made my way down the silent hall where the warded doorway to the cave was, somehow, open. A soft light poured from it. Yet the closer I drew, the more distant and quiet the voice became.

By the time I opened the door, silence had returned. I scanned the cave. My gaze drifted to the far side of the room to find The Well, usually pitch black, glowing a brilliant white. I made my way over, glancing briefly over my shoulder to see that the door had shut. As I reached the edge, I stared down into The Well to see my own face, and a scene began to play out before me. One in which I'd already made my monstrous transformation.

Only now, in this version, Mareina was nowhere to be found.

My heart nearly stopped.

Where the fuck was Mareina?

Something was wrong. Horribly, horribly wrong.

As though witnessing the event in person, I found myself standing in Zurie's throne room with my future self in front of me, along with the priestess officiating my inauguration, and what appeared to be at least half of Bastrina in the audience to witness. I turned in a full circle, scanning every corner for Mareina.

320

Panic filled me to the brim when she was nowhere to be seen and powerless to escape this fucking nightmare.

The priestess, dressed in the traditional Akashian vestments, stood before my future self.

"Nakoa Solanis, your reign rings forth an era of unparalleled peace, unity, and prosperity to the Kingdom of Atratus. As the High Priestess, I pledge on behalf of our deity, *Akash*, to bestow her blessings, protection, power, and wisdom to guide our sovereign nation justly so that you may lead us to a future brighter than the stars themselves."

A large, gilded crown appeared in the priestess' hands, placing it on my bowed head. She stepped back, and I rose, solemn words pouring forth and echoing with power throughout the temple as my wings unfurled and I drew a blade across my palm.

"By the divine power vested in me, I swear an unbreakable vow: I will protect the Kingdom of Atratus with my life. In the darkest of nights and the fiercest of storms, I shall remain the guardian of Atratus until death. With *Akash's* will and power flowing through my veins, I shall fulfill my sacred duty with honor."

CHAPTER
FORTY-FIVE

MAREINA

My sleep was fitful. Plagued by nightmares too close to a past reality that I was desperate to forget. On Zurie's dais in her ampitheater, Vesper had wielded my sword as she beheaded everyone I'd ever loved, and I was forced to watch as a crowd behind me cheered. I'd knelt beside them, chained to the ground, waiting my turn as their blood pooled around me. Only my turn never came. The blood around me rose higher until it filled my lungs, and I drowned beside their headless bodies.

The sensation of Nakoa's large, firm body curled behind mine, tugging me firmly against him, was a tremendous relief despite the lack of trust between us. At least until memories of the previous evening returned, making my wounded heart that much harder. I drew in a fortifying breath.

How could I keep this secret from him?

How could I kill his mother without him knowing?

And if I told him the truth, in what way would our world be doomed?

Leilani had pulled me aside again after *The Well* and reaffirmed the importance of not telling him the truth about Zurie. It was cruel to not tell him... But... Was that knowledge worth lives? No... I guess I couldn't say it was. And Miroslav had reminded me of the fact before the night's end.

The words were crawling up my throat until I turned in his arms to find him wide awake. His face pale and expression tense, eyes wide with fear. My heart rate kicked at the sight.

"What happened?"

His throat worked on a rough swallow, shaking his head gently. My heart began to pound furiously.

"Last night... The Well."

"You visited it?"

A nod.

"And...?"

"... I don't know that I can say."

"Is something terrible going to happen?"

He paused momentarily, licking his lips and taking a deep breath.

"I... Don't know."

The beat of my heart thumped so loudly it echoed in my ears.

"I'm not going anywhere, Nakoa..."

His face hardened as he fought back emotion, eyes glistening.

"Mareina... Last night, I... I'm sorry. I didn't mean what I said... I just... I've become blinded by my own determination. I would choose you with or without the bond... I can't fathom a more perfect female not just to rule Atratus but *for me.*"

He searched my gaze almost frantically as if trying to find evidence of my faith in his words. I nodded gently through this sensation of numbness that settled on my chest.

"... OK."

His brows knit together.

"OK?"

I took a deep breath, rolling out of his arms to stare at the ceiling.

"OK. I appreciate it. Thank you for saying so."

Nakoa perched himself on an elbow as he reached out for me,

just as the sound of movement and voices outside our room filtered in.

Vyssini... We'd be heading to Vyssini today on our way to Bastrina...

My heart leapt at the idea of being in the same place as Malekai but immediately fisted with pain, knowing that I wouldn't be able to leave with him... And just... Disappear.

What had *Nakoa seen in The Well?*

Had whatever he'd seen been why he'd been desperate to apologize?

* * *

By noon, our large group was dressed and ready to leave. With nothing more than the brief murmuring of an ancient tongue, Leilani opened a portal in the forest at the front of her glamored home. A portal large enough for the group of us, including our horses, to step through and arrive somewhere on the outskirts of Vyssini.

The restless energy surrounding everyone at what now felt like a silent countdown towards Zurie and our potential deaths had my anxiety rising. The closer we came to Vyssini, the more it intensified, though I wasn't entirely sure why. The Knowingness that had spoken to me in the past days seemed to have gone silent despite my probing.

Leilani seemed somber but relatively at ease as she gave me a firm squeeze before leaving, whispering so that only I could hear. "I have seen much of your future in The Well, Mareina. You and Nakoa have nothing to fear as long as you stay together."

My throat worked on a rough swallow as I pulled back to gaze into her dark eyes, unable to hide their worry.

"... Thank you. For everything," I managed.

She gave me a nod and a weak smile. "I'll see you at the palace..."

And I could only pray that Malekai wouldn't be there. I didn't think I could handle it if something happened to him. We had 100 years of friendship and loyalty when I'd had next to no one else along the way - only my fleeting years with my childhood best friend, Fara, and Seline, my first love. Both, now dead.

I desperately wanted to speak to Pomona to see what had passed during her encounter with Malekai. However, we still hadn't had the privacy to do so. Thankfully, she seemed relatively at ease, if not only mildly anxious, at our rapidly impending attempt to infiltrate Zurie's palace.

Roderick, Lokus, Rayne, Pomona, Famei, and Vesper crossed through the portal's edge, only quickly exchanging goodbyes with Leilani and Miroslav as I waited for Nakoa and tried to breathe away my fears.

Stay together.

Right.

How in the gods' names were we supposed to stay together when I was supposed to go inside the palace, with no one but Vesper, to kill Zurie.

Nakoa remained in the distance, discussing something even my sanguinati ears couldn't hear. Unable to disguise the tension in Miroslav's glittering diamond-like eyes, his gaze met mine.

"Worry not for what the future will bring, Mareina. You have nothing to fear," he murmured calmly within my mind.

His reassuring words did little to assuage my concern, but before my mind could formulate a response, Nakoa tugged me through the portal.

* * *

Thanks to its wealthy citizens, Vyssini was usually a bustling town boasting stunning architecture and artwork. It was one of the exceedingly few places in Atratus that seemed to have benefited from Zurie's reign. Thanks to its spectacular location, surrounded by pristine mountains and lakes, many of the Lords and other aristocrats of Atratus that fed from Zurie's bosom had secondary homes here.

However, the closer we rode, the more dread settled heavily in my gut. The town seemed all but abandoned. Businesses and homes shuttered. The streets vacant of life. Only the occasional face peeking out from behind a curtain evidence that anyone remained.

Pomona had told Malekai to retreat... Why were tendrils of dread coiling around my throat and my limbs? I suddenly felt stupid to think Malekai would have listened. Sacrificing his livelihood and, in turn, incurring Zurie's wrath simply because I asked him to.

As if reading my mind, Pomona met my gaze from where she rode beside me. She appeared equally as distressed.

The oppressive weight in the air weighed heavily, only increasing with every hoof step forward.

Nakoa's grip on me tightened the moment a soft hum began to sound in the distance. The group of us silently exchanged wary looks as the humming grew louder, eventually rising to a buzz. And then came the stench.

In all my years of battle, murder, torture, executions, and all the horrific smells associated with it... It had been a long time since it had inspired such a visceral reaction within me. I had long thought myself numb to death, yet I found my hands trembling and restless. I looked down to see my magic, reappearing as those dark red tendrils seeping from my skin. I promptly called it back to me and glanced to either side to check if anyone else had seen it, but everyone's gazes were locked on what laid in front of us.

We finally rounded the corner of Vyssini's central square, boasting beautiful bronze sculptures, gilded storefronts, and colourful awnings. Though our attention was focused solely at what laid in front of the bronze fountain depicting a female holding a large bouquet of *aetra* blossoms. Crimson water crashed from the sculpted waterfall behind her, pooling at her feet, reminding me of last night's nightmare.

That wasn't what had bile crawling up my throat. Nor was it the flies swarming like a thick fog.

At the foot of the fountain, at least 20 metal pikes had been speared through the cobblestone, boasting just as many heads, and beneath them laid their headless bodies.

I stared, slack-jawed, as that all-too-familiar numbness washed over me.

Despite the ridiculousness of my hope that Malekai would have heeded my request... I couldn't help but feel that twisting knife of defeat. Despite what had happened after I'd tried to escape Nakoa, I recognized not all of them would be corrupt, like those who'd tried to violate me. The males and females who had been executed before us were integral Uprising Members.

My breath came to a halt as my gaze snagged on a familiar face. The generically handsome features... The long brown hair, still tied in its knot... The piercing blue eyes now dulled and bereft of his life force.

Confusion, mingled with disbelief, swept over me...

I squinted, trying to make sure my eyes weren't deceiving me.

Was that...

Galvor?

"Do you recognize them? These aren't any members of The Uprising that I know...," Nakoa asked his *olana kah'hei.*

My gaze drifted across each face, all of which were familiar, to ensure that Malekai was not among them. My voice barely came out a whisper.

"That's because they're not Uprising members..."

I turned to look at Pomona, her face pale at the gruesome display but... mirrored none of the shock slackening my own.

"Who are they?" Nakoa asked, his voice almost breathy with disbelief.

"Zurie's soldiers..."

CHAPTER

FORTY-SIX

MAREINA

fter leaving Vyssini's central square behind, that sense of foreboding gradually lifted the deeper we rode into the forest and *away* from the carnage that I could only assume The Uprising had left behind... Praise the gods, Malekai hadn't been among them. Though I couldn't sense what specifically, something was off...

I kept throwing discreet glances at Pomona, who seemed intent on avoiding me. She hadn't seemed surprised in the least... Had...

Had Malekai killed them?

My stomach roiled to imagine either scenario. Either he was out there, potentially gravely injured from making a narrow escape... Or he had killed them himself? Killing so many of them certainly wasn't beyond his power... Some of these were soldiers we'd fought beside. Though a few of the ones I knew personally, like Galvor, were... Unsavoury, to say the least... They'd trusted them with his life.

Would he have really slaughtered them all merely because I'd told Pomona to tell him I wanted us to watch the world burn?

His deep, velvety voice echoed in my mind.

Katadamna kaza.

Damn the cost.

He had saved my life multiple times, and I trusted him wholly. Not to mention, finding an excuse to turn against Zurie wasn't exactly a chore. It had only been days ago she'd fucking mutilated him out of nothing more than entertaining herself.

Guilt churned heavily in my gut. If he had done this because of me... It would be my fault they were dead. Though if I hadn't, it would have been Uprising members...

Where was he?

Surely Malekai couldn't have returned to the palace as the only survivor... Zurie wouldn't accept that kind of failure...

My worry for him ratcheted higher, and I looked down to find those tendrils of magic pouring from my front.

Fuck.

With no small amount of effort, I heaved them back in, and my magic writhed indignantly against the barrier of my skin. I willed myself to take more deep, steadying breaths.

"Are you alright, *lohane thili?*"

Nakoa's voice was barely a murmur against my hair.

"Yes... Just... I knew them."

Not exactly a lie.

The leather of Pumpkin's reins creaked in his grip.

"I'm sorry... Were you close with any of them?"

I shook my head, unable to force any more words out as my mind frantically whirled. I *needed* to know that Malekai was safe.

How could I even find him?

If he had been responsible for the deaths of all those soldiers, how long would it take for Zurie to hunt him down?

I repeated my silent prayer to *Akash* like a mantra.

Please, Akash. Please let Malekai be safe.

After the longest hour and a half of my life, we finally reached a small cabin, hidden deep in the woods, to meet with a lykos male named Val, apparently the most senior member of The Uprising beneath Nakoa and his chosen family.

Val stepped out onto the porch of his cabin, arms folded across his broad chest as an even broader grin split his thickly bearded face. Thick, wavy blond hair, shaved at the sides but long on top, laid in a thick braid over one shoulder. He looked like some kind of Viking from Terrania.

"Bout time ya showed up, ya big bastard," he called out to Nakoa. The male's gravelly voice was thick with an accent only found in the mountains of *Bein Sith Mór*. A small region renowned for having some of the most spectacular and magically rich lands. Also home to Atratus' largest population of fairies, sprites, druids, witches, and shifters.

"Inconsiderate of you to live so far away, if you ask me. The three days ride to get here is a pain in my dick," Nakoa shouted back with a grin on his face as he finally drew Pumpkin to a stop and slid off her side. Before I could attempt to dismount on my own, he tugged me down into his arms and set me on the ground beside him.

Val had already descended the steps of his cabin when we turned to face him and closed the distance between us in merely a few long strides.

Nakoa opened his arms to embrace him, only to be promptly shoved aside. Val wrapped me up in his arms, pinning my own to my sides, and swung me around like I weighed nothing.

"What an absolute treasure you've found, brother!"

He inhaled deeply at my scent as I stared in shock at Nakoa's smirking face over Val's shoulder.

Val set me down, his dark blue eyes twinkling with mischief and apology.

"Sorry, lass. I cannae help myself sometimes. Ya dinnae have a sister, do ya?"

I couldn't help but be endeared by the warmth he radiated.

"No, I'm sorry to say, I don't."

Val gave a forlorn grunt. "Well, if ya ever get puggled'a this auld bawbag, ye ken where ta find me."

If you ever get tired of this old ball bag, you know where to find me.

I'd spent a considerable amount of time hovering around a fire with the good people from *Bein Sith Mór* during the war. While they were notoriously heavy drinkers, they were equally hilarious and animated. Always ready to have a laugh no matter how dire the situation. I'd frequently found myself naturally gravitating towards them. Though those I'd befriended had unfortunately met their end during the war.

I grinned up at him, giving him a wink.

"Whit's fur ye'll no go past ye," I teased.

Val's thick brows leapt towards his hairline in surprise before he burst into a heartwarming belly laugh as he clapped Nakoa on the shoulder.

"Ooooooh, better ye keep an eye on this one afore ah steal her awae'fae ye."

Nakoa chuckled appreciatively. "Brother, if you're feeling suicidal, there are more effective ways to go about asking for help."

Val's laughter doubled.

The rest of Nakoa's *olana kah'hei* greeted Val with a warmth and exuberance that left my soul throbbing with a familiar ache... What a gift it would be to have such strong bonds with so many people. To have a family. The sight of Val playfully putting Roderick, a fellow Lykos, in a chokehold and rubbing his fisted knuckles into the top of his head like they were brothers had a grin teasing the edges of my mouth.

Nakoa turned to me with an understanding smile as if reading my mind. "You belong here too, Mareina..."

Just as he stepped towards me, reaching for my hands, an all too familiar voice called to me in its deep, velvety tone.

"Mareina..."

My heart just about burst from my chest as my head snapped up

Val's porch steps to find Malekai standing in the doorway of Val's cabin.

Oh, sweet gods.

Alive.

He was alive.

Without thought, I rushed forward as Malekai descended the porch steps in a single stride to meet me. I crashed into his chest, throwing my arms around him in blessed relief.

"Oh gods, you're ok... I was so worried," I breathed, burying my face in his chest. Tears sprung to my eyes at the instant relief as my chest swelled with gratitude.

His arms held me so tightly against him I could scarcely breathe.

"You? Mareina, I was about a day away from razing the fucking Kingdom to the ground."

He looked down into my face, wiping away my tears with his thumbs.

"Fuck, I missed you."

I opened my mouth to respond but drew back suddenly, wincing at the bolt of jealousy, fear, and anger that poured into me from mine and Nakoa's tether. I'd been effectively suppressing my dread at the inevitability of this moment. Still, I gripped Malekai's arms as if he'd disappear the moment I let go. I could only pray Nakoa wouldn't try to tear his throat out.

"There's someone you should meet..."

Nakoa strode toward me, eyes already black, though he'd managed to keep his glamor in place, which... had to be a good sign, surely.

"This is my... *soulbound.* Nakoa."

The words tasted like ash, and the look on Malekai's face just about tore my heart out. I forced one of my hands away from Malekai's arm to rest a hand on Nakoa's shoulder to try and placate him. Malekai's eyes dipped to check for *soulbound* marks he wouldn't find.

"Nakoa, this is Malekai..."

And thanks to Nakoa's visions and Knowingness, he was already well aware of who he was to me. Though I wasn't about to instigate matters by proclaiming my love for him right now.

"... My closest friend and ally," I finished.

The heat of Nakoa's *olana kah'hei's* collective gaze felt as if it would burn a hole straight through me. Malekai's throat worked on a rough swallow before gradually nodding and extending his hand towards Nakoa.

Nakoa's hands fisted at his sides as his gaze fell to Malekai's hand. Tension coiled tight in the moment before he finally took Malekai's hand.

Silence weighed heavily in the air as their hands moved up and down in a mechanical motion for a painful amount of time. I couldn't help but wonder what in the gods' names his Knowingness was whispering to him.

Val approached, bless him, and clapped both males on the shoulder. Finally, breaking the tension.

"This is the lad I was telling' yew about last night... The ally on the *inside* that I mentioned."

The shock that Malekai was even here finally registered.

My gaze sought Pomona, who was already intently staring at me. With everyone's attention focused on me, Malekai, and Nakoa, she finally acknowledged me. She shrugged, lifting her brows as if to say, *your guess is as good as mine.*

"The soldiers... at the town square... That was you?" Nakoa asked, his brow tense.

Malekai gave a short nod.

Nakoa's brow tightened.

Val squeezed their shoulders, pushing them both up the stairs, before throwing me a look over his shoulder.

"What the fuck was that?" He mouthed silently to me.

I gently grabbed Pomona's arm to pull her aside as Famei, Rayne, Vesper, and Roderick followed them into the cabin.

"What happened last night?" I whispered when they'd all retreated inside.

She blew out a breath, shaking her head as we stepped further away from the cabin. "Nothing, other than attempting to thoroughly interrogate me as to where you were and to provide evidence of your safety. He agreed not to attack any of The Uprising Members. Didn't say anything about... all of *that*."

"Did you tell him about Val?"

She reared back. "*Akash,* no."

I paced anxiously, wondering what in the fuck was actually happening.

Had he been a part of this the whole time?

Surely, not...

Malekai's words echoed in my mind... "*Want me to just kill her for you, and then we can watch the world burn together?*"

Pomona's brows pinched with a hint of suspicion and deep concern. "I don't mean to pry, but... Just how close are you two again?"

I sighed, feeling the weight of my emotion crush my chest.

"I'm closer with him than I've ever been with anyone... But not romantic... We've never... acted on anything physical."

Pomona's face was tight with concern as I continued.

"We fought in the war together... Saved each other's lives on... More occasions than I can recall... He's been my best friend for the last hundred years."

"I see..." A hint of a grin tilted her lips, and a little of my tension alleviated. Her look grew coy as she gave me devilish grin, leaning in close. "And... May I ask *why* it never became anything *more* than friendship because *good-fucking-gods...*"

I couldn't help but huff a laugh, rolling my eyes. Even though I hardly knew her, I felt the need to confide in her.

"I do love him, Pomona..."

Her brows lept.

"I... Things between Nakoa and I..." I shook my head not even knowing where or how to begin. "I can't be with him... I won't disparage him to you and I recognize he has many exceptional qualities but... I will never be able to trust or give myself to him after... *All this.*"

Pomona looked genuinely pained by my admission and it made guilt clench tighter in my chest.

"I've already expressed to Nakoa my desire to leave after we finish with everything... I will help him rule... I even made a vow to do so. To support him in this as best I can. But I will not bind myself to him. And regardless... My heart already belongs to Malekai. I haven't told him yet either but... I will. Once we overcome Zurie."

Pomona nodded, gaze drifting into the distance as a look of sadness took her face but seemed otherwise understanding. And not even remotely surprised. After a few moments, her gaze finally returned to mine, offering me an encouraging smile that didn't quite meet her eyes.

"I hope that one day, however distant in the future... That you two can make amends..."

My throat worked roughly. That was definitely not something I could promise.

Her smile broadened, attempting lightheartedness.

"On a happier note... I mean... Don't repeat this to Famei, but your friend is... Wooooooohh...," she continued, fanning herself as though she were about to have a heat stroke.

A grin split my face, grateful for her attempt at distraction.

"I'll be sure to tell him you think so."

Pomona gasped dramatically. "You wouldn't dare!"

I laughed openly for the first time in what felt like... ages.

"No, I wouldn't. Don't worry."

She heaved a breath in relief, chuckling. "I still wanna know why you never had anything with him *before* you met Nakoa."

I sighed heavily. It wasn't an easy question.

"I... I haven't known many loyal people I could rely on. And those that I did... They died during the war. After that, I just... Kind of closed myself off to people because if they were worth knowing, they could be taken from me, or if they weren't worth knowing, but I failed to see it... Well, I simply didn't have enough pieces left of my heart to give in either circumstance... And the idea of losing Malekai... If things didn't work out between us... I'd have been left with *no one*. I cherished him too much to gamble with our friendship like that."

Pomona heaved a thoughtful sigh.

"Living in fear is no way to live at all, darlin'."

The truth in her words hit me like a kick to the face. *Gods, she was so right it hurt.* And it was time to fucking change that. But first, I needed to be honest with Nakoa before I confessed my feelings to Malekai... Which would perhaps be better after everything Zurie was dealt with.

I gave her shoulder a squeeze. "You're right, Pomona. Thank you. And thank you for finding Malekai for me last night.""

Her rosebud lips parted to reveal a grin bursting with affection. I'd never met someone so warm and open. It was nothing short of startling, even if it gave my heart a sweet squeeze.

"Of course. You're my sister now. With or without Nakoa."

The moment Pomona and I entered Val's cabin, both Nakoa and Malekai's eyes snapped to mine. Lest I further enflame Nakoa's rage, I forced myself to go to his side despite the ache in my chest that longed to go to Malekai. Nakoa wrapped an arm around my waist and tugged me possessively into his side. It felt like a betrayal to my emotions and to Malekai. My eyes slid shut as I tried to breathe away my tension.

Despite Nakoa being my *soulbound* and having rescued me from that basement... Something was broken between us. He'd knowingly and willfully tried to manipulate me using my emotions and my vulnerabilities... Until this morning, he hadn't been sure if he would choose to be with me if it weren't for the bond demanding it. And I couldn't help but wonder if it was only out of guilt.

I met Malekai's gaze, willing my features into something neutral, but it only made his brows furrow tighter with concern. When his eyes lifted to Nakoa's, his normally warm features shifted to something strikingly cold before returning to Val, who was currently discussing the gold and jewels Nakoa and his *olana kah'hei* had apparently looted the same day we'd met and its distribution among the various outlets through which The Uprising worked.

Impatience swelled in my chest, making me shift on my feet.

What was Malekai's plan?

Surely, he didn't intend on returning to Zurie...

How the fuck did he know about Val?

And how had he... managed to betray all those soldiers who trusted him...

Unease worked its way deeper and deeper into my veins until it rooted heavily in my gut.

Should I tell him about our plan to overthrow Zurie?

"... If we could gain the Selcarim Army as allies, we would be unstoppable," Val pleaded with Lokus, snagging my attention.

Lokus gave a sad chuckle. "The last time I spoke to my father was at the end of the war when he tossed me out of his Kingdom. Trust me when I say you *don't* want me liaising on The Uprising's behalf."

Val frowned with a look of compassion settling on his ruggedly handsome features. His eyes darted with cautious optimism to Rayne, who lifted his hands in surrender.

"Guilty by association, I'm afraid. The best I could do is get you beyond the mountain pass. I have a few friends that I've lost contact with over the years, but I'm sure they'd be open to helping. Can't make any promises, though."

This conversation was moot, considering Zurie would be dead in a matter of days if everything went according to plan. Although it would be useful for Nakoa to have the Selcarim as allies... But apparently, Nakoa had no intention of—

"The Selcarim will indeed be good allies, but we don't need them to overthrow Zurie."

Val's brows furrowed. "Koa... We've grown considerably but I don't think—

"Mareina and Vesper included; my *olana kah'hei* and I will overthrow Zurie in a matter of days when we arrive in Bastrina, where we're heading directly after you."

Val's jaw dropped.

"You've gotta be fucking kidding me," Malekai growled.

"Not at all," Nakoa growled back.

Oh fuck.

Malekai's eyes fell to mine. "And you plan to help them?"

My teeth ground together at being pulled into what I could sense was basically one ball bag's hair away from becoming a dick-measuring contest.

"Yes. I do. The plan that we've devised is a good one."

"What plan?" Malekai and Val growled in unison.

I laid my hand on Nakoa's chest to calm him as I raised my voice to speak over him.

"May I?" I asked Nakoa, my annoyance clear on my face.

Nakoa scowled down at me. "Are you sure you trust this male?"

"With my life."

If anything, Nakoa's distrust of Malekai strengthened, though for an entirely different reason.

"This male just saved about every Uprising member in Vyssini. I've made myself a fucking outlaw and executed 20 of her soldiers to join your cause."

Nakoa studied him for several moments, no doubt consulting with his Knowingness again, before he finally gave me a short nod, prompting me to explain the devised plan. Better from my mouth than Nakoa's.

As I walked him through it, his brows dipped and leapt as though oscillating back and forth between shock and frustration.

When I finished, Malekai shook his hand, huffing a mirthless laugh.

"No."

Nakoa bared his teeth. "In case you hadn't noticed, you're in no position of power to dictate what we do or don't do. If you're a part of this cause, you will fucking *cooperate* with all of us. I may be the leader of The Uprising, but this is not a dictatorship, and this is what we *all* have agreed upon. Mareina is highly capable. I have no doubt that she will have no difficulty executing Zurie. We have the element of surprise on our side. Not to mention, not only have I seen the visions, but we have two seers who can also affirm this plan will work—"

Malekai shook his head in disbelief. "I don't give a fuck about what psychic powers have *'affirmed'* this insane plan will work. There is always room for error and chaos. And you are not sending Mareina and," Malekai all but shouted, briefly gesturing to Vesper, "An *unknown* that is probably conspiring to murder her, into what will inevitably become a fight to the death with Zurie, *who is potentially one of the most powerful fae in all of Atratus.* Is that really how you plan to protect your fucking *soulbound*—"

Nakoa moved so swiftly that he was a blur as he lunged for Malekai, tackling him to the ground. Shouts erupted from Val and Famei. Lokus cackled with laughter as the coffee table they crashlanded on gave out from underneath them.

Gods...

"I made that table with me bare fuckin' hands, ya cunts!" Val cried in a voice that sounded like a clap of thunder, swiping a palm over his rugged face.

I growled, drawing in a deep breath before shifting to pull Nakoa away just as Rayne stepped in front of me, shaking his head in warning.

"If you want them to be friends, let them fight it out."

I had spent more than enough time in a testosterone-fueled environment to know the truth in his words.

I peered around from Rayne to find Malekai having pinned Nakoa to the ground. My heart gave a painful squeeze having to watch the two people I cared for most in this world beating each other to a pulp.

"He's right, lass," Val begrudgingly agreed, eyes darting to see what exactly they would destroy next before leaping forward to collect his breakables.

I watched as Malekai jabbed just for Nakoa to dodge, making Malekai punch the solid wood floor so hard that I distinctly heard wood *and* bone crack. Malekai growled through his bared teeth as Nakoa dodged, expecting a blow to come from Malekai's other hand. Malekai, being a seasoned warrior, knew Nakoa would anticipate this and jabbed with his broken hand. The tactic worked, and the *crunching* sound when Malekai's fist connected with Nakoa's face made my guts churn in empathy. Blood splattered from underneath Malekai's fist just as Nakoa gripped the front of Malekai's fighting leathers and yanked him down, rolling, pinning him to the ground and landing a bone-crunching punch before Malekai rolled them again—

Lokus stepped in front of me, whispering conspiratorially, with Pomona and Famei close behind. "Fancy a wager on who wins?"

I couldn't help but huff a dry laugh, grateful for the first time for Lokus' mischievous nature. "No... I don't..." Lokus looked me up and down, disappointment lacing his smirk as he turned to Rayne, Pomona, and Famei.

"50 silvers on the blonde fucker," Lokus announced confidently.

I gasped, making him toss me an admonishing look. "*What?* Nakoa's kicked my ass too many fuckin' times for me not to bet against him. Plus, your friend over there looks like he'd rather die than submit. Gotta admire that kinda tenacity."

Pomona narrowed her eyes at him for a moment before grinning.

"I'll raise you an extra 50 for Koa."

Famei and Rayne exchanged looks as Vesper observed all of this with interest.

Another loud crash landed, followed by another thunderous plea from Val. "Not ma plants! Ma poor bloody plants!"

Rayne glanced between Lokus and the bloody, shifting mass of bronzed muscle tumbling across Val's living room.

"Fine. 100 silvers on, Nakoa..."

Famei grinned at Pomona. "100 silvers on your fae friend."

Pomona gasped in surprise, unable to suppress her grin.

"You traitor!"

Famei beamed all the brighter. "What are you gonna do for me if I win, hm?"

Pomona swatted his thick bicep. "You are so bad." Famei gave a devilish grin as he tugged Pomona into his arms pressing a kiss to her temple. *"I want my winnings in flesh,"* he murmured softly. Pomona failed to suppress her grin, cheeks rosy with embarrassment.

I couldn't help but chuckle, watching their exchange, admiring their closeness and comfort. Their trust. Their *love*.

I leaned to the side to peek around them to find Nakoa and Malekai still going blow for blow. All the lethal grace I'd witnessed in Nakoa with that horde of bandits, and the years I'd witnessed Malekai on a battlefield inspiring awe, fear, and respect from all those around him... had all gone out the window. This was brutal fists, claws, teeth, kicks, and body slams as if it were some no-holds-barred tavern brawl.

Val rushed up to us, clutching plants and vases in his arms.

"Have we all had enough fuckin' fun here? Or did you plan on just letting them destroy the cabin I spent the last seven months building with my own blood, sweat, and tears?"

A rasping sound snapped my gaze back to the brawl to see Nakoa's tail holding Malekai about a foot off the ground by his neck.

"Oy!" Lokus cried, "That's fuckin' cheating! You're gonna cost me a hundred silvers, you dickhead!"

Malekai gripped Nakoa's tail coiled around his throat and when Nakoa didn't release him, Malekai willed a dagger into his hand.

"WHHOOOOOOOAAAA!!!"

Everyone yelled in unison as they leapt forward. Nakoa dropped Malekai like a sack of potatoes, glamoring his tail away.

Malekai coughed and wheezed trying to regain his breath.

Malekai's eyes met mine as he continued to hack up a lung. In the same moment, Nakoa turned to face me. Both of them were beaten to a pulp with swollen, blackening eyes and split lips.

Pomona approached them both, already carrying ice-filled cotton hand towels, and handed one to each.

"Alright, lads, time to kiss and make-up."

My chest ached looking between the two of them. It felt like it was only a matter of time before there'd be a brawl... I was relieved to have it out of the way and could only pray there would be peace from here on out...

I shook my head as Malekai's earlier words sank in and liberated what I'd been suppressing this entire time. Recognizing that there was, seemingly, no other way without waging a war...

Maybe it was petty and selfish, but... Although I was highly capable, the fact that Nakoa had been so quick and willing to have *me* take on the task of killing Zurie... All for his grand plan, which was also the only way to ensure my freedom from her wrath... Just didn't quite sit right. Even though I'd fought in a war beside Malekai, and he had witnessed my *lethal* efficiency... He was unwilling to let me take that risk alone. It made me feel safe. Cared for. *Loved.*

The fact that Nakoa didn't bat an eye about letting me run face-first into a battle against Zurie left me feeling... *expendable.* I knew that Nakoa was reassured by his gift of foresight and Knowingness, as was his mother and Miroslav with their gifts, but... As Malekai had said,... *error and chaos.*

There was always a chance it could all go horribly, horribly wrong.

I absently rubbed at the sore spot in my chest as I *willed* away the broken shards and dirt from the potted plants, turning on my heel to step outside for some much-needed fresh air.

I reached for Val's arm on the way out, guilt churning.

"I'm sorry for... All of this. I'll replace whatever they broke."

Val gave me a warm look of understanding. "Don't you worry your pretty head, lass. It's not your fault if these two can't behave like civilized males."

FORTY-SEVEN

S hame replaced the anger that had my heart in a vice grip as I watched that look of disappointment flash over Mareina's face.

Fuck.

I drew in a heavy breath that felt like daggers going down as I looked around at the destruction I'd wrought in Val's home. Pomona offered me a look of compassion as she handed me an icepack.

"Thank you..."

Pomona handed the other ice pack to *Malekai*... My *soulbound's* best *"friend"*, apparently. Her best friend who had only had her best interest in mind...

Gods damn it.

I was such a cunt.

Since the male had appeared, my Knowingness had been whispering information to me about him. No small portion of which was the fact that he was in love with my *lohane thili.* Had saved her life on numerous occasions throughout the war. Just as she had for him... That was an unbreakable bond.

While my own bond with Mareina was... fraying. *Rapidly.*

The fact that he, too, had fought on the wrong side of it with her only further fuelled the flames of my ire.

But he saved her life. If it weren't for him, she would have died during the war, and you would never have met your soulbound, my Knowingness chose to remind me. Again.

Jealousy, guilt, and gratitude all warred within me.

Finally, I stepped forward to where the male sat, leaning against Val's wall, icing the cut beneath his swollen brow.

The words felt like shards of fucking glass coming out, but it had to be done.

"I'm sorry."

Malekai lifted his gaze to mine, nodding in acceptance. "I apologize as well... I could have been—

"No, you're right... It's risky sending Mareina in there with Vesper alone to face Zurie."

I slid down the wall to sit next to him, draping an arm on my bent knees as I iced my swollen eye, which was healing remarkably fast, thanks to my and Mareina's bond. Pomona, the angel she is, was already *willing* away the disaster we'd made and mending the things we'd destroyed.

A woman with white and blonde hair, golden skin, and turquoise eyes screams her pain and fury onto the tile floor on which her bloodied cheek is pressed. The veins in her forehead and neck bulge as a Kahlohani warrior pins her to the ground as he pounds into her brutally from behind.

"You should have stayed in Hades, where your kind belongs."

As always, the vision left as abruptly as it came. When Malekai's face was replaced with hers, I could see the likeness is undeniable... My gut churned with a guilt that doesn't belong to me, and yet...

A Kahlohani soldier *raped* his mother.

Malekai's blood-crusted brow is pinched as he studies me warily. Thanks to my visions, it has become no small task to live two realities simultaneously, however brief, and not seem... crazy.

Before Malekai can ask any questions, I continue, trying my best to seem normal despite what I've just witnessed.

"Vesper swore her loyalty in a blood vow... Just to assuage your concerns with that... And according to my visions, along with Miroslav's, and my mother's scrying... Mareina overcomes Zurie quickly thanks to Vesper's distraction..."

I turned my throbbing head to gauge Malekai's reaction... And just as I'd suspected, not a flicker of surprise revealed itself at the mention of Miroslav.

Malekai gradually nodded. "Well, that's reassuring and all... But... I can't allow her to go in there with *just* Vesper."

It's no small blow to my ego and my conscience that this male is more protective about my *soulbound* than I have been... Begrudgingly, I appreciate that fact.

"No one else, other than Miroslav, can enter the palace... And he's promised to be there with her, but his blood vow to not cause any physical harm to Zurie doesn't exactly inspire confidence."

Malekai's expression pinched as though I were daft.

"I'm going to go with her."

I returned his daft expression.

"I'm sure Zurie is already well aware of your betrayal..."

Malekai shook his head. "No... Miroslav *folded* me and ten of my soldiers who have been vowed to secrecy back to the palace to tell Zurie that the rest of them were killed... He was the one who folded me here... He told me about Val the night before my soldiers and I left Vyssini."

My jaw dropped.

Akash almighty...

What a fucking puppet master...

I shook my head in disbelief, wondering what else this male had planned and was conspiring behind our backs... If he hadn't saved my life multiple times already... I'd have *zero* trust in him.

The orisha is loyal to your mother. Your mother is loyal to you. Have faith.

346

I gave an internal grunt to my Knowingness... The fact that he was, in fact, my mother's *soulbound* gave me enough confidence in him to trust his guidance... Even if I still found it unsettling, he was so far ahead of everyone...

He also seemed the epitome of control. It was envious. My visions had grown *so* frequent it felt like with each one, my grasp on sanity seemed to slip further and further away.

Still, I had to ask...

"Do you trust Miroslav?'

Malekai huffed, staring distantly at a smear of blood on Val's wool rug before *willing* it away.

"I mean... Until he approached me with this information and revealed to me his vow to Mareina, among a number of other things, definitely not. I wouldn't have trusted him with a pair of fucking scissors. But *now*... Yes. I do."

"He swore a vow to Mareina?"

Malekai nodded. "Yeah, he let me peer into his memories."

My brows lifted in shock.

"Did you swear a blood vow to him?"

He shook his head. "No... He didn't even ask."

Because he is loyal to Mareina, my Knowingness whispered.

I felt both relieved and jealous at the knowledge.

As if he sensed the direction of my thoughts...

"Do you wanna speak to her first, or shall I?"

I inclined my head towards the door.

"You can go first... I should probably give her anger some time to dissipate... Plus, I need to help set up camp and discuss some things with Val."

Malekai hesitated momentarily, scanning the remaining damage from our brawl, before giving me a heavy clap on the shoulder and pinning me beneath a turquoise gaze. His tone deceptively calm.

"I understand you're her *soulbound*, so I trust this won't be an issue... But I still feel compelled to make you aware of the fact that... If you were to ever harm a single hair on Mareina's head, I will not hesitate to gut you like a fucking pig... Outside of that... Let's be friends. For Mareina's sake."

The male offered me his hand with a disdainfully winsome grin. My eyes dipped briefly to a gold ring boasting a dark red jewel in its center.

"I'm glad we share... similar sentiments. On all of the afore-mentioned..."

I couldn't bother to force a smile on my face, but I embraced his hand in mine, holding firm, and leaned into his ear.

"I know you love her... The only reason you're still breathing is because I know she cares for you, but... *I still feel compelled to make you aware of the fact that...* If you ever dared to try and take her from me, I will find far more creative ways of inflicting suffering upon you before you succumbed to death... But yes. Let us have this truce, *friend.*"

Malekai's grin turned sharp as he held my gaze. Something dark and twisted glinted like a blade beneath the surface of his eyes that were far too pretty for any male to bear. My own grin blossomed at the sight.

Just as Lokus kicked my booted foot.

"Oy. I can't tell if you two are about to fight again or fuck, but it's getting late, and I don't feel like setting up camp in the dark."

Gradually, my gaze drifted up to meet Lokus. Malekai stood and made his way to Val and Pomona, offering an apology, before exiting the cabin to follow my *lohane thili* outside.

Lokus offered me a hand to pull me to standing, blowing out a breath as he clapped me on the back.

"That was a pretty decent fight, brother..."

I rolled my eyes. "You bet against me again?"

He gave me a crooked grin. "Hey, there's gotta be someone out there that can hand you your ass."

"I'll be damned if I let it be that pretty fae fucker."

He nodded in understanding. "Seems pretty keen on your Mrs."

My jaw tightened as anger sparked anew, and I took a deep breath.

"Yeah, well... The more protection Mareina has when she faces Zurie, the better."

CHAPTER
FORTY-EIGHT

MALEKAI

The moment I stepped outside, that painful knot in my chest tugged me toward where it somehow knew Mareina would be, even if I couldn't see her. Twilight would soon descend, bathing us in that haunting, ethereal blue. I found her standing alone beside a babbling creek some distance from Val's.

"Do you feel better now?" She asked without even having to glance back to know it was me.

It had always felt good to fight and blow off a little steam, and she knew it.

"*A little?*" I admitted.

She gave a soft huff before finally turning to face me, peering up at my healed face. "Let's see the damage."

I willed a barrier around us to cloak us from sight and any prying ears, closing the distance between us as her hands reached out to examine my face.

I remained silent, studying her as she scrutinized my remaining scratches. Since the day I'd laid eyes on her, thanks to Seline, *her former lover* who had introduced us, Mareina had been the most beautiful female I'd ever seen. Her beauty wasn't soft and tender...

Nor was it conventional. While her features would be considered alluring and ethereal by any standard... There was a hardness to them that lacked a feminine grace. Particularly in her expression. Which only made the tiny glimmers of softness and fragility inside that she revealed to me all the more beautiful. Or those rare moments of joy... Those rare smiles.

Sweet fucks, how her smile brought me to my knees.

Not to mention the secrets lying beneath her fighting leathers... Strength and power in her lithe muscle, layered with soft feminine curves... Made me fucking salivate.

My eyes locked onto the pillowy cupid's bow of her lips until she caught me and grinned, rolling her eyes.

"You're lucky he didn't wield his magic."

My brow pinched. "*He's* lucky I didn't wield my magic."

She sighed, turning away from me back towards the creek.

"Malekai... I've seen him steal the air from someone's lungs... Burst their blood vessels within their bodies... He wields power over elements unlike any other I've witnessed before."

My brows lifted.

Admittedly, that was an impressive gift.

Lucky for me, I wasn't quite as susceptible to anyone else's magic in the same way most wielders were, *minori* or not. Just as you couldn't wield a paring knife against a broadsword and expect to win, the magic most fae and other immortals used wasn't nearly substantial enough to do any significant harm to me. It was one of the reasons I'd survived the war and had led my soldiers to victory in every battle, even without Miroslav's help.

That being said, those kinds of abilities were gifted to a race of wielders that I had only ever read about. And I was still relatively susceptible to the impact of a physical weapon, like a broadsword, especially in my fae form.

"Did Zurie say what kind of hybrid he was?"

He was clearly part fae, but...

She hesitated for a moment before chuckling. "*Human.*"

"What?"

She shifted to look up at me, rolling her eyes. "I know, right."

Silence hung heavy between us for several moments. My throat wanted to close up and suffocate me just so I didn't have to suffer the reality of who this male was to her. The words came out like razor blades lacerating my throat.

"Congratulations, by the way..."

Still facing the creek, Mareina's eyes shut briefly as her features tensed.

"Malekai... I..."

"Mareina... It's ok. Really. I am genuinely happy that you found your *soulbound.* Honestly. I *want* you to have that kind of happiness... But I'd be lying if I said I hadn't hoped it would be with me."

After several moments, I thought she might not respond, but finally, she turned to face me. Watery emotion glistened in her eyes.

"I love you, Malekai... *So fucking much.* For years, I thought about what could be between us... I have always wanted us to have something *more, desperately,* but I am fucking terrified that the love and friendship we have would be destroyed by it. You are all that I have... And *everything* I want. I can't imagine a world without you. I *need* you here with me like I need fucking air in my lungs."

My heart thundered in my chest as it swelled to bursting.

"Mareina... There is *nothing* you can do to drive me away. There is no event that could take place that would ever make me want to leave you. You could literally shift into some demon that crawled around on all fours, hissing, spitting, snarling, and incapable of forming intelligible sentences, and I'd just be like... 'Well... I suppose a leash and a muzzle might be useful for when I have to take her out for walks.'"

Mareina gifted me one of those rare, unrestrained smiles as she burst into a laugh. The action finally caused her tears to tip over the edge and spill down her cheeks. My own grin bloomed as I bathed in her laughter, and her smile felt like water on parched soil. As her laughter settled, I nuzzled away each tear with the tip of my nose and licked the saltiness from her rosy cheeks. The scent of her arousal blossomed in the air, filling my nostrils. My grip on her tightened with need.

My conscience lurched, reminding me that she was now bound to another male, but I promptly set it ablaze, willing that it burn to ash... Yet I found myself pulling away slightly regardless.

Mareina stared up at me, lips parted and breath held as if she wanted to say something more. I could *feel* that she had more to say but finally settled on a shake of her head, seeming to think better of it, and heaved a tremendous sigh. "I fucking love you, Malekai."

Holding her tightly against me, as always, gave me the feeling that the weight of the world had finally lifted a little, and I could breathe again.

"I fucking love *you,* tessari mú. In this realm and the next."

Mareina's tears spilt as she gave me another wobbly smile. She exhaled a shuddering breath.

"There are a few other things that I wanna talk to you about, actually..."

I pulled back to catch her expression. Dread sank its talons into me.

"Don't worry, it's nothing bad," she quickly reassured, "I just..."

Mareina tortured that delicious bottom lip as she studied me, hesitating to say whatever she needed to get out. It took everything within me not to steal it from her. To not take that lip between my own teeth before caressing it with my tongue.

I thumbed her cheek, trying to encourage her.

"Whatever it is, Mareina, so long as I breathe, I will be here for you..."

Her throat worked, heaving a sigh and shaking her head.

"There are few things, one of which... Well, now would be a terrible time to discuss it... But as for the rest, whatever is happening, it's bigger than just Zurie... I don't know where this all leads... Other than taking her throne, but--

I reared back in shock... He was her *soulbound*... Of course, she would take the throne beside him and become Queen...

Oh, gods...

I had thwarted countless attempts against Zurie over the years... As had Mareina... She would have a Kingdom of people after her head.

"I can explain more later, but I have recently been shown... *things*. Which is one of the reasons I'm following through with all this... But when we made our vows, I vowed to help him rule... But... *That's all* I vowed..."

My lips parted in further shock at what she *didn't* say.

"I won't deny that I feel this bond between us on a visceral level... But my heart doesn't belong to him... Nor did I vow it to him. Or my body and soul."

Mareina stepped back, pulling up her sleeve to provide the proof of her words. My jaw slackened in shock and my own, admittedly selfish, relief at the sight of her bare arms.

"And then this... *happened.*"

She turned her right forearm to reveal the underside... My brows leapt at the intricately detailed depiction of Mors' inverted torch with wings. She despised the god despite how many souls she sent to him. My eyes narrowed at the words as I took an arm in my hand and brushed my thumb over them.

Invenitum Thanaratou.

"Do you know what this says?"

Her eyes widened in surprise. "No, *do you?*"

A grin tilted my lips. "You should, considering where your father's from. It's Ancient Aurealingan... I'm not fluent in it, but it's similar enough to Modern Aurealingan that I can still understand this at least..."

Mareina's frown looked suspiciously like a pout, causing another fissure in my blackened heart. Seeing her like this made me want to fucking squeeze her, kiss her, and take her away from all this. This fierce female had spent her whole fucking life fighting, and she was dying to stop. *And now this.*

"What does it say?"

I chewed my cheek, deliberating if I should lie to her just so I could spare her any unnecessary stress. I doubt anyone else she'd come across would be able to read Ancient Aurealingan. But... I'd never lied to her before, and I certainly wasn't going to fucking start now.

My middle finger traced the ominous words, and I selfishly relished how the hairs on her arms rose at my command.

"*... Find Death.*"

I looked up from Mareina's arm to find her staring at her arm like she was staring into the face of Death. My heart cracked a little more when I saw the glistening in her eyes. I pulled her close again, kissing the top of her head and nuzzling close to her.

"*tessari mú...*"

My treasure.

Because she absolutely fucking was. Mareina was the most precious thing in this world to me, and I'd be damned if I would let even Mors stand in the way of her finding happiness.

Mareina's body shook with the release of her soft sobs, and I held her all the tighter.

"*Shhhh... tessari mú...* Whatever this is... Whatever it means... I'll be right here with you, ok? No matter what. Ok?"

Her lips trembled again as she looked up at me.

"... Do you think he's marked me for death?"

"No?"

She reared back. "But why not? After all the fucking horrors I've committed? I deserve to——

I pressed a finger against her lips to silence her.

"Don't say that. Don't ever say that... And it's not true. You fought your way out of hell and then fought to protect your loved ones and your home. And as for the people Zurie sent you after? They were just as bad as her. You did the realm a favor."

Her brow furrowed, shaking her head...

"Not the people she had executed... Some of those were good people."

My eyes squeezed shut for a moment at the pain it had clearly caused her. I'd felt a lot of guilt since I'd convinced Zurie to promote Mareina to Irae, but none so much as now.

"You did what you had to, Mareina. If it hadn't been you, it would have been someone who didn't give a shit. And look where it led you. You're going to take Zurie's throne. I'm certain that if any one of them knew that their deaths would lead to *this*... Towards a free Kingdom ruled by *fair* leaders... They would choose to do it again..."

Her lips pressed together in a tremulous line, studying my face for the truth in my words. She didn't look entirely convinced...

One day, I'll get you to love yourself like I love you.

She sighed heavily, breathing through her emotion.

"So... What do you think the mark means then?"

I gave her a look as though it should be obvious.

"Well, for one... I'm pretty sure if Mors wanted you dead... He wouldn't tiptoe around it or warn you. I think the best thing you can do is take it literally. *Find him.* Try going to his temple... Perhaps one of his acolytes would know. At the very least."

She gradually nodded before burying her face in my chest. I couldn't resist the temptation to thread my fingers through her hair and bury my face in her neck, where her delicious scent was most potent.

I groaned, heaving a sigh against her, lifting her off the ground as I straightened with her still wrapped in my arms.

Gods, she smells divine.

My eyes popped open as another realization hit me. She didn't smell like *him*. Relief flooded me even as I admonished myself. It would only cause Mareina pain to deny herself her *soulbound.* Though... I imagined there would be nothing less than a damn good reason as to why she hadn't yet *consummated* things with him... My hackles raised to imagine him treating her with anything less than absolute reverence.

Mareina's sobs gradually subsided, and I *willed* a handkerchief into her hands.

"Thank you," she murmured softly before blowing her nose, "I'll be sure to replace it."

I huffed a laugh. *One hundred years* together, and, despite her rough upbringing, she was more courteous and considerate than any of the aristocrats I'd met in my 226 years.

"Either you keep it because you want to keep something of mine with you, or you give it back dirty so I can keep something of yours with me."

Her reddened gaze leapt to mine in shock, jaw-dropping before it spread into a heart-crushing grin as she tried to stifle a laugh by smacking my arm. "Ewwwwwwww!"

I husked a laugh, giving her a challenging look. "It has your *essence* on it. I will happily suck the snot off that thing. Gimme."

I reached for the hand holding the napkin, but she snatched it away, a shocked grin broadening further when she saw how serious I was.

"You wouldn't dare..."

Ooooh.

I see.

I grinned from ear to ear. "A dare? You dare to dare *me?*" My laughter rumbled. "Since when did you develop this fetish, you twisted little minx? I mean, I can think of other bodily fluids of yours that I'd have chosen first, but hey, beggars can't be choosers."

I leapt towards her, closing my arms around air when she dodged. Excitement blossomed in my chest, broadening our barrier lest we be disturbed.

The grin on her face, still puffy from crying, had my heart swelling with both love and relief.

When fighting on a battlefield, you'd be surprised by the wide variety of bodily fluids that manage to defy gravity and can inadvertently find their way into your mouth. Sweat, blood, bile, saliva, even ventral fluid that one time... Almost all of which came from complete strangers.

If licking Mareina's snot rag would make her smile, I'd gladly do it. I'd probably get a fucking hard-on from it just because the snot was hers, and I was indeed that fucking twisted.

She widened her stance, ready to pounce in either direction. I feinted left and right, but she saw through both. My cock was getting hard already. Thankfully, my fighting leathers were constricting enough to keep it pinned down against my thigh.

And if her brilliant smile wasn't anything to go by, the sight of her lengthening fangs certainly were. She was enjoying this just as much as I was.

"What's the matter, *Theikos?* Getting slow from all those nights at the brothel?"

I couldn't hide my low growl of satisfaction. Both at her use of my surname and her little display of jealousy. She'd never been very good at hiding it. And I fucking loved it.

"Maybe I am. And maybe that little rag is all I need to keep me from going back. It would honestly be selfish of you to keep it from me."

She cackled with laughter as I lunged for her again, and our chase began. Those had warmth and relief blossoming in my chest. And thanks to said laughter and her only half-assed attempt to get away, I closed in on her, pulling her against me with one arm, gripping her wrist with the other, and bringing it to my face. She squealed in both horror and delight.

"Malekai!"

"Such a greedy female," I teased before biting down on the handkerchief, yanking it from her hand with a jerk of my head. I pinned her freehand down at her side and held my prize aloft.

The balled-up cloth unfurled, revealing the clear goo of her snot. I hummed my delight as she gasped in horror.

I didn't hesitate a second more before I palmed the thing and licked it from top to bottom. Mareina faked a gag in between laughter.

"Oooh... Salty and... kind of refreshing."

She shook her head at me with wide eyes, still beaming a mile wide.

Worth it.

"You are..."

"Wonderful? Devastatingly handsome? Irresistible?" I finished for her, stuffing the napkin into my pocket.

She laughed, eyebrows raised in disbelief. *"Insane."*

I chuckled smugly. "For you? Always."

FORTY-NINE

MALEKAI

A s our laughter faded, she wrapped her arms around my waist and buried her face in my chest. The sound of her inhaling my scent deeply sent my heart tumbling and my nose-diving into the crook of her neck, filling my lungs with her precious scent. Savouring it all the more. Who knew how long it would be before it twined with his?

"So, Queen, huh?"

She huffed. "We'll see, I guess."

I couldn't help the smile that curled the corner of my mouth.

Queen.

Mareina would undoubtedly be the best Atratus had ever seen. Her strength and valor, paired with her life experience and compassion... She would be a just ruler. Something that I'd never even bothered to consider a possibility. The realm would be a better place with her ruling one of its Kingdoms.

Not to mention...

"You'll look fucking stunning in a crown and gown."

She gave a sad chuckle. "You make it sound like it's a guarantee."

All humor left me. "... Mareina, I'll be right there with you to ensure Zurie's fucking dead as a doornail."

"She's literally one of the most powerful fae in the Kingdom... If not the realm."

I scoffed inwardly.

"Even with the help of *aetra,* if I wanted to pick my teeth with her bones, there's little she could do to stop me."

The only reason that cunt was still alive was because Mareina hadn't told me to kill her already, and the fact that if it wasn't Zurie in power, it would be someone else just like her or worse.

Like some male who would try to exploit Mareina.

And now that I needed to protect Mareina from her... Something that her own fucking *soulbound* didn't seem terribly concerned with... Well...

I had zero qualms about sending her wretched soul directly to Mors.

Mareina's brows leapt.

"You're awfully confident."

I merely shrugged. Now was not the time to reveal the one thing I'd hidden from Mareina. Not because I didn't trust her with my secret but because my entire family in Hades had been killed because of it.

"You don't sound nearly as excited about this as most would be at such a lofty prospect."

She gave a tiny shake of her head against my chest.

"You know what would excite me?"

"Hm?"

"You remember that thermal pool we found in Bein Sith Mór?"

I couldn't help the low hum of pleasure that escaped me.

How could I fucking forget?

"I do..."

"Going there again. With you... That would excite me. Going there with you and never being forced by obligation to leave. Maybe building a little house there..."

Sudden emotion clogged my throat, and I had to take a deep, low breath to ease myself off the ledge of leaping to do something completely and utterly selfish and irresponsible.

".... Maybe we could adopt some vicious, stray animal that just needs a tender touch to make them gentle..."

A chuckle rumbled through me. "You basically just described yourself."

She giggled. *Actually giggled.* Fuck, it had been too long since I'd heard such a sweet sound. "I'm only vicious when provoked."

I sighed wistfully. "I know... It's one of my favourite things about you."

"What would excite *you* right now?"

"Hmmm... Well, the thermal pool is a nice idea, but there are a few things I can think of that would excite me even more."

"... Is that so?"

"Most definitely."

"Even if we were naked?"

My cock thickened.

"Without a doubt."

She lifted her head from my chest to look up at me, piquing a suspicious and mildly offended brow.

"And what exactly is it that's so exciting it takes precedence over the thermal pools? And I swear to *Akash*, if you say spending the evening at *Satia Fama* with your females from the brothel, I'm going to stab you."

I husked a satisfied laugh.

"The *Satia Fama*, nor its females, have never excited me."

"Are you ever going to actually tell me what does?"

"That's a very private question that I'm not entirely sure you're ready to hear the answer to, *tessari mú.*"

A coy smirk lit her beguiling features. It took no small amount of self-restraint to not lean down and kiss her.

"If that's the only thing holding you back, then I think your ability to read people must be getting a little rusty, Theikos..."

Carding my fingers through her hair and staring down into her face bearing such a pleased, open expression sent butterflies fluttering around in my belly.

"Hmmmm... Let's see... visiting a blacksmith would excite me right now."

Her brows pinched in confusion as her lower lip jutted out suspiciously like a pout, making me want to bite, lick and kiss it.

Her voice was flat with disappointment.

"A blacksmith?"

"Yes... I wouldn't deign to buy you some generic ring at a jeweller's."

Her jaw dropped, eyes widening.

"And then I would build you that little house near the thermal pool in Bein Sith Mór..."

Her chest swelled as she held my gaze, her eyes gradually swelling with emotion.

"Maybe a little garden and greenhouse so we'd have even fewer obligations to leave our haven... I don't have much of a green thumb, but I'd give it my best."

She tortured her bottom lip, trying to maintain the dam of her watery emotion.

"And yes, going to the thermal pool to watch you bathe again... Admittedly, that would be thoroughly exciting... Although, I don't think I'd be able to keep my hands off you a second time."

She laughed, her tears finally spilling. "And what, may I ask, would you do instead?"

"I would wash your hair. Bathe you. Caress you...," I crooned before bending to speak softly in her ear, "Fuck you until the world fell away and the only things that remained were the two of us. Show you in the only way I yet haven't just how much I fucking love you..."

She was holding her breath and hadn't even realized yet. A corner of my mouth quirked. The scent of her arousal, slightly floral and rich, reached my nose, making my cock twitch.

"And on a far less romantic note, I'd also make you gag on my cock, smack your thick ass until your cheeks were red and perhaps a little bruised, and fill every orifice of yours with my cum... Among a variety of other things... With your permission, of course."

A barely audible moan escaped her just as her mouth snapped shut and her cheeks flushed with color.

"That sounds... *Ideal.*"

The air became heavy with desire... and something *more.* Much to my dismay, now was not the time to act upon either of those things.

She also seemed to realize it as she cleared her throat.

"So... You wanna explain exactly how you ended up at Val's... And... Slaughtering half the men you'd brought with you."

Her words caused a painful pinch in the center of my chest. I hadn't necessarily *wanted* to kill them... Not entirely, at least...

But I had specifically selected the soldiers travelling with me to Vyssini that I knew the world would be better without. As much fulfilment as I found in living the life of a warrior and, as of the last 90 years, give or take, as a general in Zurie's army... I was under no delusions that, while not *all*, a significant number of my comrades were the absolute scum of the fucking realm. As professions that required practised murder often did.

Miroslav had shown up after *folding* Mareina to Ouvelleete and dropped the bomb on me that, basically, I had to choose between my loyalty to Zurie or Mareina. And well... I couldn't give less fucks about Zurie outside of her paying my handsome wages.

Mareina, on the other hand, quite literally, meant abso-fucking-letly everything to me.

I hadn't needed a moment's thought to give him an answer. Though it had taken him some convincing for me to trust his word and all the events he relayed to me that had been set in motion...

He'd revealed a myriad of probabilities in which Nakoa and Mareina would usher in a new era of peace in Atratus.

And, as awful as it might sound... I didn't give a fuck about any of that, either. I was entirely too jaded to have much faith in that. Even if Nakoa and Mareina ruled fairly, the Lords and Ladies that would dominate their regions certainly wouldn't. Not to mention, I was wholly reluctant to let Mareina live a life that promised constant death threats. Which is precisely what would happen if she and her *soulbound* ruled the Kingdom with a compassionate hand because it meant that all the wealth and resource hoarding those Lords and Ladies had gotten so used to would no longer be possible.

The singular thing I cared about in this world was Mareina. An era of peace would be epic, but how long would it last? I was a cynical bastard... Peace or war, feast or famine, life and death... They were all cycles, and each had their time to pass. I didn't wish suffering upon anyone... Or... Well... Let's say I didn't wish it upon *most*. But each person was more than capable of crawling out of whatever adversity they'd been born into or had found themselves in... And if not... Well... Survival of the fittest.

I know Mareina found my stance a little fucking heartless, but... If anything, she was evidence of the fact that it was possible. And look at the fucking breathtakingly magnificent, fearsome female she had become because of it.

She thought that I wasn't aware of the fact that she had been raped repeatedly, along with a variety of other sexual and physical assaults, at the Erosyan Temple. And I would never tell her. She had made peace with it. But I knew that haunted fucking look in her striking emerald eyes the moment I'd met her. A fair number of the females that had chosen to join Zurie's Army had shared a similarly violent past and had joined the military so that they could learn the skills that would enable them to drastically reduce, if not eliminate, the likelihood of them ever being made victims again.

Seline had told me before I'd met Mareina that she had been raised in the Erosyan Temple, so it wasn't too far of a leap for me to close the gap between her upbringing and the shadows lingering around her that she had been violated.

Until then, I'd been a frequent patron of the Erosyan Temple. However, soon *after* Seline introduced me to her, I'd paid the Erosyan Temple another visit, threatened a few lives, and even filled a few

CHIARA FORESTIERI

purses... Within a week, I'd managed to hunt down one of the men who had violated her. After another couple weeks, I'd found the next... And a year later, I'd procured a small collection of mismatching teeth from each male that had touched her wrongly.

After that, I'd burned the fucking place to the ground. Mareina's father had survived from what I'd heard, but I couldn't be fucked if he did or didn't, considering he'd led his daughter into that gaudy, *Akash*-forsaken shithole.

To this day, Mareina, along with the rest of Bastrina, assumed it had been something as benign as an inebriated patron's rogue cigar that had caused the fire.

I'd created this image in my mind of the day she would decide to be with me when I could present my little treasure trove of teeth as a gift to her... A token of my undying love and readiness to fucking murder anyone who dared to wrong her.

And now... Well, that little fantasy I'd never thought possible seemed like it might one day come true...

Mareina's voice snapped me out of my thoughts.

"Malekai?"

I cleared my throat, trying to re-center my thoughts.

"Yeah... Your favorite person in the world clued me into a few things..."

She reared back before her jaw dropped in shock.

"Found him sitting in my fucking living room waiting for me after he dropped you in Ouvelleete... Bastard could have *folded* me home but instead made me hoof it."

Mareina's expression paled, speechless... I couldn't help but wonder what he had told her to get her to betray Zurie... Not that she needed much convincing... It had been clear to me for years that she had been pining for a way out. I had been secretly saving my considerable wages over the last decade so that, just as Zurie had said in her private garden, I could retire and take Mareina with me. Ensure that neither of us would have to work again unless we wanted to... Even so, I'd been serious all those times I offered to burn the world

366

down for her. It would take little effort for me to reduce Zurie and her palace to ashes.

Though doing so would alert the world that at least one of my kind was still roaming the realm but, it was a risk I would have eagerly taken... Perhaps we could have hidden somewhere in *Hades,* the homeland of mine and Mareina's parents... Or *Maimyō mo Qì.* I'd heard it was a continent at peace. Maybe we still could. Somehow, someway.

"But what the hells did he say to convince you to betray Zurie?"

I smirked, shrugging my shoulders.

"I told you already, Kalini... *Wherever you go, I will follow.*"

Mareina's chest swelled, staring up at me with those big beautiful fucking eyes that never failed to take my breath away. Her lips parted as though she wanted to say something...

Mareina's mouth snapped shut. Her pretty throat - the same throat I'd fantasized about kissing, biting, licking, choking, fucking, and filling with ropes of my cum on countless occasions - worked on another rough swallow. I slid my hand up her neck to caress her cheek with my thumb as I held her gaze beneath me.

"I wasn't exaggerating all those times over the years that I'd offered to burn the world down for you... The offer still stands. You need only say the word."

I tried to maintain a calm facade as everything within my body, my soul, *strained* towards her so desperately it fucking hurt. For decades, I'd been convinced that *she* was my *soulbound...* But her ability to resist me had proven to me otherwise.

Still... Whatever this was, from the moment I'd met her, she had possessed me heart and soul.

Mareina's eyes slipped shut at my declaration, nuzzling her cheek against my palm before turning to press a kiss to it.

"I love you, Malekai Theikos. You're the greatest gift I've ever been given."

The action made my heart ache in the most beautiful way as her words stole my fucking breath. My heart thundered in my chest as I finally dipped my head to graze my lips against her cheek as I spoke.

"Mareina Kalini, I've loved you from the moment I laid eyes on you, and you're the only gift I've ever fucking wanted."

Her chest swelled against me, and I squeezed her all the harder against me, wanting nothing more than to take her far away from here. Her words mirrored my thoughts.

"Gods, I wish we could fucking leave this all behind."

I hummed thoughtfully. "You know if I *did* reduce Atratus to ashes... You'd be freed from your vow... And we could do exactly that."

Her eyes peeked open as she grinned, giving her a sly, heavy-lidded look that had my cock thickening further. Thankfully, still trapped in the pant leg of my fighting leathers.

"Always such a naughty boy."

A low growl of pleasure rumbled from my chest.

"I'll happily play the villain if you're my reward, Mareina."

Her lips parted, but a rough shout cut through the air before she could respond.

"Mareina!"

Fuck.

Though it was probably for the better, we were interrupted. While I had little to zero respect for their *souldbound vows,* I didn't want to cause Mareina any additional stress. Like fucking her until she forgot his gods-forsaken name and inciting a fight to the death between me and her *syntrifa. The Aurealingan term for fated mate.*

Mareina took a fleeting second to close her eyes, throwing her arms around me the next.

"Coming!" She called out over my shoulder.

Mareina gripped the back of my head, her nails digging in slightly, as she brought her forehead to mind.

"Katadamna kaza."

The warmth and love I had for this female swelled in my chest.

Yes. We would get through this together. Damn the cost.

"*Katadamna kaza, tessari mú.*"

She exhaled heavily, giving me one last meaningful look before she turned and made her way through the forest back to Val's cabin.

I listened to the soft crunch of her receding footsteps on the leafy forest floor as I remained standing beside the creek.

A few moments later, the sensation of a familiar presence - one that I had never liked and was now beginning to dread - manifested at my back.

"... I can see the wheels turning in your mind, General... If you think to do something... Impulsive... It will not end well."

My molars squeaked in protest at the pressure of my clenching jaw.

"Suffering is inevitable. One need only discover what makes it worth enduring."

"At the expense of how many others?"

I gradually turned towards Miroslav, already eager for this conversation to fucking end.

"If you're worried about me upholding my end of the bargain, you needn't worry."

Miroslav pressed a hand to my shoulder as I shifted to pass him and return to Val's cabin.

"It is not *that* I am concerned about..."

My gaze drifted to the offending hand, feeling my patience wind tight, ready to snap. I knew it would take little effort for this male to sever the cord between my body and soul, but I'd always erred on the side of nihilism when it came to my own well-being. Though for the sake of Mareina...

Our gazes met briefly; the sudden softness - compassion - in his eyes made my stomach churn.

"I know my fate, Miroslav... What I do between now and then is not of your concern."

CHAPTER

FIFTY

MAREINA

The camp had already been set up when I'd emerged from the forest. Val had offered his spare room and couch to anyone who wanted them. I'd taken up his offer to sleep on the couch. Nakoa's gaze had snapped to mine, but to my surprise, he didn't protest. Perhaps he was trying to weasel his way into my good graces. We still hadn't spoken since his and Malekai's brawl.

The rest of Nakoa's *olana kah'hei* had declined, preferring their own palate of furs in their tents. Which left the bedroom for Malekai.

The group of us sat around the fire eating dinner, thanks to Famei's cooking and Roderick's hunting, when Malekai finally reappeared from the woods. His expression was neutral. Unreadable. *To most.*

I could feel the air heavy around him. His magic, which I could feel on a tangible level, restless. Tension knotted in my chest at the sensation. He had been fine only minutes ago...

Nakoa, standing on the other side of the fire, only threw me a cursory glance as he discussed something with Val, Lokus, Rayne, and Roderick. Pomona animatedly conversed with Vesper a few feet away. I had to do a double-take when I saw Vesper laugh.

Malekai plopped down on the tree-trunk-turned-bench beside me, offering me a small smile as though that would disguise whatever was bothering him.

"What happened?"

Malekai's chest heaved with a loud sigh.

"Miroslav paid me a visit."

I reared back. "Just now?"

A nod.

That slippery... I'd been about to call him a bastard, but... Considering he had basically given his life to protect Leilani, Malekai, and the realm...

Still, I couldn't stifle my grumble. "Well, if you see him again, please tell him I'd like to have a word."

Malekai's gaze remained fixed on the fire.

"Care to share what you two discussed?"

"Said he didn't want me doing anything *'impulsive'*... Or interfering too much between you two."

I rolled my eyes.

"I've vowed my fucking life to this. It's not like we have much of a choice."

Silence settled heavily, and my mind wandered to the dream Malekai had painted of our future in Bein Sith Mór, giving my heart a bitter squeeze.

What I wouldn't give for that.

"I'll be right here with you, Mareina. Don't worry. And who knows what the future will bring. Look where we were less than a week ago."

Nakoa, as if his ears were burning, strode over from where he and the other males had been huddled and took a seat on the other side of me. Tension knotted in my gut at being squished between the two of them.

"I apologize for earlier, Mareina... I have no excuse for my behavior. I apologized to Malekai as well. And Val."

I had to admit, his apology took me by surprise.

I turned to look at him and saw a... startling sincerity in his eyes. Though it wouldn't be the first time I'd been fooled by his *sincerity*, I wasn't about to admonish him for good behavior, so...

"Thank you... that means something to me."

A discomforted silence stretched between us. Only seconds passed, but I couldn't fucking bear it.

"I'm gonna head inside and take a bath," I announced, rising to my feet, "Do try to behave. *Both of you.*"

After Val showed me around and got the bath running, I sat in the tub until I pruned and the water turned tepid. Mors' mark on my arm had been unavoidable in my nudity, and I'd been forced to come to terms with *whatever* it was he intended. I clearly didn't have any control over it. And Malekai giving me of the straightforward and obvious suggestion that if Mors did actually want me dead, he wouldn't bother warning me about it.

By the time I reached the couch, Val had already turned it into a cozy nest for me. Laughter echoed from outside, inadvertently calling me to the window. My jaw dropped when I took a peek from around a remarkably frilly and feminine curtain. A squeal erupted from Pomona, and even Rayne was bent over, clutching his stomach, with laughter.

Roderick sat on Malekai's shoulders, and Lokus sat on Nakoa's as they ran around trying to catch the fae lights- no *pixies* - in the air above them before placing them in a *bag.*

What in the absolute hells?

Malekai's face was broad with a grin, mirroring Nakoa's. Val, Rayne, Vesper, Pomona, and Famei stood off to the side, cackling. Still in shock, my bare feet carried me outside, dressed in only my pyjamas. Warmth suffused my chest as I took in their exuberance... How... Happy and familial everyone looked.

I sat beside Pomona and Famei, who gave me warm smiles as the latter *willed* a bottle of fae wine into his hand.

"First one to bag 10, wins. Fancy a drink?"

I nodded and gave my thanks as the big males teetered and swayed as the lights dipped and leapt away, all the while howling with contagious laughter.

"Who's winning?"

"Nakoa at the moment—

"Outta the way!" Roderick cried.

We barely leapt out of the way in time as Malekai and Roderick came barrelling towards us to catch one of the fairies zipping between us. All three of them crying with laughter.

"How the hells did you get the pixies to agree to this?"

Val's face was bright with humor, face split in a broad grin in the center of his thick beard, huffing as he caught his breath and wiped the tears of laughter from his eyes. "It was their idea! Little adrenaline junkies. I've become friends with the local glee... They are *suspiciously* good at poker."

A loud grunt sounded as Lokus was run gut-first into the side of a tree branch, leaving his feet dangling and kicking, and Nakoa ran out from under him.

"You're supposed to duck!" Nakoa wept through his laugh.

"How?!" Lokus shrieked. "I can't fold myself in fucking half, you twat!" Lokus clutched onto the branch for dear life, holding the luminous bag of pixies in one hand. Nakoa bowled over, hands on knees. "Get back here before I fall!"

Nakoa struggled to catch his breath, still laughing through his tears. "Just fall!"

"You get back here right now, or I swear to *Akash,* I'll take a shit in your fucking lute!"

My own laughter howled out of me, unrestrained and free. Alongside me, Pomona, Famei, Val, Rayne, and Vesper. As we watched Malekai juggle Roderick and Nakoa juggle Lokus, each of us met one another's eyes in this beautiful, shared moment of tear-jerking laughter.

And for the first time since the war, of all events, I felt the unmistakable soul-warming satisfaction of unity. *Family.* Or at least, the closest thing to it that I had felt since being huddled around a campfire with Malekai, Seline, and the handful of soldiers we'd once fought with our lives to protect. All of the previous stress and tension wholly gone, almost forgotten, and suddenly not nearly as important as it once was because *this*...

This felt like something.

Something precious and new. For me, at least, and I knew Malekai as well. Perhaps fragile now considering all that weighed in the balance... But perhaps something worth fighting for and protecting. Something that might make all the heartache worth it.

After Roderick and Lokus finally managed to capture the last of the pixies, we gathered for them to start counting to determine the winner as we caught our breath. My eyes met Malekai's, and he gave me a wink that made something in my stomach flutter, still beaming brightly.

A few moments later, my eyes panned to Nakoa. His eyes lifted to mine and... I had to admit that I'd never seen him look so handsome. It didn't make my heart flutter, but it soothed the wounded tether between us because he looked... *happy.*

It was then I realized I'd never actually seen him smile and laugh, so open and unrestrained. Unencumbered, however briefly, by his battle to achieve his goals and liberate his people. He looked young, happy, and carefree.

One by one, the pixies flew out of the bags, still squealing their high-pitched laughter, looking like they'd just flown through a cyclone. Their hair was wild, and their clothes dishevelled from darting through trees and bushes. No doubt being jostled wildly in the bags as Malekai and Nakoa ran.

Lokus cried out in victory when he and Nakoa had two more pixies fly out after Malekai and Roderick's bag had emptied.

"Nice try, fur ball," Lokus chided, clapping a long hand on Roderick's back. Roderick parroted the words in a mocking tone, contorting his face in a way that made a remarkable impression of Lokus. "That name's getting a little tired, brother. Nearly as tired as I am of hearing it."

Lokus stuck out his tongue, waggling it and rolling his eyes. "Is it, brother?" More eye rolling and tongue waggling, "Is it? Maybe I should start calling you 'baby balls' since you're so sensitive. Does that make you feel any better?"

Roderick giggled along with everyone else. "Oooooh, projecting now, are we?"

Lokus gave an exaggerated laugh, unbuckling his belt. "*Oooooh*, let's find out, shall we?"

Pomona swatted at him. "Don't you dare pull those saggy prunes out again, or I'll slap you."

With the weight of what loomed ahead, it seemed we'd all formed an unspoken agreement to let go of our worries for the evening.

It may be one of your last.

Our laughter continued, but eventually, our yawns became increasingly contagious, and Nakoa's *olana kah'hei* made their way to bed one by one. The pixies had even stayed for some time after drinking and were more boisterous than I'd ever know them to be. A few of them, *mainly the females,* remained hovering near or perched somewhere on Val. And I couldn't help but notice that Vesper had gone into *Rayne's* tent when she'd bid us all goodnight. *He had followed shortly after.* Just before I left, I noticed Malekai handing a few of them a gold coin, which they hauled away with combined effort.

By the time I laid back down on the couch, my abdomen was sore from laughing. A sensation I was almost certain I'd never experienced before. A tall, muscular form filled the doorway just as I'd begun to drift off.

My heart leapt, hoping it was Malekai. A streak of moonlight peeking in from the window poured onto Nakoa's face as he stepped forward. The sight of him had the tether flaring in an unwelcome way. My body tensed, preparing for an argument about my not sharing his furs with him.

"You still awake?" He whispered.

"... Yes"

Nakoa closed the distance between us and sat on the floor, leaning back on the couch.

"I just... wanted to come say goodnight properly."

"... Oh... Um... Goodnight. I hope you sleep well."

"... It was... Good seeing you so happy tonight."

"I felt the same seeing you..."

A few weighted moments passed before Nakoa broke the bout of silence. "I... It would make *me* happy to see *you* happy like that more often."

A breath I hadn't realized I'd been holding finally released.

"... Same."

"Look, I... I'm sorry that... I've been... not the best mate. I want to try harder."

That boulder returned to my chest as the realization hit me.

"... I don't know that you'll ever be able to give me what I need."

Nakoa reared back. "Why?"

"Because becoming King... Liberating the Kahlohani Islands... Ruling Atratus... Those things will always come first to you."

He remained silent for a painfully long amount of time, in which a hurt I didn't quite know how to identify slowly sunk its talons into my mangled heart. The secret I was keeping about the truth of his *mother* reared its head, but I forced it back again with the weight of my exhaustion.

"But that is what is required of a good King."

I huffed sadly. "Yes... You are absolutely correct."

Nakoa's voice hardened into something cold. "If you're to be Queen, I would want you to be the same. Nothing should ever come before our duty to our people. To the Kingdom."

Exhaustion settled deeply inside me. I only managed a soft hum of agreement.

"And I don't see how that's a hindrance to being a good mate, Mareina."

A heavy sigh of resignation left me as I could no longer hold back since I'd first learned of his manipulations. And even more so since he'd confessed that his vision had told him that *I* was the one to kill Zurie. Which would be glorious and all if I didn't feel like I was doing his dirty work for him, and he had no qualms with the fact that I might potentially die doing so.

"Because I would never sacrifice your happiness and wellbeing to achieve those things... It may be short-sighted and selfish, but if it came down to it, I would never want, much less ask, for you to risk and potentially sacrifice your life to help me fucking take the throne."

The words were bitter, finally leaving my mouth. Nakoa's gaze snapped to mine in understanding.

"Mareina..."

"I know we have no other *reasonable* choices, Nakoa. I'm going to uphold my vow... I would fucking burn this Kingdom to the ground for you if it meant protecting you, despite our differences... And as much as I can objectively appreciate what a noble endeavor this all is... I just won't ever be able to fully give myself to someone who doesn't love enough to reciprocate that."

Nakoa sat there for several moments. My eyes, blessedly, remained dry. Instead of feeling heartbroken, I just felt... A draining combination of numbness and sadness.

"... Goodnight, Mareina."

CHAPTER

FIFTY-ONE

MAREINA

T woke to strong arms cradling me against a broad, muscled chest as Malekai's sea salt and embers scent enveloped me. Overwhelming relief and warmth inspired me to nuzzle deeper. A deep hum of pleasure sounded from his chest.

"Sorry to wake you, but I couldn't let you sleep on that lumpy couch."

A few moments later, Malekai set me on Val's guest bed. "I don't want you to sleep on that lumpy couch either."

"Mmmmm... As much as I'm dying to crawl in that bed with you, I'm not sure your *soulbound* wouldn't attempt to kill me for it."

I gave a sad huff.

"I doubt it. He wants Zurie dead too badly and is relying on us to make it happen... We can both remain clothed. It's not an invitation that's sexual in nature. "

Malekai chuckled as he sat beside me, sweeping back the hair from my face. "Oh? That's a shame."

Laughter, no matter how fleeting, liberated the weight on my chest. His large hand settled on my cheek, and my own reached up to hold it there. My chest ached with emotion and gratitude as tears

378

suddenly pricked my eyes. He had a way of doing that, even with such a small gesture.

"For a hundred years, you've been my light in the dark, Malekai."

"And in the glaring brightness of harsh reality, you've been my blessed, dark reprieve."

My throat struggled to work past the clogging emotion stuck in my throat. Malekai leaned down and pressed a lingering kiss to my forehead. My eyes squeezed shut, sending tears streaking down my cheeks. He pulled back quicker than I'd have liked, eyes darting to where my hand held his against my face. A pleasantly surprised look on his face.

"Well, hello..."

I followed his gaze to see the dark red tendrils of my magic curling around his hand and up his harm.

"Oh gods, sorry..."

I *willed* the tendrils to pull back, which only made them tighten their hold on him. Malekai chuckled, his white grin bright in the dark. His words were a pleasantly surprised statement rather than a question.

"This is new..."

"Yes... It started after I got this," I clarify, lifting my arm to reveal Mors' mark.

Malekai caressed one of the dark tendrils with a single finger, and it responded by slithering over his hand and coiling around it, drawing a deep, pleased hum from his chest.

"And... Have they done this before?" He asks, quirking a brow.

The subtext of his question is clear: *Do they do this with Nakoa?*

"No, never..."

His expression is unreadable as he nods.

"Have you tried... wielding them yet?"

"No... Haven't really had the time or energy, but I probably should. I'm not used to wielding magic like this..."

Malekai grunted softly in affirmation. "Perhaps you should speak with Rayne... These look similar to his... And clearly have a will of their own," he adds with a devilish grin as the tendrils reach further and slide under the V of his top.

I couldn't help but chuckle. "Oh, my... They're... Tenacious."

His laughter escalated into a galloping boom as he shuddered. *"Too ticklish! Too ticklish!"*

The tendrils drew back abruptly, hovering just beyond one of my hands. Our laughter gradually faded as our eyes lingered on one another. I wanted to reach out and pull him against me, tell him to stay, but even if Nakoa wasn't just outside the cabin... I know it wouldn't be right. And from the look on Malekai's face, he knew it too.

He picked up one of my hands and pressed a firm kiss to the inside of my palm, magic still swirling around it. My breath caught, and I watched a little wide-eyed as my magic slipped over his shoulders and around the back of his neck as if trying to clutch him against us. His knowing grin peeked out from above where he held my hand to his mouth.

"Sleep deeply and peacefully, *tessari mú.*"

FIFTY-TWO

MAREINA

When we'd woken the next morning, Malekai's horse, Ceres, as big and beautiful as ever with her golden coat and black mane, was grazing in front of Val's cabin. Miroslav must have brought her here this morning. Shame he couldn't have spared us all the journey to Bastrina, but... Perhaps there was something that would occur along the way that was necessary to ensure our success.

Val had already been packed and ready to go despite Nakoa telling him he didn't want to risk dwindling any of The Uprising's numbers. "Learn when to pick and choose your battles, brother. Ya cannae stop me from comin'," Val said before mounting his grey, dappled horse with a graceful sweep of his leg.

I stood on Val's porch, dreading the idea of spending the next couple of days I'd have to spend in Nakoa's arms atop Pumpkin. Since the moment I'd stepped out of Val's, Nakoa had seemed resolute to pretend I'd ceased to exist. Part of me was relieved, while the other part, the tether, burned furiously because of it.

He was the one that found me so fucking disposable. How dare he give me the cold shoulder just because I hadn't appreciated being used as his pawn.

As if *Akash* herself had heard my prayers, Vesper ascended the porch steps. The look on her face was almost pitying. "You want Chihiro back?"

"You sure?" I asked, purely out of politeness, praying to the gods she would insist.

Her brows lifted. "Unless you prefer to spend the next 2 days looking just as miserable as you do now..."

I heaved a sigh that I felt like I'd been holding since the day I'd met Nakoa. "Gods... Is it that obvious?"

"Based on your expression alone, I'd hazard a guess that you'd rather sit ass-first on a pike than ride with Nakoa right now."

I scrubbed a hand down my face. "Thank you... I do really appreciate it... It won't be too much for you to ride with Rayne?"

A coy grin curled one corner of her lips. "Oh, yes... A terrible burden, but... I'm sure I'll get through it *somehow.*"

She made her way back down the stairs and strode towards Rayne, who watched her with no small amount of admiration. He glanced up at me briefly, giving me a short but no less appreciative nod as if I'd just done him a favor.

My chest tightened with anxiety as I approached Nakoa, who was silently preparing Pumpkin. My mind warring with indecision about whether or not I should heed Nakoa's Mother's warning in *not* telling him the truth about Zurie being his birth mother.

"Hey..."

Nakoa's gaze flicked to mine, sadness and resignation written all over his features even though his voice was hard and cold as stone.

"Yes?"

I reared back, my temper flaring swiftly and brightly, and lowered my voice to a whisper. "I'm not entirely sure why *you're* angry with *me*. Did you not volunteer me for the task of killing Zurie alone as if I'm just some disposable sword for hire? Did you not use our bond and pretty lies to manipulate me? Did you not try to use my emotions and developing feelings to get me to fulfill the bond so you could heighten your power?"

Nakoa's jaw flexed as the corners of his mouth turned down. "*Our* power. And nothing I said was a lie, Mareina. I know I should have done things differently, and when I told you I wanted to do better, you essentially dismissed me. You want to give up already after only having met days ago."

"Well, you've made quite an impression."

Nakoa stiffened briefly at my words as he finished saddling Pumpkin. Straightening to his full height, he stared down at me. The tether between us felt like it was on fucking fire, but I forced my chin to lift even if I did want nothing more than to run away.

Silent moments passed before Nakoa gradually nodded in acceptance. "I would have hoped my *soulbound* and future Queen would understand that sometimes we have to set aside our selfish needs and desires to do what's best for the Kingdom."

Would 'selflessness' extend to murdering your own mother, however wicked?

Intuitively, I felt his answer would be yes, but it didn't change the fact that it wasn't my decision. Still, I couldn't bring myself to make the confession just yet.

"Yes, well... I would have hoped my *soulbound* wouldn't use me as a pawn in his quest for power... But don't worry, Vesper's riding with Rayne, so I won't have to trouble you with my selfishness on our journey to Bastrina."

I turned on my heel and left, practically sagging against Chihiro when I reached him on the other end of where the horses were lined up.

* * *

As if we were all holding our breath in anticipation of confronting Zurie, the journey to Bastrina over the next two days was all but silent. I'd ridden mostly beside Pomona, and my peripheral mind had remained dually focused on both Malekai and Nakoa.

As much as I'd craved Malekai's presence throughout the journey, I hadn't wanted to cause any unnecessary animosity between him and Nakoa by doing so. Malekai, thankfully, seemed to become fast friends with Val, Lokus, and Roderick. Each evening, the three of them sat together like a tiny den of thieves.

Now that Vesper had been sharing Rayne's tent, that left me with the spare tent, and Malekai had his own.

On the last night before we'd reached Zurie's palace, we'd stopped early for the evening in a small town just outside Bastrina, having all agreed that if this was to be our last night alive in this realm, we would treat ourselves to an actual bed at an inn. And despite the sheer joy I felt at the promise of a hot bath, the fact that there weren't enough rooms for me to have my own was... a significant blow. I had to share one with Nakoa.

Everyone had chosen to eat in their rooms, including Nakoa, who hesitated silently as we stood at the tavern's bar paying.

"You can bathe first... I'll eat down here," I offered.

He gave a neutral grunt before turning and heading up the stairs towards the room.

"I'll eat down here with ya, lass," a warm, rumbly voice behind me said. I turned to face Val, who gave me a look of compassion. Roderick sidled up next to me. "Same."

My eyes wandered for Malekai. "He went up to the room he's sharing with Lokus," Roderick clarified.

The innkeeper reappeared with several clean beer steins he began filling from a keg tap. "You can have a seat. I'll have the barmaid bring it all to your table."

The tavern was only crowded by half. We were close enough to the city that unease clenched my gut when a few patrons did a double-take when they saw me, to then quickly avert their eyes.

Perhaps I should have eaten in the room.

We sat at a table in one of the rear corners, and I left my hood up lest I draw any more unwanted gazes.

Val and Roderick sat across from me. The former scratched his beard while the latter scrubbed at the stubble of his normally clean-shaven face, making a rhythmic, coarse scratching noise.

"How do you feel about tomorrow?" Val asked.

I *willed* a barrier into place to protect us from prying ears as I searched within myself to see if I felt any kind of... anxiety but instead merely found that familiar numbness. When the time came, my heart would beat a pounding rhythm all its own, but as usual, when it came to matters of life or death, I felt nothing after having been desensitized after all these years.

The only thing I felt outside of numbness was the wound of Nakoa being so quick to volunteer me for the job, like some henchman at his beck and call who mattered not whether they lived or died.

"Fine..."

Roderick and Val both frowned, studying me keenly.

"You sure about that?" Val asked, quirking a brow.

"Yes. I'll be glad to be free of her."

Val nodded, heaving a sigh. "Look, love... I get the impression that things aren't exactly peachy between you and Nakoa, but... Whatever it is, make peace with it tonight before it's too late. Just in case. I have no doubt we'll be successful tomorrow, but... Death pursues us all in this realm, and if I've learned anything here... It's just when we thought we'd escaped that he catches us in his snare."

Death...

I hadn't shown anyone else the mark from Mors.

Merely the thought of the God of Death had the mark on my forearm burning. Since Malekai's suggestion, I'd felt this undeniable pull, silently urging me to go to Mors' temple in Bastrina. I'd been desperately trying to ignore it, but now that we were almost there, every moment I denied the urge was like nails raking across my mind. The thought of his acolytes alone made me shudder.

Out of the corner of my eye, I noticed the barmaid approaching with a tray laden with our food and drinks. I dropped the barrier.

When she set down our plates, each heaping with an entire chicken, vegetables, and roasted potatoes, I stared at mine with only mild interest. Instead, my fangs ached with the need to feed, and I would likely need extra strength to ensure our success tomorrow.

And my survival.

Val and Roderick tucked into their food, devouring it with fervor.

I had to force myself to take a few bites. Ironically enough, the hungrier I became for blood, the more normal food tasted like ash.

"Is it not to your liking?" Roderick asked around a large mouthful of food.

"It would be, but now I just need... something more."

Both his and Val's brows leapt in understanding, their chews slowing.

"Don't worry, I'm not *that* hungry."

They chuckled good-naturedly. I pushed my plate towards them, opting for the wine waiting in front of me.

A look of exhaustion settled on their faces as soon as they finished eating, followed by contagious yawning. Before heading to their room, Val's hand settled on my shoulder.

"I know he can be a right, stubborn cunt... But he cares deeply for you..."

I drew in a deep breath, forcing a smile onto my face as I nodded.

"Thanks, Val... See you in the morning."

He hesitated for a moment before turning to make his way to bed.

Roderick leaned his hip against the table, arms folded against his broad chest, staring down at me like he could see right through me. I returned his gaze, deliberating whether or not I should ask his advice.

How do I go about telling Nakoa that he's sending me to kill his mother without jeopardizing the future of Atratus?

I didn't miss the fucking *astonishing* irony in the fact that she had sent me to kill him. And neither were aware of the other's plot. Not *truly.*

The words were yet again poised on the tip of my tongue just as Roderick spoke, cutting them off.

"Perhaps you guys should just try being friends?"

My brows leapt at his suggestion.

"I doubt Nakoa wants to be my friend."

Roderick gave an easy shrug. "He doesn't know what's good for him... Seems to be working well for you and Malekai."

At my hardening look, he raised placating hands. "I mean that sincerely. Maybe if you set a boundary as friends, he won't take you for granted or manipulate you anymore, nor will he feel like you're shutting him out completely."

"Maybe..."

I didn't dare give any such thing hope.

"Either way, we're here for you... You're not alone. I can't speak for Vesper, but as for the rest of us... Our loyalty to you isn't hinged upon whether or not you decide to be with Nakoa... *Or* Malekai."

My breath halted mid-inhale.

Roderick chuckled. "I've known Nakoa my entire life. He's not the *easiest* person to get along with, and considering the entirety of his aspirations all sit in *your* basket until *whatsherface* is missing her head ... I can imagine it's making him a little crazy... Or well... Even *more* crazy than his usual state of madness."

"... Thank you, Roderick. That... means a lot more to me than you can imagine."

He nodded slowly as his grey-blue eyes bore into mine, and it felt like he was seeing so much more than I'd intended to reveal.

"I hope you can get some sleep, Mareina."

"Thank you... You too."

I waited until Roderick had disappeared up the stairs before I slipped out of the tavern and made my way to the stable. Chihiro was happily gnawing away on his hay when I approached. I gave a pat on his thick neck, murmuring my apologies. He gave an exasperated huff in response.

The stable woman kept her eyes to herself as I approached, a palmful of silvers in hand. "I'll be back in a few hours if anyone asks."

"Yes, my lady."

FIFTY-THREE

MAREINA

The streets were surprisingly empty when Chihiro and I entered the city. Within 20 minutes, the smell of benzoin and myrrh drifted towards me... The scent was oddly familiar but caused my nerves to ratchet regardless. An anxious energy seemed to pulse through me as the marks on my arms tingled in an almost pleasurable, if not strange, way. A distinct improvement from the angry, burning sensation they'd had when I'd been trying to ignore this *call.*

The temple stood off by itself, carved in a pale veined marble. Torches hung from each of the many towering columns, casting ominous shadows in the dark of the nearly moonless night. Only a sliver of each of the moons remained. Silently, I made my way up the steps towards the colossal doors upon which a dark bronze effigy of Mors himself was mounted, taking the hand of a spirit as it rose from a body shed in its bed. He almost looked... *gentle.*

I also couldn't help but notice that he had four enormous wings instead of merely two.

One of the enormous doors cracked open silently, just enough for me to squeeze through.

I heaved a sigh. "Oh dear..."

While, yes, it would be the height of stupidity to walk into this strange, dark temple alone... There I was... Stepping toward the door.

Surely, those grey-robed acolytes couldn't wield any weapon or magic greater than mine... And Mors wouldn't have stalked my dreams and marked me just to lead me here to die.

"Are you actually insane?"

My mouth quirked as I turned to see Malekai striding up the steps, wearing an admonishing look on his face.

"For fuck's sake, Mareina..."

"Thank you for coming..."

He huffed, shaking his head. "Yeah, thanks for the invite. When I suggested you do this shit, I thought it went without saying that you take me with you, you fucking lunatic."

Gods, I loved this male.

I gave him an appreciative smile and slipped his hand into mine.

"Thank you for coming."

I turned back around to try the door to find a dark-robbed shadowy silhouette had appeared in the doorway.

I yelped in surprise at his sudden and silent, ominous appearance. Every hair on my body stood on end. I held my breath, squeezing Malekai's hand in terror. Ready to shove him away if that thing so much as tried to raise a finger to me.

Instead of reaching for me, the *Pharalaki* wordlessly turned and disappeared into the temple.

Malekai and I exchanged a look before he stepped ahead of me, taking my hand in his and pulling me behind him.

It was almost completely dark. Only the fae light floating in front of the acolyte that I guessed we were supposed to be following guided our steps. Columns lined the foyer and hallway that gave way to numerous doors, none of which we stopped at. The *Pharalaki* rounded a corner and passed a shadowy hand over a section of the stone wall that then disappeared. A pitch-black, arched doorway appeared, and he began descending a set of spiralling steps that led further into the dark.

Malekai looked back at me in the rapidly dimming light. "You sure about this?"

"We're gonna die at some point. Why not now?"

"Hilarious." His tone said he found it anything but.

Still, he led the way down the steps, gradually catching up with the light and the acolyte.

The scent of... fresh air and flora greeted us moments before the steps ended. Instead of a dungeon or a crypt, or whatever else one might fathom to lie beneath a literal *Temple of Death,* we found... A single, large, full moon illuminated a field filled with tall grasses and wildflowers that rippled on a breeze like silvery, docile ocean waves. A large stone house with a terracotta roof sat in the distance; the lower floor's windows facing us were illuminated and glowing the colour of a lit hearth.

Malekai and I exchanged wide-eyed looks as the acolyte strode through the field towards the house.

Behind Malekai, just meters away, a river flowed. Glowing an unearthly blue. He followed my gaze, lips parting at the sight.

The River Oblivion.

The *Pharalaki* stood patiently by a surprisingly flimsy wooden front door made of nothing more than several slats of old plywood where vertical shafts of light peeked through.

A rather humble home for Mors... *A God.*

I'd seen illustrations of a sprawling palace. Not this cozy artisan's haven that barely had a front door. I suppose if anyone didn't have to worry about safety, it was him.

Dark vapours escaped from within the hood of the *Pharalaki's* robe, disappearing from between the light-filled gaps in the wood.

"Do come in...," a silky female voice called from inside the house.

The *Pharalaki* drifted away, its robe whispering across the tall grasses as it returned to the temple. A view of ice-peaked Mountains laid in the distance beyond the single, open, doorless doorway that simply floated in the center of the field.

Malekai, still holding my hand, pushed open the door to reveal a woman with skin the color of the moon and hair as black as night to match. Large, heavily lashed, luminous green eyes took us in. The high cheekbones, the shape of her lips... All so painfully familiar.

Her features slackened as her gaze swept from Malekai to settle on me. The steaming clay pot held in her mittened hands shattered at her feet. Breath caught, voice whispering and cracking at the same time.

"*Akash almighty...* I can't believe you're finally here."

Her eyes swelled with tears as she stepped around the pile of food and clay shards, closing the distance between us. My breath felt like it had been gripped by a fist in my throat as I stared into a face that I'd seen far too many times to not recognize. Every time I'd ever looked in a mirror.

There were only slight differences. She had slightly rounder, fawn-like eyes and impossibly long lashes. Where her skin was nearly alabaster, mine had an olive complexion. And she looked only vaguely older than I did.

Something painful squeezed in my chest at the recognition.

Oh, gods...

Her hands, surprisingly cool, gripped me by the backs of my arms. She hesitated as though giving me the opportunity to protest before she crushed me against her chest with considerable strength.

Too overcome with shock, I felt like I'd just been thrown into an icy lake. It wasn't until her hand came up and cradled the back of my head in a manner so tender that my shock began to thaw.

We stayed like that for long moments. My emotion swelled, but I swallowed it back as it shifted into wounded anger.

"*Where have you been?*"

The female drew in a shuddering breath as she finally drew back from me. Her face puffy and red.

"Mareina... It's not what you think."

I shook my head in disbelief as my eyes hungrily took in the sight of my mother. The first I'd ever seen of this female.

Malekai's large palm settled on the small of my back. The action helped to steady me as a portion of my anger dissipated from nothing more than his touch.

"Your father and I—

A loud *crash* sounded from outside as a tremor shook through the floor. Malekai and I whirled just as the flimsy wooden door burst open, splintering against the white stucco wall of the house. A male at least as broad and as tall as Malekai's six foot eight inches filled the doorway. Four black wings, identical to my own, folded tightly against his back as he took a hesitant step closer.

I'd never seen a depiction that revealed the face of the God of Death before, but I certainly hadn't imagined it to be this. His black robe nowhere to be seen. Dark wisps of magic curled off of his body as though restless. His formidable shoulders and chest filled a dark tunic. Long, thickly muscled legs dressed adorned by a matching pair of linen trousers.

Chiselled features slackened, and the dark olive-tan skin of his face paled with a shock that mirrored my own. Slightly upturned, hazel eyes widened at the sight of me. Cupid's bow lips parted. His black hair, cut short on the sides and longer on top, was wind-whipped.

My mother's voice was a tremulous whisper.

"Your father and I didn't have a choice. Giving you away was the hardest thing we've ever done."

Mors closed the distance between us in a single stride and crushed me to his chest so fiercely it all but knocked the wind out of me.

"I knew you would come."

The sound of his voice sent me reeling. *This* was the voice that had filled my dreams. All this time... *All this time...*

The words from the dream echoed in my mind.

"Forget not that you are both death and eternity given form. You are never alone. Seek me, The Guardian of Life, to find your home."

My voice came out a croaking whisper. Malekai watched us with nothing short of awe illuminating his face. For the first time in many, many years, I saw tears swelling in his eyes.

"It was you..."

"Of course it was. Who else?"

All these years, the *Pharalaki* weren't stalking me... They were *watching* me.

"But in the dream, it called you the Guardian of Life..."

"I *am* the Guardian of Life... *Eternal life...*"

I shook my head in shock.

"I apologize for being enigmatic... We couldn't risk my sister, Keres, finding you... We are bound to this realm. When your mother, *Soteira,* became pregnant - something that we didn't even think was possible - we tried to find a way... A solution... Nor did we want you to be bound to this realm."

Keres... The Goddess of Violence.

Unease twisted in my gut... A deity I had, thankfully, only ever read about. She was depicted as being vicious and merciless, tearing a warpath through her every step.

Soteira curled her arms around one of Mors' large arms as she continued where he'd left off.

"We summoned Moirai, and she told us as best she could what would occur in both fates... If you stayed here with us, and if you went to Bellorum or one of the other *medí kosmoi...*"

Middle worlds.

"As beautiful as it is here, we wouldn't want you to have this place be the only place you've ever known. We wanted you to have freedom... Among other things, we wanted you to meet your *soulbound...*"

My breath caught as a flare of pain speared through my chest.

"That is how you came to be born in the doorway between realms..."

Soteira tipped her head toward the walless doorway that led from Avernus to Bellorum.

I hadn't ever realized that the words in the dream should be taken so literally.

Born *between* realms... Born in an *actual* doorway.

Every shadow observant... The *Pharalaki*.

Death and eternity given form...

Dizziness from the revelations swept over me, and instinctively, my hand reached for Malekai, who promptly draped his arm over my shoulders and tucked me into his side. My parent's eyes lifted to his.

"This is... My most loyal friend and..."

My words drifted briefly because that didn't sound nearly sufficient for what Malekai was to me.

"And the love of my life. Malekai."

Malekai's arm tightened around me as his already considerable warmth seemed to double, making me want to bury myself against him in comfort.

My parents' brows leapt in unison.

"It's an honor to meet you both," Malekai said, with warmth and reverence, offering his hand.

Mors' mouth tilted up in a soft grin as he took his hand in both his own.

"And I, you... Moirai showed us a great many things in Mareina's future potentialities... And you were in a great many of them."

Soteira embraced Malekai's hand in her own despite her brows pinching with confusion. Her smile uncertain as her gaze caught Mors.

"The tether between you two is... one of the strongest I've seen... But... Is Nakoa alive?"

My throat seemed to work over a bit of gravel.

"Yes... He is. We... Don't really see eye to eye on... anything."

Soteira and Mors exchanged a glance, something unspoken between them, before she gradually nodded, wearing a look of both compassion and concern.

"I see... Thank goodness you have each other then."

Something seemed strained about her words, and she forced a smile that didn't quite meet her eyes. It gave me an uneasy feeling that I willfully chose to ignore.

"What keeps you bound here?" I asked, desperate to change the subject and get my questions answered.

Mors and Soteira exchanged a tense look.

"Every deity that is born in service to a realm is bound to it, *but* they have an aspect of their soul that enables them to fold to and from various realms - shift forms and energies - while the greater portion still remains rooted to their home realm... My sister, Keres, with the help of an ally, stole that portion of both mine and your mother's souls so that she can wreak havoc as she pleases across the realms without our interference... If we were to try and leave my domain without it, our soul's connection to this realm would be severed... We wouldn't be able to return until we died as mortals...And by then, it would be too late because Avernus, along with everyone in it, would have been destroyed...To put it reductively."

Thankfully, Malekai was holding me, or I would have swayed on my feet.

"How do I find her?"

Mors' expression hardened, transforming his warm features into something cold and harsh, looking much more like what I'd expected the God of Death to look like.

"You don't," he said firmly, "She knows only violence and hatred. If she found you..." His words drifted, throat working on a rough swallow as he shook his head. "I do not want to imagine what she would do to you."

"... But that means... You'll be stuck here. *Forever.*"

Mors chuckled. "When you're as old as I am, you learn that very few things remain unchanged for all of eternity. I am sure that one day, fate will have its way and the pythoi that mine and your—

"Pythoi?"

Mors' brows knit together warily.

"In the dream you sent me... There was a pythos..." My eyes darted between the two of them, "Only the one."

Mors, jaw clenching, exchanged another look with Soteira.

"I never sent you any dream of a pythos."

Malekai's words were more of a statement than a question.

"Your brother..."

Mors scowled, hand fisting by his side.

"Yes... My brother... Meddlesome, fool."

Somnus. The God of Dreams.

That was how he'd sent me that dream all these years.

"He knows where it is..."

Mors shook his head angrily. "Probably, considering he can enter the subconscious mind of any being..."

"Is he in Bellorum?"

"Probably not, and you mustn't attempt to find him. I don't know why he would send you anything related to that *Akash*-forsaken pythos but Mareina, please... I implore you..."

I heaved a sigh... There was too much currently at stake with Zurie and Atratus. And adding some quest to find Somnus, Keres, and that pythos... Well... I wasn't exactly eager to heap any more life-threatening scenarios onto my plate.

I nodded in understanding. However, some part of me prayed that he wouldn't ask me to make any promises.

Thankfully, whatever he and my mother saw on my face appeased them. Still, she frowned.

"When was the last time you fed?"

Malekai huffed a laugh. "She seems to be a sucker for masochism because I am *constantly* forced to ask her the same question."

Soteira and Mors both scowled.

"Why do you cause yourself this suffering?" Soteira asked. "So long as you are in that world, you require blood to sustain you and your power. It is why we chose sanguinati to raise you."

I had no idea about how or why they specifically chose my foster parents, but... I had serious questions. Questions that would have to wait.

Zurie's reign was coming to an end *tomorrow*. And Nakoa was likely tearing the village apart looking for me.

Fuck.

This would not look good.

I looked up at Malekai before returning my gaze to my parents.

"I'll feed. Don't worry... But we should go..."

Mors' eyes looked almost pleading. Heartbroken that I'd be leaving after I'd only just arrived.

"Time here is different than in Bellorum... You've been here mere minutes, and only seconds might have passed there..."

Guilt struck a disharmonious chord in my heart.

"Even so... I'm exhausted, and it took twenty minutes for me to get here. By the time we get back, Nakoa might have torn the tavern apart already... And tomorrow is... A big day."

Mors and Soteira nodded in understanding, though neither asked me to elaborate. Thank *Akash*.

"Well, at least take some of our blood. It will strengthen you."

I reared back slightly.

I'd never fed from my father. Sanguinati, and apparently deities, didn't require any blood to survive until their magic matured during early adulthood.

"Don't worry about the venom. It doesn't have the same effect when it's between those you share blood with."

FIFTY-FOUR

NAKOA

S neaking footsteps had my eyes popping open. I'd fallen asleep with my hand around the dagger's hilt tucked beneath my pillow. My chest twisted tightly with anticipation at the feel of Mareina's magic, her presence, entering the room. I didn't bother to let her know I was awake. She could probably discern the fact regardless, even though I remained unmoving and kept my breaths slow and even. The tinkling sound of water told me she'd slipped into the bath. A tugging sensation in my sternum urged me to join her.

Not a fucking chance.

However brief our last conversations, they had pushed me away. I could understand Mareina being upset about my misgivings, but the fact that she couldn't empathize or understand the need any ruler had to put their Kingdom above all else had my heart hardening towards her.

Why her?

Why?

I would have been proud if she had felt the same.

It was my *destiny* to rule.

How could I be forced to do so with someone who didn't recognize that the Kingdom came above all else. Certainly above personal needs and desires, no matter how consuming.

"What will you do about Zurie's army after she's dead?"

I hesitated before rolling over, not entirely sure I even felt like speaking with her. I craved it entirely too much despite the amount of pain it sent spearing through the tether. Distance. I needed distance from this female. She was a disorienting distraction. My rational mind told me that perhaps it was a blessing this male of hers had shown up.

Malekai.

My *irrational* mind told me to strangle him with his own innards.

My lungs drew in a heavy breath that did nothing to bring me any form of relief.

"They will bow to me or die."

A pause.

"That sounds very much like something Zurie would do... Oh, wait. Nevermind. *She has.* To entire races of people. *What the fuck are you thinking?*"

I huffed a joyless laugh. "I'm thinking that if I let them go, they'll start an uprising of their own, and it's merely a matter of time before another war starts."

Weighted silence.

"... If you truly want people's loyalty, you will help them. Those soldiers of hers aren't loyal to her out of love or respect. It's purely out of desperation and necessity. Nearly all of whom have families who are living in squalor or are barely struggling to stay out of it. Zurie's coffers are bursting from all the profit she has made over the years on *aetra.* Why don't you give some of that money to them, not to *buy* their loyalty but as a gesture of goodwill that you will take better care of them than Zurie has. It would be a negligible sum against what she possesses. Promise them what you will promise the Kahlohani. I know that the people of Atratus weren't always your people, but they certainly are now. Or at least will be after tomorrow.

And killing those who refuse to join you will only justify anyone's distrust and reticence to join you."

This is why she is destined to be your Queen, My Knowingness whispered.

She was right. I was still thinking with an old anger and vengeance against people I had fought against since I was old enough to wield a sword.

An unwelcome weight settled on my chest. Lying on my back, I turned my head to find her green eyes glittering in the dark, already fixed on me.

"You're right... Let's try that then."

She said nothing more, and I had nothing more to say. I rolled over again, facing away from her, though I could still feel her eyes on me. Water sloshed as she quickly finished bathing and then rose to get dressed.

When her weight settled on the other side of the bed, the words left me before I'd even given them thought. As if someone or something else had pulled them out of me.

"I'm sorry, Mareina."

FIFTY-FIVE

MAREINA

Outside of my body humming with magic after drinking from both of my parents, our trip to the cave, hiding the tunnelled entrance into Zurie's palace, was uneventful. Our morning had been quiet, as if everyone were silently replaying all the possibilities of how today could unfold. Or at least that's what I was doing. Though my mind specifically replayed the best-case scenario. I refused to spiral down the numerous death traps of failure. Before any battle, I always focused my mind on visualizing victory. It had always served me well.

Hidden beneath a wall of vines that grew out from the stone, sucking at the moisture that trickled through from the surrounding snowcapped mountains, the door to the tunnel appeared as nothing more than the stone wall of the cave. I murmured the ancient fae words that Miroslav had taught me after I'd been promoted to Zurie's Irae. I imagined he had already seen this exact moment when I would need it.

A certain calm came over me as the door appeared. As if after all these years, completely untouched, if the dense cobwebs in the tunnel were anything to go by, had been placed here just for us. For this very purpose...

A flame burst into life in Nakoa's palm as he stepped forward.

That was new.

At my piqued brow, he gave me a shrug.

The cobwebs in the tunnel were so dense they'd hardly cut through them with their swords.

A shudder worked through me, imagining all the spiders and other many-legged creatures that would have sought refuge here.

Nakoa's gaze remained fixed on me until something in him shifted all at once, and he stumbled back ever so slightly. I'm not sure anyone else noticed. His eyes grew distant, and his neck craned towards the ceiling, lips parting as if in awe.

To anyone else, it might look like he's just gaping at the cavernous ceiling, but to me... I can tell that he's having some kind of vision. I can feel it in my guts, and it's deeply unsettling.

In only a few short seconds, he seems to return to himself, and his eyes snap back to mine. His throat worked on a swallow, and it's almost as if he looked... vulnerable. As if I'd just caught him in a moment of helplessness. These *visions* have been plaguing him more and more - visions of things that are anything but pleasant if the sudden ashen looks when they overcome him are anything to go by. Occasionally, I'd even caught him speaking to whoever it is that appears in them before he returns.

Part of me wants to reach out and tell him it's OK... But it's not. I'm about to kill his *mother;* I might die trying, and if I tell him - it could apparently destroy everything fate has set in place so that we can finally bring justice and peace to this realm.

I could physically *feel* the window of opportunity I had to confess the truth about his mother to him, slowly shutting right in front of me.

That window seemed to shut as his eyes left mine, and Roderick, Val, Lokus, Famei, Pomona, and Rayne all sidled up beside him. Malekai remained by my side, and Vesper beside him.

Something pulled tight between us.

Right beside the weight of my guilt.

If things go wrong, this might very well be the last time I get to look any of them in the face.

My soulbound included.

Roderick and Val had already begun peeling their clothes off, shifting into their Lykos forms. On all fours, their heads still reached Nakoa's chest. Rayne's demeanor was relaxed, though his dark shadows curled around and beside him restlessly as they began to solidify into tall, sentinel-like beings with glowing eyes, long claws, and sharp teeth. The hairs on my arms lifted as I felt them returning my gaze before drifting to Vesper, who was openly staring at them, lips parted.

Pomona gave me a winsome grin, *folding* in front of me as if to remind me that she could do such a thing. She gave me a tight squeeze, murmuring in my ear. "Be careful, new sister." She kissed my cheek before folding back to Famei, who smiled. His golden, yellow eyes glowing brightly.

Lokus gave an exaggerated yawn, patting his mouth.

"I'll send Miroslav for you at the tunnel entrance inside the palace as soon as it's done. *Akash* be with you."

Nakoa gave me a short nod. "See you on the other side."

He turned, leading the way in the darkness, and I shut the hidden door behind them as I promptly shoved away the hurt burning through our tether.

It felt like our fate had been sealed right along with it, and there was no way to know if that was a good or bad thing.

I could potentially die *doing this, and that's all he had to say?*

The soothing heat of Malekai's hand, at least a few degrees warmer than anyone could naturally be, slid over my shoulder. My magic felt as though it was purring in response - the first occasion since I'd fed from my parent's blood that soothed the tension in my body and my magic, which I could feel coiled tight and ready to strike.

"Ready, *tessari mú*?"

I nodded, meeting his gaze. "Are you?"

A soft smile perched on the corner of his unfairly perfect mouth.

"As long as I'm beside you - *always.*"

My eyes slid shut briefly, taking comfort in those words. And praying that no harm would come to him on this utterly insane endeavor.

When I opened my eyes, I looked past him to Vesper, who was openly staring at us with curiosity. Though I found no judgment beneath it.

"And how are you feeling?"

She seemed surprisingly relaxed.

"A little unsettled about pretending to be a corpse, but other than that... Ready to get this the fuck over with."

FIFTY-SIX

NAKOA

My skin felt as if it might burst. Nearly as intensely as my shoulders ached for my wings and magic to be unleashed. Not only for what we were about to do but also for having had to part ways with Mareina while she faced Zurie. As necessary as it was, considering giving Zurie 'my corpse' would yield the least messy result so long as we managed to pull this off. I was shocked by the intensity of my genuine gratitude and relief that Malekai was with her.

Rayne's beasts led the way, slithering against the walls as we strode down the tunnel that seemed more like an endless, yawning chasm with no end. More than thirty minutes had passed by the time the barest sliver of light could be seen peaking from beneath a door in the distance. The entire time, my heart pounded a deafening beat in my ears as I could only guess how Mareina was faring. If Zurie was dead yet.

The hairs on the back of my neck rose, and my steps slowed as we approached, and my *olana kah'hei* walked ahead of me.

Still wielding the ball of fire in one hand, instinct had my free hand reaching for the hilt of my sword.

I half expected a vision to overtake me, but instead, I turned to find a female dressed in a pale grey gown with silver hair and dark skin. She grinned wide at me, revealing a delicate set of fangs. Her voice a husky purr.

"Hello."

CHAPTER

FIFTY-SEVEN

MAREINA

M iroslav appeared the moment I warded the tunnel entrance to the door again. Malekai gave him a brief nod of acknowledgement. "Miroslav."

"General."

Vesper studied him warily as his gaze briefly met hers. Neither spoke, but I sensed something was exchanged silently between them. He gave me a tight smile that had a tendril of anxiety snaking through me. Miroslav didn't give tight smiles. His expressions ranged from stoic to *stoic*. So, to see something like a flicker of unease was *deeply* alarming.

"How's Zurie?" I asked, eager to skip pleasantries.

"Not dead yet," Miroslav replied flatly, "But if you mean suspicious, then no. She's had her attention consumed by an unexpected visitor."

"Unexpected? You didn't *foresee* said visitor?"

It was a genuine question. Nothing ever seemed to be *unexpected* for Miroslav.

He piqued a brow at me. "I'm not omniscient, Mareina... There are always outside factors that evade me no matter how thoroughly I search."

"And who exactly is this visitor?" Malekai asked before I could.

"The heir to Ishra's throne, Thalia. Her father's health is waning. She'll soon be Queen and came seeking to ally with Zurie."

My brows leapt. *Well, that certainly wouldn't be happening.*

I knew next to nothing about Ishra other than it was shrouded in a dense fog that caused madness if anyone attempted to enter with ill intent. Though it was known for its remarkable architecture from what I'd seen depicted in history books that were far out of date. I only knew of its King, Nour Attía, who was said to be the descendent of a demiurge and was a rather benevolent male on top of it. As far as I knew, their Kingdom hadn't seen war in thousands of years.

We could only hope that his daughter would be willing to continue that.

"Will she be a problem?"

Miroslav looked thoughtful. "I'm not entirely sure. When I try to get past her mind's barrier, I'm met with the mental equivalent of that fog surrounding their continent. This also occurs when I try to peer into her past and potential future. She's... *gifted*."

Malekai and I exchanged a look.

"Well, let's try to deal with Zurie discreetly as planned and... See if we can ally with her."

Without further delay, Vesper shifted into Nakoa's form in seconds. I almost stumbled backwards as I took him - *her* - in. At my slack-jawed reaction, she gave me a wink.

Miroslav cleared his throat. "You'll need to display his wings and tail since his magic wouldn't keep them glamoured after death."

"Right..."

An enormous pair of dark umber wings sprouted from her back, along with Nakoa's long, thick tail. Vesper, bearing Nakoa's face, gave me a sultry grin as if she *knew* as she caught me staring at the appendage and wagged it.

"How's this?" She asked, turning to model his wings and tail.

"Accurate," I said flatly.

409

I turned willing a ward into place for our horses that would remain here until we finished. Vesper mounted Chihiro and then groaned as she folded over, laying over his side.

"I'm going to cover you, alright?"

Vesper sighed, resigning herself to what was about to happen. "Yep."

With a small amount of guilt, I willed the same canvas I used on every occasion that required a corpse to remain undiscovered over her body, tying off each end with rope.

My heartbeat kicked up a notch at whatever fate we would soon discover lying ahead of us.

Malekai sidled up at me, curling his arm around my waist and kissing the top of my head. "I'll be with you every step of the way."

Thankfully, he was often at my side anytime we were both at the palace, so it wouldn't raise any eyebrows.

Miroslav nodded, wordlessly laying a hand on our shoulders as I pressed a hand to Chihiro's neck. Miroslav folded the group of us in front of the palace gates.

Miroslav's voice rang out in an imperious tone - a strange return to the only way I'd ever heard him speak until recently.

"Have Irae Kalini's horse taken to the stables and fed."

One of the guards approached, giving a slight bow to the both of us before taking Chihiro's reigns.

"After that, you can return to the barracks. You're dismissed," Miroslav added, gripping the canvas sack that wrapped Vesper's body as he placed his arm on our shoulders again, leading us towards the palace entrance. Nakoa or no, we were forced to make our way down the long, moted entrance lugging a *corpse* because no one other than Zurie's employ could fold *in* from outside the palace or its gates, even if accompanied.

Once inside, it made no difference except for the areas warded against it, like Zurie's personal chambers or harem. The guards were all too desensitized to Zurie's *antics,* so no one batted an eye when we strode by carrying a body bag.

The hair on the back of my neck rose the moment Miroslav folded us from the Zurie's giant entrance to the crypt. I hadn't actually ever been in here before. Torches of flame, not fae light, burst to life, casting moving shadows against the alabaster stone of the crypt.

My eyes were instantly drawn to the marble relief of Mors' sigil, the inverted torch with wings... Surprising warmth suffused my chest, easing my nerves considerably. His voice, from within my dream, returned to me.

"... Forget not that you are both death and eternity given form. You are never alone. Seek me, The Guardian of Life, to find your home."

Malekai squeezed my hand, drawing my gaze to his, and he gave me a secret, knowing smile.

As though Vesper, in Nakoa's long, bulky form weighed nothing, Miroslav gently set her on the bier - the platform which displayed the dead before burial - and began untying the rope at the canvas' ends.

"I'm going to glamor you so you look more... dead... and she doesn't see you breathing," he murmured quietly to Vesper before turning towards me, "As I'm sure you already planned, tell Zurie, you magicked the body shortly after death to preserve it so she doesn't think anything of it radiating off the body."

My gaze drifted as he spoke, taking in the old letters carved into several dozen tombs housing Zurie's family members. All 5 of her siblings had died young, and her parents, who weren't particularly old, had also passed. More than half of them had done so in *sudden, tragic accidents.*

How wildly fortuitous she'd had no one to challenge her for the throne.

Miroslav turned to me and gave me a look that I suspected was intended to be encouraging. "She'll be distracted viewing her *son's* body..." His gaze lingered on me pointedly.

Vesper gasped, eyes bursting open. Miroslav only gave her a narrow-eyed look. If the information surprised Malekai, he was a superb actor.

Right, so stab Zurie in the back when she's not looking.

I'd have felt guilty about that if she hadn't committed mass genocide on multiple occasions, among other things.

The guilt I couldn't seem to shake remained the fact that *I*, Nakoa's *souldbound* and Queen, was supposed to murder the female who had birthed him without him even knowing.

A silver collar appeared in Miroslav's hand. "This is what she has the males in her harem wear. It's a magical suppressant. Slip it around her neck to prevent her from wielding magic in case she doesn't die instantly."

My skin crawled as I closed my hand over the collar and *willed* it away for the time being.

Malekai held my gaze, surely sensing my increasing nerves. His warm hand curled around one of mine as he murmured a soothing spell.

"*Katadamna kaza, tessari mú.*"

My heart swelled with a love I'd denied for far too long. Though now was not the time to declare it. Instead, I squeezed his hand, not letting go, and poured my emotion into him.

"*Katadamna kaza.*"

Miroslav appeared a few breaths later, a hand resting on the middle of Zurie's back after *folding* her into the crypt. The sweet scent of *aetra* rolled off her, making me want to bury my face into Malekai's chest to replace it with his.

Zurie didn't bother to acknowledge us. Understandably so, as she took in the sight of her 'deceased' *son* and drew a trembling hand to her mouth.

Seeing any emotion outside of anger or malevolent glee on her face was unsettling. I hadn't witnessed such a thing outside of what The Well had shown me when she'd first ordered Nakoa's death just after his birth.

She quickly closed the distance between them, coming to stand at the bier, running her shaky fingers over his luscious feathers. His proud cheekbones, eventually cupping his cheek.

My eyes suddenly stung at her whispered words. So quiet they were barely audible, even to me.

"You were so beautiful, my precious darling... I'm so sorry."

Oh, gods...

My throat worked to stifle emotion.

Kill her, my instincts whispered urgently.

Though his eyes burned with intent, Miroslav's face held zero expression as he met my gaze.

I knew then and there I didn't have the heart to *murder* Nakoa's mother. Not without him knowing the truth.

CHAPTER

FIFTY-EIGHT

NAKOA

I drew my dagger, swiftly pressing it against the female's throat as she folded us into what I could only assume was one of the guest bedrooms in Zurie's palace. Her reaction was neither one of shock nor offence. Instead, she merely grinned from ear to ear. She looked... *young.* Young enough to be in her twenties. Though that meant nothing. She could quite possibly be hundreds of years older than me. Her heart-shaped face was framed by long swathes of silvery waves that spilled over her delicate shoulders. Bright grey eyes, wide and doe-like, were made even more striking by her dark skin as she looked up at me from her petite but curvy stature. Her head only reached my chest.

"I mean you no harm. Just wanted to have a little chat in private... *Your Highness.*"

My glare would have caused a lesser spirit to crumple as I pressed the blade harder against her throat. A trickle of blood dripped over the edge and onto the low neckline of her pale dress.

"You have about four seconds before I remove your head."

"My name is Thalia. Princess Thalia Attía of Ishra. I wish to ally with you."

Her reply only served to make my hackles rise further.

How the fuck did she know?

"I have a great number of other allies, all of whom possess rather extraordinary gifts... I've been watching you for quite some time."

I scowled, finally removing the blade from her throat. She swept a finger over the blood dripping from her neck and the top of her breast, licking it from her fingertip.

Whatever war was destined to come to our doorstep, having allies from the continent would be exceedingly advantageous. Ishra's King was the descendent of a demiurge. Several generations back, and had now been mixed with various other formidable *wielding* races, but even so, the male would be exceedingly mighty.

A vision bled over present reality.

A bedridden male with white hair and dark skin lies in an ornately decorated bed of white and gold. He gazes up weakly in bewilderment with pleading eyes. His voice is little more than a rasp. Hands trembling, he reaches for a person in front of him that I cannot yet see.

"Where is my daughter?"

A soft voice comes from behind me.

"I'm right here, father."

The vision clears so quickly that it's possible Thalia didn't notice that I'd momentarily disappeared. She only continued to study me as she waited for my reply.

"What is it exactly that you have to offer as an ally? And why have you come all the way to Atratus seeking allies? Surely, there are larger, more formidable allies on the continent who would join you."

"I have acquired them as allies already..."

My patience has already grown exceedingly thin. I could practically *feel* my *olana kah'hei's* panic from here. My voice comes out a growl that only seems to spur her on.

"That only further confuses me as to why you wish to ally? Surely you realize there will be an era of turmoil as I take the throne... Atratus is a small region with even fewer resources. "

I didn't dare mention *aetra*, though she was undoubtedly well aware.

Her fingers nervously twisted a tiny bit of fabric at the side of her figure-hugging gown. Decorated with ornate, silver beading woven into the tight fighting bodice that appeared to be strangling her breasts.

If anything, the sight made me all the more wary. She no doubt knew what she was doing. Or at least trying to.

"My father has fallen ill. With no King beside me when I take the throne, I have no doubt that members of my father's court will make attempts on my life."

Ah.

"I have a *soulbound,* female," I grit out, nearly holding up the arm that was supposed to be covered with *soulbound* markings. *But wasn't.*

I was angered by both her attempt to *woo* me and the fact that it reminded me my *soulbound* was someone who wanted nothing to do with me and did not share the ideals with which I would rule.

"A *soulbound* who would rather seek the company of another male..."

My magic slipped, eyes burning black and wings flaring at her harsh but factual words. Her lips parted in awe as she took in my true form.

"If this is your attempt at a proposal, you're fucking miserable at it," I snarled with barely restrained rage.

Her expression turned to one of compassion.

"I... I'm sorry. I just... I also know this pain. My own *soulbound* has also sought another."

My jaw dropped momentarily, but I quickly snapped it shut. In all my years, I'd never heard of such a thing. My scowl softened.

"Truly?"

She nodded, throat working on a swallow.

"It is one of *many* reasons I sought you out."

I shook my head as I tried to breathe away the phantom fist squeezing my throat.

"I have to return to my *olana kah'hei.*"

She nodded in understanding.

"There is one last thing."

I piqued an eyebrow at her as my impatience reared.

"It's about Zurie... She's not who you think she is."

My expression tightened.

"What?"

"Zurie is... *Your birth mother.*"

CHAPTER
FIFTY-NINE

MAREINA

The dark red whorls of my magic seeped from me, writhing in anticipation. I seized what remained of my minuscule window of opportunity, *willing* my sword into my hands as I lunged forward. Zurie, likely thanks to her already considerable power and *aetra* heightened senses, spun toward me just as my sword slid through her abdomen with no more resistance than butter. A gurgled cry tore through Zurie's throat as I forced the blade up, severing her sternum into two halves until it reached her heart and *willed* the palladium collar to slip over her throat.

Shock widened her eyes. Blood dribbled from her lips, diaphragm, and chest. The words she rasped were unintelligible before she slipped off my blade and collapsed on the floor. I hardly noticed as Vesper rose from the bier where she laid, shifting back to her true form, and stared down at Zurie with wide eyes.

My rage, for all the horror she had committed and that I had blackened my soul for and committed on her behalf, rose swiftly. I stared down at her crumpled, bloody form, half in shock.

No.

That was too easy. Something dark within me craved

more... *More* for everyone who had died because of her greed. *More* because of every person I had killed for her. *More* because I had blackened my soul to serve her all these years.

I had too much pent-up rage for it to end like this.

It took everything within me not to finish her off here.

My body trembled with fury, only gradually calming as my conscience echoed my decision.

I would give Nakoa the choice. I would tell him the truth.

I heaved a shuddering breath as I finally turned and nodded towards Miroslav.

"Go get Nakoa."

He hesitated, eyes snapping to mine in realization. *He knew I was going to tell Nakoa.*

Despite his and Leilani's insistent warnings *not* to tell Nakoa... He didn't look angry. A few tense moments passed between us.

"This is a different path that you are choosing, Mareina... Are you sure?"

Doubt trickled in.

His expression became resigned... Exhausted. "If you have any hope of..." His words cut short, shaking his head as though deciding against it. "I cannot... ensure your survival in this path. It is a violent one."

I had blackened my soul enough. I would not betray my *soul-bound* in such a way, and violence was all I'd ever known.

"I'm certain."

Miroslav took a deep, slow breath as if coming to terms with this as well, jaw tightening.

"As you wish."

Miroslav *folded* away before I could change my mind. Not that I would have.

Malekai rubbed southing circles on my back as I tried to breathe in steadying breaths. Something like fear worked its way through me.

More violence.

"I cannot ensure your survival."

How bad could that be? My father was Death... Surely...

You have far too much blood on your hands. And not even Mors can clean it off.

At least we'd basically succeeded. Entirely unscathed...

My muscles, however, were still taut and primed for *war*. The tremor in my hands still hadn't subsided.

Why did I feel like something else was coming?

Because Miroslav just told you, you might die.

Because you're about to confess, you hid the fact that Zurie's his mother, and you nearly murdered her without even telling him.

Because you're soulbound to a male who hates you and has tried to use and manipulate you every step of the way.

The same male who was willing to task you with killing one of the most powerful fae in the realm. Even if it was only because of the amount of aetra she consumed.

Miroslav returned in the next breath, Nakoa's *olana kah'hei* in tow. My heart pounded so loudly it echoed in my ears as my gaze drifted over the group of them. Every face is tight with worry.

Where the fuck was he?

My eyes darted back to Miroslav, whose normally relaxed brow was drawn together, his sharp jaw flexing.

Before the words could even leave my mouth, low and behold, Nakoa appeared. With a strikingly beautiful female dressed in an equally stunning gown that left far too little to the imagination. My gaze narrowed between the two of them as rage and jealousy twisted through me, further priming me to unleash whatever it was that I could feel building up inside of me like a fucking volcano.

Nakoa's eyes *burned* with murderous intent when they settled on me.

"Did you know?"

I steeled myself for his onslaught.

"Yes."

I could feel the heat of his *olana kah'hei's* stares. Their eyes darted between us with confusion. Nakoa looked like he wanted nothing more than to remove my head from my body. And part of me wanted him to fucking try.

Maleki shifted to step in front of me just as Nakoa's tail lashed out for my neck. Malekai's sword appeared, nothing more than a flash of steel. The bottom third of Nakoa's tail hit the polished stone floor with a wet slap.

A chorus of gasps rang out, and Nakoa's eyes widened at the sight of his mutilated tail. His face contorted into a rictus of rage as he launched himself at Malekai, sword in hand.

I could have cackled with laughter.

Oh no, no, no.

My body shoved Malekai out of the way as I raised my own sword to meet Nakoa's. The sound echoed with the clang of our clashing blades, and I shoved him backwards with a burst of strength and power that surprised even me. Deep scarlet tendrils of magic seeped out from beneath my skin as I *willed* him frozen in place. I could feel his magic hammering against mine, but it was a useless endeavor.

All four of my wings burst from their glamor. Every muscle in my body trembled with barely restrained rage as my mind oscillated between unleashing it and just letting it all burn.

He's your soulbound. He's your soulbound. He's your soulbound, some distant voice in my mind chanted.

Nakoa's eyes were wide with shock, as though he were truly seeing me for the first time.

Distantly, I could hear and *feel* other magic outside of Nakoa's, warring against my own. In my peripheral, I could see the silhouettes of the others battling against the shield my magic had instinctively drawn up.

"*I should have killed you when I had the chance,*" he rasped, his black eyes filled with hatred.

Something deep within me fractured, and my magic *detonated*.

CHAPTER
SIXTY
MALEKAI

Never in my life had I ever experienced such an intense level of terror as I had when blood sprayed across the interior of Mareina's barrier. She'd collapsed to the ground, drenched in blood.

For those initial moments, I thought...

Gods...

With a still shaking hand, I swiped away another tear.

Praise Akash, it had only been that dickhead of a soulbound of hers.

Though he had survived.

Somehow.

Barely.

Last I saw, he'd been lying unconscious in a bed located in the remote northern wing of the palace, with Thalia hovering at his side and the rest of his friends nearby.

Miroslav had *folded* an unconscious Zurie somewhere. I hadn't bothered asking where. I didn't actually care and - although I still held moderate disdain for the male - if he was anything, he was capable. I had no concern about Zurie getting free. Especially because, if she managed to get free, he'd likely be the first one she killed, considering his betrayal.

And *now*, Mareina was lying in my bed. Also unconscious.

Miroslav had folded us here with one of the healers from my army, Bohyun. Not only was she arguably one of the most gifted healers in all of Atratus, she was one of the few people in the world that I trusted. Swaying her loyalty away from Zurie had taken almost no effort. Not that she would trust or vow her loyalty to Nakoa.

Bohyun had as much faith in politics and those seated in positions of power as much as I did.

Which was to say, *not at all.*

Her loyalty lied solely with those she loved and helping the most vulnerable - *minori* and humans. She'd only joined my army perhaps a decade ago, so Mareina had barely met her, but I was certain they got along. At the very least, Mareina would trust my judgement in telling this woman what had occurred at the palace and tending to Mareina's unconscious body.

Not a single scratch marred Mareina's skin, other than those fucking claiming marks on her neck and shoulder from fucking Nakoa. I wanted to ride back to the palace just to gut him. The only thing that had held me back from doing so was that I was terrified to leave Mareina's side, *and* I imagined Mareina wouldn't want me to murder her *soulbound.*

Even if he was an absolute cunt.

I knew Mareina well enough to know that she hadn't wanted to wear his marks... Perhaps Bohyun could do something about them. Though now wouldn't be the time to ask.

"I'll pay you triple what Zurie does. *Did.* To stay here and tend to her. *Please.*"

Bohyun heaved a sigh as she straightened from where she'd been hovering over Mareina's painfully still, supine form around which whorls of her dark crimson magic seeped and writhed. Even now, it stretched towards me, curling itself around an ankle or arm. When

Bohyun had first tried to touch her, strands of Mareina's magic had lashed out to restrain her before they sniffed out her and her intent.

"There'd be no point... There's nothing I can do for her... Not to mention... I have no experience in healing *gods.*"

My eyes flicked up to hers from Mareina. I hadn't given her that information... Though I imagined it would be blatantly obvious if any healer worth their gifts went *poking* around.

"Tell no one, Bohyun. *Especially* not that mate of hers."

Bohyun reared back, horrified by the suggestion. "I would *never* break patient confidentiality."

I nodded, giving her an apologetic look. "I know... Thank you. You're one of the few people I trust. I just..."

My throat worked roughly against the emotion clogging my throat. I'd never seen Mareina so... *vulnerable.*

Even before I'd found out that she wasn't sanguinati but a literal *goddess,* she had always been *my* goddess. My fucking *Queen.* My warrior.

My everything.

I had witnessed her overcome terrifying odds long before she'd come into this power. We'd fought in a *war* together, for fuck's sake. And this female had become the heart and soul of me. If something happened to her, I would fucking break down Mors' temple doors and force his creepy-ass acolytes to open that hidden entrance into his after-realm to find her.

I'd throw myself onto my own sword to get there if I had to.

So to see her like this...

It made me feel something I'd never truly experienced before despite having faced death on a battlefield countless times.

Fear.

"If she were *actually* sanguinati, I'd say she needs to feed... But I have no idea how gods sustain themselves..."

My face slackened in realization.

Bohyun's black brows pinched together.

"General?"

"When you see Miroslav, please send him here. It's urgent."

She looked disappointed that I wasn't going to clue her in on the epiphany I'd had. As much as I trusted her, I wasn't about to tell *anyone* about who her parents were. As soon as I could get Miroslav back here, in the off-chance he didn't already know, I'd simply convince him to bring us to Mors' temple because of his mark on her wrist.

"Yes, sir," she said begrudgingly. I willed a small purse of gold coins into my hand and palmed it to her.

"I want you to research everything you can about healing gods and their magic—

Her eyes narrowed. "You do realize I have other patients to take care of..."

Like Nakoa. The soon-to-be King.

"Indeed, I do. Which is why I'm incentivizing you... You *do* realize she's your future *Queen.*"

A glare simmered somewhere beneath Bohyun's slightly pinched expression before lifting her chin as she relented.

"Fine."

"I'll send for you as soon as we return."

"Where are you going?"

Instead of answering, I gave her an appreciative nod.

"Thank you, Bohyun. I am truly grateful."

Bohyun's glare returned.

"General."

At that, she turned and left.

When I heard my front door snick shut, I finally exhaled a breath I felt like I'd been holding since Mareina and I had entered the palace.

Mareina, of course, hadn't moved an inch. I went and collapsed on the bed on the other side of her, rolling over to face her. My hand slid over hers. It felt... unnaturally cool. My eyes dipped to watch the steady, gentle rise and fall of her breath. It was the only thing keeping me from completely falling apart.

My eyes narrowed at the sight of the blood on her chest. I'd *willed* it all away... I reached for the spot where it peaked out from between her breasts before examining my fingertip, which came away with nothing. I slightly lifted the linen shirt I'd replaced her fighting leathers with to discover... scales? Such a dark red on Mareina's skin they were nearly black.

I rose onto one elbow, pulling down the loose neckline of my shirt on her to get a better look. *Willing* my eyes not to ogle her luscious breasts. However, as soon as I saw what laid between her breasts, it wasn't difficult to do.

A snake.

A third eye rested in the center of its head. While it still appeared as ink on her skin, it moved. The creature appeared to tilt its head to examine me, briefly flicking out its tongue before it slithered into the shape of an Ouroboros.

I stared at it in shock. Squeezing my eyes shut and opening them again to see if my vision was... lacking.

It had only been a handful of days ago that I'd seen Mareina's blessedly bared breasts... And that snake certainly hadn't been there.

Though neither had those magnificent wings at her back...

Gods... What else had transpired that she hadn't yet told me about?

Not that we'd had the time to discuss anything.

I covered her breasts and laid back down beside her. My mind reeling at everything that had transpired over the last several days.

The fucking *world* had changed.

CHAPTER

SIXTY-ONE

KERES

My thumb idly pushed at the *Kassarmaya* adorning my ring finger.

I'd spent the last 600 years scouring the realms for the blasted thing, and now that I'd finally found it, I could pay my brother and his *wife* a little visit. Who'd have guessed it would only be a hop and a skip away across the San Al-Mani Sea... It had been no easy feat getting through that fog of madness that shielded the entire region.

Willing away the glamour of the pretty demiurge princess, I padded my way up the steps of my brother's temple, rolling my eyes at the enormous bronze relief of himself in all his compassionate glory on the front doors of the building. With nothing more than a press of my hand, the *Kassarmaya's* ward-breaking power cut through the wards like a blade through flesh. Electrifying glee split my face as the door pushed open easily. It had been over half a millennium since I'd been home. Since I'd seen my *soulbound*.

The cavernous foyer was dimly lit by torches casting ominous shadows. My loud scoff echoed off the black, veined marble.

Clearly, my brother was still as dramatic as ever.

427

This was supposed to be a temple. Not a bloody mausoleum.

And it was broad daylight. I may be the Goddess of Violence, but even I appreciated a little sun.

Even his acolytes shared Mors' love of theatrics. One of them appeared in a nearby doorway, a dark hood drawn over his head, looking exactly like the ridiculous, fantastical depictions of my brother.

Even without being able to see his face, I could still *feel* his shock. And something much, much sweeter.

Terror.

He attempted to flee down a hallway. My wings burst from my back to propel me towards him, sword raised high. A diagonal portion of the top half of his body slid away from the lower half, both thumping against the floor.

Mors' *Pharalaki*, his *phantom guardians*, spilled from the dark hallways rushing towards me. Another of the gifts the *Kassarmaya* imbued its wearer with was that it could also project wards as unyielding as the ones it had broken. *I willed* a warded barrier to block their progress. They couldn't be killed. Fighting them would be like trying to battle a cloud of smoke.

I pushed back on the barrier, shoving them back further down the hallway. One on top of the other, heaps of them pressed against the transparent barrier. They pounded on it with the weight of a heavy, corporeal fist.

Flashing them a victorious grin, I stopped in front of the stone wall where the doorway to my brother's realm was carved, hidden by his magic.

With a caress of my ringed hand, the stone blocking the doorway disappeared. Just as I extended my foot to descend the steps, a hair-raising sound, like a steak knife shrieking against porcelain, stabbed my ears.

I scowled at the offending *Pharalaki*.

"Stop that."

As if I'd encouraged them, all of them began to run taloned

fingers against the barrier. The sound so shrill it made my knees want to buckle. I snarled, pressing my hands over my ears as I rapidly descended the spiral stone staircase.

The moment I stepped onto the soil of the *Elysio Agaro's* - one of the many paradises Avernus had to offer - for the first time in 600 short years, I felt like I could breathe again. Like a tremendous weight had been lifted off my shoulders. I didn't allow the sight of my brother's perfect little home with quaint little puffs of smoke whirling gently in the air against the gentle breeze to ruin the relief I felt at finally having returned.

At long last.

Home sweet home.

Slightly lifting the skirt of my gown, I waded through the silky, tall grasses. Savouring the feel of it against my skin. I yearned to just lie here in peace, stare up at the clouds, and just let the world turn around me until it was consumed by entropy.

Maybe then I would have peace.

Maybe then this insatiable thirst for vengeance and violence would finally leave me.

Maybe then I wouldn't have to feel the cavernous, gaping wound of betrayal that had sat in my chest for the last 600 years, festering in perpetuity.

Tears of righteous anger burned my eyes as I marched through the grasses, no longer able to enjoy the beautiful feeling of finally returning home.

My breath caught in my chest at the sight of Soteira, my *soulbound*, watering the plants outside her house. As though the tether that had once bound us as fated mates still existed between us, her gaze lifted from across the field to meet mine. The ceramic pitcher of water in her hand slipped and shattered on the ground.

Willing away the wet emotion tarnishing my face, I folded in front of her, and she stumbled backwards. I caught her by the wrist.

"*Keres,*" she breathed, chest heaving in shock.

It took everything within me to maintain my composure. Still gripping her, I pulled her against me. And despite 600 years of betrayal, the peaks of my breasts still strained towards her, and my core became slick with my arousal as her scent filled my nose and my breasts grazed hers.

My lips curled with delight at the faint scent of her own arousal. It brought me no small amount of satisfaction that I could still affect her this way. Even though I knew she was loyal to my brother, despite the fact that he'd destroyed *everything*.

I pushed the thoughts away.

"Lovely to see you again, darling."

"How did you... You—"

I lifted my hand, wiggling my ringed fingers to boast the *Kassar-maya*. It was a rather plain-looking thing - simple polished black stone from *Akash* knew what realm, fitted into a simple silver setting. But I imagine that was the intent of the *demiurge* that had created it. The only discerning feature was the glowing rune on the *inside* of the ring.

Even so, her lips parted in recognition.

As if trying to summon Mors, her nervous gaze flicked to our surroundings.

"He's not home, is he?"

I already knew the answer. Thanks to my allies, I'd known he wouldn't be home until it was too late.

Soteira's delicate throat dipped.

The moment I turned my back on her and strode into their home, my mask of amusement shattered. I steeled myself for what I was about to do.

You can do this, Keres. You've driven countless beings from their mortal forms. There is no such thing as death. Partiality is for the weak. This is the only way.

The sight of Soteira's and Mors' stupid, cozy hearth and all the precious little knickknacks decorating the mantel was all it took to harden my resolve hardening once more.

Soteira and I had once had a mantel and hearth decorated like that.

Forcing a lightness I didn't feel, I whirled to face her.

"You know... I saw the damnedest thing today..."

Soteira was abominable when it came to guarding her emotions. As terrifying as this little goddess could be when provoked, she had a heart of fucking *goo.* No matter how much she'd try to pretend otherwise, I knew that she'd missed me all these years. It was the way of *soulbound.*

Even if my brother had severed our tether.

Realization lit her eyes with *fear.*

Oh, yes, precious mate. Your betrayal truly knows no bounds.

"I saw a female today... She had *breathtaking* wings..."

There were only a handful of beings that had wings like ours. Black and boasting four of them instead of two.

Her brow hardened, eyes darkening with the promise of violence.

There she is.

My grin stretched, my heart kicking up at the unspoken confirmation.

"What have you done?" She seethed, power crackling at her fingertips.

I gave her a look of mock offence. I was petty enough to enjoy the sight of her barely leashed wrath. After all, it was the most I'd gotten from her in 600 years.

"My darling, you *wound* me. What reason at all do I have to wish grave harm upon my own niece?"

Her jaw feathered furiously. I chuckled with delight. It felt *good* to be in the *right* for once. I had every reason in the world to take something precious from my mate and my brother after everything they'd done to me.

"I have... a bargain I'd like to make with you."

The suggestion was met with a scowl.

"You remember how I stole that little spark of your soul and put it in that pythos, trapping you here for all of eternity?"

She growled. It was adorable.

"Well... I dare say I'd like to give it back."

"Why do I have a feeling that whatever stipulation you have attached to that bargain, I'll want nothing to do with it."

My grin grew so broad my cheeks ached.

"Oh, my love... Ye of little faith. *Of course,* you will. That's the best part."

I could *feel* her rage growing.

No matter.

I knew she didn't have it in her to kill me.

Even if that's what would be best for her.

For the realms, a dark, insidious voice inside me murmured.

"How about this... I'll give you the pythos, *and* I won't lay a finger on your precious daughter... All I want you to do is..."

The last word seemed to get stuck in my throat, and I felt my resolve cracking. Tears stung my eyes, and I suddenly had to turn away from her.

The pressure in the room seemed to deflate slightly as I began to pace in front of that gods-forsaken hearth.

Emotion clogged my throat. Each word I spoke came out with increasing fervor, my demands ending on a shout.

"You're going to drink from The River Oblivion, *I'm* going to shatter your pythos, and *we* are going to fucking be together!"

There was just one little part that I'd omitted, but... I couldn't bring myself to speak it aloud.

Soteira's gaze softened.

"And if I don't?"

I scowled, unable to keep up my charade of amusement any longer.

"You want your daughter to live happy and free, don't you?"

Soteira's gaze hardened again, and I couldn't fucking stand it.

"For 600 years, you've forced my hand. You don't get to fucking look at me like that," I seethed.

She continued to anyway.

I strode out the front door. The sound of soft footsteps trailed behind me.

My bottom lip quivered its disloyalty. I was trying *so* fucking hard to keep it together, and the blasted thing insisted on buckling now when we were so fucking close.

Soteria trailed after me towards The River Oblivion, located only meters away from her house. As I approached, I turned towards her, not giving her my back. Lest she shove me in, foiling my entire bloody plan. She had the audacity to look disappointed as she stepped up beside me.

I willed the pythos into my hand. It was terribly pretty. Like my mate. Such a shame to shatter it. *Them.* Her eyes widened at the sight of it. I willed a coffee mug into my free hand, passing it to her.

She hesitated, staring at the thing like it had threatened her.

"Unless you'd prefer to take a bath?" I asked, voice dripping with impatience and sarcasm to mask my broken heart.

She snatched the mug before squatting at the river's edge. A trembling hand carefully scooped up the river's glowing pale blue water. My heart pounded furiously in my ears.

She would forget me. She would forget everything.

Including my brother.

Her eyes, filled with tears and resignation, bore into mine.

If I didn't force her to reincarnate, she would begin to remember, little by little, perhaps in within the span of a human lifetime or two... Which was the blink of an eye to ones such as us. And that look in her eyes told me she knew it. And all of this would amount to nothing but more hurt and betrayal.

My words came out little more than a whisper on a broken laugh at the ridiculousness of it all. My emotion sliding down my cheeks, on display for her.

"I missed you."

She studied me for several moments as if she were trying to memorize every detail. Every feature.

She shrugged helplessly, huffing a soft, joyless laugh.

"I missed you, Keres. There hasn't been a day that's gone by that I haven't."

It took everything in me to not crumple.

"At least now, I won't have to feel this way any more," she added mournfully.

Soteira brought the cup to her lips, quickly tossing it back.

The pythos in my hand shattered.

A dazed, exhausted look came over Soteira's face as it scrunched up in confusion. Tremors wracked my whole body as I stepped toward her. She stumbled, dropping the cup, and again, I caught her.

She looked up at me with those big, beautiful green eyes that I'd fallen in love with from the moment I'd laid eyes on her.

"Hello, angel," I murmured softly. Sadly.

Her brow pinched with confusion before relaxing at the sight of me. The warmth of my love suffused my chest and seemed to spill out of me as though it would try and swim the distance between us, even without the tether to bind us.

She felt this, too.

Her voice breathless with something like recognition.

"Hi."

Slowly, I leaned in close.

She allowed it. Some unwitting instinct had her even tilting her head back as if to bare her throat for me to mark her. Again. My gaze dropped to her neck, where my claiming marks were still visible.

I closed the tiny distance between us, pressing my lips to hers. A sigh left her, and she opened instantly for me. She tasted like my first drink of water after traversing the fucking desert for too many lifetimes. My heart swelled so wholly, with both overwhelming love and relief, that I had to choke back a sob.

My breath shuddered out of me, and I knew if I hesitated a moment longer, I wouldn't be able to go through with it. And if I didn't, my brother would hunt her down and steal her away from me all over again.

I *willed* my dagger into my hand. The dagger *she* had gifted me all those years ago.

I slipped it between us, and it pierced her chest plate, her heart, with ease, thanks to the magic it had been infused with.

Her magic.

The god-killing kind.

Soteira sagged in my arms, and I collapsed, clutching her against my chest.

Soon.

She would reincarnate with no remembrance of any of this pain and suffering. Of the betrayal.

Of him.

And I would find her because she was the other half of my soul, even if we were no longer bound together.

CHAPTER

SIXTY-TWO

MORS

"W ell, if it isn't Grigori Rozenkra, my favorite little ice prince... Fancy seeing you here. How are you, darling? Keeping warm?" "

The hunched grey silhouette was all sharp, bony angles, draped in little more than a burlap sack even though he was sitting on a mound of snow at the top of a mountain peak with icy winds that could freeze your eyebrows off.

He didn't bother to turn around.

"All those people... I... I... *Children.*"

My shoulders sagged their disappointment.

Grigori had spent the last 150 years inhabiting this mountain peak, seeking the shelter of an icy cave at night when the wind and snow became unbearable.

"I can feel their pain. Their suffering," he continued woefully. Voice wavering and cracking.

More often than not, in religion and mythology, people got it wrong when it came to what they envisioned to be hell. Torture and imprisonment inflicted by demons and other bloodthirsty monsters.

The thought would have made me chuckle if my dick wasn't

about to fucking snap off like a blasted icicle in this *Akash*-forsaken place.

No, no. Certainly, demons and the like could be found in Avernus, my underworld, but not to serve the purpose of inflicting torture and imprisonment... Such things belong to the so-called *living* realms. And those who inflicted said torture, whether 'demon' or not, were the harbingers of karma and... sculpting, so to speak.

They wielded the pointy end of karma on those with or who had once had wicked ways. *Or,* guided by their own wickedness, they unwittingly helped to hone and sculpt their victim's strength and compassion.

The pain and suffering they inflicted could one day lead to their victim's selfless action, valour, wisdom, and growth. Just as a warrior's body did not become skilled and hardened by sitting in a field of flowers for all their days, neither did those who were destined for greatness.

When a soul came to the afterworld after having lived a life that revolved around inflicting suffering on others, I didn't torture them. Nor did I employ any *demons* to do so. I didn't need to.

They did it all themselves.

After a soul had passed on, there would be a period of purging, where they would have to experience all the pain and suffering that the soul had inflicted on others during their last lifetime. And when they reincarnated, they would be on the receiving end of their former transgressions.

Conversely, if they led a life helping or benefiting others in some way - whether it be making people laugh from behind the counter of a cafe or rescuing someone from a burning building - that soul got to experience all the love and joy they had brought to others.

And Prince Grigori here, had inflicted *a lot* of suffering in his royal lifetime.

This, of course, had nothing to do with why I had come to this wretched, frozen wasteland to visit him. Although even *it* had a beauty all its own, albeit harsh, with its striking snow-capped mountain peaks, vistas, frozen lakes, and sprawling valleys.

Hate the fucking cold.

My half-frozen legs protested as I forced myself forward and sidled next to him, squatting beside him.

"Oh, look! It's your favorite fruit...," I announced hopefully, praying that he would ask me to fly him somewhere blessedly *warm*. His head finally turned as I *willed* a mango into my hand as an offering.

The male's face had a bumpy layer of frozen tears caked onto his cheeks. He didn't have eyelashes or brows anymore. They'd long been frozen off. His lips cracked and blistered. His toes were little more than black and blue stubs.

A flicker of longing passed over his face.

Just let go, just let go, just let go, I chanted silently to him in encouragement.

150 years of freezing to death was enough suffering. I knew every one of Grigori's most heinous crimes, and I'd say he'd served his penance by now. I could feel the karmic debt of each soul, and even if it had been paid off through the purge and self-inflicted suffering in places like the Kurian Mountains... Sometimes, they grew attached to their suffering out of fear. Habit. Familiarity. Safety, oddly enough.

Because at least if they were here, they wouldn't have to take the leap of faith required before drinking the waters of The River Oblivion and being sent back into the unknown, where they might revert to their old ways because of ignorance, influence, and circumstance.

Depending on what stage of evolution their soul was in, it was a possibility... but eventually, every soul was destined to ascend and return to our *true home*. In all my years, now nearly an eon...

I had too many transgressions to count...

When my time came, would I end up in a place like this?

Torturing myself until *Akash* devoured the world once more, and we all returned to her cosmic bosom.

If I had learned anything over the countless millennia, watching an infinite number of souls who either suffered the effects of their iniquities or savored the many rewards of their virtues... It was that every act - whether done out of love or malice - was returned to you.

Your time is nigh, God of death, that quiet voice whispered within my mind.

Fear clutched my heart in its bony, unforgiving hand.

I attempted to block it out as Grigori's gaze lifted to mine, his half-frozen tongue snaking out to lick his parched lips.

"How about we go somewhere warm? How about a nice beach, hm?" I offered, taking in his frigid form, "Or perhaps defrost in a nice thermal spring...?"

Grigori's expression shuttered once more, and I knew he wouldn't take me up on my offer. Or the mango.

Sure enough, a moment passed, and he heaved a sigh, returning his gaze to the unforgiving landscape beyond the vista.

Groan.

My teeth chattered as I sank down beside him.

"I've come for a favour, Your Majesty."

Silence.

"I need you to help me find something. Or something*s*, rather."

Grigori, even in his most weakened state, was *still* the most capable seer to grace Arvernus in at least a millennium.

Still more silence.

"It would mean a great deal to my wife and I. And our daughter."

Grigori's gaze snapped back to mine, his blue-grey eyes suddenly bright with life. With hope.

I knew that even if I offered him relief from his suffering, he would refuse me. He would say that this was what he deserved.

But what he did desire was *redemption*.

The prince's voice held a sudden sparkle of hope.

"Daughter?"

"Yes... Helping me would enable my wife and I to reunite with her. It would bring us all tremendous joy and fulfilment."

Why the male practically had stars in his eyes.

Until now, I'd never noticed just how dazzling they were. I wondered if, beneath all the frostbite, starvation, and self-loathing, there was a handsome male somewhere in there.

A tremulous smile split his face, eyes dazzling with unshed tears. After all his torment and suffering, seeing him like this for the first time was truly a breathtaking sight. So much so that my own eyes began to burn as I caught his contagious grin.

Grigori threw his arms around me, knocking me backwards into the snow, and I couldn't help but laugh.

My arms embraced his seemingly fragile body, and when he finally drew away from me, hauling me up with a surprisingly strong grip, there were tears of joy melting the ice crusting his face.

"What is it exactly you're looking for?"

"Two pythoi. My sister, Keres, has hidden them somewhere."

"What's inside of them?"

"A fraction of mine and my wife's souls."

If he'd still had eyebrows, they would have leapt towards his hairline.

"Well... Let me... I'll see what I see, I suppose."

I gave his arm a squeeze in gratitude, stomach-churning when it felt like little more than a humerus bone. He held out a large, callused and cracked upturned hand between us.

"It helps sometimes if I can connect with you and your memories, even if they're not directly tied to the objects in question."

I held his hand, squeezing slightly with my gratitude and excitement.

Grigori's eyes slipped shut, and I couldn't help the wandering of my eyes, taking in his bony frame and bare feet. The sight alone was painful.

"I only see one..."

My head jerked back up to find his eyes still closed, the skin of his forehead scrunched in concentration.

"What?"

440

Gods.

Maybe my sister was keeping Soteira's pythos on her nightstand. *Probably.*

He shook his head, shifting from one foot to another on the snow as if he'd stepped in something sticky. His voice became breathless. Another wavering smile.

"I'm standing in warm water... *Akash almighty, I forgot what that feels like...* I'm in a cave, though. It's... small... Or perhaps part of a larger one, because the water isn't stagnant. It's lapping at my feet as if I were standing on a shore... But I see it. At the back. It's on a stone pedestal..."

Grigori took small stationary steps in the snow, a fragment of what was occurring in his mind and... wherever else he was. He raised his free hand as if trying to block out a glare.

"It's so bright I have to shield my eyes... It's like trying to look directly into the sun."

Wingbeats pounded the air from above, and I turned to find Lathrimos flying towards us.

"Your grace... Forgive me for the disturbance, but... There's a female here. She insists on speaking with you. For seven rotations, she has not stopped pleading with every winged being she could find on *Sosiadarap* to find you."

Grigori dropped my hand, Lathrimos' eyes dipping at the action, but said nothing.

"Who is she?"

"Princess Thalia Attía of Ishra... She claims she was killed by your sister."

CHAPTER

SIXTY-THREE

MORS

J ust after I'd arrived in *Sosiadarap, and* Thalía had informed me
that Keres had stolen the *Kassarmaya* from her family, the
panic and rage of my *Pharalaki* filled my mind as they'd fed me
images of her breaking into my temple. I'd flown faster than I
could remember in my eon of life. And the whole time, the merciless
voice of my conscience chanted in my mind.

This is what happens when you try to take what doesn't belong to you.

Dirt sprang from the ground as I landed in front of my house,
leaving a small crater.

Push-kicking the front door open, the wood burst into splinters.

My voice came out a roar.

"Soteira!"

Even before I rushed through the empty house, I knew it would
be a fruitless endeavor. I could feel it. She was gone. Our home bereft
of her essence. Terror filled my veins like an ice colder than the
Kurian Mountains.

An invisible fist gripped my throat as I burst back out of the
house, eyes scanning the horizon. My gaze caught on the shattered

442

ceramic pitcher on the ground beside the bed of poppy flowers. My breath caught in my throat.

No.

As if drawn purely by some inner knowing, my feet were carrying me through the tall grasses toward The River Oblivion. A gentle breeze parted a thicket along the river, and I caught a glimpse of pale flesh and midnight blue fabric.

I could have died right then and there if it weren't for the hope that she was still alive.

A foolish hope indeed.

"No."

My knees caught me as they buckled beside her unmoving form.

Shaking hands slipped over her smooth, *cold* flesh to gently roll her onto her back. Blood smeared her chest and the grass beneath. Her features suspended in a blissful expression.

"No... No. No. No. No... Soteira, please."

A broken sob burst from me as I gathered her in my arms. My head tilted to the sky, and an inhuman roar tore from my chest. I clutched my wife against me, burying my face in her neck to fill my lungs with her scent for what would be the last time. Her blood smeared my face and chest in the process, but I was beyond caring. If anything, I wanted her blood on me. *In me.*

At least then, I'd still have part of her with me.

This was true hell.

Akash had no need to create any hells because we had no problem creating them all on our fucking own.

You did this, that spiteful voice whispered in my mind.

"Mors," a hoarse voice sounded softly behind me. My head snapped up so fast; if I'd been human, it would have given me whiplash.

Hatred like nothing I'd ever known burned through me swiftly and viciously. Carefully, I laid Soteira back on the ground and rose.

Keres stood only a couple dozen feet away. Her face swollen and puffy from weeping. Her hands and pale grey gown stained with my wife's blood.

Wordlessly, I drew my sword, *Charon*, from thin air. The same one that Soteira had imbued with her magic.

It had been 600 years since I'd had to truly wield it. On no one other than the fucking plague of a female before me.

"You're going to die, and then I'm going to bind your soul to the *kasma ostyra* until this universe is consumed by *Akash* herself."

Kasma Ostyra.

The Chasm Doorway.

It was a place where not even light could survive. A gaping hole in the very fabric of this universe, leading from this one to another. It remained unknown which realms laid beyond it. No one dared to get close to it. Anything that did was sucked in and disappeared. We only knew that it led *somewhere* because as much as it consumed anything in its vicinity, it radiated a soul-shuddering magic.

Magic that not even us deities understood or had ever seen before. It was entirely something *other*.

If I bound Keres' soul to its horizon, she would spend an eternity being torn to shreds.

Instead of fear, only sadness is shown in her expression. The fury normally burning in her eyes extinguished.

"Then you'll be stuck here with me."

My rage burned so brightly that divine fire sprang to life over my hands and along the blade of my sword. Perhaps I'd let her burn to ashes over and over for the rest of eternity if we were stuck in this realm together.

She *willed* the pythos containing that fragment of my soul into her hand, nodding in the direction of the river.

"Drink... And I'll free you."

My breathing stilled.

"Unless you'd prefer to live in agony for all of eternity. Which would be no less than you deserve."

Hope burst to life, bright and nourishing. Only one thing gave me pause... If I drank from The River Oblivion... I'd forget my daughter... My precious daughter that was... destined for *so* much. It was why we had sent her away from here, and it had nearly fucking killed me. I couldn't abandon her like that. And I'd only just found her again...

"If you think of your daughter, you needn't worry."

Every muscle in my body went taut, primed with rage.

"If you think to harm her, I would gladly suffer eternity to prevent it. And spend all of it peeling your skin from your fucking flesh. If you think I would grow bored of such an endeavor, let me remind you that I am *easily* entertained, sister."

She huffed a bored laugh.

"I have no desire to harm her. She is my blood, after all. The daughter of *my soulbound.*"

What a shame my glare couldn't *actually* burn a hole through her wretched form.

"As you well know, she has a long and violent journey ahead of her... Perhaps you could even help her... If you're free to roam the realm, that is."

"Speak plainly, witch."

"Vow to not seek out my *soulbound*—

"*She's not your soul*—

Keres roared to life, her fast flushed with fury.

"*And you made damn sure of that, didn't you!*"

She... *had a point.*

I remained silent.

Keres drew in a calming breath before continuing.

"Vow to not seek out *my soulbound*, and if by some wretched twist of fate - if you should ever cross paths with her - that you will not entertain *any* form of relations with her. *Then*, you will drink from The River Oblivion—

"But if I vow—

"Shut. Up. *You thorn in my fucking tit.*"

She heaved a dramatic sigh.

"And I *won't* kill you afterwards and force you to reincarnate. It will only be a matter of time before you begin to remember her. "

I nearly laughed.

"Do you think me naive? You'll likely leave me stranded in the desert or put me in a dungeon to rot. And I'll have nothing *but* my memories of her to keep me company."

Keres frowned as if that was *exactly* what she had planned.

"*Fine.* After you drink, I'll be sure to place you somewhere *pleasant* with a very large purse of gold—

"And Charon."

My sword was nearly as old as I was and had protected me through countless wars.

She rolled her eyes.

"*And* Charon. Completely free from threat or harm. You'll be free to do as you please and in a splendid place to seek out every pleasure Bellorum has to offer. Happy?"

No. I was not fucking happy.

Everything within me urged me to tear her head from her body and dance on her foul fucking corpse.

But that would leave me imprisoned in my own realm for, potentially, eternity, and my daughter, surrounded by enemies in Bellorum.

I took a deep breath, biting back my heartbreak. The evidence of my pain would only bring this wretched creature joy.

I folded my arms across my chest, feigning a nonchalance I didn't even remotely feel, as I drummed my index and middle fingers on my chin.

"Hmmm... Not quite... What else..."

Keres' jaw tightened.

"*What else?* How about I change my mind and fucking *drown* you in The River Oblivion, and then there's no bargain!"

My lips quirked at her threat.

"Oh, my darling sister... I do so wish you would try."

It wasn't that she *couldn't* beat me... But it was a *considerable* risk for her to even try.

She groaned loudly.

"Make your demands, brother. I'm *quite* bored of you."

SIXTY-FOUR

A hollow ache, like my heart had been carved out of my chest, woke me. Every bone in my body ached like I'd fallen from a great height and landed head-first on stone. Like my skull had been split in half. Still crawling out of the dregs of a deep sleep, that perceived hole in my chest had my hand fisting the shirt covering it as memories returned to me from the... *How long had I been unconscious?*

A groan escaped me.

Delicate hands slipped over mine. I didn't have to open my eyes to know that it wasn't Mareina's. Thalia's magic brushed against mine, gentle and inquisitive.

Caring.

The polar opposite of Mareina's magic.

"Hey... How're you feeling?"

Hushed murmurs erupted around us, and half a dozen others' magic pressed against mine. My *olana kah'hei.*

Forcing my eyes open felt like ripping open parcels sealed shut.

It took several bleary moments for my vision to settle.

Thalia stared down at me with wide eyes, her brow furrowed

448

with concern.

Pomona shoved past her, gripping my hand in hers. Her face was sheet white, wrought with worry. Her bright hair had a messy red halo around her head as if she'd relentlessly been running her fingers through the strands.

"Koa... Thank Akash..."

Val and the rest of my *olana kah'hei* huddled around the bed, luxurious and so ornately decorated it was gaudy.

Val's expression held none of its usual warmth or joviality as he gave my blanketed foot a squeeze.

"Gave us right scare there, brother."

"I gotta say, the horns suit you," Lokus grinned.

Oh gods.

No.

The transformation.

Val elbowed him in the gut.

"Now you can be the one to find him a mirror, ya cunt."

Lokus gave a smug grin, *willing* one in front of me.

Of course, the bastard had one off-hand.

My heart thundered so loudly it echoed in my ears.

Lifting the thing felt like lead weight in my hand.

Twin black curling horns, similar to those of a gazelle, not unlike the ones Famei possessed, rose over a foot in the air. Sharp, black bone plating protruded shallowly from the outermost edges of my brows and cheeks. My eyes dipped to the back of my hand, holding the mirror to see the same plating peppered my knuckles and fore-arms and...

Oh fuck.

I dropped the mirror to examine both of them.

Claws.

I had fucking claws.

Gods... I looked like some hells-spawn demon from mythology... Exactly as I had seen in my premonitions... There was only one thing missing...

I sat up, swinging my legs over the bed.

Thalia reached out for me, curling her fingers around my bicep to ensure I was steady on my feet. I wasn't sure whether to shove her away because it might feigned concern to soften my heart towards her so she could get what she wanted... Or allow my heart to be softened by the action because it was genuine.

I did neither. Instead, I ignored her. A few gasps sounded, and someone made a choking noise. My gaze dropped to the mutilated sight of my tail... Though it appeared to be growing back. Thank *Akash*.

No, that wasn't what had caused the gasps.

I scanned the room, looking for a full-length mirror, my eyes landing on a gold-framed, floor-to-ceiling one on the opposite end of the room. My breath punched out of me at the sight before me.

My wings.

My beautiful wings...

All of my feathers...

Gone.

Instead of the wings that only Seraphi, rare bird shifters, and the odd fae who likely had hybrid blood from the two...

Mine were now like that of a gargantuan bat.

Or demon.

Instead of my lush, lustrous feathers, my wings were now made up of thin dark membranes, slender, curved and flexible-looking bones that ran through them, and sharp thumb claws at their angular peaks.

I flexed them wide... In equal parts horror and admiration. They looked... terrifying.

And I liked it.

Thalia appeared at my side, head tilted in open curiosity. She tentatively held a hand out, lifting her eyes to mine in permission.

"May I?"

Some foreign feeling invaded my chest.

Was I... Nervous?

I nodded, and her petite hand reached out to stroke the delicate membrane and one of the top bones.

A full-body shudder worked through me, and arousal flared to life deep in my belly.

She snatched her hand back as my wings snapped shut, folding tightly against my back.

Fuck.

"Sorry... I didn't mean to—

My response came out gruff.

"It's fine."

She nodded, her gaze running over me with admiration.

"They are... Truly breathtakingly beautiful."

My heart flip-flopped in my chest, and I quickly shut out that entirely too warm and unwelcome feeling.

I left Thalia standing there as I returned to my *olana kah'hei*. My thoughts steadfastly on Mareina.

"Where's Mareina?"

Everyone remained silent, their unease practically cloying in the air.

Dread sank its talons into my gut.

Finally, Pomona's throat worked on a rough swallow.

"She's... She..."

"Miroslav took her and the blonde male somewhere," Thalia finished for her as she sidled beside my *olana kah'hei*.

The ember of my jealousy and rage flared to life once more.

Had my own *soulbound* tried to kill me? And now left me for *Malekai?*

A flurry of questions infested my mind, each more crazed than the last. None of which they could answer.

"And ... Zurie?"

The female who was apparently my mother.

At least by birth.

The very female I'd sent Mareina to kill. The Queen I'd loathed and spent the entirety of my life seeking to destroy.

451

All because the female I'd trusted most in this world, the one that I *had* unwittingly called mother and had raised me, had also lied to me and helped pave the way for me to murder the woman who'd birthed me. Even if she was a foul creature and deserved to die... *I deserved to know.*

And my *soulbound* had known.

How cruel was fate the people I should be able to trust most in the world had lied to me for as long as they had known me?

"She's in the dungeons... We thought you might want to... speak with her," Roderick said gently.

So alive.

I couldn't help but wonder if that had been deliberate or unintentional on Mareina's part. Though considering the fact that my mate was a veteran of murder, I found it hard to believe that she'd make such a mistake.

A minuscule and traitorous part of me found relief in that. That perhaps Mareina hadn't killed her for my sake. And due to the fact that, no matter how horrific Zurie was, I felt a visceral need to meet the woman from whose flesh I'd been born.

"The dungeons... *In her own palace?*"

"Miroslav and Malekai ordered the palace guards away from the western wing of the palace... The dungeon is in the north wing. Where we are now."

"So... No one knows yet...?"

"No... But... Suspicions will start rising if we don't do something soon."

"Take me to her."

Thalia seemed to know her way around this part of Zurie's palace. And not a soul in sight. I could only hope that Miroslav and Malekai would manage to keep anyone from asking questions for the time being. It had been such a remarkably successful and seamless ordeal, it seemed... Too good to be true.

The dungeon, to my surprise, was empty. Either they'd cleared the dungeons, too, or Zurie didn't keep any prisoners.

She kills them all, My Knowingness whispered.

Yes... That seemed highly probable.

Even with the palladium collar Mareina had put around her neck, I could feel her magic. The palladium collar just kept it out of her reach.

The cells appeared to have been carved directly into the stone beneath the ground on which the palace sat at the foot of the Falcweard Mountains.

Without any spoken direction, we were drawn to the furthest cell at the right of the long, musty corridor. At the end was a stone archway leading into an alcove where a single spear of light illuminated the space. As we approached, runes I didn't recognize were carved into a stone dais in the center of the floor. The shaft of light came from where a hole had been carved into the ceiling, allowing sunlight to peek through. Something seemed to beckon me to this space, though I had no idea why. When I reached for my Knowingness, it remained utterly silent, as it so often had as of late.

I reluctantly turned away from the door towards the thick wrought iron door of the last cell on our right. Thalia placed a hesitant hand on the door of the cell, casting me a compassionate glance as if to ask, *are you ready?*

I gave her a subtle nod. A second look at the door revealed it was nothing more than an iron barrier indicating the location of a cell. Under her breath, she murmured something in ancient fae, and the barrier disappeared. How exactly she knew precisely which words to invoke was something I would have to ask her later.

It took no small amount of effort to train my face into something coldly neutral.

Zurie sat on the floor directly across from the entrance, leaning against that wall, still dressed in her torn and blood-soaked gown.

Her eyes widened at the sight of me, her breath stilling. After only a few silent moments, something I hadn't fathomed her capable of glistened in her eyes.

Emotion.

Had she given me away?

My mind reeled, trying to imagine the life I'd have had growing up in this palace. *As a prince.*

Would I have turned out as wicked as her if I'd been raised by her?

I finally managed to take a single step forward into the cell. The question cut through me to reach her.

"How?"

Zurie's expression shuttered as she rose to standing, her gaze flicking to the crowd of people behind me.

"Leave us," she growled.

If this female hadn't been the bane of my entire existence, I'd have appreciated the fact that even a dank dungeon didn't strip her of her pride. Thalia and my *olana kah'hei* remained exactly where they were, at my side. I could feel their magic, restless in the air, as they watched.

"In case you hadn't noticed, you're no longer Queen."

Her jaw flexed with anger, hands fisting by her sides.

"We have much to discuss, and it is not for outside ears. You wish to take the throne and rule as King? *Trust no one.* Not even your family."

Whether or not she knew anything about me or the betrayal that had come to light, her words hit home.

"Vow that you will speak only the explicit and clear truth to me."

Her expression cooled, lips pursing. "Gladly. Only if you make a vow in exchange."

I huffed a dry laugh. "You're not exactly in a position to make a bargain, Zurie."

Instead of being cowed by the reminder, a knowing grin tilted her lips before she burst into an abrupt, sardonic laugh."

"Oh, how wildly naive you are. You think I have no power because you've given me this little necklace?" A petite hand brushed a fingertip across the palladium collaring her throat as if it were a precious jewel. Large, blue, doll-like eyes took on a malevolent glint.

"I don't need my magic to be powerful, *my son*. And you'd do well to not rely on yours either, no matter how mighty."

I gave her a bored look.

"You've done a lot of talking yet have somehow told me absolutely nothing."

A sly grin returned. "I will *allow* you to take the throne. I'll even help you rule—

A hoarse laugh bubbled up and quickly escalated. Despite what had inspired it, it felt good.

Zurie scowled impatiently at me as I wiped tears from my eyes as my laughter oscillated repeatedly between a breathless chuckle and an unhinged cackle.

"Are you *quite* finished?"

Fate certainly had a sense of humor.

"You've destroyed an entire Kingdom. Committed mass genocide on multiple occasions... I just can't help but find humor in the sheer level of delusion you must live in to think I would actually value *your* assistance."

Like any truly delusional person, she didn't even acknowledge the truth I'd just thrust in front of her.

"Whether you like it or not, you're going to need my help."

"Give me one reason not to kill you, Zurie, because it's all I've dreamt about for years."

Her expression almost became wistful as she stared at me, gradually shaking her head as a sad smile curled her mouth. She heaved a sigh, suddenly looking as though a wave of bone-deep exhaustion washed over her.

"You'll soon discover there are many reasons you need me..."

I frowned my increasing boredom. So many words yet so little meaning.

She gave me a sly and frustratingly smug look.

"Least of all being that I know where your father is."

SIXTY-FIVE

MAREINA

W aking up felt like crawling through mud. My eyes peeled open, landing on a floor-to-ceiling glass window that ran the entire length of the room. It was dark out. Even from the bed, I could make out the luminous blanket of stars in the night sky. And the *singular* moon. I rose, feeling surprisingly... *light.* My gaze scanned the entirely unfamiliar room... It was sparsely decorated in a way I hadn't seen before. Clean and elegant lines, monochrome shades of grey... I tried to search my mind for any sense of recognition, but all my memories seemed just out of my grasp. I found I didn't mind... I felt oddly at peace. Safe.

My feet carried me across a fluffy wool rug towards the window, mildly surprised to find my form draped in dark silk grey pyjamas I also didn't recognize.

Peering out of the window revealed that there was indeed only one moon... Which seemed... wrong. Though I couldn't quite recall why.

The silhouette of a mountain range loomed in the distance.

The amber light of several orbs flickered on. I whirled to find a remarkably tall, broad, olive-skinned male leaning in the arched doorway. Hands inside the pockets of his pale, loose-linen trousers. His black hair was shaggy, framing a rather breathtakingly handsome face. Curious, dark eyes studied me.

His features were wildly familiar, yet I still couldn't place how or why.

"You look so much like your father. Though you have your mother's eyes."

His voice was a thing of dreams. A soothing, lush, deep velvet hum that could lull me to sleep if it so chose.

My mind searched like a seeking hand... *My father...*

My eyes rounded when a fragment of memory returned to me like the pearl of an oyster at the bottom of a dark, placid sea.

"You're my uncle..."

A corner of his mouth quirked as he padded towards me on bare feet.

"Indeed I am..."

"Somnus..."

A soft smile.

He leaned against the window, hands still in his pocket, and as I stared up into his eyes, I realized that his eyes weren't merely dark. They were black. And the flecks of light I'd mistaken for light reflecting off their darkness... I realized they were stars. A galaxy of them. The more I stared, the more I found myself drifting towards them. *Into them.*

A soul-deep desire to do exactly that overcame me. To fall into the safety and warmth that deep sleep promised, if only—

"Don't..."

The word snapped me out of the haze. I drew a sharp breath, shaking my head of the haze that had blanketed me like a drug.

"Sorry about that... You'll be more susceptible here..."

"Where are we?"

"My home."

"... How did... What—

Trying to recall anything felt like trying to part a thick fog, but gradually, more pearls... memories, drifted towards me... And the memories of...

Oh god...

"I'm asleep..."

A nod.

"Is Nakoa...?"

"Alive and well."

Nakoa's last words returned to me.

I should have killed you when I had the chance.

Something tightened in my chest and knotted in my gut.

"What of Zurie?"

"Also alive."

"Why am I here?"

He drew in a deep sigh, his gaze shifting to stare out of the window.

Somnus paused, his starry eyes searching mine for any sign of recognition.

"But most importantly, you need to go home.

"Home?"

"To Avernus..."

My breathing stilled.

"Why?"

"In a nutshell, your father's karma came back to haunt him. And now he is no longer there, nor does he remember it..." Somnus paused for a few moments, holding my gaze. "Or you," he added gently.

My heart just about stopped. Somnus shook his head as I opened my mouth to reply.

"In time, his memories will return..."

"But what about Atratus? I made a vow."

"And there's nothing stopping you from keeping it. After all, the very doorway you were born in leads there."

"So you're saying you want me to rule my father's underworld *and* Atratus."

Somnus shrugged.

"If you don't, the two realms will bleed into one another. Avernus will be breached by demons and untold horrors. Every soul craves their home, Mareina. The depraved most of all..."

His words settled on me with the gravity of a cosmic void.

"The dead will flood the living world, and vice versa. The realm of the dead is supposed to be a place of respite. Of healing and rest. Of repaying of karmic debt. Of cleansing. Without that... The world would descend into chaos and unimaginable suffering... And if that weren't enough, the hole in the fabric of the realm would catch the attention of those residing in hell realms.

"Your father is naive in thinking that hells do not exist. Though they are not places for the dead. They are very much alive and very much hungry. I have seen them. I have travelled to the darkest depths of their minds. Their dreams. And the things they dream of are... the stuff of nightmares."

Dread settled low in my gut. Deeper. Into my soul.

Never in my life had I ever felt so... incapable. I was a honed warrior. Becoming Queen of Atratus, while I didn't feel worthy, I knew I was capable. Certainly more capable than *Zurie,* and she had been ruling it for hundreds of years.

But *this...*

An entire realm, with countless souls...

"Your father's power not only facilitates the healing of these souls once they arrive but also protects them and the entire realm by holding the very fabric of the underworld together. Without him, it will begin to fray."

My heart thundered in my chest.

"But I don't have that kind of power..."

A soft chuckle and a pinch of his brow like I'd just said something inconceivably silly.

"But of course you do, child. Your father *and* mother's power runs through your veins and animates your very life force. When you met the *Seraphi,* their spirits - the very beings your father's life force helps to sustain - the power that had been *buried* inside you because you were born in the living world - burst free."

The Seraphi...

"The Seraphi are part of your father's domain. As are demons. Or at least the image of what folklore paints them to be."

"But I thought..."

"What? That your vow to Atratus and to rule beside Nakoa activated your power?"

When I remained silent, he chuckled. The sound deep and warm. As if it were an absurd notion.

"The more time you spend in your father's realm, *your realm,* the more you'll come into your power. You remember how Phaedra explained the *Seraphi* feed?"

Fragments of their resting souls... Wander the realm seeking a certain energy source... Just as a flame is not diminished by sharing its fire, it only grows.

"What about my mother? Surely she..."

My words drifted off as I took in his grim expression.

"What happened?"

"Karma... In a nutshell."

My frown deepened. "Surely, there's more that you can tell me about my parents apparently just *disappearing* and forgetting everything. If anyone has a right to know, I would think that—

"It is not my story to tell. Perhaps your aunt will explain it to you."

I reared back. "The Goddess of Violence..."

"Keres is often misunderstood... She and your parents have a rather tumultuous history."

"Will I ever see them again?"

"Without a doubt... I'm going to pay your father a visit in a few moments, in fact."

"Where is he?"

"Lying on a beach in Nissi Tis Pillis."

My brows leapt in disbelief.

"Then why can't you at least bring him back?"

"He'll come back eventually. But for now, it would be better for us all if history didn't repeat itself."

"So I'm supposed to go back to Avernus and do what? I don't even know where to begin."

"Just as you don't have to tell your heart to pump blood or your stomach to absorb the nutrients of your food, your mere presence in Avernus will ensure that your realm is preserved. Though you will have duties to perform. Lots of them. You'll have plenty of support... I'll send word before you arrive."

"But... Mors has spent time away, and the realm didn't collapse..."

"Only for brief periods of time. It's like when you swim underwater and hold your breath. Except it's not you holding your breath when you dive underwater; it's the ocean... Every time your father left, the underworld was essentially holding its breath. And going too long without oxygen... Without *him*... Well..."

I shook my head in disbelief.

"And you can't help?"

Somnus merely gave me a look of compassion.

"I'll visit regularly. As often as I can, I swear it. You're my niece, after all, and we have only just met."

My scowl only softened *slightly*.

"So what exactly *are* you going to do?"

The corners of Somnus' mouth curled, eyes twinkling.

"I'm going to find Persephone."

YOU ARE THE FULFILLER OF DREAMS

By reading this book, you have directly contributed to the betterment of not only my life but that of my two boys (17 & 4, as of 2024). And for that, words cannot even begin to express my gratitude.

But please know that you are the granter of wishes and the fulfiller of dreams.

With all my heart, I hope this book brought joy to your life and nourishment to your soul. If so, I would truly be *eternally* grateful if you could leave a review and/or spread the word on your social media or in your book clubs. As an indie author, things like positive reviews make all the difference in the world.

If you did not enjoy this book, that is heartbreaking for both of us and I would be more than happy to receive a verbal lashing as punishment.

Either way, I am always overjoyed to hear from my readers and would love to hear from you on instagram. (@authorchiaraforestieri)

YOU ARE THE FULFILLER OF DREAMS

:)

THANK YOU

Thank you to my family and friends, who have been so unwaveringly supportive and believed in me even when I had a hard time mustering the strength to believe in myself.

Thank you to my readers. Words cannot even begin to express how grateful I am. The impact you have on the lives of my two boys and me is truly the stuff of dreams. I wish, from the depths of my heart and soul, that my writing has had at least a fraction of that positive impact on you.

Thank you to that source energy, guiding light, inspiration, the universe, the divine, God/Goddess, or whatever you wish to call it. I don't dare claim to 'know' what else is out there, simply that I feel there is something *so* much more beyond what we can even begin to comprehend or perceive.
And that it begins and ends with love.

ABOUT THE AUTHOR

Originally from the US, Chiara Forestieri is a single mother of two [not-so] tiny little love muffins (a 17-year-old and a three-year-old, as of 2023) that spends her days taking care of her small family, practicing Brazilian Jiu-Jitsu and Muay Thai [with the grace of a failing inflatable tube man], pouring her heart and soul into creative and entrepreneurial endeavors, such as this book. All with varying degrees of success, of course. Ranging from 'well, at least no one died' to 'have you lost your mind?'

Currently, she lives in wonderful London praying desperately for sunshine and warm weather. And while many of her prayers have been answered, this one is most often not.

Some of her favourite things (outside of family and friends) include:

- Her Kindle
- Brazilian Jiu-jitsu
- Muay Thai
- All things nature and wilderness
- Animals
- Clean sheets (*drool*)
- Dirty humor
- The sea (her home)
- Hot-warm-and-squishy freshly baked cookies
- Sun

- Kindness
- Cuddles
- A fiery hearth
- Pyjamas
- Oh, and love. Love, love, love. :)

Wanna see more of your favorite characters? See excerpts from upcoming books? Or just general juicy, steamy, romantasy content?

Follow the journey instagram! :)
@authorchiaraforestieri

Printed in Great Britain
by Amazon

38213947R00273